LUCK'S HOLDING

LUCK'S VOICE BOOK 5

DANIEL SCHINHOFEN

Copyright © 2022 Daniel J. Schinhofen
No parts of this book may be reproduced in any form by an electronic or mechanical means – except in the case of brief quotations embodied in articles or reviews – without the written permission from the publisher.
The characters and events portrayed in this book are fictitious. Any similarities to real persons, living or dead, are purely coincidental and not intended by the author.
Copyright © 2022 Daniel J. Schinhofen
All rights reserved.

CHAPTER ONE

Doc stretched as he got off the black gelding— three days out of Deep Gulch had him looking forward to reaching the city. Patting his horse, he watched the others getting off their mounts or out of the wagon.

Fiala smiled as she spoke softly to the mare she'd been riding. Her black tail and cat ears twitched as she did, clearly happy with her ability to ride as well as she was. Seeing Doc watching her, Fiala's smile grew wide and her single longer canine peeked out over her lip. Her blue eyes twinkled with happiness.

His gaze shifted to Sonya next. Her horse was the second shortest among the group, which she needed as a dwarf. She wasn't as graceful with dismounting as Fiala had been, but it was clear she'd taken her riding lessons to heart. She brushed at her bangs, her black hair slick with sweat, before putting her hat back on. Glancing his way, she smiled softly, her brown eyes filled with love.

Doc gave her a wink before looking at the next woman in his life. Ayla leaned a little against her mare. She rode well, but it was clear that she would need healing again tonight. Her hand rested on the massive Express rifle Doc had given her as one of her wedding gifts. The rifle wasn't her primary weapon— her ability to deal with numbers was her greatest skill. She touched the brim of her hat, but her blond hair still flowed down her back. Feeling his gaze on her, she looked his way, her hazel eyes apologetic. Doc gave the half-elf a warm smile in return.

The last of his wives to get off their horse was Lia. Lilliana looked born to the saddle, and her white stallion nudged at her, looking for affection. She wore her buckskins with ease, her double pistols hanging naturally on her hips. She'd been known as Death Flower back when she'd fought against the government, but now, she went by Lia. Doc was still touched that she'd left behind Deep Gulch to go with them. Lia's sharp elven eyes fixed on him questioningly. Her odd tricorn hat sat on her head, not obscuring her blond hair at all. Jade eyes peered at Doc with love, curious as to why he was watching her like he was.

Doc gave Lia a small smile and shrug before he looked at the two women getting out of the wagon. Rosa, his insatiable dryad wife, was stepping down from the back. She didn't know how to ride, but honestly, she didn't need to— if she really wanted to, she could travel from tree to tree. Her emerald eyes found his the moment he looked at her. She touched her short tangle of blue-tinged green hair before smirking. He called her his weed most of the time, as their relationship was decidedly outside the norm.

Shifting his gaze to the last woman, who wasn't yet truly his wife, Doc smiled softly. Sophia Sagesse had left behind her family to go with him. She was with him not only as the attorney of his company, but also because they were going to wed once they reached Furden, the capital of Coalrud Territory. Sophia had some decidedly different features from Lia's pointed ears or Fiala's feline tail.

Sophia stretched when she got off the driver's bench. Her legs from the knee down were bird's legs, her feet especially. Four taloned toes that could score wood when she walked, and here, they dug into the ground as she reached for the sky. Doc's eyes traveled up her body, taking in her firm figure, trailing up to the small feathers where her hair would be. The small brown feathers had tiny white splotches to them, and they were downy soft when Doc touched them. Sophia blinked, her orange eyes finding him watching her, and her cheeks heated just a little.

Besides the women he loved, there were two other people on this trip with them. Harrid, Doc's dwarven bodyguard, was clumsily getting off the shortest horse they had. He could ride passably, but he didn't care to ride at all. Even with the hot weather, Harrid still wore his full gear. Though the breastplate, chain mail, shotgun, pistol, and axe had to make things worse, Harrid wore the outfit with ease. Doc knew he'd have to heal the dwarf, but he didn't mind helping the man who would stand between him and harm.

The last person wasn't as well-known to Doc. Clyde Rossal was a badger bestial by heritage, his white and black hair attesting to that. His black eyes were serious as he got down off the wagon. Clyde had been a driver for bank wagons before a knee injury retired him. Doc had healed him, and then Clyde signed a contract with Luck's Holdings. The man moved with assurance around the animals, getting things ready to camp for the night.

The sun was still hours away from setting, but stopping earlier let them set camp. They'd paused in a place that had been used as a camp before, making setting things up easier. Doc, like the others, made sure the animals were settled first.

Lia was the first one done getting her horse taken care of. She went to help Harrid first, as the dwarf was having the hardest time of it. Doc was the next to finish and went to assist Ayla. Fiala went to help Sonya when she finished, and Clyde and Sophia got the wagon team settled before pulling out their camping gear from the wagon.

"This is different than I thought it would be," Ayla sighed in relief when Doc healed her aching thighs.

"Oh?"

"All the books make trips seem... romantic?"

"True," Doc chuckled just as her horse lifted its tail to drop its own opinion. "We're done. I'm going to help Harrid."

"I'll assist with the camp," Ayla said, waving her hat in front of her face.

"All the animals are in good health, Voice," Rosa said, meeting him on the way over to Harrid.

"Good. Horses can get sick or injured easily, and we don't want that."

"I think you can manage it tomorrow," Lia was saying when Doc got closer.

"As long as my legs support me," Harrid grumbled.

"I got you," Doc said, reaching out to touch the dwarf. Green light glowed around his hand as he touched Harrid's arm, sending healing into him. "And it's done."

"Thank you, Shaman," Harrid sighed in relief. "I'm beginning to think I should ride in the wagon."

"Won't improve if you don't strive."

"That's true... I'll do my best to endure."

"Time to help with camp," Lia said.

"Before you all go," Rosa said, "Doc, you've been thinking of hot springs today. There are a few of them nearby, about two miles that way." She pointed off the trail toward the west.

"Really? Are they good?" Doc asked.

"They are not the sulfur springs that you worry about."

"Hmm... a couple miles should take less than an hour," Doc said, looking toward the direction Rosa had pointed. "Get camp set, then go check them."

"Check them?" Lia asked with a raised eyebrow.

"Yes. If they're good, I'll buy the land. Hot springs will bring people this way. I've had ideas about what can be done to really help bring people to Deep Gulch."

"Should probably talk with Ayla and Sophia, then," Lia said a touched distracted. "Camp first, either way."

"That's fair."

* * *

Since they'd had a few days of practice, the camp was ready in short order. Their food was the rations they'd brought with them, along with two pots on the fire for coffee.

"Now that we're set and sated, I wanted to go check out the hot springs," Doc said.

"Hot springs?" Fiala asked.

"A natural upwelling of heated mineral water," Rosa explained.

"It feels amazing on tired muscles," Lia smiled. "Explain what you had said earlier about getting people to Deep Gulch, please?"

"Rail," Doc said. "I want to see about buying up the right of way to drive a rail line from Furden to Deep Gulch. If the springs are what I think they are, then I'd want to buy the land they're resting on, too. I'd put a stop in at the springs and use it to bridge the two."

Ayla's lips pursed. "We can probably manage it, but it's another massive expense. Just getting the rights for the rail is a large expense... adding in construction of the line, and it will quickly add up."

"Which is why I'm going to get a partner for it," Doc said.

"Roquefell?" Sophia asked.

"Yes. He's from wealth, probably has all the connections needed, and seems interested in me."

"The Roquefells are bankers and businessmen," Ayla said softly. "We'll need something to entice him."

"I have a few ideas, but I want to meet him first," Doc said. "I'll only work with him if he's free of corruption. First, before anything else, I want to see if the springs are even worth the investment for the ground around them."

"Let's go," Lia said, standing up. "It's been a long time since I soaked in the ones here."

"Yes, it has," Rosa said gently.

"Uh..." Harrid looked uncomfortable.

"I'll have Rosa and Lia with me," Doc told Harrid. "I think those two in the wilds are enough protection. Stay here with Clyde and keep the camp safe. We'll likely return after dark."

Harrid nodded, but was clearly unhappy.

"Once we're back in a town or city, you'll be the point of my protection again," Doc said, seeing Harrid's face, "but in the wilds, who would you think is the best for keeping me safe?"

"Rosa and Lia," Harrid admitted. "It's why I'm not arguing, but again, I wonder if I'm entirely needed."

"I'll be glad to have you in camp," Clyde said; the bestial rarely offered his opinion unless asked. "With all the stuff we have here, just me being here would make me very nervous."

"It's not likely anyone will come by, but yes, two is better than one," Lia said.

"Okay," Harrid said. "I'll stay with Clyde."

"I'll grab the cards," Clyde chuckled. "We'll play for pennies."

Harrid snorted. "Don't stay out too long. He'll clean me out."

Doc laughed and clapped Harrid on the shoulder. "A few hours, at least."

"Should we take anything with us?" Fiala asked.

"Some towels to dry off afterward," Sophia said. "I'll want my bathing cap, too. My feathers are delicate at times. I'm not sure if the minerals in the springs would hurt them."

It took a few minutes to gather their things, but after they had, Doc, his wives, and Sophia headed into the woods. Thinking over Deep Gulch and the route to Furden, he thought he might know where on Earth the hot springs would be.

If I'm right, this area will grow up. The rail going into it will make it boom, and people from all over will come for the waters. Doc smiled as he followed Rosa. *What would that make the town... Coalrud Springs? We can name it something better than that... I'll have a chance to give it some thought.*

CHAPTER TWO

Their walk through the woods in the evening light was pleasant enough, even with the warmth of the day. Doc had taken to wearing his travel clothes, having changed out of his suit after the first day.

"You've been here before, Lia?" Sonya asked.

"Before I rode the plains, seeking death," Lia replied, "this used to be the territory of the Heartwood tribe."

"Used to be?" Doc asked, thinking he already knew.

"Slaughtered to the last member," Lia said tightly, "much as my tribe almost was."

"Most of the tribes from this region were killed," Rosa added. "If you go west out of the mountains, or even east to the plains, you can find other tribes."

"But they've been combined and pushed into reservations made by the church, not on the land they call their own. It might be hard when you meet them, but you'll give them hope, Doc."

"I hope to do that and more, Lia," Doc murmured.

"We'll help in every way we can," Fiala said, taking his hand.

"Which helps me a great deal," Doc smiled at her. "Rosa, are you doing something to keep the insects down around us? I've been expecting to be a smorgasbord for mosquitos."

"Yes," Rosa nodded. "I'm keeping the majority away, but a few will still come in to feed. I know you dislike them."

"Thank you."

"Doc, besides the rail to Deep Gulch, what other plans do you have?" Sophia asked.

"Nothing solid yet," Doc admitted. "I'm thinking that going west would be best for now. The frontier would give us an easier time of trying to build Luck's worship. I know about a few things that happened over the next few decades on my world that might apply here, as well— financial windfalls that would bolster the hell out of our bottom line."

"Making it easier for your plans," Ayla nodded.

"That's my hope. I know about a major gold strike, and another of silver. What that'll mean on this world where soul stones and mythrium are a thing, I don't know... what's the name of the territory on the far western side of Uta?"

"Vedana," Lia said. "It's mostly desert."

"My old home used to be in that area," Doc said softly. "Pahrump, Nevada. Rumor always said the name translated to 'Water Rock,' but I have my doubts."

"You want to go see it?" Lia asked.

"Oh, we'll be heading that way. North of that were Goldfield and Tonopah, decent gold and silver mines. I'll be buying up the spots and hiring dwarven miners to work them," Doc smiled. "The mines in Nevada were something I had at least some knowledge of, so I'll make sure to snatch up all the decent spots that are open."

"It's a tough place to live," Lia said.

"It can be," Doc agreed. "I know there are tribes in the area, and I'm hoping to make contact with them. If possible, we can make it habitable for the miners, and they'll work with the tribes."

"That would be good," Sonya smiled.

"I want to get the old animosities set aside. If we're to make real progress, we'll need to unite elf and dwarf. We can't let them stay divided."

"It'll be tough, but we'll do all we can," Lia said.

"We need to cross over the river," Rosa said as they got closer to the water.

"Hmm... can you make a bridge that'll hold up to heavy wagons?" Doc asked her, stopping beside her. "The rail should be on this side of the river, but we'll want to build near the springs."

Rosa licked her lips as she looked at the river. "I can, but it'll tax me, Voice."

"And we'll refill you, Weed," Doc said gently. "If your sister wasn't already going to be with Posy, I'd have her helping out here when she's reborn."

"I can ask Mother to send another of my sisters to this area to aid you," Rosa said, "but without someone trustworthy here, it might end badly."

"Fair. Let's just worry about what we have before us now. A bridge wide enough and strong enough to support the bank wagons."

"Step back and give me some time, please," Rosa said as she knelt down.

"We'll entertain him, Weed," Lia said as she snagged Doc's arm. "When you're ready, we'll have something to help you."

Rosa shivered, her eyes flaring before she closed them. "Thank you, Lia."

* * *

Doc was grinning when they crossed the bridge an hour later. "Good job, Weed."

"Thank you, Voice," Rosa murmured, happy to be walking with his arm around her waist. "It will stand for generations."

"Went above and beyond," Fiala said. "This has to be able to easily handle two wagons."

"It can," Rosa nodded. "If this becomes what Doc believes it will, then it is best to make it ready for that future."

"Onto the hot springs," Sonya giggled, "though I think our husband is as relaxed as he can be already."

"With all of you, I find life to be *very* relaxing," Doc laughed.

A giant pool of steaming water wasn't far on the other side of the river. The scent of minerals was strong, but not repugnant to Doc. Lia looked at the steaming water with melancholy, old memories coming back to her.

Doc went to Lia's side, taking her hand. "We've got you."

The others surrounded her, and Lia sniffled once. "It's okay... My old family came from the Heartwood tribe. They married into my tribe when they married me. We came here every winter to visit with their tribe."

"Do you want to talk about them?" Sonya asked.

"No. They are past. I remember them every year, as is our way. The memory just touched me."

All of them kissed her briefly to remind her of the love she had around her at this moment.

"Let's strip and enjoy the waters," Lia smiled. "There are dozens of pools up and down the bank from here, along with the caves."

"Caves?" Doc asked, something nudging his memory.

"Vapor caves," Rosa answered before Lia could.

"They were sacred to the tribe," Lia said softly. "A place to let the impurities of life out while seeking a better connection with Mother."

"Natural steam caves made by the springs, right?" Doc asked, still searching for a memory from his old life.

"Yes," Rosa nodded.

"Lia, would it be okay to modify them to bring tourism to the area?" Doc asked her.

Lia was quiet as she started to strip off her clothing. The others slowed in their own undressing, wanting to hear what she had to say.

"Can we do it to honor Mother?" Lia asked.

"Yes," Doc said. "We might want to stay another day or two. If we do, Rosa can sculpt the caves to represent Mother's presence. We can even see about naming them to reflect that ideal."

Sophia sighed at his words.

"Sophia?" Doc asked softly.

"I know and agree, Doc," she said. "I just want to get there now, not later... I'm being selfish."

Doc went to her, touching her cheek gently. "I understand. There's nothing wrong with feeling that way, either, but Rosa being able to set things up for us before we go will be better for us in the long run."

Nodding, Sophia stepped into his arms. "I know... I'm for the idea of preparing the area for the future."

"You know that, when we get there, it'll still be a day or two for us to get things in order for the wedding, right?"

"Yes, and that's fine. I just want it now. The trip means we're getting closer, but each day we stop, I feel my heart twist. What if you decide against it when we get there?"

Doc lifted her chin, meeting her orange eyes. "Never. I wouldn't turn away from you. Our wives would never forgive me if I even considered it, either."

"We would be very upset," Ayla said.

"Doc isn't the kind to turn from someone he loves," Sonya added.

"You're already part of our family in everything but legal name," Fiala said.

"A member of our small tribe," Lia smiled.

"He loves you deeply, Sophia," Rosa added. "I can see his love for all of you. It is deep and powerful."

Sophia leaned against Doc. "I know it's stupid. It's just fear. I'm not letting it stop me; it just lingers. I won't ask you to rush just to assuage my fears, Doc. Making things better now makes sense. Doing this will make Lia happy, too."

Doc kissed her gently before letting her go. "Thank you, Sophia. Can I undress you now?"

Sophia blushed, then nodded. "Can I hold you while we soak?"

"I think we'll all be taking turns holding each other," Fiala smiled. "After all, we want our turns with you, too."

"I would love that," Sophia admitted.

* * *

They spent a couple of hours enjoying the water. Doc knew that, during the winter, the pool would be even better than it was now in the summer heat. After they'd dried off, Rosa led them to the vapor caves. Lia asked them to strip before entering, so they did as she asked.

The caverns were dark, especially as night fell outside. Luckily, they all had better-than-human eyes, so even with the darkness, they could make out the caves. A small stream of hot water flowed through the single cavern.

Doc looked it over before he nodded slowly. "Rosa, this will tax you again. If it's doable, I'm hoping to turn this into a couple of caverns... enough for a dozen people in each, at the most."

"If I extend it that way, it would be possible," Rosa replied, pointing at where the water came from.

Doc touched the walls, then frowned. "I think marble would make for better benches... Shape in spots for two-inch marble slabs to be placed as benches along the walls, please. Would any luminescent moss grow in here?"

"Yes," Rosa murmured as she knelt beside the wall she was going to work on. "I can even grow it for you."

"That'll be tomorrow, then," Doc said. "I want enough that a human can move reasonably around the caves without it being bright."

"For the best," Lia nodded. "How do you think to tie this back to Mother, Doc?"

"Carving the stone," Doc murmured, "or Rosa shaping it to look like natural carving. I'm sure the tribes have pictographs of Mother. We want to incorporate them into the walls... faint, but here."

"Oh... can we add a few from the clans, too?" Sonya asked.

"Yes."

"There are very old ones from history," Sophia said. "I've seen reproductions in old texts. There is debate if humans or bestials made them."

"All of them... maybe one type per room?" Doc murmured. "That would be wonderful. It would give the idea that she accepted all forms."

"What will you name the caves?" Fiala asked.

"Mother's Warmth," Doc smiled.

"And the community you want to build here?" Ayla asked.

"I was still debating that, but I'm thinking Heartwood's Tears."

Lia's breathing hitched at the name. "A lament to them being gone?"

"Yes. If the name remains, then the tribe's memory remains," Doc said. "Everyone who comes here will learn about the tribe, and the name will remind everyone who ever thinks of it."

Lia grabbed him, holding him tightly as the far wall of the cave began to erode away into nothing. "I love you, Doc."

Doc held her back. "I love you too, my dear elf. We can't undo the past, but we can make people think about the future."

The others folded around them while Rosa worked. She smiled as she felt the love from the group. She would make this place a memorial to the tribe, but also a place of reverence to Mother. Doc would praise her for it, then reward her when she'd finished.

CHAPTER THREE

They ended up staying at the springs for two days. Rosa created a path from the road to the bridge; with her work, the new path was infinitely better than the road they'd been using. That had Doc wondering what else Rosa could do to make things better for the budding communities he had planned.

Clyde and Harrid used a couple of the smaller pools farther up the bank from the giant one Doc and his wives used. Both men were glad to get a good scrub to pull the travel dirt off. Harrid stood in awe when he saw the vapor caves. The only thing missing were the marble slabs Doc wanted as benches. Clyde thought it was interesting, but wasn't as amazed.

When they headed down the road toward Furden again, Doc asked Rosa to help fix the worst of the road conditions. She even made a couple of one-wagon bridges in spots that would benefit from them, instead of having to ford the river. Doc and his wives made sure to re-energize her every night, causing a bit of discomfort for Harrid and Clyde, but the family did their best to keep the noise down.

It was a little more than a week after they'd left Deep Gulch when they finally rolled into Furden. The small city was built mostly of wood, but a few stone buildings were dotting what would be the main street. The outskirts of the city held a few large manor homes that spoke of wealth. A small river wound through the settlement— Doc's mind supplied the name 'South Platte River,' but he wondered what it was called here.

"Furden, capital of the territory," Clyde said. "The Flat River is the reason it survives, though it does flood sometimes."

"Nicole said there are over ten thousand people here," Ayla said. "A far cry from the cities of the east, but far more than Deep Gulch."

"It's going to be unpleasant," Sonya said. "I can imagine the noise and smell."

"Yeah," Doc agreed. "Probably not great, but we have business here, the most important of which is a wedding."

Sophia's cheeks pinked, but she was smiling when she looked back at him. "Getting the rail and Heartwood's Tears started is more important for your mission, but thank you, Doc."

"We need to secure lodging, first," Clyde said as he got the wagon rolling again, having paused so they could all see the city.

"There's a decent hotel near the bank called Palace Hotel. It's where many of the wealthy stay when they're passing through," Ayla said. "Peabody told me about it."

"There for the night," Doc said, looking at the afternoon sun. "Tomorrow, we get things going for a longer stay. I want to find a home that will suit us, and another place for Clyde to stay with the horses. We'll send word to the bank that we're in the city afterward so Roquefell knows where to find us. Sophia, I want to wait for the wedding until we see him."

"Because inviting him to your wedding shows that you value him," Sophia nodded. "Okay. I can wait a few more days." Her lips tugged down at the corners even though she tried to keep her tone upbeat.

"We can marry right now, if you'd rather," Doc said, riding up so he was beside the wagon.

Sophia glanced at him, then away. "I'm being selfish again, Doc... No. I can wait. I just want..." She shook her head. "I'll wait. What's better for our family overall is what we should prioritize."

Doc reached out to her, and she took his hand briefly. "Ayla, find a place for a wedding. Fiala, Sonya, help her, then arrange for flowers, music, and food, please. Sophia deserves as close as we can get to what you had."

"We'll manage it, husband," Fiala smiled brightly. "That'll help with the wait, I bet."

Sophia nodded meekly. "Thank you…"

Rosa touched Sophia's shoulder. "We all care for you, Sophia."

"Before I go to the hotel," Doc said, slowing to ride alongside the wagon bed, "I need to take someone to the soulsmith. I want to cut off any trouble before it happens."

"That'd be for the best," Sophia said. "Having her paperwork in order will stop a mountain of trouble."

Doc held out his arm. "Come on, Weed. We're splitting off."

Rosa slid to the side of the wagon, then carefully— with Doc's help— shifted to sit behind him. She held on to his waist, her chest pressed to his back. Saying goodbye to the others, Doc rode ahead into the city proper, with Harrid grimacing behind him as his thighs protested.

Doc was aware of the people staring at them when they rode past. Expressions ranged from shock, anger, and lust, but Doc ignored them all. He wasn't sure exactly where the soulsmith would be, but he figured it was likely near the main street.

As he got to the bustling thoroughfare, he had to slow the gelding. Joining the slow-moving traffic of horses and wagons, Doc angled toward a man with a badge on his chest.

"Sir?" Doc called out. "Deputy?"

The man with the badge broke off his conversation with a grizzled old man, turning to Doc. "How can I help you?"

"Where's the soulsmith, sir?"

The deputy's eyes widened when he saw Rosa behind Doc. "You managed to collar one?"

"Have to get the paperwork signed off, but yes." Doc turned the horse so Rosa could be seen, her collar visible.

"Damn, that... you going to sell her? I know the demand for them back east is high."

"I had no idea," Doc said, his tone neutral. "I need to get her collar checked and paperwork signed off before anything else."

"R-right," the deputy stammered. "Uh... two streets down," he pointed as he spoke, "right next to the bank. It's the small building with barred windows. Never thought I'd see one in the flesh... Thank you for making her cover up. I'd have had to bring you in for indecency if you hadn't."

"Which is why she wears it," Doc chuckled. "Thank you."

"You staying in the city long?" the deputy asked.

"For a bit, at least. Business to get done. Is there a problem?"

"No, but I can warn the sheriff and others so if they see her out, they aren't taken by surprise. You do know she has to be with you or someone from your family at all times, right?"

"She always is," Doc nodded. "Just let them know she might be with my wife."

"Will do. Make sure they have the right paperwork to prove the claim."

Doc's brow furrowed for a second before he nodded. "Will do. Thanks, Deputy...?"

"Oh, right. Deputy Hays McGee, sir."

"Thank you, Deputy McGee."

Doc rode off, and McGee turned back to the old man he'd been talking with.

Rosa whispered to Doc, "He was thinking about how the sheriff might try to find a way to get you to sell me."

"I'll break them if they try," Doc murmured back. "It's why we're going to do this now."

"Thank you for your revulsion at the idea of selling me."

"You're mine and no one else's, Weed. They'll have to take you over my dead body."

"Which I won't allow," Rosa shivered as she soaked in his thoughts.

"Guess we'll be together forever, then."

Luck's Holding

"Yes, please, Voice."

Doc patted her hands around his waist as he slowly guided the horse down the street. He sent her images of loving her well into old age, then felt her press more into his back.

The bank he'd been directed to was Emerita First National. Doc nodded, knowing he'd be back to visit it after they found a place to stay. A couple of horses were tied out in front, and a guard with a shotgun was standing on the porch. Doc nodded to the man as he rode past.

The brick building right next to that was much smaller, and the front windows had thick bars which would make it impossible to use them for entry or exit. Doc came to a stop in front of it, getting down after Rosa and tying the horse to the hitching post. Eyeing the front of the place, the sign declaring it to be the soulsmith, he felt a wrongness to it.

Rosa shivered, looking at the ground. "This place is steeped in twistedness. Not Darkness, but a twisted perversion of Mother's ways."

"We'll be in and out as fast as we can," Doc said. "Come on."

"Yes, Voice."

"I'll keep an eye on the horses," Harrid grunted as he got off his own mount.

Doc gave him a look, then shifted over and healed him quickly so he would not catch any attention. "Thank you, Harrid. We'll be right back."

Entering the shop, Doc was glad for the light, but then frowned—the lights were coming from soul stones. They were behind glass, glowing softly, much like electric lightbulbs, but softer. The front was a small space with only a single chair by the door and a counter. A bell rested on the counter with a sign telling customers to ring and wait.

Doc tapped the bell as he shifted uneasily. The room felt wrong, setting his teeth on edge. Rosa stood beside him, her leg pressed against his as she stared at the floor.

The door behind the counter opened and a gray-templed, black-haired man with thick glasses came out of the back. "Hmm, customers...? A dryad!" His eyes were bright as he stared at Rosa. "Ponderosa pine, isn't she?"

"She is," Doc said, pulling out the paperwork. "I need you to verify her paperwork. Also, what paperwork does my spouse need to prove she's also able to have the dryad beside her?"

The soulsmith gave Doc a long look for a moment, his fingers tugging the edge of his waxed mustache absently. "Hmm... Interesting... Keeping a dryad outside of being a mage is flamboyant. You don't look like you have that kind of money, either."

"Looks can be deceiving," Doc snorted amiably. "Look, I've been on the road for over a week. I wasn't about to wear my suits when out on the trail."

The soulsmith chuckled. "That is a fair point, sir. I do know some who would, but they're fools. I'd thought you were just a trapper when you brought her in."

"No, she's mine. I won't sell her or trade her."

"Can I get your name?"

Doc set the paperwork on the counter. "Doc Holyday, owner of Luck's Holdings."

His eyes sharpened on Doc. "Luck's Holdings? I've gotten a lot of stones from the mine owned by them."

"My mine," Doc smiled.

"The rich are entitled to a few eccentricities," the soulsmith chuckled. "Keeping a dryad when you have no use for one is that." Picking up the paperwork, he read through it. "Hmm... yes... this is all in order." He set it down, then tapped the counter. "Get her up here so I can examine the collar."

Doc moved the paperwork, then patted the counter. Rosa lifted herself onto it and laid down, her face impassive.

The old man stared down at her, then sighed. "A lovely tree. I always liked the pattern to the ponderosa pine." Pulling out a monocle, he put it on before staring at Rosa's collar, his finger gently tapping the stones. After a moment, he grunted. "Roll over, please."

Rosa did as directed, having been watching Doc's mind and doing as he wished her to.

After a minute of the soulsmith checking the back of the collar, he nodded. "The collar is secured and empowered. Now, for the test: I need you to order her to do something outlandish."

Doc frowned for a moment, wondering what he could order her to do that would prove the collar was functional. The idea hit him a moment later. "Tell me you love me."

"I love you, sir," Rosa whispered.

"That'll work. No dryad wants to be collared. They all resent and hate the one who collared them," the soulsmith nodded. "Get her down so I can finish the paperwork, please. As for your wife's paperwork, there is a spouse's form. I'll get it when I'm done with this."

"I'll need five copies, please," Doc said.

The man had pulled a feather pen and ink from under the counter, but he paused. "Five?"

"I have more than one wife," Doc replied.

"I did say the rich were eccentric..."

"I haven't gotten your name, sir."

"Hmm, there is that," the man said as he uncapped the ink. "I'm Richard Steward, soulsmith, graduate of Rockhill College... er, pardon me. It's Apoc University, Summit City campus now."

"Ah, I should've realized you'd be an educated man," Doc said. "Never attended, myself."

"Well, Rockhill was for those who wanted direction from a higher source," Steward chuckled as he wrote on the forms. "Apoc University takes over all the smaller colleges. Says they need better direction. I graduated in 1850, which was a few years before they took over."

"I didn't think you were that old, sir."

Steward laughed. "I'm nearly fifty, young man. Clean living has helped me stay strong."

"I would've put you in your thirties," Doc said. "Outside of the gray decorating your temples and a few in your mustache, you don't look that old."

"I don't drink or smoke, which helps that. Many don't understand that hard lifestyles mean an early grave."

"I'm all too aware. I don't smoke. No chew, either. I do favor a drink now and again, truth be told."

"Your body will make you pay for that in the future," Steward said as he pushed the paperwork to Doc, holding back a single page in his hand. "Your copies. I'll get this filed tomorrow. Let me go grab the spouse forms for you. Five, you said?"

"I enjoy a good woman as well as a good drink," Doc grinned.

"Ah, a vice I still have, myself. With wives, though, you'll not be visiting the establishments I do. But, in case you like a bit of... wild fun," Steward said slowly, "the Iniquitous Den has women of a certain type."

Doc knew "iniquitous" could mean sinful, so he figured he knew what the man was saying. "Ah. Not just human?"

"No humans at all," Steward replied. "Some of them can be quite... spirited. I enjoy those ones."

"Good to know. I doubt I'll be visiting it, but perhaps I'll stop by. I'm assuming that just getting a drink is on the menu there?"

"They have a full lounge. A man of your wealth could visit it. I wouldn't mention it to anyone who doesn't have... standing."

"Got it," Doc said as he put the paperwork away. "Thank you."

"Be right back," Steward chuckled. "Oh, just one question: do you have any personal stones to sell?"

"I do have some on hand. Interested?"

"All of the stones I get from your mine are slated for government work. I'd been hoping to get my hands on the ones not sold to them. I have experiments to test, but without free stones, I'm stuck."

"I don't have them on me. Let me get back to you."

"Of course," Steward nodded. "I'll stop delaying and get those forms now."

CHAPTER FOUR

Unhitching the gelding, Doc led the horse across the street toward the massive hotel. Rosa followed him with her head down, her eyes tracking people nearby. Harrid was in step behind them, also scanning the street. Doc tied his horse up in front of the hotel, then led Rosa up the stairs to the front doors. A man in uniform was standing there, watching Doc and Rosa approach with a curious expression.

"Can I help you, sir?" the doorman asked.

"Checking in. Not sure if my group already did." The sound of horses behind him got Doc's attention— everyone had arrived just behind him. "Ah, there they are now."

Lips puckering slightly, the doorman cleared his throat. "Sir, this establishment is for the *wealthy*."

"I've heard," Doc said, turning back to the doorman. "Is it humanist?"

The doorman frowned slightly, but replied crisply, "No, sir."

"Then we'll be fine. Which livery do you use?"

"Franklin's. It's down the street," the doorman said primly. "Please wipe your boots before entering, sir."

Doc looked at his boots. "Need to see about shoes while we're here, too..." he muttered. Scraping his boots, he looked at the doorman. "Going to need help with the trunks."

"Yes, sir," the doorman replied tightly. "Please step inside. As soon as you register, we'll have the bellman help."

Harrid moved up beside Doc, scraping his boots off, as well.

"Ladies," Doc called to his wives, "I'll bring the bellman back in a moment."

"We'll get it out of the wagon," Lia said.

"Ayla, this is a business expense. Come help," Doc said.

The half-elf had just tied off her horse. "Yes, husband."

The doorman's eye twitched, but he stayed otherwise impassive as he opened the door for Doc. His eyes tracked to Rosa's bare feet; they didn't have any mud or manure on them, so he stayed quiet. Doc entered the lobby, looking over the rich décor with a critical eye.

The lobby was an atrium with a stained-glass ceiling to allow light in. There were silk dividers to separate out the middle of the room, allowing people to sit in peace. Balcony walkways overlooked the lobby floor, allowing all seven floors a clear view. Doc paused just inside, waiting for Ayla, knowing this was clearly an upscale place.

Ayla came in a minute later, her clothing as travel-stained as his. "We'll be met with skepticism, but I can manage," she told him.

"Let's get this done so our things can be brought in," Doc said before offering his arm like a gentleman should.

Ayla took his arm, letting him lead her to the receptionist's desk where the woman on duty eyed them critically. Her eyes darted to Rosa, her lips pursing as she tried to place the oddity with the couple coming her way.

"We need your largest suite, along with two other rooms," Ayla said before the receptionist could speak. "We'll be staying for at least one night, but maybe longer depending on how long it takes to find a suitable home."

The receptionist was caught off-balance by the forward address. "Yes. That will run quite a bit," the receptionist said, trying to reestablish her footing. "This is the most expensive hotel in the city."

"This is the best the city has, hmm?" Doc asked, looking disappointed. "Well, we'll make do, I guess."

Harrid kept his face impassive, chuckling internally at Doc's quick thinking.

Now, the woman was *really* off-balance. No one had dismissed the Palace as less than stellar in all of her time working there. "Uh... yes. I mean..."

Ayla pulled out a checkbook. "Shall we get to the bottom line? I have others who need assistance with their luggage. We'll need the name of the livery the establishment uses, too. We have a half-dozen riding horses and a team with a wagon that'll have to be stabled for the indefinite future."

Seeing the checkbook and the name of the account, the receptionist nodded: it was a name that her manager had told her to be aware of. "Of course." Her tone was now very professional and accommodating. "The best suite, plus two more rooms. We can arrange that for Luck's Holdings."

Ayla glanced at Doc before smiling. "Good. Can you send the bellman out right away? Also, someone to help the coachman get the horses and wagon down to the livery, please."

"Yes, ma'am," the woman replied crisply. "Just give me one moment."

The receptionist was quick to go to the manager's office.

"Roquefell?" Doc asked softly.

"Probably. He would've left word here, figuring we'd use it," Ayla replied softly.

"She'd been told by her boss about the business. He'll be coming out soon," Rosa whispered.

"That tracks," Doc nodded, then promised mentally to thank her later.

Rosa shivered, loving the images he'd sent her.

A thin, severe-looking man in a quality suit followed the receptionist to the front desk. "You're Doc Holyday, the owner of Luck's Holdings?"

"That's me," Doc said as he watched the receptionist hurry off to another door.

"Ah, we've been told to expect you. The owner, Mr. Roquefell, thought you'd eventually be in. Might I just see some paperwork proving you are who you say?"

Ayla tapped the check which was still sitting on the counter. "I was going to pay for our stay."

The manager picked up the check and looked it over before returning it. "That will not be necessary. Standing orders from Mr. Roquefell are to accommodate you. I'm also to inform him you are in the city so that he can extend an invitation to you."

"We'll be finding a home in the city," Doc said. "We won't be here long. Please inform him that, once I have a residence, I will be glad to meet him."

"I see. Very well, sir. In the meantime, your stay is on the house," the manager smiled professionally. He glanced over as two bellmen came out with the receptionist. "And our staff will see to your needs."

"Very well," Doc said. "Thank you…?"

"Ah, yes. Mr. Volenite." He extended his hand, and Doc shook with him. "If you encounter any difficulties, just let me know."

"I will," Doc smiled. "Your best suite can handle six, can't it?"

Volenite looked distant for a moment. "I… can arrange that, if you give me an hour."

"Please. In the meantime, the baggage will be brought up. Is the bathing in the room or communal?"

"In the room? Goodness, maybe in time," Volenite laughed. "Each floor has a bathing room that contains a few tubs along with dividers so you can make sure you have some privacy."

"We'll need the bathroom closed for the next two hours, and the one on the floor below it for my guard and driver. We've just finished a week-long trip and need to refresh."

"Of course, sir," Volenite nodded. He glanced at the receptionist, who went to arrange things.

"Please see to the bed, as well. You'll have two hours once we can get to our clothing."

"Yes, sir. It'll be ready by the time you finish."

"Excellent. I'll make sure to tell Mr. Roquefell about the wonderful service," Doc smiled.

A moment later, the front doors opened and his wives began to file in. Volenite's eyes widened as he took in the assortment of people. It was clear he was a little shocked, but he was able to hide most of it.

"Clyde said he'd get the wagon and horses to the livery, then come back," Lia said. "I made sure he had money for it."

"The top floor's bathroom is ours for two hours," Doc told them. "Harrid, you and Clyde get the sixth floor's for the same amount of time. When we finish, Mr. Volenite here will have your rooms arranged. We'll be in the best suite."

"I'll take the one next to yours," Harrid said. "I can share with Clyde."

"Clyde can have his own," Doc said. "Just in case he finds... distractions."

"Ah, yes. Thank you, Sha... sir," Harrid corrected himself with a grunt when Sonya elbowed him.

"Room seven-ten for you, Mr. Holyday. Your man there can have room seven-nine, and your driver can have room seven-eight. The baths are the first door at the top of the stairs on each floor. Is that acceptable?"

"Quite," Doc nodded. "A pleasure."

The front doors opened and the two bellmen came back in, struggling with the trunks.

"I will ask if you'd like us to secure your weapons while you stay with us," the manager offered. "We do provide that service."

"We'll keep them with us," Doc said, "but thank you."

"Of course. However, we do have a 'no firing weapons inside the building' policy," Volenite said carefully, as if worried that he might upset them.

"The only reason we'll discharge our firearms is if we're fighting for our lives," Lia said simply.

"Yes, of course," the manager coughed. "Rooms seven-ten, seven-nine, and seven-eight," he advised the bellmen.

Two more bellmen came rushing out to assist the others, one of them having to put his hat on as he crossed the floor.

"Yes, sir," one of the newcomers said.

"Ladies, shall we?" Doc motioned to the stairs.

"Thank you, sir," Ayla said, collecting the check and tucking it into her folder. "Can you arrange dinner for all of us, plus for our staff? Delivered to our rooms in three hours?"

"Of course. The dining room is open from six to nine every day, but for you, we can arrange room service."

"Perfect," Doc chuckled. "Good evening. I believe we'll be staying in for the rest of the night."

"Yes, sir," the manager said, watching them go.

He was still there when the receptionist came back to the front desk as the group began climbing the stairs. "I'll send word to Mr. Roquefell. Arrange to have the carpets looked at after they leave. The one woman with him will damage them badly. If they aren't who they say they are, I will see them pay or be jailed."

"Yes, sir," the receptionist said softly.

Doc paused on the second floor to heal the few who could use it, trying to make their climb up all the stairs more bearable. He then trailed the others with Rosa beside him. "Tell me, Weed."

"He was telling the truth about what orders he was given, but he is doubtful if we are who we say we are. He is unhappy to have so many... others... here. That's the worst he thought of us, but it was still there. He was also displeased with Sophia's talons and the carpets."

"Is he a bigot or not?"

"I'd say he's much less than some, but has an edge of bigotry. He wants to do the best he can to show himself useful to Roquefell. He believes that he will be sent east to a better establishment if he can prove himself."

"He might be right. Roquefell sounds like he's the kind to reward his subordinates."

"Peabody, Rondle, and this man all hold him in high esteem," Rosa said.

"We'll see if he's going to be an ally or not in the next few days." Doc shook his head, then remembered the paperwork he had on him. "Oh, right. Ladies, I have papers for each of you…"

CHAPTER FIVE

The full group, including Clyde and Harrid, ate in the dining room of the hotel the next morning. All of them were glad to have full meals again, and the chef's dinner last night was just as good as their breakfast was.

"We'll need the marriage form, set up the reception hall, food, and other sundries, then get in to see the judge for the wedding," Ayla was saying as they finished eating. "It'll still be a smaller wedding... oh, we need to invite the Ironbeard clan."

Sonya nodded. "Which means the wedding won't be as small as you thought. Only part of the clan will come, though. The elders will, and maybe some of the others. He's marrying a non-clan member, and we don't have the same ties here that we did with my clan."

"Is there a tribe from here, Lia?" Doc asked.

"Like the Heartwood clan, they were wiped out," Lia said a little stiffly.

A pall of sadness fell over the table for a moment.

"We need to find a house today, if possible," Sophia said. "I also want to visit the printer. Do you mind if I manage that, Doc?"

"Not at all, but I'd like Lia to go with you," Doc replied. "We don't have trouble here, but this is a city, and I'd rather petty crime didn't touch you, either."

"Lia?" Sophia asked.

"I'll go with you. He's right; it'd be best to not go alone," Lia said.

"I was thinking of asking the manager here if we couldn't close this room off for the reception," Ayla said, pulling the conversation back to wedding ideas. "We know the chef is good, and this room would be big enough if we moved things around a little. It would also be easy to get a room for the night." She gave Sophia a smirk when she said that.

Sophia blushed, then nodded. "It makes sense."

"We can ask before we go. He might know who to ask about homes, too," Doc said before draining the rest of his coffee. "I want shoes to go with my suit. When we eventually go east, I'll need them."

"You want to go west first, and boots work both here and out west," Lia said. "I'd wait on the shoes."

"Agreed," Ayla said. "Any businessman here knows to take the ruggedness of the frontier into account."

Lia's eyes went past Doc. "Someone is coming."

Doc waited, watching Lia to see if he would have to act.

The man walked around until he could see Doc. "Excuse me, sir? You are Mr. Holyday, right?"

"I am, but who are you?" Doc asked.

"I'm Robert Robin," the man smiled broadly. "Mr. Roquefell sent me. You are looking for a house, are you not?" Taking his hat off, the man's canine ears became visible.

"We are, but we also need a place for our driver to care for the wagon and horses," Doc said.

"Yes, of course. I'm the owner of Robin's Realty. We handle many properties in the city, sir. If you'd like to come with me, I'm sure we can find you a home before the day ends."

"I'll be right back," Ayla said, getting to her feet.

All the other women rose with her, leaving just the three men at the table.

"When they get back, we'll go with you," Doc said. "Well, most of us will. Clyde, we'll see about getting things shifted tomorrow, probably. Take the day."

"Appreciate that," Clyde smiled. "I was going to visit an old gambling hall I used to enjoy."

"Don't lose your shirt," Doc chuckled.

"It'll be fine. The games are honest at Silvered Dreams."

"Oh, Colin's place," Doc said, thinking back to the man from the tournament. "Tell him I said hello, and that I'll try to stop in while I'm in the city."

"Will do," Clyde said before getting up. "See you tomorrow."

* * *

Their carriage arrived on the outskirts of the city— the river ran not more than a hundred yards from the manor. It was a grand Tudor-style manor with two floors, with windows dotting the front that faced the south, toward the city.

Harrid jumped down from the driver's bench where he'd been riding shotgun. Opening the door, he stood aside when Doc got out. As he helped his wives out, Doc hoped that Lia and Sophia were okay, as they'd gone off to run their own errands. The last person out of the carriage was Robert.

"Here we are. This manor was built by one of Mr. Roquefell's associates, but the man went back east, having to take over his family when his father fell ill. It was barely lived in for about five months. There is a staff of two: a maid and gardener, currently in the servant quarters around the back," Robert said as they approached the front door.

"River might be a problem if it floods," Doc said.

"It could, but I doubt it will happen," Robert smiled.

Doc glanced at Rosa, and she bowed her head— she would handle what he wanted if they took up residence here. Turning his attention back to the manor, he had to admit that he liked the exterior. It felt like the home of a socialite, which would suit him for his time in Furden. He spotted at least six chimneys, meaning the inside could be heated easily enough, as they were spaced out across the entire building.

When they reached the front door, it opened to reveal the maid. Her oblong ears were covered in dark brown fur, and her large size made Doc think of a black bear. The hints of gray in her hair and dusting the fur on her ears spoke of her age. "Master Robins, good morning."

"Mizzi, this is the Holyday family," Robins smiled. "I'm showing them the home."

The maid turned to them and curtsied. "Welcome. I'm Mizzi, the maid, if you keep me as such. I have decades of experience with the job."

Fiala stepped forward with a bright smile. "If we do, I'm sure I can use the help with keeping a place this large in order."

Mizzi's eyes tracked over the group, and she curtsied again. "I will do my best, mistress."

"Let me show you the interior," Robert grinned.

"Robert," Doc said, "let Mizzi show them. I'd like you to show me the grounds."

"Of course, sir," Robert said. "Mizzi, I leave them to you."

"I will do my best, sir. Ladies, if you will follow me, I will show you around the inside. There are plenty of rooms for all of you."

Ayla went to follow the others, but had a question for Robert first, "Is there someone who could alter a room for us that you trust here in the city?"

"I do know a few who can modify the home to a limited degree," Robert said, unsure of what she was asking for.

"I ask just in case the master bedroom isn't large enough," Ayla said before she went inside.

"Large enough?" Robert murmured.

"We'll need a bed made to order, as well," Doc said. "There's someone who can do that, yes?"

"Of course. The Ironbeard clan has just started taking orders to make spring mattresses."

"Excellent," Doc smiled. "Shall we?"

"Right. The property is fifty acres, so you'll have all the room you could want," Robert said, leading Doc around the side that was closer to the river. "Plenty of room for whatever you fancy to do."

Doc looked over the area; the property had been cleared for a few hundred feet in all directions. Beyond the cleared space, the land was still wild and natural. Turning toward the back as Robert exposed the potential, Doc barely listened.

A man was near a house set at the back of the cleared area, working on a small garden. Straightening up when he saw the group, the man dabbed at his forehead, brushing against his curled ram's horns. His hand paused when he realized one of the three was a dryad.

"Ah, there he is. Radley is the gardener, married to Mizzi. Radley?" Robert motioned the man to them.

Setting his hoe aside, Radley headed their way, his eyes darting back and forth between Rosa and the men. "Sir?"

"Mr. Holyday is considering buying the property. Your wife is showing his wives the home, but he wished to see the grounds."

The man lowered his gaze away from Doc. "A pleasure, sir."

"Call me Doc," Doc told the gardener.

Radley jerked slightly, his gaze coming up to meet Doc's. Seeing Doc's extended hand, the gardener took it on reflex.

"Pleasure. I know you have your work cut out for you just maintaining this clear area," Doc said.

"It's good work, sir," Radley said, bewildered by this finely-dressed man treating him well— the former owner had completely ignored him and his wife.

"How often does the river flood?"

"Every ten years or so. It depends on the snowmelt."

"Going to have to find a way to make sure the house is kept safe," Doc said.

"It rarely floods enough to come this far in, sir."

"I'd rather be safe," Doc said amiably. "Rosa, why don't you go ahead and check the river for me?"

"Yes, Master," Rosa said as she walked away from them.

"She's yours?" Radley asked with hesitation.

"I'm not a mage, so you'll be fine," Doc chuckled.

Both Robert and Radley were clearly thrown off by the comment; who other than a mage would keep a dryad on hand?

"The exterior looks good," Doc nodded. "Radley, let's go back around the front. I have an idea about how I'd like the driveway to look."

"Yes, sir," Radley murmured, not able to regain his mental footing quickly.

"I thought maybe you were... not many can afford to have a collared dryad. The hunters charge a lot, and the mages buy them up right away," Robert said.

"I collared her," Doc said amiably as he started to walk around the far side of the home to circle it completely. "Did it when I was getting my mine in order."

Both men were again shocked at the news, trailing Doc reflexively. Harrid walked behind all of them, his beard hiding his smile as he watched Doc throw people off-kilter time and again.

* * *

Doc shook Robert's hand, handing him the check. "A pleasure."

"The pleasure is mine, Doc," Robert said. "Didn't really expect you to go for the first property."

"I like it, my wives like it, and it has room for growth," Doc smiled. "Just make sure to send the workers out there tomorrow. They need to be respectful to my wives."

"Of course. I know just the ones," Robert nodded.

"Good. Have a good day."

"You, as well, Doc." Robert left them in the hotel lobby— he had a check to deposit at the bank.

"They're only building a stable?" Fiala asked, as she figured she'd be the one at home tomorrow.

"Yeah. The servant's quarters had a spare room for Clyde. Make sure they add a living space to the stables, though— he deserves his own space. I'll be there tomorrow with Rosa making sure the property doesn't flood, just in case."

"We'll check out tomorrow," Sonya smiled. "Things are moving quickly."

Sophia smiled at Sonya. "Yes. Oh, Doc, I got my errands done. I had a limited run on these for you right now, but more will be made up in the coming week."

Doc took what she'd handed him: it was a business card, printed on cardstock. It had the name of the company across the top with their logo underneath that, followed by Doc's name and title. "Hmm... probably going to need them."

Sophia handed Ayla a small stack of the cards, as well. "Yours. I have mine."

"I haven't said this recently, Sophia, but thank you for all you do," Doc murmured. "I'll be informing the bank to tell Roquefell we're ready to meet when we leave tomorrow. The sooner I can see him, the better."

Sophia nodded eagerly. "Agreed."

"The restaurant here will be used as the reception hall for the wedding," Ayla smiled. "I have it under contract already."

"I also made sure we can see the judge in three days," Sophia said softly. "I'm hoping that'll be okay?"

"I'll let the clan know tomorrow," Sonya said. "Fiala, will you come with me?"

"I'll stay home tomorrow," Lia said when Fiala looked uncertain. "Better for you to go with her than me."

"I'll talk with Clyde about getting a carriage. If we're going to be in town for a bit, it's best to get one now," Ayla said. "I need to see about the properties for the hot springs tomorrow, too. Sophia, I'll need you for that."

"We can get the framework in order, at least," Sophia nodded.

"Let's go wash up, have dinner delivered to the room, and turn in," Doc smiled. "Tomorrow might be busy again."

CHAPTER SIX

Doc crossed the street— Rosa just behind him, and Harrid was on his right. The Emerita First National Bank was massive, made of the same stone as the hotel across the street. The front had columns supporting an awning that stretched across the majority of the first floor. Outside the double doors was a guard, casually standing with a shotgun.

Doc nodded to the guard when the man gave him a quick scan. "Morning."

"Morning, sir," the guard replied, his eyes going from Harrid to the dryad. "Keep her on good behavior."

"She'll behave," Doc said amiably.

The guard looked doubtful, but didn't contradict Doc.

The lobby was massive, easily taking up half of the first floor. Three guards stood at evenly spaced points inside, holding their shotguns loosely as they watched everyone. Offices took up the left side of the lobby, with plaques denoting what each office was for. The back of the room had a door where one of the three guards was standing, and Doc figured it would be the manager's office. The right side of the room held the tellers, along with the secured vault area.

The handful of people there were being seen by the tellers, or in line to do so. Doc had only one reason to visit, so he walked over to the guard near the manager's door. Much like Deep Gulch, the guards inside the bank were bull bestials. The man by the office had sharpened his forward-facing horns to give himself an imposing presence.

"I'm Doc Holyday. I need to speak with the manager about Mr. Roquefell," Doc said once he'd gotten close enough.

"Wait here," the guard said. He knocked on the door, then stepped inside. He was back a moment later, leaving the door open. "Mr. Buchon will see you."

"Thank you," Doc said as he entered the office, Rosa right behind him. "Good morning, sir," Doc greeted the manager.

Harrid followed Doc inside, but stepped to stand just inside the door.

The man behind the desk grinned as he stood up, his gut making him scoot his chair back first. "Mr. Holyday, a pleasure! I've heard a lot about you. Mr. Roquefell has been looking forward to meeting you. I, myself, am a little upset with you, as you cost me two of my best people."

"Rondle and Peabody," Doc chuckled. "Good men. You'll never get Peabody back."

"Yes, I've been told that he is marrying and staying in Deep Gulch to run the bank there," Buchon sighed. "A pity. I still hope to get Rondle back in a year. Sadly, though, I'm beginning to think I will not. Your business in that town is deemed an important account to the bank."

"Sorry, not sorry?" Doc chuckled, shaking hands with the manager.

Buchon's brow furrowed. "What an odd saying."

"I don't want to waste too much of your time," Doc said, taking his seat. "I was told to inform you when I got to town so you could tell Mr. Roquefell that I was here. I'll be at my new estate. I believe it was called the Yorkton estate before."

"Oh, yes. A very good home. Barely been lived in," Buchon nodded. "Robin wasted no time getting you to see it."

"He said Roquefell sent him," Doc shrugged. "But I'd originally been told to inform you, so that is why I came. You'll be seeing a lot of business from Luck's Holdings in the near future."

"Already got irons in the fire?"

"Quite a few," Doc chuckled. "Just don't be surprised when my financial officer comes in. You know of her, I'm sure?"

Buchon barked a laugh, his belly shaking. "Yes, I've heard of her. It was because of her that the records from Deep Gulch suddenly became easier to understand. I've heard you married her; is that true?"

"It is," Doc nodded.

"Interesting," Buchon said, his gaze drifting to Rosa. "Very interesting. Well, I shall pass the message to Mr. Roquefell before the day is out. You should expect a message from him in the next day or two."

"I'm already looking forward to the meeting," Doc smiled. Standing up from the short meeting, he waited for Buchon to do the same, then shook hands again. "Thank you for your time. Not sure I'll need to see you again, but it was nice meeting you."

"The pleasure is all mine," Buchon said. "I'm sure we'll end up seeing each other again. A man of wealth and influence like you will surely be attending social events."

Doc kept his face impassive, but nodded. "Probably, though I'm more a frontiersman than a socialite."

"We have a number of them that have recently started to attend events. I'm sure you'll do better than they are, at the very least."

"We'll see," Doc said. "Have a good day."

"Good day, Mr. Holyday."

Rosa trailed him silently all the way out of the bank. The moment they crossed the street, she spoke softly, "He is unpleasant. Goodman promised to bring Ayla up for him to have before you appeared in Deep Gulch. He was also thinking of ways to try to get me from you."

"People are people wherever you go," Doc sighed. "I'll warn Ayla about him. Has he done anything that we can point to for Roquefell?"

"He didn't think of anything this time."

"Pity," Doc said. "As long as he does his job and doesn't cause problems for us, we'll leave him be."

"As you wish, Voice."

"You'll be getting plenty later, Weed," Doc murmured. "I'm putting you to work as soon as we get to the property."

Rosa's eyes glowed briefly as she watched his ideas play through his mind.

Clyde was pulling the wagon up to the hotel when Doc got there. "Ready to get things moved over, sir."

"Thank you. We'll be getting the stables set up at the property as quickly as we can. Until then, we'll keep using the livery you've been using."

"Yes, sir," Clyde said, setting the brake.

Lia came out of the hotel with four bellmen behind her, each carting the trunks. "Husband, we're ready. The others have already left on their errands."

"Once it's loaded, we'll be off, then," Doc said as he pulled a couple of dollar coins out of his pocket. Once the bellmen had the trunks in the wagon, he tossed them each a dollar. "Thank you, gentlemen."

They thanked him back before going back inside the Palace Hotel. Doc looked at the building again, wondering why the builders had opted to make it a triangle. It worked with its location, but it was just so odd; he mused that the shape might be another attraction point for it.

"Sir?" Clyde asked.

"Sorry, we're good," Doc said before climbing up onto the bench. Lia, Rosa, and Harrid were already in the back. "Take us home."

Clyde released the brake and flicked the reins. "Yes, sir."

* * *

Doc was glad it didn't take them longer in the city, as Radley was speaking to a group of six men who were standing beside a couple of wagons. "Robert moved faster than I thought," Doc chuckled. "Lia, can you and Radley get the trunks inside? I'll be getting the workers started before coming inside."

"Of course."

"I'll help," Clyde said as he pulled them up.

Radley and the workers looked over as the wagon rolled down the drive. "There's the master of the house now," Radley said.

"Good," the lead worker snorted. He turned away from Radley, then slowed upon seeing Lia and Rosa in the wagon.

As soon as the brake was set, Doc got down, advancing on the men. "Guys, if you'll follow me, I'll show you where to build and what we need."

"Yes, sir," the lead worker said slowly, rubbing at the sawed-off horn nub on the side of his head.

"I wasn't expecting a full crew today, honestly," Doc said, already walking away. "Robert sure moved quickly for me."

"Bring the wagons around," the bull bestial told his crew. "Yes, sir. He said you'd pay top dollar, and that you wouldn't care that we're bestials."

"True on both counts," Doc said.

The man kept glancing back at Rosa walking behind them. "Uh, sir...? Are you a mage?"

"Hmm... not like you think," he said as he walked toward the back of the property. "I'm thinking over here would be best. It'll need enough room for a dozen horses, two carriages, and a wagon. I'd also want a small suite attached to it for the driver and grooms. Need to see about a groom, too."

"I know a few young men who can do the job," the bull bestial said.

Doc paused, looking back at the man. "Sorry, I forgot. I'm Doc Holyday, and you are?"

"Simpson, sir."

"Well, Simpson, if you want to send them along, I'll talk with them."

"I'll send at least two out. They're boys who are extra hands where they are now."

"That'll be fine," Doc said. He looked at Rosa, who nodded fractionally. "I need at least two suites, with room for beds and a living area, and a joined bathroom that they can share," Doc went on.

"I'll need to bring in another man for the plumbing."

"Bring in the best you can get," Doc said. "As long as they do quality work, I'll be fine."

"Yes, sir. I can get this moving. Do you want updates?"

"Periodically, but mostly when it's finished. I have horses in a livery in town, but I'd rather you take your time to build a lasting structure than slapping one together."

Simpson nodded. "Very well, sir. We'll get started."

"Radley can help with things you might need. I'll make sure you have water on hand, too. I don't want anyone getting heatstroke."

"We appreciate that, sir."

"I'll be down by the river for a good portion of today," Doc told Simpson. "If you have a real problem, just let me know."

"Yes, sir."

"Come on, Rosa," Doc said. He headed back for the house as the wagons came around the corner.

Harrid trailed Doc; he was a quiet shadow, ready to defend him if needed.

CHAPTER SEVEN

Doc yawned as he took a seat in the dining room. He gave his wives a tired smile. "We'll need to refresh Rosa later tonight. I did what I could for her while we were outside."

"With the workers here?" Sophia asked with a little shock.

"He took me into the woods," Rosa told her. "He fed me quickly, then we went back to work."

"We got back later than I thought we would," Fiala said. "I hope dinner is okay as it is."

"I'm sure it'll be fine," Doc told her gently.

"We arranged for deliveries of groceries," Sonya said. "Milk and meat will be twice a week, and the rest will be once a week."

"Delivery? Probably for the best. We are a little far from the city," Doc said. "I'm sure we can afford it."

"We can," Ayla said. "Sophia and I have also asked for a carriage or two. That way, the trip to town can be done in accordance with what your standing in society should be."

"Why don't we trade off stories so we can eat at the same time?" Doc suggested as he pulled a steak off the platter. "I'll start: the workers are decent enough people, and you probably saw that they got the frame up. They were shocked at how easy Rosa made it for them to get the foundation posts in."

Rosa smiled at him when he touched her head; she loved his soft affection during meals.

"As for the river, she improved the bank so we won't have to worry about flooding. If it does, it'll surge to the other side, instead… whoever builds over there will hate it. I expect to hear from Roquefell tomorrow, with me seeing him either then or the day after." He paused. "I also asked the builder if he knew a couple of grooms. We'll need someone for horse care besides Clyde. He said he'd send two people over. Don't be surprised if that happens and I'm out. Just talk to them and hire who you think would be best."

"We'll handle it," Lia said.

"I'll go next," Sonya said. "The Ironbeard clan was happy enough to meet with me. They did request that you stop in to see the elders. All of them promise to be at the wedding, and think that fifty other couples might attend. Elder Alaric also asked if you had business in the city that would interest the clan. I told him I would let you know he was asking."

"Hmm… I'll make sure to talk with him when I stop in there, but that'll likely be after the wedding."

"Besides that, we did some shopping and got things set up for the home. I like the bathroom we have here," Fiala said. "The man who built this place must've spent a fortune on sanitation and water."

"Probably did," Doc agreed. "Would explain the price."

"It was expensive, but if we're here for any length of time, it'll be worth it," Ayla said.

"That's it for Sonya and me," Fiala said. "Go ahead, Ayla."

"We arranged for the hot springs property to be purchased by Luck's Holdings. I know what we had in the account to work with before, so the deposit was fine. I'll have to stop by the bank tomorrow to make sure all the money is set to be paid in the installments we set in the contract."

"It wasn't as hard as we thought it might be," Sophia added. "The clerk we spoke to thought we'd be by. They were the one Ayla worked with before to get the property between the mine and Deep Gulch."

"He was very interested in why we wanted that stretch of property and the right of way out to it."

"Were the hot springs not marked on the map?" Doc asked.

"No markings at all, besides the river," Ayla grinned. "That means we got it much cheaper than we would have. I also got a deal on the right of way next to the existing road for cheap. I made sure to secure it all the way to Deep Gulch. Because of that, the rail line can run to the mine over your property instead of over the state's right of way."

"Damn. Good job," Doc said between bites.

"We'll just need to find the right people to build up the hot springs and the rail," Sophia said. "We should improve the road between them at the same time. It'll make it easier to attract people that way."

"Since we'll have workers right there anyway, it makes sense," Doc agreed.

"Now for the bad news," Ayla sighed. "We saw the city church while we ran our errands. It's pretty big. I doubt it's only a single preacher. If we end up causing trouble, it'll be even harder to deal with them."

"I'm not hanging out a shingle for healing here. Not right away, at least. I want to get a feel for the city, and that all starts with Roquefell. He'll either be a major ally or a huge stumbling block."

"Doc," Lia cut in after a few seconds of silence, "I want to get a laundry maid. Mizzi asked about expanding the staff, and I agreed that we should. She knows a few people who have children at the right age to take on the tasks."

"If you think it needs to be done, then do it," Doc smiled. "Fiala, do you want a cook on staff?"

Fiala licked her lips, a bit torn on the idea. She wanted to be a housewife, but a manor plus staff was daunting to her. "Maybe? Give me a day or two to think about it?"

"Take as long as you want. All of us, plus the extended staff we're going to be adding, is a lot of work. I know you had talked about being the housewife, but at this point, you'd be the Lady. You'd direct and the staff would do for you."

"Mother talked about how Lady Fullerton ran her manor. I'll do my best to do the same here."

"We'll help," Sonya said, covering Fiala's hand with hers.

"Thank you," Fiala exhaled slowly. "I just want to do the best I can for all of us." Looking up, she met Doc's eyes. "A cook would be helpful. We can put them in charge of the larder, as well."

"It's a manor," Sophia said. "We might want to see about hiring a full staff. The servant's quarter out back was built for twenty people."

"We'll do it right, then," Doc said. "Talk with Mizzi. I'm sure she knows others who do similar jobs. We'll promote her to head maid and her husband to groundskeeper. That only leaves the butler as the most important position open."

"We'll speak with her tomorrow," Fiala said. "Those of us that are here and not running other errands."

"Should be most of us," Ayla said, "if everyone can wait for me to just do my small jaunt to the bank and back."

"Best if it's as many of you as possible," Doc said. "The more eyes and opinions on staff, the better. Make sure to arrange it around the upcoming wedding, though." He looked at Sophia. "Go with Ayla into town and tell the judge we'll be there in three days. That's the longest I'm willing to wait, with or without seeing Roquefell."

Sophia's smile was bright. "I will."

"I'd suggest one or two men as guards for the estate," Harrid said. "Even if you don't make enemies, it'll be known that someone of wealth is living here."

Doc gave the normally quiet dwarf a nod. "A good point."

"Two should be enough, but they need to be the right two. Clyde might know another couple of retired bank drivers. Those men have the required personalities."

"Solid idea. We'll talk to him tomorrow about it."

"Yes, sir," Harrid nodded.

"Excuse me," Mizzi said, coming into the room. "If you're done, I'll take those away for you."

"Might as well broach this now," Doc said. "Mizzi, we have a couple of questions, if you don't mind?"

"What can I answer for you, sir?" Mizzi asked, a little uncertain.

"We were considering expanding the staff. You'd be promoted to the head maid, and your husband to groundskeeper," Doc said, "but we need solid advice on other staff. A butler who can work with the two of you is the first priority, as they'd be the last of the senior staff."

Mizzi stared at him for a moment before she curtsied. "Thank you, sir. Umm... would you mind if they're... like my husband and I?"

"I don't care what their lineage is. That's not who I am. All I care about is if they can do the job."

"They would also need to hold a few things in confidence," Ayla said. "Not secrets as such, but things that we'd prefer to not become common knowledge."

"I have a cousin who can do the job. They were trained for it, but the position they were going to take vanished," Mizzi said.

"The position was for here?" Doc asked.

"Yes, sir."

"Have him come around. At least one of my wives will speak with him. If it pans out, we'll hire him. But we'll be adding a full staff, like a laundry maid and others. Can you reach out for us?"

Mizzi looked around at each of them, clearly trying to understand. "You want *me* to select the staff?"

"We would like you to help with it, at least, but it'll mostly be your advice to lead us to the people we interview," Fiala said.

"I... yes. I'll arrange it all for you, mistress." Mizzi curtsied deeply to Fiala.

"Perfect," Doc grinned. "Ayla, you'll need to set the contracts and pay."

"I'll do that after the bank," Ayla nodded.

"We should retire," Lia chuckled. "We all have things to do tomorrow."

"See you for breakfast," Harrid said, the first one to stand.

"We'll talk to Clyde right after that," Doc told the dwarf.

"Yes, sir."

Mizzi began to gather the dishes as everyone left the room. When she was alone, she looked back at the door. Her new employer was odd, but he seemed to care, and his wives proved that he truly didn't mind people's ancestry. A smile came to her as she worked— if it worked out, she'd be getting paid more and have others to do more of the work for her.

CHAPTER EIGHT

Doc followed Harrid out to the servant's quarters, Rosa trailing them with a bright smile. Radley asked if he could help them, but Doc explained that they were just on their way to speak to Clyde.

The interior of the servant's quarters wasn't fancy, but was built as well as the manor. The entry room held a single staircase to the second floor and halls that extended farther on the ground floor.

"Not sure what room he took..." Harrid said.

"Clyde?" Doc called out, figuring the badger bestial would hear him.

A door opening upstairs told them that he'd heard him— Clyde came hustling down the stairs almost immediately. "Yes, sir?"

"Ease up," Doc said. "Sorry, I just wanted to ask you a favor."

Clyde nodded. "What do you need?"

"Harrid suggested a couple of men to keep an eye on security, then went on to suggest that you might know people from your old line of work who'd be interested."

Clyde looked up for a moment before nodding slowly. "You could do for them what you did for me?"

"Easily."

"I can get you a dozen men if you want, then," Clyde snorted. "Lingering injuries plague those of us who retired."

"Say... two for security here, and another as shotgun for the carriages we're going to be getting? Hmm... and a second driver, just in case."

"Four? That'll be stone simple. If you were anyone else, I wouldn't be so sure about it." Clyde met Doc's eyes. "You take care of your own. That'll go a long way with all of them. Uh... wait... can you have the room for the stables extended for very large men?"

"Elephant bestials?" Doc asked.

"For the ones who will stay here. I know two who have lingering pains that would be happy to watch the grounds. One is married with a kid, and the other is a confirmed bachelor."

"I'll tell the workers when they get here. Rosa, we'll need you to help sink another few posts, I'm sure."

"As you need, Voice."

"Another driver and one for shotgun are even easier to get," Clyde went on.

"Bring them by to talk to Ayla; she'll be handling the contracts," Doc told him. "Just remember, the best we can get. It doesn't matter what their heritage is."

"It's one of the reasons I like working for you," Clyde chuckled. "I'll head for town in a minute."

"Thanks," Doc said, shaking hands with him.

Stepping back outside, Harrid smiled. "That'll make me feel better about keeping this place secure. I know how you feel about your wives. Keeping them safe at home will make keeping *you* safe easier."

Doc paused before laughing. "You're right. I didn't think of it that way. I won't be as nervous about the manor being attacked once the guards are here."

The sound of a wagon and people caught Doc's ears. "The workers are here. Good. We can ask about adding onto the stables."

Simpson led his crew around the manor, two horses pulling a

fully laden wagon behind him. The man waved to Doc, wondering if the property owner was going to give him trouble after all.

"Simpson, I need to ask for a change to the building," Doc said apologetically. "Looks like I'll be having a couple of elephant bestials working here. I want to add homes for them on to the stables. Add another fifth onto the current estimate for it?"

Simpson stared at Doc for a moment, then shook his head to clear the shock. "Uh, yes, sir. We can manage that. Just rooms for them?"

"A suite for each would be better," Doc admitted. "You'll really need that plumber."

"I'll handle it, sir. Could you have your dryad help with the ground again?"

"Rosa. Her name is Rosa," Doc said amiably. "Let's go see where you think you need the holes."

* * *

It was almost noon when a carriage rolled up the driveway. Doc stepped outside to meet it, his wives joining him. The young man sitting beside the driver was wearing a fine suit. When the carriage came to a stop, the man stepped down, then bowed to the assembled family.

"Mr. Holyday?"

"That's me," Doc replied.

"I come from Mr. Roquefell, sir. Do you have time to come to his estate?"

"Thought he might ask today. I have a guard to come with me, along with my pet."

"That is fine, sir."

A rat-tailed man came around the carriage to open the door. He had on a bright blue jacket with large silver buttons. It looked a little out of place until Doc remembered that footmen often wore uniforms that denoted their boss' station. That meant that the young man in the suit— who, when Doc looked closer, had yellow eyes— was one of the servants from Roquefell's interior staff.

"Doc, the staff should be showing up soon, but we'll handle it," Fiala said.

"Thank you, Fiala," Doc murmured, then kissed each of his wives goodbye.

The footman was clearly shocked, but the messenger was impassive as he waited.

Doc got into the carriage, followed by Rosa, then Harrid. The velvet padded seats spoke of the money invested in the vehicle. Rosa sat beside Doc, looking at the ground until the door shut, then she leaned against him. Doc put his arm around her waist, relaxing as best he could with the meeting that was coming.

* * *

The ride was long enough that Doc wondered about it, but they didn't once come close to the city. The road was rough in a few spots, causing them minor discomfort when they were jostled.

Wish I knew how to improve suspensions, Doc thought. *That book series with the guy who could Shape things made it seem easy. Then again, hadn't he been a mechanic? I'm more a jack-of-all-trades; a little knowledge here and there, but nothing specialized like that.*

The ride smoothed out, and Doc twitched the curtain away from the window to look out. He let out a soft whistle when he saw the manor coming up. There was a lavish garden— trees, bushes, and flowers of all kinds could be seen. Several men in work clothing were tending to it, and beyond the garden, a manor thrice the size of his new home rose up.

"He's got wealth to spare..." Doc muttered.

"To be fair, Doc, so do you," Harrid snorted.

"True enough. This is obviously where he wanted his house. If I was settling down, I might do something similar, I guess."

"For all the children, if nothing else," Rosa murmured. She sat up, kissing Doc's cheek. "Silent pet?"

"To start with. We need to gauge him."

"I will do my best to learn all I can about him and his staff, Voice."

"I know, Weed. I'll make sure you get a lot of rewards later."

"I still have moments where your abilities worry me," Harrid said, "but you use them for Doc's benefit, so I'm trying to adapt as best I can."

"I rarely look at your thoughts since you asked me not to," Rosa told him.

Harrid exhaled a rough snort. "'Rarely' isn't never... but it's to keep Doc safe, and I know that, which is why I do my best not to complain." He shifted, wondering if he should add his other thought. "Besides," he went on, deciding he could since Doc always told him to speak his mind, "I'm sure you help keep the large relationship from having as many problems."

Rosa smiled. "I have only stepped in twice. They, like us, only want Doc safe and happy."

"Luck blessed me with understanding women," Doc smiled.

"Sophia was near ecstatic that you gave a firm wedding date last night," Rosa giggled. "Her worry had been fluctuating, but slowly rising, because you didn't wed her right away, and kept saying it would be soon, but later."

"I don't want to wait, but I also want to firmly establish solid allies, too. In the end, I'd rather marry her and apologize to a new ally, then to wait even longer."

"Should you send word to the Ironbeard clan about speaking with them the day after, then?" Harrid asked as the carriage rolled toward the front of the estate.

"Might be best to schedule it. I wonder if they're fully on board, or if they'll want to test me. Depends on Elder Ironbeard's report to the others, I bet." Doc gave Harrid a grin. "Going to toss your line out to see if any of this clan bites?"

Harrid shifted, but nodded. "I was thinking about it, especially if we stay in the city for any length of time. I think it'll end up like my clan, though; mild interest that vanishes when they know I'll be going with you."

"Yeah," Doc said a little sadly. "You still have decades, though, right?"

"I'd say longer than you, but... not sure that's true, considering you're backed by a goddess."

"Hmm... I wonder if my healing can turn back old age? I haven't tried it in that regard. If it can... none of my family would need to suffer a shorter lifespan," Doc mused.

The carriage slowing down snapped him out of the moment. Smoothing his jacket, he rolled his neck. "Okay... this will either be a good thing or the start of a war. Goddess, please smile down on me today."

"She will," Rosa murmured before adopting her act of being even more submissive than she was.

"Be shocked if she didn't," Harrid added as he got ready to get out. "Sir, you do know I should be the first one out, right?"

Doc chuckled, thinking back to the book series about the Tuatha again. "Yeah. I remember hearing about guards doing that."

"Good."

The carriage came to a full stop, and Doc felt the footman jump off the back. A moment later, the door opened and Harrid stepped out. After he checked around, he shifted away from the door. Doc stepped out and saw the young bestial was already waiting for them. He held his hand back to the carriage, helping Rosa down.

The front doors of the manor had an inscription that made Doc's lips purse. They were written in a language he didn't know, but he thought it looked like Latin. The double doors were split down the middle of an emblem that looked very much like some kind of ancient coin.

The servant who'd come to the manor cleared his throat. "Welcome to Roquefell's estate. If you will follow me, I shall take you to see him."

"We will follow," Doc said as he moved to the front of his small group.

CHAPTER NINE

They were led into a parlor to wait— the butler who'd taken them inside got their drink preferences, then left. The walk to the parlor hadn't been long, but enough to let Doc see the manor was done in understated wealth; everything was quality, but not flashy. Doc thought he might like Roquefell just from what he'd seen so far.

The butler was back with the drinks before taking up his station by the door. Doc leaned back in his chair, one hand idly stroking Rosa's hair while he sipped his whiskey. The first sip warmed his throat, and he had to admit the stuff had a burn, but was smooth enough to enjoy. His second taste let him place it: the drink was dwarven-based, he'd sampled a similar whiskey when he married Sonya.

"This is from the Ironbeard clan?" Doc asked the butler.

The bestial bowed his head. "It is, sir."

Doc took a moment to study the butler. The outfit was what he expected, but he had trouble placing the bestial's bloodline. Doc knew he had canine roots, but he couldn't pin what type. The only thing he had to go on were his ears, as the butler had no tail; his ears were slightly larger than the wolf bestials he'd seen. *Maybe coyote... or a fox?* Doc thought, unable to figure it out.

Rosa, having been reading his thoughts, used a finger to trace a word on his calf out of sight of the butler. Doc glanced down at her with a smile, mentally thanking her for identifying him as part fox.

Harrid stood a few feet behind Doc in a relaxed, parade rest posture. At Doc's request, Harrid had left his shotgun at home. It gave him a slightly gentler cast, if a dwarf in chainmail and breastplate, with an axe on his back and a pistol on his hip, could be considered "gentler."

The door opened, admitting a man in his middle years. Perfectly coiffed hair, a rich suit, and the stride of a man who was unworried about anything identified him before he could speak.

Doc stood up, setting his whiskey aside to greet his host. "Mr. Roquefell, thank you for inviting me."

A smile touched the man's face as he advanced and shook Doc's hand firmly. "I'm glad to finally have the chance to meet you, Mr. Holyday." His eyes flickered to Harrid and Rosa before settling back on Doc. "And your companions."

"My guard, Harrid, and my dryad, Rosa," Doc answered, seeing the request for what it was.

"A pleasure. Please, sit. You, as well, Harrid. I promise no harm to your employer, and every guard can use a rest. Miss, would you care for a chair?"

Harrid was unsettled— Roquefell had a very charismatic manner that made him seem like a friend. "I'll stay on station, sir. My job is not done until his is."

"My place is at his side," Rosa replied to the question sent her way.

"Of course," Roquefell smiled. "As you'd prefer." He took a seat across the small coffee table from Doc. "I'm sure you are fine speaking with them present, yes?"

"They'll hold everything in confidence. As your butler will?"

"Alfred," Roquefell smiled, addressing the butler, "bring us the decanter of Louis. Two... no, three glasses, and then retire from the room. Unless... do you smoke, Mr. Holyday?"

"Never been one of my vices," Doc replied.

"That will be all."

"Yes, sir," Alfred said, bowing to Roquefell.

"Let us just wait a moment for him to return," Roquefell smiled. "I've heard you prefer using your given name. Is that true?"

"'Doc' is how I prefer to be addressed," Doc admitted.

"Very well," Roquefell smiled. "Then you can call me David."

"Very generous," Doc said, knowing society placed more weight on family names for the time period; given names were usually only for trusted friends. "I appreciate the thought, David."

"It's nothing. I'm hoping that our conversation will lead us to a point where that would be a given in the future, anyway. My associates have kept me apprised of your work in Deep Gulch."

"Peabody and Rondle. They informed me that they were passing word along."

"The woman Oliver took up with, Heather, I heard she is a wonder with music. He also informed me there would be next to no chance for me to entice her out of the town."

"The Lily is her home," Doc said. "I'm sure that, if you let things settle a bit, you might be able to have her visit the city. The two do dote on each other."

David leaned back with a broad smile. "Good. I worried he'd never find a woman. Oliver is a genius with numbers and has a keen love of music, but... well... you've met him. His chance of finding a woman who actually loved him was not great."

"He is socially awkward," Doc agreed.

A knock came on the door before Alfred came back in with a tray. A well-known bottle of cognac sat on the tray, along with three snifter glasses. Setting the tray in front of David, Alfred bowed, then departed.

"Harrid, have you ever had the pleasure of King Louis the XIII?" David asked as he sat forward to pick up the bottle.

"No, sir."

"Please sample a small taste, at least. I know the elders of Ironbeard have found it worth their time," David said, pouring a half-ounce into a glass and setting it to the side of the table. He then poured two ounces into the other two glasses, setting one before Doc. Taking his, he sat back, sniffing the top of the glass briefly. "It is such a wonderful cognac. When they started selling them by the bottle, well, I had to get a few. For moments like this, if nothing else. I firmly believe the idea behind the bottle will help keep it as something to remember for decades."

Doc picked up his, then sat back as he sniffed at the top of the glass. The aroma seemed to linger— it was rich, warm, and aromatic. Part of him had always wanted to try what was known as the king of cognacs, but it cost hundreds of dollars on earth to even get a small serving. He'd at least seen enough movies to know how to hold the snifter correctly.

"I believe you're correct," Doc told David. "This cognac sold in that bottle will be around for a century easily." He took a small sip, not swallowing right away, just letting the liquid pool for a moment on his tongue before he did. Smooth warmth slid down his throat, and a smile came to him. "Wonderful." His brow furrowed a second later when his inner ear began to warm. It wasn't unpleasant, but it was something he'd never encountered before.

David chuckled as he watched Doc's face. "It takes you by surprise, doesn't it?"

"Never felt that before," Doc admitted.

"It only happens a few times before it stops, sadly," David sighed.

"Harrid, go ahead. I know this won't impair you, and it's worth the memory."

Harrid stepped forward to pick up the glass. He sniffed at it, his eyebrows rising before he took a sip. His beard went up as he smiled. "Thank you. It is very good." He finished the glass, then set it down and stepped back.

"Now, Doc, I'm sure you are wondering about why I've taken an interest in your work?"

"I am," Doc admitted.

"Probably a bit worried about my reasons, and if I'm really an ally or an obstacle."

"Very straightforward, and yes."

"You prefer the straightforward," David chuckled. "I'm partial to it myself, but many want extra words to get to the same point, as if the number and quality of their words will make the difference."

"The longer a man of your position takes with them, the more they feel they're worth."

"Exactly," David said, sipping from his glass. "That can be used to benefit if you know who and when to use it on. But between us, I'll be straight: a goddess brought you to this world and asked you to help. That is what I've heard, but I wanted to hear more from you. Straight from the horse's mouth, as it were."

Doc took another sip of the expensive cognac. "Lady Luck asked me to confront the Darkness that's killing this world. She brought me to Deep Gulch. Having done what I could there, it's time to expand."

"Lady Luck, the personification of good fortune," David murmured with a sad smile on his lips. "Did she speak of any of her siblings?"

Doc shook his head. "Not really. She did say they'd all given up on this world."

"Can't blame them," David sighed. "Have you studied history?"

"Not studied, but I've had lessons in both elven and dwarven lore."

"From your two wives... I should say two *of* your wives to be accurate," David nodded. "Lillianna Treeheart, the Death Flower herself, and Sonya Redblade from the Oresmelter clan. Not great teachers, but good enough to help you learn the basics."

"You seem to have a point in there," Doc said slowly.

"Long before Apoc became the only religion, the other gods and goddesses had Voices. They were killed off as humanity turned away from them. I always wondered why the gods didn't react to the change."

"Do you think this is the only world they looked over?"

"I don't, but others did," David sighed. "That is how Apoc spread, because there were no reprisals. Why believe in a god who doesn't care if you silence their Voice? The few who weren't killed outright went silent, blending into the background to try surviving longer."

Sipping his cognac, Doc felt a revelation was coming, but David was building up to it.

"They eventually passed. Some told their children, who told their children, who disbelieved their parents until the story was nothing more than a rumor in a family. To have a new Voice show up, and begin speaking, well... some have heard." David met Doc's eyes with an intensity that told him of the man's interest. "Is she the only god that has looked back at the world?"

"Who was it in your family's history?" Doc asked.

"Yes, I did basically admit it," David nodded. "She was called Trade, according to the story. I had to find my many-times great-grandfather's diary to even get that. He was just the last to believe, until me. Our family has always had fortune when it came to business. My brother is currently locking up oil, but he doesn't believe in the story. Luckily, he isn't enamored with Apoc, either."

"Trade was likely her initials if she was anything like Luck," Doc said. "I don't know if she's turned back to this world, but it would take belief to even try contacting her."

"I can see how that would be. Hard to build belief in today's world. Apoc takes a very dim view of 'false demons.'"

"I know," Doc snorted. "I had to put the preacher in Deep Gulch to rest."

"The church isn't likely to care for years," David said as he took another drink. "The two priests here are... pliable. Both have become disenchanted with the church as they languish in the city. They've tried for years to go back east only to be rebuffed again and again. I made sure they were gently led astray. They put on the front, but neither care enough about the church to think about Deep Gulch's preacher no longer reaching out to them."

"Thank you."

"It was for my hopeful benefit, as well. My hope is that you'll get the chance to ask your goddess to ask Trade to look my way."

"I see. What would you do if she did?"

"The same as you," David replied. "Start chipping at the grip Apoc has, and help bring belief back to what was."

"Why?"

"I could ask the same of you," David chuckled. "But because my family had a task, one that we failed. I hate losing. I believe that, if given the chance, I could do what my family should've done. If you work with me... well, Luck and Trade together...? We'd be quite the force. A non-violent force of change."

Doc set his empty glass down— he hadn't even realized he'd finished it, the drink had been so smooth. He extended his hand to David. "Your hand, please?"

Davis set his own glass down, then reached out to take Doc's hand. "We have a deal?"

"This is just to check something," Doc said before murmuring under his breath. "Lady, is this man free of corruption?"

Green flames with golden sparkles infused Doc's hand, and David stared at it in awe. Doc nodded as he felt the problems with David's body, but even with his minor lung and liver issues, there was no Darkness in David. Doc infused his energy into David, healing the damage.

Sitting back, Doc exhaled and placed his hand back on Rosa to replenish his energy. "Your lungs and liver are good again. You don't smoke or drink in excess, so they weren't terrible."

David swallowed, then pulled his handkerchief to dab at his eyes, putting it back in his breast pocket when he was done. "I felt the warmth of being loved... Was that your goddess?"

"That was her energy working through me," Doc said.

David bowed his head. "Thank you, Lady Luck. If you hear me, please tell Trade that I would love to do what my family failed to do generations back."

"I'll be marrying in a couple of days," Doc said after a moment of silence. "I'd like to invite you to the reception. I believe the Ironbeard clan elders will be there, too."

"I'll attend," David replied as he cleared his throat. "Now, what can I do to aid your grand endeavor?"

Doc grinned. "I have a few things started, but there's so much more we can do together. Some of it comes down to if you'll throw in fully with me. I'll start a second company as an offshoot of Luck's Holdings; you'll get two-fifths of it, and I'll hold the rest."

David picked up his glass, draining it before pouring more for him and Doc. "Tell me about the plan."

CHAPTER TEN

"Okay, Weed, tell me," Doc said as they rolled away from David's.

"He was open and honest the entire time," Rosa murmured. "His great hope is that Trade will speak to him, making him her Voice."

"Is he going to back us?"

"Fully. He never had a single thought of duplicity. To hold to that so firmly means he is either honest or capable of lying to himself. The idea for the hot springs excites him; he wants a draw to the territory. His current plan is to build himself up enough to be able to spread different ideas without as much backlash. He'll work behind others who will take power positions for him."

"Proxies, so he's free to do what he wants, while also still having a say."

"Yes. He is certain you also held back on him. His thoughts on that were complimentary to you."

"Going to need Ayla and Sophia to work the contract with him," Doc sighed. "All of that after the wedding, though."

"Sophia will be happy," Rosa purred as she snuggled up against him.

"He was more approachable than I thought he would be," Harrid said. "Rondle was right about him."

"Might be a lingering trace of the old goddess," Doc said. "Having the ability to put everyone at ease would help a great deal with trade. I'd guess she'd be the goddess of commerce instead of trade, now."

"The wedding is still two days away," Harrid said. "What're you going to do before then?"

"Nothing," Doc said. "I'm putting everything else on hold. Might go check the Silvered Dreams and say hi to Colin. I wonder if they had anyone show up to be interviewed?"

* * *

Arriving back at his home, Doc helped Rosa out of the carriage. The sun was heading for the horizon, telling him it was well into the evening. "Thank you," Doc told the driver.

"Pleasure, sir."

"Ah, good, you're home," Sonya said, coming outside. "If you'll come with me, husband, I'd like you to meet the new staff."

Doc gave her a warm smile. "Of course."

She took him into the parlor where his wives were chatting with three new people. Mizzi stood near Fiala, speaking softly with a happy smile on her lips.

"Doc's here," Sonya announced to them.

All eyes went to Doc as he entered the room, then shifted to Rosa and widened.

"Hello," Doc smiled. "Rosa is harmless to those who are harmless to us. I'm Doc Holyday. I prefer my given name, so just call me Doc."

"Let me introduce you to them," Fiala smiled. "First, Mizzi's cousin, Bernard Burniss."

"A pleasure, sir," the black bear bestial bowed formally, standing to greet Doc.

"We have Charles Patter next. He'll be our chef."

The dog bestial— obviously a basset hound— gave Doc a wide grin. "I have ten years of experience in preparing fine meals, sir."

"And lastly for now, Aylss Washington, our new laundry maid," Fiala finished.

The barely-teen had pronounced otter bestial features. She curtsied deeply to Doc. "Thank you, sir."

"Welcome to our home," Doc smiled back. "If my wives have agreed with you, then I'm sure you're the right people for the jobs. Honestly, I didn't expect a chef to be here already."

"He was in the same spot as me, sir," Bernard said. "When Mizzi told me you needed staff, I told him."

"Aylss was supposed to originally fill the position too," Mizzi added softly. "I've asked around for the other jobs. I expect to have people arrive in a day or two for those spots."

"Excellent work, Mizzi," Doc told her. "Ayla, do you have the contracts?"

"Signed already," Ayla smiled. "I also have a carriage arriving tomorrow. I believe Clyde has people for you to meet. He went with us into the city and said that, if he'd known, he'd have at least had the wagon here."

"I'll head out back to talk to him, then," Doc said. "I have news on Roquefell for after dinner."

"Good news?" Lia asked.

"Yeah, good news. See you all for dinner in an hour?"

"I'll get started right away," Charles said, getting to his feet. "Mizzi, can you show me the way?"

"I've got it. I'll go out the back," Doc said. "So Charles, not Chuck?"

The man winced. "I don't care for that shortened name, sir."

"Got it," Doc said as he led the chef out of the room.

He dropped Charles off in the kitchen before going out the back door. The work crew was clearly winding down for the day. Doc headed over to Simpson, who was chatting with Clyde.

"Gentlemen, how did the day go?"

Simpson was the first of the men to speak up, "Good, sir. As you can see, we're making progress. We've been asked to focus on the staff rooms first."

"I asked them," Clyde grinned. "I have solid yeses from all the people I talked with today. Drivers and footmen are here, but they need your help. The guards will come out once the rooms are ready."

"The plumber will be here with us tomorrow to see about tying into the existing pipes," Simpson added.

"Sounds like a good day," Doc replied. "Thank you, Simpson."

Simpson said his goodbyes and got his crew moving.

Doc turned to Clyde. "Introduce me?"

"Sure. This way," he said, leading Doc into the servants' quarters. "How did your day go, Doc?"

"Good. Roquefell looks to be a solid person. I'll be working with him to get things established. Ayla mentioned at least one carriage being here tomorrow?"

"Not ideal with the lack of a place to store it yet, but yeah. We'll need it with you going into the city. I'll make sure it's as good as we can make it... at least you have plenty of grazing for the horses."

Doc spotted the wagon to the side of the quarters. "Where's its team?"

"Around back. I've got an improvised shelter for them right now."

"Understood. As long as you think it'll work."

Inside, Clyde called out, and a set of doors on the second floor opened. Radley came from the first-floor hall, as well.

"Sir?" Radley asked.

"Meeting the new staff," Doc told the groundskeeper. "We have a chef, butler, and a laundry maid."

"Good. I was hoping they would get the positions. Thank you, sir."

"All I care about is quality work," Doc said. He turned to look at the stairs where a trio of men were coming down. Two of the men both looked shorter and stockier than a human, but they weren't the right build for a dwarf, either. The third had antlers trimmed down to just above his hairline. "Gentlemen, I'm Doc Holyday. Call me Doc."

The antlered man said, "I'm Vic Runn, sir. I'll be the groom."

"Nice to meet you," Doc replied. "Glad we have someone who can help care for the horses."

"These are Darren and William Driver," Clyde chuckled. "They're brothers who can drive, be shotgun, or be footmen."

"Clyde says you can help with old injuries?" Darren asked. "We took the job more for that than the pay."

"If not, we'll be leaving," William said.

Doc grinned at them. "Lady Luck, these two men need your help." His left hand reached back to Rosa, who had knelt to place her head under his hand.

All four of the staff stared at Doc's glowing hand with wide eyes and open mouths.

"Either one of you, take my hand," Doc said.

"Well, I'm the eldest." Stepping forward, Darren gripped Doc's hand tightly, then exhaled in relief when it didn't burn.

Doc nodded when he felt the injuries that the half-dwarf had accumulated. "Rough life. Give me a moment." A minute later, he let go of Darren's hand, shifting to offer William his hand. "Your turn."

Darren was slack-jawed at the lack of pain as he flexed his knees, taking a deep inhale as he did. "It worked...?"

William lunged forward eagerly, taking Doc's hand.

Doc frowned at the missing pinkie on William's left hand— he couldn't replace digits or limbs yet. He did heal everything else before letting the magic fade. "That's the best I can do. I can't replace fingers."

William shook his head, pulling a handkerchief to wipe at his eyes. "No, it's fine... I felt it work."

"Umm, sir?" Vic asked slowly.

Doc looked at the groom, then nodded. "Sorry. I didn't know. Lady, please, once more?"

Vic took Doc's hand, stiffening for a moment as the healing worked on his injury. He sobbed once when the magic faded. "Thank you, sir..."

"You can have children again," Doc said softly. "Kicked by a horse?"

"Mule," Vic sniffled, turning away. "Sorry."

"No apology needed. It's a big thing being able to have kids. Not sure if you have a woman in mind."

"I've been seeing her, but she was talking about wanting children, and I... I stopped courting her a month ago because..."

"Might as well see her again," Doc said, clapping his shoulder. "Apologize for disappearing, first."

"Yes... umm... thank you. Clyde, I need tomorrow."

"Take two days. I can handle things while you get everything in order."

"Thank you," Vic said before he rushed upstairs.

"We thank you, too, sir," Darren said. "Having the clause about leaving if we weren't healed seems silly now."

"Would've been useful if I wasn't able to do it," Doc said. "Settle in. The carriage should be here tomorrow. Clyde, they're under your direction."

"Yes, sir," Clyde grinned.

William grunted. "Clyde the taskmaster is back."

Clyde chuckled darkly. "Just for that, I'll need your help with the horses tomorrow."

Darren laughed. "You did it to yourself, Will."

William sighed. "Dammit."

"Have a good night," Doc said, shaking hands with both men.

"Sir," Radley asked slowly, "can you do that for anyone?"

Doc gave the man a questioning look. "Problem?"

"Mizzi and I... no kids..." Radley mumbled.

"Ah. Come with me. I'll see about healing both of you," Doc said.

*　*　*

Once dinner was done, Doc explained his meeting with David to his wives. "He'll be ready to meet you both two days after the wedding," Doc finished. "As soon as the contract is in place for the new company, I'll work with him on the bigger plan."

"We'll get it done," Ayla grinned at Sophia, then nudged her. "Told you he'd wait until after."

Sophia's face heated. "I... yes..."

"Two days?" Doc asked.

"Two days from today, in the courthouse," Sophia nodded quickly.

"We arranged for a room just for you two," Ayla smiled fondly at Sophia. "This way, she gets you alone for an entire night, like we did. So we're all equal."

"It doesn't—" Sophia began.

"Good," Doc cut her off. "I want you all as equal as possible. Sophia, you deserve that. I'm sorry I made you wait a month to get married."

Sophia shook her head emphatically. "No, Doc, it's fine."

"She loves you and felt like she was causing issues," Rosa said from her spot between Lia and Doc.

Sophia slumped. "It wasn't...! Yes... I was... sorry."

Ayla leaned over to kiss Sophia's cheek. "It's okay."

"It really is," Doc said. "Ladies, I think we need to remind our lovely lawyer how much we love her."

"Perfect," Lia smiled. "Fiala, will you help me lead the evening?"

"Hmm, yes. I like the small acts of control," Fiala smiled. "Sophia, tonight, we'll all be with you. Tomorrow night, Doc will have Rosa while we're with you before the wedding. The night after, you'll have him all to yourself. You deserve it. You've done so much for our family."

Sophia met her eyes before she bowed her head. "Thank you, Fiala."

Harrid got to his feet. "I'll see you in the morning."

"Shall we?" Doc chuckled, standing up as Harrid left the room.

CHAPTER ELEVEN

Doc was thankful for having the wagon; it saved him the walk into the city. A carriage would make things better— even the worst would work— but most of the horses were still at the stables. Besides, he had another reason for the wagon: Clyde wanted to take him to meet the elephant bestials who'd be serving as guards, and Mizzi had asked Clyde to pick up a few people to be interviewed for staff positions.

"The estate is growing really fast," Clyde said as the wagon went around the outskirts of the city, then followed the river.

"Faster than I thought, too," Doc admitted, "but it'll mean things run smoother while we're here."

"And it'll be safer," Harrid added from his spot beside Clyde.

"It will be," Clyde agreed. "Uh, about that bit, Doc? You'll need to invest in guns for them if you hire them. Only a few guns are made for people of their size, but they can handle the kick."

"If they sign, then I will," Doc nodded. "Have to make sure they have the best they can get. That does remind me, do the others need me to get them better equipment?"

"Everyone but the two we're going to see have their own weapons."

"Got it. Do they live by the river?"

"Yeah, they do…" Clyde grumbled.

"Ah, understood," Doc said, hearing the undertone.

"We're almost there."

Doc looked at the hastily-erected shacks ahead of them. "All the bestials live here?"

"Not all, but most of them," Clyde replied.

"Hmm…" Doc murmured as he considered what he could and should do. "Hands up, not handouts. What does that look like for here and now?"

"Doc?" Harrid asked, looking back at his boss.

"Thinking of how to help the people who live here."

"Lasting help, you mean," Clyde said. "That's tricky."

"Always is," Doc agreed. "Giving people a hand up is what I want. I refuse to give people handouts, as that doesn't teach them to work for more."

"Besides giving them jobs, I'm not sure how you'd manage that," Harrid said.

"I'll think about it," Doc sighed.

"Well, we're here," Clyde said, pulling the wagon up to a building; it was better built and larger than most of those near it.

The home looked good from the outside, and it was obviously cared for. It was just in a terrible part of the outskirts, which diminished it.

Doc waited for Clyde to lead him and Harrid to the door. He felt the eyes on him from those nearby, clearly wondering what business the three of them had there.

A massive elephant bestial answered the door, then smiled when she saw Clyde. "Come in. This is your employer?"

"Mr. Holyday, this is Mrs. Tusken."

"Velma will be fine, sir," the woman smiled at Doc. "Come in. I'll get my husband."

Doc took a seat in a chair that was obviously not going to be used by the larger bestials. Harrid stood behind Doc and Clyde took the other normal chair.

A minute later, Velma returned with her husband. The male bestial limped slowly, clearly not wanting to put too much weight on his left leg. He groaned in relief when he sat down. "Mr. Holyday, nice to meet you. I'm Orville Tusken. You've met my wife already. My son is out at the tutor's at the moment."

"A pleasure," Doc greeted him back. "Clyde said you'd be willing to work as a guard for my new home."

"House or estate?" Orville asked. "Clyde mentioned something about a full manor and grounds."

"Sorry. Estate," Doc clarified. "We have another to see, as well."

"Jason will be along shortly, I don't doubt. He lives just down the street."

"That'll make things easier. I trust Clyde, but wanted to meet you myself before you signed on."

"We wanted to meet you, too," Orville said. "Clyde said you're the one who healed his leg. Said you're a faith healer."

"He's right. My goddess is Lady Luck. If you want, I'll heal you right now."

"Without the contract?" Velma asked with disbelief.

"I won't hold that over someone's head. I heal anyone who asks and can have a little faith in my goddess." Doc told her gently. "Lady, there's a man here with old wounds that trouble him. Can you help him?"

Two gasps filled the room when Doc's hands started glowing green. Before anyone could move or say anything, a knock came on the door. That jerked Velma from her shock as she hurried to answer it.

"What do I have to do?" Orville asked slowly, staring at Doc's hands.

"Just take my hand," Doc said as he stood up.

"What in the hell?" another man asked when he saw Doc's glowing hands.

Doc glanced back at the elephant bestial man who came into the room. "Healing."

"Jason Hyde, this is Doc Holyday," Clyde said. "Doc, this is Jason, the other potential guard."

"Ah, that makes sense."

Jason limped closer to the others. "He can really heal?"

"He hasn't yet," Orville said. "He was just offering to."

"You already signed?"

"No," Doc said. "I'll heal you, regardless."

"Try me first," Jason said, moving as quickly as he could.

"Why?" Doc asked.

"I don't have a kid," Jason said bluntly. "If you fuck up, at least it'll be me and not Orville."

"Jason—" Orville started to say.

"Shut it!" Jason snapped. "Well, can you or not?"

Clyde snickered. "This'll be entertaining."

Doc just smiled as he turned to Jason, holding out his hand. "Just take my hand."

Jason eyed the glowing hand, then grabbed it.

Doc winced at the strength in that grip, but he let his energy flow into Jason. *Hmm, decent health... his right foot was messed up. Shit, a caltrop, maybe? That would be terrible for an elephant. I didn't look at the other guys as closely before, but they are very flatfooted.* Pushing the thought away, Doc poured healing into Jason.

Jason stared at Doc, his grip loosening as he felt the comfort ease his pain away. He had vague memories of his mother soothing old hurts, and that's what he felt as his foot— which had pained him for years— finally stopped hurting.

The glow faded when Doc stepped back. "All done."

Jason blinked slowly for a moment before he looked at Orville. With slight hesitation, Jason took a step forward, then another, and another, before he started to laugh. "It's gone... it's gone!"

Orville watched his friend with wide eyes; they'd both been hurt on the same job. To see Jason walking with no pain made his heart clench. His gaze drifted to his wife, who looked hopeful as she watched Jason, before she met his eyes.

"Sir?" Orville asked, shifting to get up.

Doc closed the distance before Orville could stand, his hand glowing green again. "All I ask is that you thank her."

Orville nodded, taking Doc's hand. The energy that flowed into him had Orville choking back tears. It was the comfort his wife gave him when he'd come home three years ago, nearly crippled. They'd barely survived since then, solely relying on her doing the odd jobs that she could and his small pension from the bank. When the energy faded, Orville blinked away tears.

Doc stepped back, feeling a little drained. Not having Rosa with him always reminded him of how much he relied on her. "You're healed."

Orville pushed himself to his feet. The first step was awkward, as he still half-expected the full, or even a lesser, pain. When his foot came down firm and sure with no pain, he nearly stumbled. Then, he crossed the room with fast steps to grab his wife into a crushing hug. The pair of them cried as they held each other.

Harrid nodded, pride that he worked for Doc flaring in his heart. Clyde grinned smugly, knowing how much the healing meant for them, just like it had for him.

After a minute, the couple and Jason were composed again. The men were seated and Velma hurried off to get drinks.

"We'll sign," Orville said simply.

"Yup, right now," Jason nodded.

Doc pulled out the contracts that Sophia had given him. "Here you go. It's what Clyde told you: pay and days off."

Both men picked up the contracts, reading through them slowly. Doc could hear them mumbling the words as they read.

Well, it is the old west. Mandatory education wasn't really a thing, Doc thought as he waited. *Never did ask about it... I know Posy was studying. Something to ask later.*

"Here we go," Velma said, bringing mugs full of beer back into the room. She handed them out to the men before standing behind her husband to read over his shoulder. Her lips didn't move at all, and Doc could see her eyes going over the words faster than Orville.

"I'll sign it," Jason said. "I trust Clyde."

Doc was sure Jason hadn't read through it all; he'd just given up. "Very well."

Clyde pulled off the messenger bag that he'd been carrying. He had a pen and ink on the coffee table in short order. "It's exactly what I told you it would be."

"It even has a clause for if you die while working," Velma murmured softly to her husband.

"It's not in the contract," Doc said, "but you said that your son was at the tutor's. I know we'll have a few younger people on staff. The laundry maid, for instance. I can see about hiring a tutor for all of them. That way, he wouldn't have to come all the way into the city just to attend."

Velma and Orville looked up in surprise.

"The more we know, the less likely we are to be taken advantage of," Doc said softly. "The easiest way up in life is through education."

Velma nodded. "As I tell Lance all the time."

"I'll sign, even if that doesn't happen," Orville said, taking the pen after Jason.

Doc understood what Clyde meant about needing to get them the right guns as he watched Orville sign— the pen was a small twig in the large hand of the bestial. "It'll be a few days until your rooms are done. Once they are, Clyde will let you know."

"Enough time to tell the landlord we're moving out," Velma said.

"Thank you," Jason said, standing up and handing his contract back to Doc.

"No, thank you. Knowing my wives will be safe when Harrid and I are out helps ease my mind."

"Wives?" Velma asked.

"I'm marrying again tomorrow," Doc smiled softly. "Sophia, the one who wrote the contracts, will be my fifth wife." Doc felt bad for not including Rosa in that number, but as far as the world would know, she was just his dryad, not his wife. "I should've asked, but you'll be okay with my dryad being around, right?"

Velma stiffened slightly. "Dryad?"

"She won't harm anyone unless they mean to harm my family or her," Doc said gently. "Rosa is special."

"Doc speaks the truth," Clyde said. "I've been traveling with them for weeks; she's well behaved. She's collared," he added to help ease Velma's fears.

Velma exhaled. "Oh... umm, yes... that'll be okay. Sorry. I just worry for my Lance."

"Your son will be safe," Doc said. "When you meet her, you'll see."

CHAPTER TWELVE

Doc thanked Clyde as he got out of the back of the wagon. Dusting off his suit, he knew it was why the guard outside the gambling hall was staring at him. A rich suit riding in the back of a normal wagon was well out of place. Add in Harrid, fully-armored and armed beside him, and the incongruencies added up.

"Welcome to the Silvered Dreams, sir," the guard said when Doc approached, his eyes locked on Harrid. "You'll have to surrender the weapons if you go into the hall."

Harrid's lips thinned, but he nodded. He'd still have his armor and could use his body, if needed.

"Is Mr. Montgomery in?" Doc asked the guard.

"You'd need to ask inside, sir."

"Very well. Thank you."

The front room of the gambling hall reminded Doc of the Gold Strike. There was a partitioned area where the cashiers stood ready to turn cash into chips. Beside the cage was a bear bestial, casually holding a shotgun. Another stood beside the double doors that likely led into the gambling hall itself. On the other side of the room, a rabbit bestial woman smiled at them from behind another counter.

Doc understood the rabbit bestial's role from what the guard had told them. He angled Harrid toward her first. "Check for weapons?"

"And coats if you'd like, sir," she smiled back at him.

Harrid grunted as he opened the shotgun and pulled the shells out of it. He shoved them into his pocket before pulling his pistol and taking the rounds from it, as well.

The woman waited, then licked her lips. "The axe, too, sir."

With a grimace, Harrid slipped the axe off his back, adding it to the pile with his guns.

The woman pulled out a small tag, writing each weapon on it. Doc watched her work with interest; she knew the make of each weapon, even noting the axe as dwarven-made. She made a second copy of the tag and handed it to Harrid. "Just present this when you leave."

Harrid took the tag slowly. "You keep them back there?"

"Each tag is for a specific cubby," the woman explained as she took the tag and axe.

As she walked into the small nook behind her, Doc could see a bit of the room. It was basically a closet with cubbies of various sizes. Since there was an axe, Harrid's weapons went into a larger cubby. She returned and collected the shotgun and pistol before returning to her station.

"Thank you for unloading them," she added softly. "I always feel better knowing they've been rendered safe."

"Rather not have them discharge without reason," Harrid said.

"Me, neither."

"Thank you, miss," Doc smiled. "Come on, Harrid. Time to get chips."

Doc ended up before one of the cashiers. The woman looked sleek, and with her small, brown-furred ears and solid dark eyes, Doc tagged her as a mink. "I'd like to get some chips, please. I was also hoping that Mr. Montgomery might be in?"

The woman took the cash from Doc, counting it out to provide chips as she said, "I'd have to check to see if he is, sir."

Doc pulled out one of his business cards, setting it on the counter near the chips that she was placing. "Hand this to him and let him know that I'm fulfilling my promise to visit his hall."

She picked up the card and looked it over before nodding. "I'll pass the message along, sir. If he's in."

Doc collected the chips. "Thank you. It's okay if my guard comes with me, right?"

"Yes, but he'll have to stay back from your table unless he is actively gambling. You'd want the second floor, but that won't open for a couple of hours yet."

"Understood. Thank you."

With chips in hand, Doc led Harrid toward the double doors. The guard on duty there opened one of them up for them, wishing them a good time.

The main room was a lot like the Gold Strike in Deep Gulch. A bar took up most of the back wall. Up near the front was a small lounge where a couple of older men were sitting, just sipping on their drinks. The rest of the room was filled with different gambling tables. Both sides had staircases with velvet ropes blocking them off.

Women in saloon-girl attire walked the room with trays, delivering drinks to the players. Doc didn't see any working women at the tables, for which he was glad. There were a couple of female dealers, making him smile and notice that those tables were doing more business than the others.

Sex sells... or in this case, a pretty face and low-cut top, Doc chuckled as he took in the room. *Bestial women, even. It looks fine; the customer base seems evenly split right now. That speaks well for Colin.*

Harrid trailed Doc as he took a slow circuit of the room. His eyes scanned the staff, including the few guards stationed along the walls. Then, his gaze went over the patrons, noting the ones who were sizing Doc up.

Stopping at the bar, Doc grabbed a beer before going to find a table. He settled at a blackjack table, the only player there. The dealer gave him a professional smile as he started shuffling.

"Poker seems to be popular," Doc said as he set out the quarter minimum the table had.

"New type of poker," the dealer said. "The owner brought it back from a tournament southwest of here. Seems the town of Deep Gulch was the first to have it."

"What's special about it?" Doc asked as he watched the dealer's hands.

"Ah. It has a communal set of cards to use while you get two in your hand. It's called hold'em. Played a bit, myself. It's more engaging to me than draw or stud." Finished shuffling, the dealer cut the deck. "Good luck, sir."

Doc let a couple of hands go, counting cards as he did. It wasn't exactly something he should do, but single-deck blackjack with no other players made it far too easy not to.

Doc went from the table minimum to the maximum, betting five dollars. "I notice those tables have female dealers."

"And they're busy most of the time," the dealer said with a trace of bitterness to his tone. "I've heard the boss say, 'a pretty face makes it easier to play.'"

Doc gave the man a look, then nodded. "Bet you get the female players who do come in."

The man jerked slightly before nodding. "True... My heritage helps me there." The slightly-pointed tips of his ears showed off his partial-elven blood. "'Exotic,' as they say."

"I understand. Do you find it demeaning?"

"Not really. I'm glad my mother at least gave me a pretty face that I can use to my advantage. Most of the time, it's no help. More of a hindrance."

"People can be stupid." Doc smiled when he saw the two queens he'd been dealt. "Stand, by the way."

The dealer nodded— he had a nine showing, then turned over his hole card, showing a king. "Winner. Nice time to jump your bet. Just in time for the shuffle."

Harrid shifting got Doc to look up. Colin Montgomery was coming toward the table with a wide smile.

"Ah, looks like my message was passed," Doc said as he collected his chips, leaving the winnings on the table. "That's for you."

"Oh, thank you, sir," the dealer said. He collected the five-dollar chip, tapped it on the edge of the table, then pocketed it in his vest.

"A generous man," Colin laughed as he reached the table. "I hoped you'd stop in. What do you think?"

"Nice place. You really should get rid of the faro tables, though. They can't get much business."

"Ever since we started hold'em, they've been dead. Going to flip them into more poker tables," Colin said, motioning for Doc to follow him. "Let's have a seat to talk more easily."

They ended up in the lounge near the front of the room, settled in the corner of the area. Colin waved one of the women over and ordered them drinks; he understood that Harrid was on duty when the dwarf waved off the offer and shifted to stand behind Doc. Once the two of them had drinks in hand, Colin relaxed.

"What brings you in?" Colin finally asked.

"My word that I'd visit. I was curious about the set up and how you handled things."

"Any comments?"

"A little resentment about the new dealers getting a lot of business. Not overly much, but it's clear that there's a bit of hurt. The dealer I was with understood how and why it was the way it was. I'd say throw him on a hold'em table. Some will want a guy dealing, I'm sure."

"I've had a few players complain that women shouldn't be dealing," Colin snorted. "I was planning on it when I got faro out. Good to see you had the same idea, though. Your business is said to be booming. Rumor is that you just bought up a chunk of property between here and Deep Gulch."

Doc sat back slowly. "Really?"

"I have a regular who's big in property," Colin chuckled. "Has a brother in the office that handles it. He told me all about how Luck's Holdings bought up a few square miles just off the main road to Deep

Gulch. Add in the deal to build the right of way up and he was very interested."

"Hmm... Who is he?"

"Owner and operator of Western Expansion, Michael Strongarm. Surprised you never heard of him. He was talking about buying property down near Deep Gulch. He backed out of the deal shortly after you started making waves. I think he knew Goodman."

"Nope, never heard of him," Doc said slowly. "Goodman and I never got along, though, so no surprise there."

"He's a charismatic man; he's asked about buying me out. I've been thinking it over. As the biggest gambling hall in the city, I'm a little hesitant to let it go. The price had been decent, and he recently upped his offer."

"Must see the potential," Doc commented as he sipped from the mug he had. "If it's enough to retire on, I can see the appeal."

"It is, but I do make good money with my hall. I'm basically retired now, as it is. I just oversee my manager."

"Tough call, then."

"Not here to offer me a better deal, are you?" Colin asked with a twinkle in his eye.

"No," Doc laughed. "It's a nice place— bigger than the Gold Strike by double, and better in every way. I wasn't looking to buy you out. Though... maybe me coming to town has Strongarm worried? Might be why he suddenly increased the price."

"Don't mind if I casually mention you dropping by, do you?"

"Business is business," Doc chuckled. "Just don't paint me as edging in on his attempt to buy you out. I don't need an enemy."

"I'll phrase my words carefully," Colin said.

"Care to attend a wedding?" Doc asked.

"I thought you were already married."

"I'm marrying again. Tomorrow, in fact. Have a few people who are going to attend the reception, and thought you'd like to be included."

"I wasn't expecting that," Colin said. "I didn't think I was a close enough associate to be invited to something like this."

"I wouldn't have asked before today. But you've been even with me and, honestly, I'll be in the city for a while and could use a friend."

Colin sat forward, extending his hand. "I'll be there. When and where?"

CHAPTER THIRTEEN

Doc walked with Harrid out of Furden. They'd spent some time talking with Colin and playing a few more games at the Silvered Dreams before calling it a day. The sun was past midday and heading toward evening as the pair went home.

A man in decent clothing was coming the other way, a grin on his face as he whistled happily. Seeing the two of them, he nodded. "Heading out to apply at the new estate?"

Doc grinned back at him. "What about you?"

"I was just dropping off a carriage. They had a gaggle of people up there, mostly bestials. They'd probably take the dwarf as a guard. Not sure if they have a butler, so you have a chance."

"Good to know," Doc chuckled. "Thanks for the heads up."

"Best of luck... though I'm not sure if the new family will take humans. It was all non-humans that I saw. Even the mistress of the house was bestial." The man wasn't being rude about it— he was just offering up what he knew.

"Love knows no bounds," Doc shrugged.

"I'm not against it," the guy said as he passed them. "Just wanted to let you know in case you have a stance."

"I'm pro-equality. Nice to see others not being closed-minded."

"Might be different if the church seemed to care, but it's nice being able to not have to worry about holding to their dogma. Good luck."

Doc watched the man go before shaking his head. "That was nice."

"Roquefell said he'd helped ease the church's stance on things," Harrid said.

"Looks to be working, at least."

"Sounds like your wives will be filling all the positions for the manor."

"It did sound that way. I'm sure I'll have some more introductions to get through."

After a few minutes of walking, Harrid asked, "Are you not going to set up a house of worship?"

"Huh?"

"When Colin talked about selling the gambling hall, I thought you'd be interested. Instead, you veered away from it."

"For the reason I said: I don't really need another enemy right now. I'm hoping this Strongarm guy will just ignore me while I get things in motion."

"But you invited Colin to the wedding reception."

"I was honest about that. Having friends in the city is a good thing."

"You didn't consider that, by inviting him, Strongarm might still see it as you making a play for the Silvered Dreams?"

Doc fell silent for a moment. "Fuck…"

"That's a no, then."

"I didn't. My intent was just to see about building a friendship. Since you mentioned it, I can see where someone outside of it could see it as a slow play. Befriend him, smooth talk him, then push for the business being sold… as a friend."

"Goodman would've done it."

"Yeah, and if he was friends with Goodman, Strongarm might see it the same way."

"I'm glad we'll have guards on the estate."

Doc could only agree with Harrid as they kept walking. He chewed over the problem that he might have inadvertently created.

They were getting closer to the estate when Clyde came their way, driving the wagon. Doc and Harrid stepped aside as Clyde came closer. He slowed the wagon when he drew near them, a dozen people in the back.

"Sir, dropping off hopefuls," Clyde said, starting the conversation.

Doc looked at the people in the wagon; all of them were non-human and clearly depressed. "Sorry, folks. Thank you for coming out to apply for the positions. Did you leave your names with my wives? If we have more positions open up, we'll more than likely contact one or two of you again."

A handful said they had while the others grew more sullen.

Doc pulled out enough coins for everyone and approached the wagon. "My thanks for spending your day applying. I'd hate for you to feel like you wasted your time." He handed each of them a dollar.

The declined applicants were surprised, and a few even offered smiles at his generosity.

"Clyde, see you later," Doc said, waving before he turned for home again.

As the wagon got moving, Doc caught snippets from the people riding in it.

"Wait, was that the husband they spoke about?"

"He was way nicer than..."

"He gave us money just for applying?"

"If I hear about them needing help, I'm going to..."

Doc smiled as he walked, glad he could bring a little happiness to them.

"Money really means nothing to you... sometimes I forget."

"It makes life easier," Doc said. "I've dealt with not having it for decades. The difference between having it and not is stark. Honestly, I probably should care about it more... make sure I always have it, as most with money do. I told Luck that I would help those around me if I had her favor, so that's what I'll do. Maybe people see it as foolish, but that doesn't matter. As it is, I'm going to cheat as hard as I can to make sure money never becomes the problem."

"If what you talked about on the way to Furden happens, you won't ever have a shortage."

"That's my hope. Then, I just have the hard road of trying to bring society back to the gods. It's not an easy task, but it's made easier by not having to worry about money. I'd be in a real pickle if I only had twenty dollars to my name."

"That would make your task near impossible."

"Yeah... try convincing people to follow your goddess if you're wearing rags and screaming from a soapbox."

"Would likely just turn them away faster."

"Exactly."

* * *

When Doc and Harrid got back to the estate, Doc smiled as he saw everyone moving about— there was a definite influx of people on the grounds. Rosa was the first to spot them. She rose from where she was kneeling, hurrying their way with a bright smile. Doc's reflexive smile back was just as happy.

"Welcome home, Voice," Rosa said when she got to him.

Doc pulled her into a hug, squeezing her tightly. Inhaling, he caught the scent of pine. He smiled as he lowered his head and nipped her ear. "Helping Radley with the grounds?"

"Yes. Lia asked me to. She promised I'd be rewarded by you tonight. I get you all to myself."

"Because they'll be with Sophia, getting her ready for the wedding tomorrow," Doc murmured in understanding.

"She is very happy now. Even with her mind whirling with joy, she is managing to get all the contracts done perfectly for you."

"All of them make my life better, including you, my precious Weed."

Rosa moaned lightly when Doc nipped her ear again. "Thank you, Doc... thank you... I want all of what you plan for me."

"I know, Weed," Doc murmured, "but that's for later. Explain what you were helping Radley with."

Rosa led him back toward Radley and a younger man, who'd both paused in what they'd been doing when Rosa rushed off. Radley took his hat off as Doc approached, and the other man was quick to do the same.

"Evening," Doc greeted them.

"Sir, this is Aran. He's my helper for taking care of the grounds," Radley was quick to explain.

"Thank you for the opportunity, sir," Aran said, ducking his head.

"Out of curiosity, gopher bestial?" Doc asked, feeling like he was right.

Aran jerked, his head snapping back up to stare. "Uh... y-yes, sir. Most get it wrong."

"Just seemed to fit," Doc shrugged. "Welcome to the house, Aran. Radley will get you settled in. I was curious about what the work was."

"We're plotting out the front gardens, sir," Radley explained. "Rosa was helping us with the ground so it'll be easier for us. Mistress Fiala explained that we'll be given the money to get the right plants after the wedding, but I figured we could get the ground prepared now."

"Good plan," Doc agreed. "Decorative garden or useful garden?"

"Sir?"

"Just flowers and shrubs that look pretty, or are you going to add in fruit trees?"

"Oh, we were going to make sure the trees had a secondary purpose, sir. If you want, I can make sure the bushes are berries, as well."

"Please do. I don't mind the decorative, but I do prefer the useful. I'm sure, in time, the chef will like having some extras to work with. Add an herb garden out back, too. I know the cost of some spices can be high."

"Lia already asked them," Rosa murmured. "We worked on that plot, first."

"Ah, that makes sense," Doc chuckled. "Carry on, gentlemen. Rosa, when they finish, come find me."

"Yes, Voice," Rosa smirked as she bowed her head.

Doc imagined her being tied up and unable to do anything with him as he walked away. Rosa shivered— she wanted what he'd promised earlier, not that, but even being helpless like that had an appeal to her.

"He's very easy to talk to," Aran whispered.

"Only been here a few days," Radley said, "but he feels like a man I can work for until I'm old and gray."

Rosa smiled to herself, knowing Doc had overheard them. Kneeling down, she touched the soil, focused on making it the best she could for the plants that would come in the next few days.

* * *

Doc was met just inside the front door by Bernard. The man was in full butler uniform and bowed slightly, clearly having had training for the job. "Welcome back, sir."

"Thanks. Where are my wives?"

"Mistress Sonya is in the parlor, sir."

"I'll go there," Doc said. "Carry on."

"Yes, sir."

Sonya looked up as Doc entered the room. "Husband, welcome home. Let me introduce Bitum. She's our parlor maid."

The mousy-looking woman curtsied to him. "Greetings, sir."

Doc realized that him thinking of her as mousy was correct when he saw her ears and tail. "Welcome to the house, Bitum." He took the seat beside Sonya, looking back at Harrid. "Relax, Harrid. I'm not going back out tonight."

"I'll go put my equipment away, then," Harrid nodded before he left the room.

"How did your day go?" Sonya asked, taking Doc's hand and resting it on her lap.

"I got the contracts signed before going to see the Silvered

Dreams. Colin was nice to see, and I invited him to the reception. He had some news about a friend of Goodman's in the city who hopefully won't be a problem."

"We'll handle adding him. We have a dozen potentials added for you, just in case."

"'Because a good wife thinks of everything, and my wives are very good wives,'" Doc chuckled, quoting a book series he liked.

Sonya giggled, then leaned into his side. "We want to be the best we can for you."

"Mission accomplished for you all, then. Tell me about your day, please?"

"Of course. We found staff for all the positions," Sonya said. "Do you want to meet them all?"

"Sure," Doc murmured, leaning in to kiss her first. "If you'll be my guide, I'm all for it."

Sonya beamed as she got to her feet, still holding his hand. "I'll be happy to lead you to meet our new additions."

CHAPTER FOURTEEN

Doc let out a shuddering breath as his toes uncurled, his hands releasing Rosa's head. "Not sure I should've let you do that, Rosa. Today is supposed to be Sophia's day."

Rosa slid farther up the bed, nuzzling against his side. "Me being at my best means I can assist if anything happens. Besides, Lia would have said something if you were to not have me this morning."

"Can't fault that logic. Did they tell you how this is supposed to work today?"

"Maybe..."

Doc's lips twitched at Rosa acting coy. "Are you hoping I'll give you more, Weed?"

"Yes." Her voice hitched as she watched his thoughts.

Doc shut down all the ideas he'd let fill his head. "No more today."

"As you decree, Voice," Rosa sighed.

"Now, now, pouty little Weed," Doc chuckled and kissed her blue-tinged green hair. "You get plenty from me."

"I do," Rosa murmured. "You take very good care of me, far better than I thought you would to start with. I can still recall my fear of what might happen the morning after our first night together."

"When you entrapped me?"

A small nod of her head was her only reply.

"Might've been bad, but I wasn't upset with you. I'm glad Mother listened to me liking you."

"She was mad, but your words soothed that anger. Your willingness to see me again had me so excited and worried. What if you changed your mind? Maybe you'd want me only as a power source."

Doc stroked her hair, thinking back to the time he'd found her with Fiala at his side. "We put those fears to bed."

"With Fiala," Rosa giggled. "She was so shocked and excited that you made me sit and watch you be with her. That moment took her love for you and made it explode in wonder. She had a slightly negative view of herself... she was afraid of me, of my looks. You blew those concerns aside when you loved her over me."

"She's precious."

"To all of us, because she allowed us to have you, as well. We all thank her in small ways, reminding her of how grateful we are. She worries again about being the lady of the home. She was just coming to terms with the idea of being a housewife, and now, she's a lady. Fiala won't tell you, but she worries. Just love her and praise her as much as you can. That's the best you can do."

"What about the others?" Doc asked, holding his lovely dryad to his side.

"Lia is fine; she knows her role. She will help with the tribes and be your gun when needed. Part of her worries that you might try to coddle her and keep her from doing what she can."

"I won't. I'll worry if she's in danger, but I know she's far better suited for some things than I ever will be."

"Sonya is happy that she's able to help with the Ironbeards. Her goal is to help you bring all the clans we meet under your leadership as shaman. Honestly, she's the one who worries the least. She's steadfast in her love of you. She would be the first to endure any hardship to help you, Voice. Her only worries are about the others finding fault with her needing more time with you in intimate settings. They've all told her they never will, but that faint kernel of doubt remains."

"I tried to run from her," Doc chuckled as he remembered Sonya's drive to claim him.

"She's stubborn and we all love that about her," Rosa smiled. "Ayla... she was so conflicted in the beginning. Logical, yet a romantic at heart. Ayla fought to be the one in charge, as she never wanted another to control her again. But you just kept giving to her, over and over, never hinting or suggesting that you'd push. She heard of how you were with me, and a part of her heart yearned fiercely for that, to stop being what society wanted her to be: all prim and proper. When you accepted her being in charge, part of her broke more. She wanted to be in charge, but not with you, the one who saved her. When you accepted her depths, she melted. Her whole world shifted with you at the center. She molded to her true desires because you accepted them. Then, you gave her more by letting her be aggressive with me and the others."

Doc's mind drifted back over those moments with Ayla, going from their wedding night to her meeting Rosa, and everything after. "I'm glad I could bring her the happiness she wanted," he said softly. "That's all I want with my wives— for them to be as happy as I can make them."

"Which is why Fiala has started trying to do more," Rosa smiled, kissing his chest. "We've all noticed how excited you get when you watch her gently dominate us. That started a passion in her to do more to bring you more pleasure and love."

"Silly kit... shit," Doc stopped himself.

"I'll never tell her, Doc," Rosa whispered. "I know how often you stop yourself from saying that. You've done amazingly well in training yourself away from it."

"She hates it, so I won't say it," Doc said simply. "I try not to think it, too, but I know I fail there... a lot."

"She knows. She asked me, and I told her the truth."

Doc's heart stopped for a moment. "Shit."

"No. Her love grew when I told her. That you have never uttered that phrase past the first time means you want her to not feel slighted. I told her the truth about how you try to stop even thinking it. She waffled on allowing you to say it in some settings to give back to you. I told her you wouldn't want that... Was I right?"

Doc's chest warmed as he thought of Fiala considering bending on that point. "You were. I love her. Please tell her to let it go. I'll do better. She deserves only love, not hurtful words. She isn't a humiliation sub, unlike some, Weed."

Rosa shivered as she clung to his side. "Thank you, Voice. I will tell her tonight while you are with Sophia."

"What about my dear lawyer?" Doc asked.

"You shattered everything she knew. You were a stranger who saved her life during a shootout. Sure, you don't see it that way, but she still does. She knows you went to help Wenn, but the fact that you risked yourself and saved her is what matters to her. You put yourself at risk to heal her father; the preacher could've come for you then, and it would've gone badly. You didn't bat an eye when you tried to help. Even when you came back after her father's death, you didn't flinch at the idea that he might've gone to the church. Instead, you offered to help find out why he'd died."

Doc's mind drifted back over those moments.

"When Ayla came to her for help, she agreed because she felt like she owed you, but also because she wanted to be closer to you. You accepted her as a true friend, trusted her implicitly, and during it all, never leered at her or tried to get more from her. Ayla saw what Sophia hoped for, but she was fighting for her own spot to start with. Once Ayla was accepted, she started to help Sophia accept what it was she wanted."

"Little troublemaker," Doc chuckled, thinking about Ayla.

"You having her move in had Sophia so hopeful and worried at the same time. Your wives were all on board with her joining the family by then, but she knew she had to hold to what her family would want. When you agreed to allow the others to play with her... well, that's when everything changed. Ayla purposefully left the door cracked open that night."

Doc swallowed as he considered what Rosa was saying. *Had Sophia not known?*

"Fiala teased Sophia about how, when you got home and went for clothing, you might hear them, possibly even see them. Curious how neither of them looked at the door, wasn't it?"

Doc started to laugh— he thought he'd snuck a peek, but they'd set him up. "Oh, Ayla... you'll pay for that, then be rewarded."

"She'll thank you for both. Sophia was so worried about how you'd see her, but if it was an 'accident,' then she'd have her answer if you found her attractive without having to flatly find out."

"So timid," Doc sighed softly, thinking back to the morning after the peek. "She was so timid, but eager."

"And she still is... she yearns for tonight, Voice, craves what it will bring. Seeing you with us ever since that first morning has made her nearly frantic to be underneath you. Part of her worries that she'll fail to please you. Silly little lawyer," Rosa giggled. "As long as you are you, she will know how wrong her fear was."

Doc let out a slow breath. "I'll treat her just as she needs. I'll always be me, worried entirely about the one I'm with."

Rosa began to kiss down his chest. "We know, dear Voice... I seemed to have caused you a hardship. I'll help relax it for you."

Doc laughed as he let her have her way, knowing he could use the release. He gently stroked her hair as she went, praising her mentally for telling him everything she had. His faint worries for his wives had been laid to rest by his precious weed.

* * *

Stepping out of the hansom cab, Doc exhaled slowly. Dressed in his best suit, he smoothed the jacket as Harrid got out behind him. Lia had explained the plan for the wedding when he'd finally left the bedroom.

Harrid shifted a little uncomfortably, not happy being without his armor and weapons. Lia had asked him to wear his best clothing and just his pistol. Once he was sure she'd be wearing her guns, he begrudgingly acquiesced to her request. He understood the reasoning, and Doc had even asked him to be the best man, but not being in guard mode made him edgy.

"You okay?" Doc asked.

"I'd feel better with my armor and weapons," Harrid answered honestly.

"Thank you," Doc said, patting his shoulder, "for being honest, but also for doing this."

Harrid nodded, looking around as a guard. "My speech won't be any good."

"Probably be better than Lia giving me another one," Doc chuckled.

Harrid's beard twitched when he remembered the speech she'd given during Ayla's wedding. "I'll do my best, but is it okay mentioning that you're the shaman of my clan?"

"Do what you think best," Doc said. "I do trust you, Harrid. I know I'm hard to work with at times, and I'm doing my best to make it easier."

"The one who looked after me once called me rocks-up-my-nose stupid," Harrid said. "I was stupid enough to shove rocks up my nose because I had nothing else to do. Even at your worst, you've never been that bad, though I have wanted to slap you a few times."

Doc laughed as he started walking up the stairs of the court building. "I'm not against being slapped if I need it. Just check the swing; you might break my jaw, otherwise."

"I doubt it," Harrid snickered. "After all, you're rather hard-headed and stubborn. I think that's why you and Sonya get along so well."

"Fair enough," Doc agreed, still chuckling.

The courthouse here was larger than the one back in Deep Gulch. The clerk and records departments looked to take up three times the amount of room. The far end of the hall had three sets of double doors leading to the courtrooms. Doc's steps slowed, as he had no idea which was the one to sign off on the marriage.

Harrid glanced at Doc, then pointed to the right. "Lia said it's the right courtroom."

Luck's Holding 103

"Glad she told you," Doc replied.

"Just the family for the courthouse. Everyone else will be at the reception, right?" Harrid asked.

"We didn't see the need to ask people to show up for the signing. Makes it easy to keep it off the radar of anyone wanting to disrupt things, too."

Harrid just nodded as he opened the doors to the empty room. Doc hoped Harrid was right about this being the correct courtroom. Doc crossed to stand just behind the small wall that separated the front from the viewing area, and Harrid stayed by the door so he could keep an eye on the hall.

Minutes slowly ticked by as Doc waited. His nerves had been increasing as the wait went on. He knew Sophia wouldn't back out, but his mind kept trying to spin different 'what-if' scenarios.

Harrid coughed once, standing up even straighter than normal. Doc's heart clenched, then relaxed— Harrid was just telling him that the others were here. A second later, the door in the back of the room clicked open and Doc jerked slightly.

The judge was an older man with a long, droopy, mustache decorating his face. The thick eyebrows and mustache were solid white, and his head was bald. Giving Doc a look, the judge chuckled as he moved to the bench, taking his seat.

"Grooms are always nervous. Just be patient, son. If she agreed, she'll be here." The judge's voice was calm, but clearly spoke of his years of smoking.

"Thank you, sir. I believe they're coming now," Doc said. He pushed the gate open to the court proper and waited, resting it against his hip.

"Another witness is coming with her, I hope? You need two."

"She has her friends, sir," Doc replied.

"Good. I hate having to make those who want to get married come back."

A minute later, Sonya stepped through the open doorway that Harrid was next to. She gave Doc a bright smile when she entered, moving aside to face the aisle. Doc's breath caught a moment later when Sophia appeared in the doorway.

Her gown was a bright white that flowed to her ankles. The sleeves were laced to her wrists, with silver filigree in the form of owls flying up her arms. She carried a journal in her hands as she approached him. Her orange eyes were filled with happiness while she crossed the room to his side.

The others filed in behind her, smiles on their faces as they took places in the waiting area. Sonya and Harrid followed Doc and Sophia to stand before the judge. Another woman who'd been mostly ignored was the last one in the room— she went to stand to the side of the judge's bench, handing him the paperwork.

The judge took a moment to look over the forms before he nodded. "Yes, everything is in order." Looking up, he gave Sophia and Doc a smile before his eyes narrowed slightly. He looked back down at the paperwork and his smile grew wider. "Ms. Sagesse, it is always a pleasure to see one of the learned marrying."

"Thank you, sir," Sophia smiled back at the judge.

"I do know of your family's tradition, having presided over a ceremony before. I will begin." Clearing his throat, the judge raised his head and spoke formally, "Mr. Holyday and Ms. Sagesse, you are both here today to see your lives joined together. This is a momentous occasion. The Sagesse family has long kept the traditions and laws of civilization strong. You marry into a long family line, and that is good." He paused to clear his throat again. "Ms. Sagesse, you may speak."

Sophia swallowed, her eyes on Doc's. "Doc, you've brought me a lot of happiness. I hope that I can give you even a tenth of what you've given me." She presented the journal to him. "This is who I was. All of my family chronicles our lives so that our children can learn from us. When we marry, we give the journal of who we were to our partner. It is theirs to keep safe for our children. As of today, I will be keeping a journal that chronicles our life together as a family."

Doc took the journal with care, using one arm to press it against his chest. "I'll do my best to not only give you the happiness you already have, dear Sophia; from today on, I will strive to give you even more. You've been a balm for my nerves time and again. I doubt I'll ever be able to express how joyous today is for me."

"Well said," the judge chuckled, then coughed. "Please step forward and sign. Witnesses, you will step forward after them."

Doc signed before handing Sophia the pen. When she finished, she handed it off to Sonya, who in turn, gave it to Harrid. The moment they were done, the judge signed off on the paperwork, as well.

"By the right of law, you two are now married," the judge intoned, his mustache pulling up high as he smiled. "You may kiss your wife, sir."

Doc pulled Sophia to him gently. He was still holding the journal so he couldn't dip her, but he did kiss her soundly. The moment drew out as Harrid and their family cheered for them. A light laugh joined the cheers when the clerk giggled as the kiss drew out.

"Goodness, that's certainly a lot of love," the judge muttered.

Doc broke the kiss, then gave the judge a nod. "Sorry, sir. We've waited far longer than we intended to."

"That is fine, Mr. Holyday. I remember my own wedding, decades past now. Clerk, I'll be taking the rest of today off. I believe I'll go home and spend it with my wife."

"Yes, sir," the clerk said as she took the paperwork from him.

Hand in hand, Doc led Sophia from the room. The others fell in line behind them, with the clerk being the last. The judge watched them all go, tears starting to fall from his eyes. The loss of his wife was over a decade past, but the love the newlyweds had reminded him keenly of his loss. He would go home, polish her urn, and tell her about his day.

CHAPTER FIFTEEN

Doc and Sophia rode in a two-person enclosed hansom cab over to the Palace Hotel. Holding hands and exchanging small kisses the entire way, the pair felt the rush of happiness that tonight would be their night.

"I'm not dreaming, right?" Sophia whispered.

"I am if you are," Doc murmured. "I wish we could've gotten married once your mother took over as judge in Deep Gulch, but she asked us not to. Something about conflict of interest."

"She wanted to make sure no one could say she married us because you forced her. Your enemies will try to find every possible way to cause trouble. All of us being married will be one way. With me getting married to you here, it'll be harder for others to find the trail. My cousin is also helping… muddy things further."

"What do you mean?"

"She's misfiling the paperwork. It'll still be in the office, just not where it belongs."

Doc's lips twitched. "Never anger the one who handles the paperwork. Your life will be hell if you do."

Sophia ducked her head. "I suggested it before we left. The others agreed with my reasoning."

"I wasn't brought in for that discussion."

"We handle a lot of things for you... husband."

Doc was silent for a moment. It came down to if he trusted the women in his life to do what was best for him, even if he didn't know everything. The previous times they'd all colluded on matters he hadn't known about came back to him; most notably, the parties with others before they left. They'd gotten everything in order before asking him. A tiny part of him was still uncertain if leaving the children behind was the right choice.

"Doc? I'm sorry."

Doc blinked, pulled from his thoughts by Sophia's tone. "What? Oh, no, Sophia, you're fine. *I'm* sorry. I was lost in thought. I agree with what you did, and the fact that you all try to make things easier for me." Pulling her back to his side, he kissed her gently.

Sophia sniffled— her panic at his silence had started to spike. His words soothed her emotions, and she melted into the kiss. She'd talked with her mother a lot about what marriages should be, and had read as much as she could get her hands on. Doc was one of the better men she could ever hope to have. There was a small part of her that was sad he wasn't hers alone, but honestly, she didn't want to give up Ayla or the others, either; they'd been so kind and loving to her.

The carriage slowing, then stopping, had them break the kiss. They made sure they were presentable before Doc stepped out. Helping Sophia out next, he smiled broadly when she took his arm as the rest of his wives climbed out of the carriage behind their cab.

"The guests should already be here," Sophia whispered. "Let them go in front of us, and then we're the last ones into the room."

"Okay," Doc murmured. He gave Harrid and his wives a smile, letting them climb the stairs ahead of him.

The doorman held the door open for them, watching the procession with a grin and tipping his hat to Doc and Sophia. "Happy day to you both."

"Thank you," Doc replied.

The staff on duty watched the group heading toward the dining room. Soft comments complimenting the bride and groom followed them.

Doc paused just outside of the doors as the others walked in. With a smile to Sophia, he finally led her inside. A soft, happy cheer went up from the nearly hundred people in the room. It was almost packed full, with the only open space being the dance floor. Most of those present were dwarves from the Ironbeard clan, though others did fill out the reception party.

Doc didn't know a few of the faces, but they were all at a table with David Roquefell; he figured they were people he should know in time. The newlywed couple accepted the celebration before Doc led Sophia to the head table, his wives filling out both sides. The only man at the table with them was Harrid, sitting on Doc's right.

Doc seated Sophia, then cleared his throat and held up his hand, waiting for silence. "Ladies and gentlemen, we'll be having dinner first. Then, of course, the speeches. We'll try to keep them brief. We'll finish the night with dancing, as is tradition. Thank you all for coming to my wedding with Sophia Sagesse." He clapped his hands, and the servers began to bring trays into the room.

***

Dinner was amazing— the chef had gone all out to make the best he could, as the budget he'd been given had been overly generous. He'd been around the rich and powerful enough to know that an event like this could raise his name up, and possibly earn him a place as a personal chef to someone like David.

With dinner slowly coming to an end, it finally came time for the speeches. Doc stood, letting the crowd slowly quiet. "We have no father of the bride to give a speech. Sophia's father died a few months back, sadly. I can say he loved his daughter and wife deeply. Without him here, I will begin with the groom's speech. Then, we'll move on to others that many of you don't know, but are a tradition for me."

A small murmur had gone through the room at Doc's news about Sophia's father, but they quieted again.

Doc turned to Sophia seated beside him. "Where to start...? Maybe with your mother telling me in no uncertain terms to leave you be?"

Sophia laughed along with the crowd.

"I can't say when I felt real love for you the first time. The first day I saw you, I thought you were beautiful, but I respected your mother's wish and tried to banish any ideas that might've arisen. There was a point when I sorely needed you, and you were there for me, protecting me in ways I couldn't do for myself. That led to you becoming the head of the legal department for Luck's Holdings. In time, we worked closely together, and I found myself falling for your intellect. I've been blessed to be loved by intelligent women."

A soft murmur went through the crowd.

"You'll always be a shield for us in some ways, dear Sophia, but I will do my very best to protect you, as well. I can promise without fear of failure to always love you. Having you beside me will make me smile brightly, no matter how dark the moment we face. When you speak, I will listen. You have wisdom far beyond my own, and I'm not an idiot to ignore your advice. Please, be kind to me when I make mistakes? To you: the wisest love I could ever hope to have."

Sophia beamed brightly when she touched his glass with hers. The crowd drank to his toast, then murmured in confusion when Sophia stood up.

"My husband's traditions include the bride speaking, along with the maid of honor and the best man," Sophia said. "I'll keep mine shorter than even my husband's." She looked at Doc with bright eyes. "You saved my life, did all you could for my father, and gave me hope and a goal to work for. My love for you has only ever grown, and I think it will continue to do so forever. I'll do everything in my power for our family. To you, dear husband, please be gentle with me. I give you my very heart and soul, but I fear not, for you are the kindest man that has ever walked this planet."

Doc touched his glass to hers, accepting her toast.

The crowd was surprised at the brevity, but also the depth of emotion Sophia had shown. They quieted again when Ayla stood; a few murmured about her heritage, but very quietly.

"Sophia, thank you for choosing me as your maid of honor," Ayla said softly. "We worked so closely together to improve Doc's business and now, his life. I will always treasure you as my dearest friend and hope you will do the same."

Sophia reached up, taking Ayla's hand and kissing the back of it. That got more murmurs from the crowd.

"As for a story..." Ayla's lips twitched and her eyes glinted mischievously. "I could tell them about our first long night working to improve our understanding of Doc."

Sophia's eyes shot wide and she started to object, earning a giggle from Ayla.

"I won't. I'll tell the story of how you came to be a part of Luck's Holdings when we needed you most. Doc had been arrested on false charges by a corrupt sheriff and was going to be railroaded by a judge who took bribes. I was in a near panic; I didn't know the law well enough to truly save him. When I came to you, I was so afraid you'd tell me to go away. You listened, and I can still clearly recall your face. It was then that I knew you cared for Doc, even if you refused to see your heart for what it was. All of us know how you will guide, guard, and care for him, Sophia. We wish you all the love and happiness you can have, and then a little bit more. To Sophia, the brains of her new family." Ayla was turned away from the crowd, so they didn't see her wink when she raised the toast.

Sophia giggled as she tapped glasses with Ayla.

Those who didn't know were still oblivious to the layers the speech contained, but those who knew could see the depth of love the two women had for each other.

Harrid stood slowly, the last to give a speech. When the crowd quieted again, he cleared his throat. "Doc asked me to be his best man, but I'm really his bodyguard. This might be the only time I can openly criticize him, even in jest. He should've considered that before asking me."

A ripple of laughter went through the room.

"Doc is a man who cares too much," Harrid said. "I've seen him time and again help people he had no reason to help, but there's one story that personifies this man more than any other. There's a young girl where he had his lodgings, a precious child Doc doted on, seeing in her a daughter he didn't have. The girl was snatched up by evil men intent on strong-arming and killing Doc. He didn't hesitate or try to consider when he got news; he rushed to save the child who had no involvement, other than that Doc cared for her. He put himself in a deadly situation for someone with no relation to him for no reason other than he cared too much."

Doc grimaced, recalling everything about Suez's trap.

"He got ahead of those who could aid him, but even going into a clear trap, he calculated his way to emerge unscathed and with the child unharmed. If Doc calls you a friend, he'll do all he can for you, even at a cost to himself. Not many people are as selfless as he is, but I swear in front of those here: Doc, if you ever rush off without me to help you again, I will kick you so hard, *you'll* need a doctor."

The crowd murmured as Doc bowed his head.

"Sophia, I don't need to tell you about your husband. You know as well as I do who he is. Any father who loved their daughter would see him for the great man he is. You'll never want for love, safety, or security. I hope you both have a very long life of joy. And your mother asked me to ask a single question, knowing I'd be here when you two got married."

Sophia covered her face with her hands.

"How many and when?" Harrid asked, his stern face cracking with laughter. "She wants grandchildren."

The room erupted in laughter.

"Doc, your wife is precious to her mother, as you well know, but I'd wait to see her again until you have a grandchild for her to dote on," Harrid finished, getting more laughter. "To the newlyweds: may their love shine brightly for all time."

Everyone in the room raised their glass to the toast.

CHAPTER SIXTEEN

Doc walked up the stairs with Sophia leaning against him. "Was it what you hoped for?" he asked softly.

"It was very nice. I appreciated them all dancing with me, even if it did cause a stir. It's not as if our marital situation will remain unknown forever."

"True. The dwarves seemed to be mostly prepared for it, at least."

"How many of them got a handful?" Sophia snickered.

"I stopped trying to correct them after the third one," Doc sighed. "I didn't realize that most of the guests were father and daughter until we started dancing."

"They were very forward," Sophia said. "Just respectful enough."

"If they'd gone any further, I would've made sure it stopped. Tonight's your night."

"Thank you... I'm nervous."

Doc gave her a soft smile. "I'll go slow, Sophia. The last thing I want is for you to hate tonight."

"I doubt you could do anything to make me hate it."

"I'm going to do my best to make it the best night of your life."

"Mmm, I hope you do. I've been wanting this for... a while now."

Doc chuckled as they reached the top floor. "So have I. Not as long as you probably have, though. It took longer for me to admit that I was okay with wanting you, too."

"I was so afraid of Ayla not closing that door..." Sophia flushed as she trailed off. "I had no idea you heard about her taunting me to join her the next morning. We'd thought you'd just see the two of us together. It wasn't until you just accepted it the morning after that I wondered if you'd heard more."

"I heard a bit," Doc murmured as he recalled the scene, pausing outside the room. "But right now, there's only one thing that matters." He unlocked the door and pushed it open before scooping Sophia into his arms.

She let out a small gasp of surprise, then giggled and pressed her face into his neck. "I wasn't expecting that."

Doc carried her into the room, using his foot to close the door behind them. He got her to latch the lock, still in his arms, before he carried her through the suite to the bedroom. There were a couple of candles lit on the small table near the bed, the only things providing any light in the room.

Laying Sophia on the bed, Doc collected a kiss the moment she was down. The kiss started soft, but quickly grew in passion. Doc broke it as he stepped back, smiling at her while he took his jacket off.

"Let me get out of this and then I'll help you get out of that," Doc said.

Sophia nodded, licking her lips as she watched him. Her heart thundered in her chest— this was the moment she'd waited for. Doc met her eyes, slowly taking his clothing off to build the tension in the room. Sophia swallowed when he finally stood naked before her; she knew what she was getting with him, but tonight, he was hers alone.

"Now to help undress my lovely wife," Doc whispered when he reached the bed.

Sophia shivered as she rolled to her side, exposing the buttons to him. "I should probably stand."

"No. I can manage if you just help a little." He began to unbutton her dress, leaning over to kiss each inch of skin as it was exposed.

Sophia's face flushed. He was treating her with all the kindness she knew he had in him. She'd had him command her a little every time they'd done things before, but here and now, he was focused on building the moment for her.

"Are you going to be like normal, Doc?"

"Not tonight, unless you ask me to be," he whispered as he got the last button undone. "Tonight, I'm going to focus solely on pleasing you as much as I can."

"Going to make me pass out? They all warned me about their first time with you."

"I've got a perfect record on that front so far," Doc chuckled as he gently rolled her to her back, then peeled her dress off. "But that doesn't matter. The only thing that matters is bliss for you."

Her spine goosebumped when he drew her dress down her torso. Her corset was more lace than solid fabric, made in a shade of sapphire blue that really made her orange eyes stand out. Biting her bottom lip, she watched his face with worry.

"Exquisite," Doc murmured, bending to kiss the gentle slopes of her breasts. "I'll get your dress off before doing more. Please raise your hips for me?"

Sophia did as he asked so he could slip her dress off her. He managed to take her petticoat at the same time, leaving her in just a corset and underwear. Her breath came faster as she was rapidly exposed to him.

"I am curious, Sophia. Do you get anything from foot or leg massages?"

Sophia blinked slowly at him; that was not the question she'd expected. "Um... yes. The center of my foot is always stiff and tender."

"I see," Doc murmured, trailing light kisses back up her body. He kissed all the way back to her lips, claiming them for a passionate moment before breaking away. "I'm going to finish stripping you down, kiss you all over, and then I'm going to massage your feet."

Sophia swallowed the lump in her throat. She was sure Doc had no idea that such a massage meant so much to her. For her family, someone easing the stress of their unique feet was very intimate. She hadn't even told Ayla that little tidbit, wanting to keep it a secret until marriage. Seeing his questioning gaze, she quickly nodded her head in agreement.

Time floated by as Doc did just as he said he would. When his hands dug gently into her feet, she let out a soft moan. Doc didn't comment about it, just continuing to work. When he finally finished, he cleaned his hands off before going back to her.

Sophia was a puddle of relaxation when he kissed up her legs. She knew where he was going, so she spread them wider for him. Doc kissed his way up her thighs, aiming for her slick sex. Her light-brown trimmed patch just above his target beckoned him. A part of him was glad his lovers trimmed themselves— only Rosa would go completely hairless, and the rest helped keep each other neatly groomed. Rosa had even helped Doc with his own grooming when he'd asked.

His mind drifted to the moment his wives found his new neatly trimmed appearance and the thankful looks they gave him. He understood; no one likes hair in their mouth. Ever since then, all of them had been even more fastidious about staying neat.

Sophia gasped when Doc's tongue traced a lazy line up her wet mound. "Oh, Doc... thank you."

Doc didn't answer vocally. Instead, he replied by focusing on his desire to bring her pleasure. They'd done this before, so he knew exactly what she wanted and made sure she was given exactly that. When she cried out for the third time, he brought a single finger into play.

Sophia's eyes shot wide open, looking down when he gently penetrated her. "Oh... mmm... yes..." Her eyelid twitched as more pleasure joined his active tongue. She let out a ragged gasp when he crooked that finger slowly, finding the spot that made her buck as she came hard.

Doc worked her G-spot with his index finger and continued to ply her flesh with his tongue. Sophia's orgasm stretched out— instead of multiples, she just seemed to have one long one. In time, he eased away to shift into position. He waited for her to regain some awareness first, just smiling down at her while lightly trailing his hands over her body.

When her eyes finally focused on him and where he was, Sophia's breath hitched. "Slowly?"

"As you wish, my dear wife," Doc whispered, doing as she asked.

Sophia moaned in pleasure, gasped in pain, and then moaned in pleasure again as Doc took her with exquisite slowness. She was lost in the sensation as he worked in and out of her with tenderness. Smaller waves of euphoria built and broke over her time and again, leaving her near mindless when he stopped.

"Sophia," Doc's voice was ragged, "I'm done. Are you okay with me going faster?"

"Please... like Fiala... please?"

Doc swallowed as he nodded. "As you wish."

He started again, but built speed and urgency as he went. Sophia's eyes shot open, unseeing, as pleasure greater than anything she'd felt before grew in her. Her legs wrapped around his waist and one of her talons nicked him, not that either paid it attention at the time. She grabbed him, pulling him down and kissing him with need as she felt another release coming. This is what she'd wanted; she'd seen the others experience it, and now, it was hers... *he* was hers.

Doc grunted as he came closer and closer to his end. He ignored the pain from her talon, then completely forgot about it as he feverishly returned her kiss. Spasming when he finally hit the end, he pushed fully into her. His hips bucked as he filled her with thick spurt after thick spurt of his semen.

Gasping when he could, Doc shuddered, having just enough energy to pull himself out and lay beside her. Sophia was unconscious, and Doc let out a feeble chuckle as he pulled the blankets over them. *Every single one of them... it's so odd...* His thoughts faded as sleep claimed him.

* * *

"Doc? Doc?! Are you okay?" Sophia's urgent voice pulled him from sleep.

"Hmm? What?"

"You've been bleeding... I... I cut you..." Sophia sniffled, touching his chest with a trembling hand.

Doc frowned as his brain tried to make sense of what she was saying. With a grunt, he used *healing hands* to check himself. He had a cut along his rear and a dim memory of her wrapping her legs around him during their final moments. He healed the wound, then took her hand in his.

She sniffled, looking at him with worry.

Finding that she was okay, Doc exhaled slowly. "It's fine. It was only a small nick on my ass."

"I woke up to get some water and saw the blood next to you..." Sophia sniffled again. "My talons..."

Doc sat up, grabbing her and gently easing them both onto the bed. "Shh... It's okay, Sophia. It wasn't bad. I didn't even realize it because it was so minor. Calm yourself, okay? I'd gladly take a dozen more of those for just a single kiss from you, much less what we had last night."

Sophia began to cry, clutching him. Many of the people in her family had hurt their lovers because of their talons. It was a known risk when sleeping with a Sagesse, but few outside their family knew that. Her fear that he'd hate her for it had claimed her before she'd managed to wake him.

Doc soothed her, stroking her back and whispering his love. He didn't understand what had caused her meltdown, but he knew she needed him. In truth, the cut had been bad enough to make him lose enough blood to stain the sheet under him, but it wouldn't have killed him.

When Sophia finally calmed down, Doc eased her head back, then kissed her gently. She returned it with trembling lips, wondering if he truly did forgive her.

When the kiss ended, he rested his forehead against hers. "I don't know what worries you, Sophia, but I'm going to tell you the flat truth: even if you cut me five times as bad every time, I'll come back to you again and again."

Lips trembling, she could see only love in his eyes. "But... but I hurt you."

"Sometimes, love hurts," Doc said gently. "Sonya hurts every time I'm with her, even after spending time to make sure she's as good as she can be. This is basically the same thing."

Sophia wanted to object, but she paused as she took his argument in. After a moment, she sniffled once. "Really?"

"Really, so please dry your tears, my love?"

Sophia's heart warmed at how easily he was accepting it. "Sorry."

"It's okay." Doc held her, looking at the curtained windows. It was late at night still— the sun not even a glimmer.

Sophia sniffled once more and kissed his neck. "I didn't get to return your attention last night."

"True, but that was because I wanted it to be all about your pleasure."

"Can I make it all about you now?"

"If you want to."

Sophia pressed into him, rolling him onto his back. She looked down at him, not used to being the one in charge. "Uh..."

Doc chuckled softly, touching her cheek. "It's okay. Do you want me to lead you?"

"Like normal, please... until I can straddle you?"

Doc's smile grew wider as he caressed her cheek with his thumb. "Gladly."

Sophia's face was hot, but she felt her heart swell again. "How may I serve you?"

Doc rubbed his thumb gently over her cheek until he held her chin softly. "You can do exactly as our wives have shown you, dearest. Make me feel all the pleasure you can give."

Sophia smiled as she lowered her head to his chest, then trailed a slow line of kisses down his torso.

CHAPTER SEVENTEEN

Doc woke up to soft breath tickling his ear. He opened his eyes and blinked slowly as he tried to place where he was. Glancing to the side, he caught the sight of brown feathers with white splotches on his shoulder.

Memories of the previous night came back to him— his lovemaking with Sophia was high in that quick replay, but more so was her moment of crisis. His heart softened for the vulnerable woman beside him. He just lay there, wondering if he could do anything to make her realize that he truly was fine with her talons and that she might cut him again. With a smile, he gently eased out from underneath her. He watched Sophia as he did what he thought best.

Sophia murmured as she shifted in her sleep, dreaming of being with Doc the night before. Her mind focused on the massage he gave her. A sleepy smile came to her, as she could easily feel the moment again. Her toes curled slightly inward, loving the memory of him caring for her feet.

"Good morning, my beautiful lawyer," Doc murmured, his hands still working on her.

Sophia's eyes fluttered open; it took her a moment to realize that she wasn't dreaming. Her eyes widened when she saw him sitting at the foot of the bed, her legs on his lap as he worked at the center of her foot. "Doc...?"

"Yes, dear?"

Sophia bit her lip for a second. "Uh... t-that..."

"Should I stop?" Doc asked.

"No! I mean... it's just... it's special for my family to have our feet rubbed. One of the better ways to show love... How did you know?"

"I know that you enjoyed it last night, is all. Now that I know that, I'm even happier to do it. Are you feeling better?"

Sophia swallowed her worry; she knew what he was asking about. "Will they be okay if it happens?"

"I'm sure they will be, because it'll be an accident, but we can talk with them. Maybe one of them will have ideas on how to make it less likely to happen."

"Making me sleep alone wo—"

"Never," Doc cut her off as gently as he could. "You've slept with us for weeks now and you've never once cut us before."

"When I sleep, I normally curl my feet in. It helps with the ache. All my talons touch me, not any of you. But when we're intimate..."

"This is the first time something's happened, dearest," Doc said, continuing to work on her foot. "None of the others will be between your thighs the same way."

Sophia wanted to argue, but he was right. The others did get between her thighs, though not the way he did. Her whole body warmed with love and lust as he kept massaging her. "Doc... thank you."

"Thank you, Sophia," Doc whispered back. "Thank you for trusting me, for letting me pamper you. I can see how much this moment means to you. That's what I want most for those who love me. I want you to have as much love as I can give."

"We want that for you, too."

"Which is why we all get along. If you have any doubts or fears, talk to them, okay? You know the guidelines we have about trust, truth, and communication. Don't hold back. We're all here for each other."

Sophia sniffled as she watched the honesty on his face. "Doc... can you stop for now?"

Doc glanced up at her. "If that's what you want."

"I do, because I want a bit more of last night before we meet the others for lunch."

Doc's smile became knowing. "Ah, I see. You want me to give more parts of you attention?"

Sophia nodded. "But maybe you can be gently demanding again?"

Doc slowed the massage as he met her eyes. "As you need or wish."

*** * ***

Lunch with his whole family was good, but they were looking forward to heading back to the manor, as they didn't have any other business in town.

"We do have things for tomorrow," Ayla was starting to say when someone approached the table.

"Shaman," Karl Ironbeard, dressed in his best suit, said, "apologies if I'm interrupting."

"What can I do for you?" Doc asked.

"I was sent by the elders, sir. They want to speak with you tomorrow. Since we didn't have a solid date for the meeting, they asked to arrange it."

Doc gave the stoic dwarf a long look. "Surprised you're the one to bring the message to me."

"My cousin asked me to come, as you've at least met me before," Karl explained.

"Do I have prior obligations?" Doc asked Ayla.

"Sophia and I were going to speak with Roquefell," Ayla replied. "That's all I know of for tomorrow."

Doc nodded, having seen Karl's eye twitch slightly when Ayla mentioned David. "I'll be there just after noon," Doc said.

"Very well." Karl bowed his head fractionally. "Sorry for interrupting your meal with your family."

"Clan is family, too," Doc said, thinking of Sonya's lessons on dwarven history.

Karl was slow to stand straight again, clearly caught off guard. "Yes, as it should be. I will let the elders know." With that, he turned on his heel.

"Stiff," Lia murmured.

"He's uncertain if the clan should ally with Doc," Rosa whispered. "The meeting is to establish if Doc is the shaman they need or want."

"I'll go with you," Sonya said primly. "I have no doubt they'll bring up our wives, and I'll shut them down."

"Good. I would've asked you to come if you hadn't offered," Doc told her. "Ayla, when you get the business contract lined up with David, set up another meeting with him for me. For that one, I'll need you and Sophia there, too."

"You want him tied to the new business before you tell him of the plans beyond the hot springs," Ayla nodded. "I will set up a follow-up meeting with him."

"Thank you," Doc sighed.

"Fiala and I will make sure the home is in order," Lia said, touching Fiala's hand lightly.

"We'll make sure things smooth out," Fiala nodded.

"Then I have nothing to worry about," Doc smiled at them.

Fiala flushed at his certainty in them. "I'm learning as quickly as I can, Doc."

"She's already doing well," Lia said. "Mizzi is a great help."

"Tomorrow will be busy," Doc sighed again before standing. "Before then, we have the rest of today without things pressing on us."

"Sophia and I need to start work on the contract," Ayla said.

"I could check out weapons for the staff with Harrid," Lia added.

"Home first," Harrid added from his spot at the table. "Have to make sure he's safe there."

"Agreed," Lia nodded.

"Guess I can check in with the workers," Doc said.

"Sonya and I can join you for that," Fiala said.

"Gladly."

* * *

Once they got home, Lia and Harrid went right back into the city. Ayla and Sophia went inside to start drawing up contracts, leaving Doc, Fiala, Sonya, and Rosa to walk the exterior. Radley and Aran were working on what would be the front garden.

"How's it going?"

"Good, sir," Radley said, taking his hat off.

"Radley?"

"Yes, sir?"

"You can keep the hat on when outside," Doc said. "Maybe it's not normal, but I'd rather you stay as protected from the sun as possible."

Radley hesitated, then slowly put his hat back on. "If that's what you want, sir."

"It is. I'd like to have you healthy for years to come. I see you got some trees today."

"Yes, sir. Currently, we have three apple and three cherry." He pointed out each trio of trees in different parts of the yard. "By the end of the week, I'll have pear and peach trees."

"I do miss a good crisp apple," Fiala sighed.

"It'll be a while before these bear fruit, mistress," Radley said. "It normally takes a few years."

"Pity, but in time, they'll be a good addition."

"Doing the trees first?" Doc asked.

"Yes, sir. Start big, then go small," Radley nodded.

"I'll leave you to it," Doc said as he looked over the front yard. "Thank you."

"Thank you, sir," Radley replied. "Never thought I'd have an assistant. Makes this much easier."

"He always tries to help," Sonya smiled.

Aran watched them walk away before he exhaled. "He's odd."

"Can be as odd as he wants," Radley said softly, but tightly. "If any other socialite heard you say that about them... you'd be lucky to just be fired. And his wives probably have very good hearing."

Fiala's ears twitched, and Rosa smiled at what they heard behind them. Doc kept his face impassive, as he'd heard it, too.

Simpson looked up as they approached the group of men, going over to greet them. "Sir, as you can see, we're hard at work."

"Looking good so far," Doc said. "Any problems?"

"Not for us, sir. Everything is moving as you wanted."

"Keep up the good work," Doc smiled. "I might have more for you in the future, depending on if you want to work away from the city."

Simpson looked back at his crew for a moment. "Depending on the job, sir."

"I'll let you know after this is completed, but it's a massive job. I'd ask the Beavertons to do it, but my business in Deep Gulch keeps them extraordinarily busy."

Simpson looked thoughtful. "You work with the Beavertons, sir?"

"Have a small family of them in Deep Gulch doing all the work for my mine and budding town," Doc replied.

"We'll do our best," Simpson said, standing up a little straighter.

"I'll look forward to it," Doc replied. "I don't want to keep you. Just wanted to check-in."

"Yes, sir," Simpson said before he turned back to the project.

The group headed for the house. When they were far enough from the workers, Rosa said, "He was impressed at the offer and is intent on proving to you that his crew can do as well as the Beavertons."

"Good," Doc smiled. "And Radley?"

"He and Mizzi are very happy that you bought the manor and kept them on, then expanded the staff. Mizzi told him last night about how happy she is to have an understanding family who appreciates her advice."

Fiala smiled at that. "I can't let on, but that's good to know."

"Our husband brings the best out of people," Sonya smiled brightly.

"My wives bring the best out of me," Doc smiled back at her.

CHAPTER EIGHTEEN

"You two keep the carriage," Doc told Ayla and Sophia. "Sonya, Rosa, Harrid, and I will grab cabs here in town to get back to the estate."

"Very well," Ayla said. "I'd think it would be easier for us to get a cab out to David's."

"No guarantee you'd be able to get a ride home."

"Doc, you're not being realistic," Sophia said. "David has shown that he wants us as an ally. He'll gladly send us home in his carriage."

Doc gave it a few moments thought before nodding. "Okay. We'll tell Clyde about the change when he stops at the Ironbeard's clan hall."

"Thank you," Ayla said, kissing his cheek. "We'll be home after we have the contracts signed and delivered to the clerk."

"We'll make sure he's happy with the contract," Sophia said.

"I have no fear when it's you two handling the business," Doc smiled.

The two of them smiled back at him— the reminder that he trusted them so much still brought them both surges of happiness. Sonya and Rosa both grinned as they watched the exchange.

The small jostle of the carriage slowing to a stop told them that they'd arrived. Harrid opened the door for them, letting Doc and the others out, then frowned when Ayla and Sophia got out.

"Clyde, change of plans," Doc told the driver. "Ayla and Sophia will be getting a cab up to Roquefell's."

"Yes, sir," Clyde replied. "I'm sure they have a place out of the way here for carriages. I'll be ready to go when you are."

"Good, because I have no idea how long this will take."

Having heard the new plan, Harrid stepped away and flagged down a cab.

"Sonya, can you ask that gentleman where Clyde can park?" Doc asked, seeing one of the dwarven guards in front of the single-story building.

"Of course, husband," Sonya said before heading toward the guard.

Doc turned to help Ayla and Sophia into the cab that had pulled up for them. "See you for dinner tonight." He kissed them both briefly.

"We'll be there with good news," Ayla assured him.

"Everything will be in order and we'll let you know when he'll be good to see you again," Sophia added.

Shutting the door after another set of goodbyes, Doc stepped back and watched the cab roll away. Turning back toward the others, he found Sonya standing with Rosa and Harrid. "All good?"

"I told Clyde where he can park," Sonya said. "He's just waiting for us to go inside."

Doc offered his arm to Sonya. "Shall we?"

Smiling, she took his offered elbow with her hand. "Time to bring a second clan into the fold."

Rosa and Harrid followed the couple, both watching everything nearby, doing their best to keep Doc safe.

The guard on the front door nodded at them as he opened the door, but he stared at Rosa with wariness. The hallway inside was exactly like the one in Deep Gulch, and Doc walked the path out of memory. They came to a set of double doors with another guard standing in front. The guard drew himself up, clearly meaning to stop them.

"Who comes to speak to the elders?" the guard asked formally.

"Doc Holyday, shaman of the Oresmelter clan," Doc replied.

Nodding, the guard knocked on the door, then stepped inside. Doc heard him inform the elders before he came back out. "Welcome, Shaman, please enter."

"Thank you."

The elder's chamber was similar to the one in Deep Gulch, but the furniture was more expensive and the stone was carved with murals of dwarves hard at work. All three elders watched the group enter.

Alaric Ironbeard, the elder in the middle of the group, had met Doc during the yearly tournament at the Lily, but he didn't know or recognize the other two. Both were male, and one had a thick beard that was mostly white.

"Shaman Holyday," Alaric greeted him. "Please, sit. We wish to converse with you."

Doc noted that only two chairs had been set out; he was glad he'd only brought the people he had and not his entire family for this. He and Sonya took the seats while Rosa knelt between them, and Harrid stood behind them.

"Thank you, Elder Ironbeard."

"Call me Alaric," Alaric said. "The reason why is obvious once we are introduced. My granduncle, Itoniv Ironbeard," he motioned to the eldest of the trio. "And my brother, Werner Ironbeard."

"A pleasure, gentlemen," Doc bowed in his seat. "Call me Doc. I would hate to be the only one being addressed by his surname."

That had Itoniv looking disgruntled. "Shamans should be addressed with respect."

"Then I ask you to respect my request, sir."

"Before we get too sidetracked," Alaric cut in, "we asked you here because you have been acknowledged as the shaman of the Oresmelter clan in Deep Gulch. My cousin was not sure you should be acknowledged as shaman while I, after our talk, felt that you could take on that role. This meant that we needed you to speak with Itoniv and Werner to see how they feel on the subject."

"I'll answer the questions you put forth."

"Is it true you have married an elf, a half-elf, bestials, and sleep with *that*?" Itoniv snapped the question with distaste, his eyes on Rosa.

Doc's friendly mood soured instantly. *Why is there always one?* he thought as he turned his gaze to the eldest dwarf. "I married the women who love me and help me in my mission with the blessing of my other wives."

"Sonya Holyday, you are from the Redblade family, a notable family with a long history. Your father, Otto, is currently a barber, but your mother became an elder of the Oresmelter clan. Is this correct?" Werner asked before Itoniv could speak again.

"That is true," Sonya replied. "I'm also the one who helps my husband learn about dwarven customs."

"Yet you agreed to these other women, including Sagesse?" Itoniv sneered.

"I did. They love our husband as much as I do. They each help him in ways I cannot. Why should I not let him have more love?"

"It is said he marginalizes you," Werner said gently. "That he favors the others over you. Even the... dryad." The last word was tacked on, obviously changed from something else.

"Elders," Sonya said gently, "I would advise you not to denigrate our wives, or Rosa. The dryad beside us gave herself to him willingly. Mother herself is doing what she can to assist the shaman in returning the old ways, or at least removing Apoc. My husband will not tolerate disrespect to his wives, *any of us*. As for him marginalizing me, in what way do you mean?"

Werner looked uncomfortable at the sudden onslaught. He still replied without too much hesitation, "I apologize for the forwardness of this, but I meant as a husband and wife."

Sonya laughed. "Fool. I get more time than any other wife in that regard because he treasures me and doesn't want to harm me. Where he might spend an hour with any of them, I get nearly two."

All three elders suddenly looked uncomfortable.

"If you're done asking about my sex life," Doc said, stepping in, "I thought we were going to discuss my fitness to be a shaman to your clan."

"Yes, yes we were," Alaric said, grateful for the opening. "My fellow elders were concerned about your stance on young women being allowed to do work."

Doc turned his gaze to Itoniv. "Your mother or grandmother, did she not work as well as have kids?"

"That was different. We were warring with the elves," Itoniv tried to dismiss the claim.

"So the women worked because the men were needed to fight, correct?"

"Yes, of course."

"Did any of them take up arms, as well?"

Itoniv grunted as if he didn't want to answer. After a pause, he finally spoke, "Some did before the halls were attacked directly, and then they all did when trying to defend the home."

"I've been told the war never led to the death of women and children on either side. The men were killed, but even when attacking a clan hall or tribe encampment, the women and children were left alone as long as they didn't raise a weapon themselves."

"The histories do say that the shamans made it a firm point..." Itoniv agreed slowly.

"Because both sides knew that they would eventually stop the war, and they would need the women and children to rebuild."

"Exactly," Itoniv said as if Doc had made his point for him.

"So the women worked during the war and some after the war, but even then, they still had children. Why is that different than now?"

"We are not at war!" Itoniv snapped as if it was obvious.

"Aren't you?" Doc asked gently. "Not all wars are fought with weapons. Surely you've seen how dwarves are being treated by humanity."

Silence fell in the hall, and Doc looked over the elders.

"Gentlemen, you are being slowly marginalized and squeezed out, just like the elves. The bestials are being bred into slave stock or into humans, all because the church decrees that only humanity should stand at the end. Apoc has firmly stated that you are nothing but tools to be used. Humanity took your remaining shamans from you after the war ended. Why? To keep you from the spiritual guidance to hold to Mother and the gods."

"You would lead us to war?" Werner asked, shocked.

"No. I'd lead you to prosperity and a chance to show that you won't be easily pushed down. Not all change needs war. War is just another tool of forcing your views on another. My goddess is Luck, not War. I'd fail if I tried to lead a coup."

"A wise man knows his limits," Alaric said. "Eight younger women of the Oresmelter clan followed your dictate of working. I explained it to my fellow elders, but can you tell them the limits you set on it?"

"I can," Sonya said with a smile. "One of my best friends is one of those women and is likely courting right now. Her name, if you wish to check with the clan, is Gretchen Oresmelter. As for what the shaman decreed; 'Turn not aside the men who show interest. Give them a chance, but be allowed to follow your heart.' That was the word of the shaman. Now, for you to understand better, Gretchen is a smelter like her father. It's not a glamorous life, as it's one of the lower stations one can have, yet she had *five dozen men* asking for her hand."

That had Werner sitting back in his chair. He knew, like many did, that most looked to marry higher. The fact that that many men had asked to court a simple smelter was jarring.

Itoniv's beard bunched up. "Eight women have done this in the Oresmelter clan?"

"And all are like Gretchen," Sonya replied. "Just as our forebears could work and raise a family, so can we. We've just let ourselves be boxed into bad thinking."

"I have spoken to my daughters," Alaric said, cutting in when there was a pause. "I asked them if this way was accepted by the clan, what would they do? My eldest was wistful. She is already married and will not try to find work now, but she wished she could have before. My youngest said she would look for work that she felt suited to, and that she would still raise a family."

"I have no doubt my son would accept that," Werner said. "He has always wondered why we stopped letting the women work, too."

"Wasteful! They could have more children if they just focused on family!" Itoniv snapped.

"Could they? Really?" Doc asked. "From what I've seen, having two children isn't even the average, and that's why the clans are slowly dwindling. Letting women work is a first step. It'll make them happy. That emotional state will make it more likely they want to have more children."

Sonya laughed. "Oh, it will. All eight of the women I spoke of have been vetting their potential partners in earnest. They want to bear a child as quickly as possible. They want to prove the shaman wise. Trust me when I say that the Oresmelter clan will be having a boom of children in the coming years."

"We have concerns about the church, as well," Werner said. "If you become openly recognized as a shaman, the church will come looking for you."

"I know," Doc said. "There are contingencies in place for the worst that could happen. How quickly will they move if more clans and tribes look to me? Both the Oresmelter clan and the Treeheart tribe call me shaman. In time, there will be more of both. I'm here to see you first, but I will move on to bring more to Luck."

"Why us first?" Itoniv asked.

"Because I had business here, and I thought Alaric could be trusted."

"What business?" Werner was quick to ask.

"That is separate from me being a shaman," Doc said. "The short answer is that I'm working with Mr. Roquefell on a few things."

"We know you just bought property between here and Deep Gulch. Is it another mine?" Itoniv asked.

"No, it'll be something entirely different. I will say that it'll be a destination to relax, refresh, and recenter. The land used to be home to the Heartwood tribe. I'll be dedicating the place to them. Clans and tribes lost should be remembered."

"They should," Itoniv said softly, clearly thinking of a lost clan.

"Tell me?" Doc asked gently.

"My father's side came from Dussle. His father's clan, the Rhinestein, were wiped out during the Reform."

Doc looked at Sonya, who grimaced. "We haven't covered that yet, husband. I apologize. The reform was when Lex Martin helped the church of Apoc grow in Dussle. His teachings led to a lot of the clans being killed or pushed out of their homes."

Doc's lips pursed, then he nodded slowly, making the connection to his world's equivalent. "I see. He helped reform the church into what they are now?"

"He made a major push in the church. It has adapted and changed since then, but it attacked our race the most during that time," Itoniv said tightly.

"The clan was called 'flowing stone,' but in dwarven, correct?" Doc asked.

Itoniv gave Doc a long look, then nodded. "Yes."

"I'll do my best to bring their name back to others' lips," Doc said. "It would be best done in Dussle, but I can think of a few places here in Emerita where it would still fit."

"I say we accept him," Alaric said. "What do you say?"

Werner nodded slowly. "He has done a lot of good for the Oresmelter clan. I would like him to do the same for us."

"Doc... will you swear on your goddess that you truly want to see the world brought out of the Darkness?" Itoniv asked, staring at him intently.

"She gave me that charge herself before I came here to this

world," Doc said. "I know Alaric talked to the Oresmelter clan. He should've told you that story."

"You really are an elf-dwarf half-breed?" Itoniv asked.

"Luck wanted both of your races to come together," Doc fudged the truth slightly. "Divided is how we've come to this point. It's time to come together, to unite back into a shining light of hope."

"Alaric heard a rumor that, when we die, our souls are not lost to the abyss of hell. Is this true?"

"Your soul is caught by Mother and you come back again, reborn into the world. How you lived your life dictates your new life. Negative actions might mean you come back as a fish for that turn of your cycle, but the better you live, the better your next life."

Itoniv paused for a long moment before he nodded slowly. "I have not been a good man... I did the best I could for my clan, though. Will she take that into account?"

"All actions come from the lens of your life," Doc said. "Mother is not harsh; she is loving. She can be stern, but she still loves."

"Shaman, please give us time to adapt," Itoniv said. "If we can assist you, we will. We would offer you a guard, but you already have one. You already have a wife, but would you be willing to take another wife from our clan?"

"Unlikely," Doc said. "My wives have to be approved by my current wives. I believe I have reached my limit."

"Pity," Alaric sighed. "I would have introduced you to my youngest. She just reached her majority."

"That puts her as my peer," Sonya smiled. "I'd welcome her as a friend."

"I will let her know."

"As for business," Doc said, "my wives can come to speak with you soon. Sophia, the woman you saw me marry, is my lawyer and handles the contracts. Ayla handles the finances and helps make sure everything is lined up. If you want?"

"Please," Werner smiled.

"If nothing else, we will have a lot of work to be done for the property we bought on the way to Deep Gulch, and I'd prefer to see friends and family enriched first."

"As would we," Itoniv nodded.

"We will make arrangements for the announcement to the clan," Alaric said. "Once things are ready, we will inform you so that you may formally take the position of shaman."

"Thank you," Doc said, getting to his feet. He shook their hands, wishing them good days before leading his group from the clan hall.

CHAPTER NINETEEN

The group left the clan hall and made their way to the edge of the street to wait for Clyde. They'd just barely gotten there when a man came walking toward them. Harrid was the first to notice him, which had the guard turning to face him. Rosa glanced at the individual, then whispered who he was to Doc.

"Excuse me," the man with the thick handlebar mustache asked, "are you Mr. Holyday?"

"I am, sir, and you are?"

The man chuckled, then slowly moved his jacket aside to show his badge. "Your guard is a might twitchy, but with who you are, maybe there's a reason for that. I'm Sheriff Franklin Donadin."

"Harrid, I doubt the sheriff means us harm," Doc said smoothly, though he thought of Grange.

Harrid relaxed his posture slightly. "My job."

"Understandable," Franklin chuckled. "If people knew how much he was worth, they might be lining up to take a chance at cashing in."

"What can I do for you, Sheriff?"

"I'd just heard you came to town and I'd like to have a chance to talk with you. I know businessmen are always busy."

"Did you have a place to talk in mind?"

"I know a saloon just down the street. It's an upscale place, so you won't have to worry about the clientele. It's as good a place as any."

Clyde pulled the carriage around the corner, slowing when he saw the conversation.

"We'll give you a ride if you can direct my driver," Doc offered.

Franklin glanced at Clyde, his eyes sizing up the driver with a slow nod. "Good man to have at the reins. With your guard beside him, people would have to be idiots to think of casually stopping your carriage."

"I've been lucky to find the people I have around me."

"Driver, the saloon just down that way. It's called the Silver Spittoon."

"I know it," Clyde replied.

"We'll be going there to have a chat with the sheriff," Doc told him.

"Understood, sir."

Doc opened the carriage door, helping Sonya and then Rosa in before climbing in himself. Franklin nodded to Harrid as he got in with Doc. Harrid shut the door, then climbed up to sit beside Clyde.

Clyde got them moving and, as soon as they were, Harrid leaned over. "Heard of him?"

"Must've gotten elected when I was in Deep Gulch."

Harrid grunted, scanning the road for any trouble.

"I must say, Holyday, I wasn't expecting you to have a dryad."

"Did your deputy not tell you about her?" Doc asked pleasantly.

"My deputy?"

"Hays McGee. I ran into him on my first day in town. He'd said he was going to warn you and the others so there was no surprise over her."

"Ah, so you're the one he was talking about," Franklin chuckled. "He didn't have a name, just someone with a dryad. I'd been meaning to go by the soulsmith to check on who it was, but that place gives me the creeps."

"It is unsettling," Doc agreed.

The carriage was already slowing, so the conversation stopped. Clyde said he'd pull around to the alley and wait for them there.

The saloon was mostly empty. There were no poker tables, nor a stage for dancing girls. A piano was off to the side, but it was covered. The two patrons inside were at a single table, talking in whispers. They glanced at the group, then away, one of them taking a long drink of his beer.

The bartender was dressed in a crisp shirt with suspenders. His mustache was a fine waxed point that barely reached the edges of his lips, and his hair was starkly parted and oiled. With his hair parted as it was, his softly pointed, half-elven ears were easily visible. He gave them a professional smile. "Sheriff, your usual?"

"Thank you, Jerome. One for my guest, Mr. Holyday, as well. As for his lady…"

"Sorry, my manners," Doc said. "Sheriff, this is my wife, Sonya Holyday."

"I'll take your best beer," Sonya said.

"Make that three, then. It's a pleasure to meet you, Mrs. Holyday." He glanced back at Doc. "I had no idea you'd married into the clan."

"She's from the Oresmelter clan in Deep Gulch," Doc replied. "I don't know what I'd do without her."

Sonya's smile was bright.

Jerome pulled the pints, but his gaze kept darting to Rosa. He was quick to set the mugs in front of them. "If I can get you anything else, just let me know."

"We'll be taking the back table," Franklin said, clearly dismissing him. "This way, Holyday."

Doc sat Sonya before taking his own seat. When he finally sat down, he pulled his hat off and handed it to Rosa, who knelt between him and Sonya. "Nice place. It's quiet."

"I prefer it," Franklin smiled. "Try the beer."

Doc took a drink, nodding. "Not bad. A little light compared to some of the dwarven alcohol I've had."

"They don't let their stuff out of the clan for reasonable prices," Franklin snorted.

"So what can I do for you, Sheriff?"

"Not so much for me, but for the community. Rumor has it you got married and have a home outside the city."

"True on both counts."

"I'm not sure if you know, but both Mr. Roquefell and Mr. Strongarm have been very generous in helping grow the city. I was hopeful you'd be looking to do the same."

Doc took another drink to give himself a moment. "In what way?"

"Well, they've both donated funds to the sheriff's office. It's helped me fill out the deputy roster, pay for the jail that just finished being built, and with other odds and ends."

"I see. I'm not against helping keep the public safe. Does the city have a planner?"

"A what?"

"A planner. Someone who helps design things so you don't end up with a factory right in the middle of a residential area. They help plot out where a city office should be located, and if a secondary sheriff's office might be useful in a certain section of the city. Those kinds of things. They'd also keep track of expenditures so all the money is accounted for."

That last line got the smallest twitch of an eye from Franklin. "No, I don't think the governor has appointed one."

"It'd be the mayor's job to handle it. I should drop in on both of them."

"Mr. Dodd is both. I doubt he'd want to hand off his job to someone else."

Doc wondered how odd it was for the mayor to also be the governor. "I see. I still need to meet him, at the very least. I'll ask Mr. Roquefell for an introduction."

"Probably for the best, but would you be willing to help your new home?"

"Of course," Doc smiled. "How much were you thinking?"

Franklin grinned widely. "Not much for a man like you. A mere thousand would go a long way."

Doc pulled out his wallet, then a check. "Who do I make it

out to?"

"Furden Sheriff's Office," Franklin chuckled. "Everything will be handled from there."

Doc nodded as he pulled the pen from his inside jacket pocket. Ayla had gotten it for him in Deep Gulch, and he hadn't used it much. Taking the cap off, he poised it over the edge of the check, marking the corner to make sure the ink was still good.

"Furden Sheriff's Office," Doc murmured as he filled out the check.

"On another note— the dryad. How did you come by her?"

"I caught her in the wilds and collared her," Doc said offhandedly, as if anyone could do it.

"Ah. Even mages struggle with managing that, I hear."

"Do they? Hmm." Doc capped the pen and tucked it away. "I'm not a mage, so I wouldn't know."

"Then why keep it?"

"Prestige?" Doc half-asked. "Not many have a dryad at their beck and call, do they? Besides, she can be useful even if I'm not a mage. She helped my groundskeeper make sure the soil was prepared for the garden going in."

"What?"

"Dryads are connected to nature. They can do more than just be an energy battery for a mage," Doc said, then suddenly wondered if that wasn't known. "The trouble is finding the right phrasing so she does what I want and doesn't twist my words."

"Oh... that could be a problem with your estate being so close to the river."

"Exactly. If I gave her any wiggle room, she might flood the property to 'help' water the plants."

Franklin sat back. "I've been told they only get energy back if you sleep with them."

Doc laughed. "False, but I'm sure that's true, as well. If they're left to enjoy the sun and weather, they recharge. Other than that, blood and semen can help them, too, so your statement isn't completely wrong."

"Damned mage," Franklin muttered. "One of them university boys told me it had to be blood and semen."

"Maybe that's all he knew. I had to drag the information out of her," Doc shrugged. "It's slower— much slower— but it gets the job done."

Franklin looked like he wanted to ask something else, but his eyes darted to Sonya and he sat back, taking the check. "Of course. It's been a pleasure meeting you. I'll just take this off to the bank. If you ever do decide the dryad is too much hassle, let me know."

"I will, but you'd have a bidding war. The soulsmith already asked after her."

"Of course that freak did," Franklin snorted as he got to his feet. "Have a good day, sir. Ma'am."

Doc watched him go, finishing off his beer.

"He wants to use me for sex only," Rosa whispered. "He doesn't think he can manage it on his own. Most of what you just gave him is going to go into his personal account."

"Yup. Just checking how corrupt the sheriff was. Worth the cost to know for sure."

"He's not beholden to anyone, but he thinks Dodd is an idiot who will be replaced by Strongarm in the next election. He does think David could take the spot, but knows David doesn't want the job."

"Good to know."

"He also hates the clan," Rosa went on. "He firmly believes Apoc is right— that humanity is the only race that deserves to lead— but he doesn't believe in Apoc."

"What about the elders?" Doc asked, watching the room to make sure they weren't overheard.

"Alaric is fully behind you. Werner wants to see you do for his clan what you did for the Oresmelter clan: bring them more money. Itoniv is still doubtful that you should be shaman. He has heard of your heritage, but he thinks it's a lie and that you're a human. His deep worry is that you will lead the clan into decline."

"Not terrible," Doc sighed.

"It's actually good," Sonya added, keeping her voice down. "The differences will get them to talk more, and when they see what you do for them, it'll slowly bind them tighter. It's like smithing steel. You need repeated strikes to forge what you want."

Doc gave her a smile, then touched his face. "Time to trim the scruff again, my dear."

"Oh, we need to get more shaving things," Sonya beamed. "I really love that you asked me to keep you clean. I'm still sorry for cutting you like I did at the springs."

"No shaving gear, and using a knife," Doc said gently. "I blame the equipment, not the handler."

Sonya flushed, but a small smile touched her lips. "Can we shop for the items, then head back?"

"My thoughts exactly. I was thinking of leaving the mustache and this section of beard, but shaving the sides," Doc said, showing her with his hands.

"Hmm, I can manage it. If it doesn't look good, though…"

"If not, then just the mustache," Doc said. "I think you'll find you like the way I look."

Sonya leaned over to kiss his lips lightly. "Of course, I will. It's you."

Rosa giggled. "She wants to do more than shave you."

"Hmm… maybe after the shave?" Doc asked Sonya, staring into her brown eyes.

"Depending on who's home, we can add others, too," Sonya murmured. "Our dear Rosa, at the very least."

Rosa kissed her knee. "Thank you, Sonya."

"Well, let's get going, then," Doc said, standing up. He looked at Harrid a few feet away. "After you."

"Yes, Shaman," Harrid said, turning to lead them from the saloon.

As they went, Doc slowed by the bar to toss a five-dollar coin onto it. He'd seen the sheriff leave without paying. "Thank you, Jerome."

"My pleasure, sir," Jerome said, collecting the coin. He'd started to make change, but when Doc didn't stop in walking away, he just pocketed it. "Nice guy," he murmured appreciatively, following the group with his eyes.

CHAPTER TWENTY

Doc gave the women in the carriage with him a smile. "Think he'll jump at it?"

"There's no reason to think he wouldn't," Ayla said.

"He was serious when we went over the contract with him. He asked for a few small changes, and nothing we didn't agree with. He only asked for forty percent of the hot springs, but was willing to split the cost of getting it all set up," Sophia added.

"Hmm... and we'll be using his people for most of the work," Doc said. "He has all the connections."

"Not all. Most of the rail in the territory was done by the clan," Ayla corrected him. "I'll be working with them on the costs and setting it up under the new company we made with David. I made sure the account is set up with the bank and that the paperwork was filed. Tomorrow, besides the clan, I'll be speaking with the accountant he has lined up to handle the money."

"David is not likely to leave the city, so the contract has a clause for him to get an extra five-percent to manage the new business," Sophia said. "This way, we can turn it over easily when we go."

"If I can get Luck to get his old goddess interested again, he might leave, though," Doc said slowly. "We'll ask him if he knows the right people to install as operators for it all."

"I didn't think about that," Ayla nodded. "That might be for the best."

"Doc, did you think you'd end up a property magnate?" Sophia asked.

"No. I had no idea what I'd really do when I was sent here. Everything just sort of fell into place. Helping Lia with the Lily was the start of it. That made me go look for a mine, and... well..." He shrugged as he trailed off.

"It really spiraled quickly," Ayla giggled. "You came in with that first load from the mine..."

"And a certain half-elven temptress tried to ply me with her feminine wiles."

"I felt terrible when you basically rejected me. Honestly, I didn't want to trade one lech for another, but you stopped that idea and instead gave me one I was shocked to be offered. That made me want to prove myself even more."

"All of that made Grange and the others hate you more," Sophia added, "and then you ended up needing me."

"Kind of a wild ride, all told," Doc smiled. "From Fiala to you, Sophia... didn't think I'd get a single woman to love me, yet now there are six."

"Will this be all?" Ayla asked, clearly curious.

"I'd say it's too many already, but I can't imagine life without any of you," Doc replied. "I don't foresee anyone else ever being special enough to join us. I'm not counting friendly fun, like Lotus and the others, but wives. They'd have to be *very* special to even have a remote chance."

"I like the family how it is," Sophia said softly. "I know I'm the last of us, but I'm with Doc. There has to be a limit, doesn't there?"

"Not according to Rosa," Ayla snickered before growing serious. "I'm very happy with our current family. I was just curious if you were thinking of others. You know every clan or tribe will try to tie someone to us."

"Yeah..." Doc said, looking into the distance.

"Doc?" Sophia asked gently.

"Sorry. Just got lost there for a moment."

"What was it?" Ayla asked. "You went distant when I mentioned the clans and tribes..." She was clearly looking for a hint of what had caused him to zone out.

"I was an orphan. Never really had a family," Doc said. "I know I've told you both... I know those kids will have great mothers and people around them to help, but part of me still twinges to think that I left children behind."

Ayla and Sophia beside him snuggled closer to his sides.

"Doc, did you not want to?" Ayla asked, concerned. "You agreed, but if you didn't—"

"Shh..." Doc whispered, placing a finger over her lips. "I agreed. My reason was serious. If bad things happen, Luck will have other chances besides just me. It was a hard thing to agree to, but even though the path is hard, it still needs to be walked."

"I was jealous of them," Sophia admitted. "They got to be with you fully before me and would get your children long before me. Now, I feel awful."

Doc's arm snaked around her waist, holding her to his side firmly. "None of that. I'm fine with what happened; it's just small twinges of worry for them. As for jealousy, well, I can understand your feelings on it. Do you still feel jealous of anyone?"

"No, because I'm here with you," Sophia murmured as she rested her feathered head on his shoulder. "I think being loved and beside you is worth more than anything else."

"Agreed," Ayla added.

"Okay. Remember that communication is one of the pillars. I won't hold back my thoughts if asked, just as I know you'll do the same in return."

"Always," Ayla said. "I'll hold to the rules."

"And me, even if it's hard to admit some things," Sophia nodded.

"I like the new look," Ayla said, changing the topic slightly. "Several kings have had similar beards."

"Yes, they have," Sophia agreed. "It's a nice blend of bearded and clean. Sonya was beyond happy to shave you again, too. All of you, as we found out last night."

"She got carried away," Doc coughed. "If she was even a little bit less skilled than she was, I wouldn't have let her try it. As it was, the one nick had my heart in my throat."

"She let you return the favor," Ayla snickered, "though you didn't do as thorough a job."

"I have good hands, but no, I wasn't going to do what she did. Besides, I like a little something above it."

"Which is good for us," Sophia giggled. "I would be petrified of a straight razor down there. The small scissors are enough for me."

"I'll stay with them in the future," Doc said. "I just didn't have the heart to tell her no. It wasn't until this morning that I remembered why shaving down there is a problem... the itchiness when it grows back."

Ayla winced. "Oh... that would be unpleasant."

"As will be the stage of prickle-fuzz when it starts to grow back," Doc said.

"We'll talk with her," Sophia said. "None of us wants you or us in less than comfort."

"Works for me," Doc said. The carriage slowing got him to take a calming breath. "Almost there. This is the groundwork for the mine claims in other territories and countries. I'm sure David will have the contacts needed."

"So do I. His family has a lot of fingers in many pies," Ayla said.

"Soon, he'll be helping us," Sophia smiled brightly, "which makes things easier."

Doc gave a small prayer to Luck that Sophia was correct.

* * *

"Welcome back to my home, Holydays," David greeted them when they entered the parlor. "Please, sit."

It took a few minutes to sit and get drinks before business was broached.

"I'm intrigued to know what else you have up your sleeve," David smiled. "Your wives wasted no time getting the paperwork filed and the new account set up when they left yesterday."

"The hot springs was just something that dropped into my lap on the way here," Doc said. "My wife knew about them and the history they had with the elven tribe that used to live on those lands. It's why the company and property are named Heartwood's Tears."

"Effectively a memorial? Interesting. I didn't mind the name at all. If we can keep the oldest trees up there, as well, it'll sell the area even more."

"A valid point," Doc agreed. "Ayla, remind me to ask Lia if she can find anyone even remotely related to the old tribe who would take on the task."

Ayla made a note in her binder. "Of course."

"But that isn't the business today, is it?" David asked, sitting back with his drink.

"No. Today is setting up Lucky Claims, a business to set and build up claims in some very specific spots."

David nodded slowly. "You seem sure of this business."

"I'm near certain that the spots I'm thinking of will have enough raw ore to make it worth the investment."

"You've been there and checked?"

"Not on this world," Doc replied.

David's eyes lit up, a bright smile flashing into existence. "Ah, I had wondered. There are stories, mostly forgotten, about past speakers of the gods that said the same."

"My old world had a period of time that is very similar to this. The country was called America, not Emerita. There's a lot the same and a lot that's different. Mine didn't have magic or races other than humans. Didn't stop us from hating people based on differences, though. I've found that people can always find someone to hate."

"That is terribly sad to hear," David said.

"There was a rich family from my world that came into their riches during this time period. They were known as Rockefeller. They made their money in oil and pretty much took over the industry in the country."

"As my brother is doing now... hmm..."

"There were mines where I founded Lucky Strike— not as rich as mine, but still in that general area— which gives credence to my wild idea to buy up property and claim the mine sites in them."

"A gamble, but a slanted one. Well, you *do* have Luck on your side. It would be foolish of me in the extreme to doubt you. What did you envision as the divide for us?"

Ayla sat forward. "We'd like to offer the same deal as before: Doc will stay as majority holder, but we'd give you two-fifths. You'd both put up half of the starting funds to purchase the property he has in mind. The contract will have a non-compete clause in it so neither of you can try to snatch the property up before the company could."

"I'm willing if the numbers fall right," David said amiably. "Why even bring me in?"

"Because I want to work with you. You have connections I'm sure I'll need and, honestly, you want what I do."

"To bring the gods back," David nodded.

"Exactly. So why not enrich us both and try to make that happen?"

"Most would only aim for their greater good."

"You gave up things before we even spoke," Doc said. "Peabody, for instance. You're the one who got the governor to appoint Nicole. I know that wasn't just me."

"True, but that was because I wanted to meet you. It was a gamble on my part, but a good one, as it turned out."

"My only goal isn't to make me rich; it's to achieve what Luck wants from me. It's to bring light back so the Darkness is driven out."

"Hard to do. I noticed you haven't tried to set up a house of worship yet. Are you waiting to find the right place, or is it something else?"

"The right place is part of it, but painting a larger target on my back is a bad idea."

"Hmm... the preachers here won't cause problems, but word will eventually get back to the east. Why not spread her name as quickly as you can on this side of the Big River?"

Doc frowned, then nodded. "Ah, I think I know it. What's the name of the big river that runs through this part of the country?"

"Coalrud River."

"Should've seen that coming. It was called 'Colorado' in my old world."

"Hmm... I can see the similarity."

"As for your question, I was thinking of going west. It'll be easier to spread her name in the less populated side of the country first. I guess I could make a bigger point if I start here. It might distract them from Deep Gulch for a bit, too."

"It could, indeed," David nodded.

"I'll look into it."

"If you do, tell me. I heard of your healing. I can send you people we would want to be friendly toward us."

"I see."

"But before that, tomorrow is the opening of the new opera house in the city. All of the socialites will be there. You need to attend with only one— sorry, ladies— of your wives. Best to ease that you're a polygamist into the consciousness and *then* push their faces into it."

Doc nodded slowly. "Two?"

David considered it, then nodded. "Any more than that and it will cause waves."

"Diversity would help a great deal, too," Ayla added. "It might be written off more that way."

"Ah, I'd be seen as eccentric," Doc chuckled.

"Yes," Sophia nodded. "You should take Lia and Sonya. Both sing, so they might enjoy it."

"I'll ask tonight," Doc said. "First, let's get this contract signed, and I can explain the properties I'm thinking of. You'll need a map of the continent. One of the spots is north of Emerita."

"In Alyseka?"

"Wow, that's similar. Alaska's next to the place I'm thinking of."

"Kanata, then. The territory next to that is Pale River Land. The elven tribe there called it that based on the water running off the glacier."

"Yukon for me, and yeah, it's in Pale River."

"That'll be trickier, but manageable," David said, looking into the distance. "Getting the tribe up there to be okay with us using the land might be the worst of it."

"We'll deal with it when we need to," Doc said. "Before that, Vedana has property rich in silver, at the very least."

"That'll be easier. Let me acquire the maps first. I'd also like to see the contracts."

CHAPTER TWENTY-ONE

"That went better than I thought," Doc said.

"He was very receptive," Ayla agreed.

"Once we get the contracts recorded, he'll reach out to people he knows about possibly acquiring the lands in those two places," Sophia smiled. "At least the railroad goes in roughly the right direction for the Vedana property."

"We'll have to build up to it, but that won't be as bad as building all of it like we're doing for the hot springs and Deep Gulch," Doc said. "You'll both be going with Sonya to talk with the Ironbeards tomorrow?"

"For the best," Ayla said. "Nailing down as much as we can now will make it obvious that you're a new force in the city and territory."

"We should have you meet with the governor soon, as well," Sophia added. "Officially, I mean. You should end up meeting him during the opera."

"I'd have thought you two would want to go," Doc said.

"I do love a good opera," Ayla smiled.

"As do I, but for this, I think it'd be better to have Lia and Sonya beside you. Most of those you meet there will meet us eventually," Sophia added.

"At the very least, Sonya should go. It'll show you stand with the dwarves," Ayla said. "Those who would disdain you for that aren't anyone you'd want to work with, anyway."

"I was actually going to ask Fiala first," Doc said. "I know she feels like she doesn't have a place to help more."

"She's eased off that with the new manor and staff," Sophia told him. "We should have her meet some of the other matrons. That might help her more with her new role."

"Have to see who we run into during the opera. I'd bet good money there's no matron school."

"That would be different," Ayla snickered. "When to scold a servant and when not to?"

"How to check the mantle without it being obvious?" Sophia joined in.

"How white the linens should be?" Doc offered.

The three of them shared a small laugh as the carriage took them into the city— they were going to get the contracts recorded before heading home.

"What about the idea of a place of worship for Luck, Doc?" Sophia asked when they settled down.

"Gambling hall is what makes the most sense," Doc said. "That means buying one and shifting things around, or building one to compete. It would give me a place in the city to conduct business. My connection will come out in time, and David had a good idea about being in control of it."

"You mentioned Silvered Dreams," Ayla said. "Do you think we could buy it from Colin Montgomery?"

"He mentioned he already had another looking to buy, but wasn't sure if he wanted to. It could start a bidding war between me and Strongarm."

"Strongarm is as much of a pig as Goodman was. Maybe even worse, if the rumors about him are even half-true," Ayla said.

"He has a lot of sway in the city, from what I've heard," Doc murmured, "but if we're going to leave the city behind, it won't matter as much. It'd be weird having a place of worship but no one there who can help the people who come with problems."

"Making one and being available might increase your faith enough to leave another helper behind, right?" Sophia asked.

"It could... it would take a good amount to pick up that option, but with the clan adding in, and if we can make a difference for the city... maybe?"

"Set it aside for now," Ayla said, softly touching his knee. "We can't do everything all at once."

Doc exhaled slowly. "Yeah. I know that, but I also feel like I'm further behind than I should be."

Sophia squeezed his other leg. "We know, but you aren't, just like we aren't."

Silence fell as they got closer to the courthouse.

* * *

Arriving home, Doc smiled at the greenery slowly populating the front of the manor. The front garden was taking shape, and Rosa beamed at him when the carriage went past her. Her sundress fluttered as she sprang to her feet and rushed after the vehicle.

Radley and his helper glanced up, but went right back to work. They were grateful for her help and not about to stop her from chasing the man who owned her. Radley was especially grateful—the ground was unyielding in spots, as he'd found out before Doc had bought the place. With Rosa, those difficulties were gone and the ground was richer for plants to grow easier.

Doc gave Rosa a smile as she came rushing up, but he turned to help Ayla and Sophia down before he hugged her. "Doing good work, Weed?"

"Yes, Voice. The ground is all set. The plants will flourish as if made for the area. I also helped the plumber so he could get the pipes laid easier."

Doc's lips twitched and he kissed her cheek, thinking of how he'd reward her soon. Rosa shivered against him, whimpering lightly as she let the thoughts flood her mind.

"Husband, if you're done playing with her, we should gather the others and discuss tomorrow night," Ayla snickered.

"For now," Doc murmured as he let Rosa go.

Rosa shivered in place again when she caught Ayla's thoughts. "The mistress is right, Voice."

It didn't take long to round up everyone and retire to the study. They dismissed the staff so they had the room to themselves. Doc filled them in on what the day had been, including the opera.

"Which leaves us with who I should have beside me for it," Doc finished.

"I suggested Sonya," Sophia said. "It would make it very clear that he sides with the clans."

Sonya beamed. "I enjoy singing, but I've never been to an opera."

"I was going to bring two of you so the idea of me having multiple wives is out there," Doc said.

"Fiala," Lia said gently, "you should go."

Fiala fidgeted. "I'm not sure... Having any of the rest of you might be better."

"Fiala?" Doc asked.

Fiala exhaled a ragged breath before swallowing. "I'm just... I'm not sure having me beside you for that event is the best idea. I'm not as refined as Ayla or Sophia. Lia would make a strong point for you." She hesitated, then spoke the rest of her thoughts, "Having a former whore beside you—"

"No," Doc said, gently cutting her off. "Having you beside me would make me happy all night. Regardless of what others might or might not think, my love starts with you."

Fiala looked up, as she'd been averting her eyes. Meeting his, her lips trembled— the deep love in his eyes was clear. "I don't want to make things harder for you."

"I'd have to be blind for that to be true," Doc said, trying to joke with her.

Rosa giggled.

Fiala shook her head. "You know what I mean, Doc."

"I do. I also know that your happiness matters more than strangers' opinions. You're the lady of the manor, my first wife, and the one who led us all to this point. If you want to go with me and Sonya, to shine brightly on my arm, I'll be the luckiest man in attendance."

Tears escaped her eyes as she blinked. "How do you always make my heart swell to bursting with love?" she sniffled.

"The same way you make mine do the same," Doc said, going to her side to hug her. "Will you?"

"Yes. I want to go... I want to be beside you always."

"It's decided," Lia smiled softly. "Fiala, we're with you as you are for us. Don't hold yourself back out of fear. If we all did that, Doc would be alone again."

"Oh, tangent," Ayla said, remembering something Doc had asked of her. "Lia, could you see about finding someone related to the Heartwood tribe in the area?"

Lia's brow creased. "I can ask around. Why?"

"To create a tie for the hot springs," Doc said, still holding Fiala. "I figure it'd be someone with only partial tribal ties, but even that would be good."

Lia nodded slowly. "I see. I'll ask. It might take a few days."

"That's fine. We have time."

"Are you going to ask after the gambling hall, Doc?" Sonya asked as she rubbed Fiala's back.

"Yes. David had a solid point; if I work on spreading Luck's name on this side of the Mississip... err... Big River as quickly as I can, it'd be a good start to doing what Luck wants. I'll set up another house of worship here. It gives me a goal to earn enough faith to pick up another gift to both make Posy stronger and to choose another priestess for the goddess."

"We should start a slow search for someone we can trust to take that position," Fiala sniffled, calming down. "That'll be harder here than it was with Posy."

"Yeah, it will be," Doc agreed. "We have some time, though." He looked over at Harrid, who was standing next to the door. "I'll wait to hear who you think would be a good choice."

"I doubt I'll have the answer again."

"You had the perfect answer last time, so it's fine if you don't find one again."

"Nothing else is planned for today," Lia said. "We'll all have things to handle tomorrow. Some of us early, and then three of you late... Hmm... Ladies, the day is far from over yet. We should go into town."

"Oh, yes, we should," Ayla nodded, getting to her feet. "Rosa, you should come with us. As his companion pet, you need to start reflecting that, as well."

Rosa bowed her head. "I'll miss my sundresses for the ease of allowing me to get naked quickly for him."

"You'll wear them most of the time, but in some instances, you should wear something more fitting," Ayla said.

Fiala pulled back from Doc a little. "Shopping?"

"Dresses. We have one or two that'll work for the opera, but we'll have other events to attend and will need to act like the wealthy persons we are. Society has some silly rules, but we have to adhere to some of them to make things easier for Doc."

Doc got out of the way. "I'll see you when you all get home. My suits are still okay?"

"Yes, but I'll talk with the tailor to have him make a couple more, along with a variety of shirts and ties. We'll need to see about some shoes, too."

"Better make me an appointment for that," Doc sighed. "Not that I'll use them much."

"Boots will work on this side of the Big River," Ayla told him. "It sets the tone of you being business, but knowing hard work. The ultra-socialites will view it badly, but others will see it in a positive light."

"Okay. I'll still get a pair of shoes for special events, like the opera."

"Not a bad idea," Ayla agreed. "We'll let the cobbler know you'll be by tomorrow."

Doc gave his wives kisses, marveling again at how lucky he was to be loved by all six of them.

CHAPTER TWENTY-TWO

Doc sat in the carriage as it slowed to a stop, thinking about what the opera might mean. *A chance to rub elbows with other movers and shakers, but it also presents the chance to make more enemies who have the means to cause trouble... Just stay calm, be civil, and ignore any digs that make me want to hit someone.*

Harrid opened the door. "Cobbler."

Doc got out and looked around. The street was moderately busy with foot traffic, horses, and a couple of wagons. The carriage got a lot of interest, as only the wealthy had carriages. Buttoning his jacket, Doc headed into the shop.

The jingle of the bell announced him to the large-nosed, broad-shouldered man behind the counter. The gentleman's trimmed beard ticked up into a smile when he saw Doc. "Greetings, sir. How might I help you?"

"My wives stopped by yesterday. I need dress shoes fit for social events," Doc said.

"Ah, yes, I remember them," the cobbler smiled as he came out from behind his counter.

Doc's face was impassive as he took in the man. He was barely four feet in height, and nearly that across at the shoulders. The large nose reminded Doc of Sigmund, while the man's build reminded him of Harrid.

"I should look at getting a new set of boots, as well," Doc said.

"This way, sir, please," the cobbler said, directing Doc toward a seat.

Doc took the offered seat while the cobbler brought a stool over. "How's business?"

The man's lips thinned briefly. "Good, sir. I'm going to take your boot off so I can get proper measurements."

"As you need," Doc said. "I'd like to see about acquiring a set of dedicated riding boots. I'll point my wives back here for the same. I know we'll end up back on horses eventually."

"That would be most welcome, sir. Are you sure you don't want to see the finished product before you say such?"

"Call me Doc," Doc said. "I probably should, but I have a good feeling about you. You remind me of a friend."

"Not many people would say that about me," the cobbler said slowly.

"What's your name, sir?" Doc asked.

"Lionel Shodden," the cobbler said.

"Because many surnames come from professions," Doc murmured.

"They used to. Apparently, a lot of people are slowly moving away from that," Lionel said as he started measuring Doc's foot.

"I'm not one to speak against it," Doc snorted. "My full name is Doc Holyday."

The cobbler's hands stiffened for a moment. "Ah…"

"I'm not with the church," Doc said softly.

The relief on the man's face was quickly replaced by panic, then suspicion. "You say that like I should worry about the church."

"I think most should worry about the church," Doc shrugged, having gotten a feel for the cobbler already. "My name comes from the fact that I'm a spirit healer. My goddess is Lady Luck."

Lionel's head jerked up, his eyes wide. "A spirit healer?"

"Yes. I don't have a house of worship in the city yet. I probably will in the near future, though."

"I see..." Lionel quickly went back to measuring Doc's foot before he slowed again. "You said 'wives' earlier. I'd thought that the group of women who'd come in might've been friends with your wife, but you mean more than one of them was your wife?"

"I have more than one," Doc agreed.

"The church is *really* going to hate you," the cobbler said, going back to work.

"In time," Doc shrugged. "Doesn't matter. One day at a time is how we live. Do you know why I chose your shop as the one to work with me?"

"No," Lionel said slowly.

"Two reasons. You'd done footwear for my wife's best friend, who told us you'd be the best person to use when we got to the city. Secondly, because I don't hold to prejudices."

Lionel put Doc's boot back on, then moved to his other foot. "Everyone has prejudices. Sometimes small, other times large, but everyone has them."

"Normally, I'd agree with you," Doc said. "Being half-dwarf has to have given you no end of trouble."

Jaw tightening, Lionel kept quiet as he measured Doc's foot.

"Being half-gnome has to have made it especially tough," Doc said after a few moments.

Lionel sat back, glaring at Doc over his bulbous nose. "Where did you hear that?"

"I have a good friend in Deep Gulch; Sigmund Hutmacher, the hatter. Good guy. He's been treated for the mercury that was killing him. He didn't tell me— I just saw the similarities between you both and, along with your stoutness, put two and two together."

"Are you mocking me?"

"No," Doc said softly. "I was trying to be friendly, and I've angered you, instead. I apologize. I won't tell a single soul what we talked about."

Lionel's eyes went to Harrid standing near the door. "You have a dwarf bodyguard?"

"The Oresmelter clan in Deep Gulch appointed him to me," Doc said. "I'm their shaman."

Lionel's mouth fell open. He looked from Doc to Harrid, who nodded silently. Looking back at Doc, the cobbler was still at a loss.

"I don't hold to prejudices. One of my wives is a dwarf, and another is an elf. I work with everyone as long as they can work with others. Take that as you will, but I do apologize for making you uncomfortable."

It took a minute before Lionel went back to work, the room silent as he did. Doc sighed internally, a little upset at himself for making a mess of the situation. When Lionel put the other boot back on Doc's foot, he stood up and went back to his counter.

Doc got to his feet, following the cobbler over. "What's the total for all the shoes and boots?"

Lionel held up a finger as he used a scrap piece of paper to jot down numbers. After another couple of minutes, he nodded, then looked up. "For a set of social shoes, a pair of good boots, and a dedicated pair of riding boots, it comes to twenty."

Doc met Lionel's gaze. "Deal. Again, my apologies." He pulled out a golden twenty-dollar coin and set it on the counter.

"I accept."

"When should I return for them?"

"I'll send a message to your estate, sir."

"Very well. Thank you."

Doc turned to go, his disappointment clear.

"Sir… Doc… I hope you have a good day."

Looking back at Lionel, Doc gave the cobbler a smile. "You, too, Lionel."

Stepping outside, Harrid gave Doc a questioning look.

"I don't know why I thought of broaching the topic," Doc said. "Obviously, I made a mistake doing so."

"You meant well," Harrid said. "Just most are going to take it badly, Doc."

"Live and learn," Doc sighed. "I won't make that mistake again, at least not for a while. I hope."

"Home?" Harrid asked as he flagged down a horse-drawn cab.

"Silvered Dreams," Doc said. "Might as well talk to Colin about the gambling hall."

* * *

Colin smiled as Doc and Harrid were brought into his office. "Welcome back. Didn't expect you today."

"Kind of impromptu," Doc replied. "Thanks for making it easier to speak with you."

"Figured you'd be back to talk to me again at some point," Colin chuckled, offering his hand to Doc. "What can I do for you?"

"When we spoke last, you said that Strongarm was asking to buy you out. I dismissed being interested in your business, but I'd like to reverse that standing now."

Colin sat back down in his chair after shaking hands with Doc. "Well... that's not what I expected."

"After some discussions with my business associates, it was deemed a good idea to get my foot in the city. I could see about building up my own gambling hall, but I'd rather buy this place instead. Or perhaps a partnership?"

"A partnership? How do you propose that to work?"

Doc chuckled as he pulled a few folded pages from his inner jacket pocket. "My wife put these together for me. It's a rough idea of what we were thinking."

Colin took the papers, but didn't open them right away. "Let me get a drink before we go too much further. Would you like one?"

"Please."

"And you?" Colin asked Harrid.

"On duty," Harrid replied.

"Very well." He poked his head out of his office. "Two of the finest, please, Ms. Sena."

"Right away, sir," the secretary said from her office.

Colin came back to his desk. "She'll be right back with them. Now, let's see what surprises you have for me."

Doc sat back and waited as Colin unfolded the papers.

The drinks were brought in as Colin read. He thanked his secretary, a rabbit bestial, without looking up from the pages. When he finished, he picked up his glass and took a sip of the whiskey.

Doc had found it smooth, but not as good as some he'd had before. He didn't press Colin, who was obviously still thinking about what he'd read.

Taking another sip, Colin set his glass down. "I'm not sure I want to outright sell it. If I did, I'd of course get you and Strongarm to bid against each other."

"I wouldn't fault you for it, either," Doc said. "There's nothing wrong with getting all you can for what you own."

"Not many businessmen would be so nonchalant about getting bid against," Colin chuckled. "You could easily just outbid him with your mine."

"True, but even if it wasn't cut and dry, I'd say the same."

"This partnership idea has merit. I'd retain the majority of the business, and you'd buy in for a percentage… It mentions turning this into your house of worship for Lady Luck. Is that why you're interested?"

"Yes," Doc said truthfully. "I could easily just build up a small place myself, as you know, but tying myself to the most well-known gambling hall here is better."

"The prospective idea mentioned you needing an office so you can conduct business as the spirit healer. Do you have an idea of where you'd manage that?"

"I was considering sectioning off part of your lounge, actually. I don't need much; just enough for a desk and space for a couple of people."

"This would put a target on Silvered Dreams for the church," Colin said, picking up his glass to down the rest of his whiskey.

"It would, but I think it'll weather any ripples created. I'm not going to broadcast my intentions on the street. Just a word here or there and let those who need it come for themselves." Doc finished off his own glass. "I wanted to leave the idea with you so you have time to give it a good think. No rush, no pressure." He stood up slowly. "I have an event to attend tonight, as it is."

"The opening of the new opera house?"

"Yes. Roquefell arranged my attendance."

"You have business with him?" Colin asked.

"I do. Big money projects, here and beyond."

"Hmm... I'll let you know, but I will say I'm intrigued, Doc." Colin got to his feet, shaking Doc's hand. "Let me show you out. You know that Strongarm will be at the opera tonight? All of the movers and shakers will be."

"Not you?"

"Small beans compared to them, and honestly, I dislike most of them."

"Don't fault you," Doc snorted. "Whatever you decide, you know where to find me."

"I'll have an answer one way or another in a day or two."

"A pleasure, Colin. To think Suez is the only reason I knew enough about you to find you here."

"I know you and he were having problems," Colin said. "What became of him?"

"He kidnapped someone and a marshal killed him," Doc said. "Apparently, he killed most of his staff and associates in some twisted idea of power."

Colin shuddered. "He seemed wrong to me... wait, the women...?"

"They both died," Doc nodded sadly.

"Goodness. That makes me queasy."

"Me, too, Colin. Me, too."

CHAPTER TWENTY-THREE

Doc waited on the porch— the late summer evening was still warmer than he liked with his suit, but he'd survive, even as he mopped at his brow with his handkerchief.

Fiala was the first one to come outside. Her blue silk dress hugged her curves above her waist, but then became a flowing gown. Her shoes were hidden by the long skirt as she walked. Her social hat, that she'd gotten with Doc what felt like an age ago, was perched on her head. The blue ruffle hid her ears, but her black tail lightly lashing behind her was obvious.

Sonya was right behind her in a maroon dress that made her chocolate-brown eyes pop. Her dress didn't flow past her waist; it hugged her hips, then loosened enough to make walking easy. Practical shoes peeked out of her dress as she moved, becoming hidden when she paused.

Doc smiled, as their choices of dresses reminded him of the first time the three of them had dinner together. It was the night he proposed to Fiala. The only differences were the material and cut of their dresses. "You're both lovely. I'll be the envy of every man tonight."

"They are tempting," Lia added as she came out behind them. "I'm just here to see you off. We'll be waiting for you."

"From what I understand, there will be hors d'oeuvres during the intermissions," Doc said. "So we should be okay with the early dinner we had. Make sure the rest of you have a good dinner."

"I'll handle things while Fiala is gone," Lia said. "Ladies, enjoy your night."

"We will," Sonya said, giving Lia's hand a squeeze. "Thank you."

"Thank you," Fiala said, placing a light kiss on Lia's cheek.

"We won't stay too long after the show," Doc told Lia. "Enjoy your night in."

"I intend to," Lia winked.

Doc shook his head at her meaning, then turned to help his two wives into the carriage. Harrid shut the door behind them and, a moment later, they were on their way into the city.

"You both look very lovely," Doc said again. "Reminds me of our first night together, when I proposed to Fiala."

"I told you he'd remember that," Sonya smiled.

"I wasn't sure. I don't think most men would," Fiala said.

"I remember a lot of things that involve the women I love," Doc said. "I recall getting knocked down and kissed, too."

"It was very sweet," Sonya said softly. "My heart ached that night. I was happy for you and Fiala, and I was hopeful that I would have my own turn, but watching the two of you be in love while I just sat there waiting to be remembered… that hurt a little."

"We didn't mean—" Doc began.

"I know. I'm not angry or hurt now."

"I know the feeling," Fiala said. "I remember the spike of fear and worry when he accepted you."

Sonya giggled as she thought about the moment. "And then you kissed me."

"Yes, I did," Fiala giggled with her. She leaned around Doc to kiss Sonya softly.

Doc cleared his throat. "Ladies, please don't tease me."

"Sorry, husband," Sonya murmured.

"Wasn't my intent," Fiala snickered.

"How has it been for you, dear?" Doc asked Fiala.

"A bit nerve-wracking. I'm doing my best to learn as I go."

"I have faith in you," Doc said. "We might make a friend or two during the opera. If so, maybe they can help, too."

"That would be good," Fiala said. "I want to do the best I can for you like all the others are."

Doc snaked his arm around her waist. "You already do. None of us are perfect, so you don't need to be, either. Knowing that you're taking care of the home helps me relax. I don't want you getting wound up over how things are supposed to be. As long as you're okay with how it works, it's fine."

"Which is what we've told her," Sonya said.

"Sometimes, it just feels like I don't do enough," Fiala said. "When it was just a house, I was better about it, but with a manor and the staff... I feel like a fake. I should be one of them, not a lady."

"Silly," Doc murmured, kissing her cheek. "You're amazing. I know we can't really do anything to make it easier for you, but try to remember that we all believe in you."

"The staff is respectful," Sonya said. "None of them look at her in question. They've fully accepted her as the lady of the home. The rest of us, too, but her more so, because we've made it clear that she's first in all things related to the home."

"As it should be," Doc said softly.

"I'm doing my best to accept it, but it eats at me," Fiala murmured and leaned into his side.

"Talk with Rosa?" Doc asked.

"I have a little, and I will again," Fiala replied. "She's working hard on the grounds for us. I heard Radley praising her to his wife last night. Mizzi was quick to explain how generous I am with the staff, overlooking the small mistakes as they learn. That dug at me—it wasn't me overlooking them. It was more I didn't know."

"Maybe we do it the easy way, then," Doc said. "Ask Mizzi to explain each of the staff members' jobs to you. Spend a couple of hours with each to learn what they're supposed to do. It'll make them nervous, but I know you, Fiala. If you're honest and forthright, they'll understand and be happy to help."

"You think so?"

"I do. Talk with Mizzi first."

"I think it's a good idea," Sonya added. "If that feels too embarrassing, we could ask Rosa to shadow them, and then she could explain it to you."

Fiala's lips pursed as she considered it. "No. I'll ask. It's my job, and I'll manage it."

Doc kissed her cheek. "As you wish."

* * *

Arriving at the opera house, Doc was impressed. A massive block of a building made of red and white stone dominated the street corner. A tower on one side rose a good story above the rest of the newly-opened opera house.

Doc helped his wives out of the carriage, aware that other wealthy people were also arriving around them. Both Fiala and Sonya quailed slightly at the mass of people gathered before the edifice. They took his arms, singling him out amongst the crowd where it was only single men or a couple for the vast majority.

All three of them wore clothing that fit in with the best around them, again pointing to them being in the rare circle of the ultra-wealthy who were attending. As they approached the front door, Doc walked as if he belonged, and his wives slowly adopted his posture.

At the entrance were two guards and a man with a clipboard in hand, checking people in. Doc and his wives lined up for entry.

"A bestial? Well, *he* won't be getting in. Doesn't matter if you put them in silks; a beast is a beast."

"With a dwarf, as well? Doesn't he know how foolish he looks?"

"Must've spent all they had on their clothing, but it's invitation-only tonight."

The comments passed over the group, making Fiala's tail lash in agitation and Sonya's hand ball into a fist. Doc leaned in to kiss both their cheeks. The kisses soothed them, even when more comments about public decency started up.

"Ignore them. They're just jealous," Doc said firmly.

"Jealous of a *beast*?" a woman scoffed. "If you could get a real woman, you'd know how ridiculous you look."

"Name?" the doorman asked stiffly, having been watching the commotion as Doc's group approached.

"Doc Holyday."

The man glanced at his list, about to decline them, when his eyes widened and he nodded. "Ah, yes. Mr. Holyday, with wives. Your private box is ready for you, sir. One of the ushers will take you to the VIP lounge."

That bit of news shocked the naysayers into silence.

"Thank you. Is Mr. Roquefell already here?"

"Yes, sir."

"Very good. Thank you," Doc said as he entered with his wives, both of whom were wearing proud smiles.

Fiala glanced back at the crowd with a haughty smile on her lips. That broke the shock, and more mutterings started up, but she didn't hear them once they'd entered the opera house. As the trio walked into the grand lobby, a man in uniform came up to them.

"Name?"

"Holyday," Doc said.

"Ah, yes, I thought I heard right," the usher smiled. "This way, sir."

They were led to the right, away from the grand staircase and toward another set of doors with a guard. The usher took them past the guard and into a lounge. A quartet played softly to give some sound to the room while servers with drink trays circulated among the fifty or so people standing around or sitting in groups.

The moment they entered, a woman in uniform smiled and presented them with perfumed silk programs. "This will explain which pieces will be performed by Emma Abotta."

"Thank you," Doc said as Fiala took them.

"Holyday!" David Roquefell's voice lifted enough that some people turned to look. "Glad you could make it."

Doc smiled broadly when he saw David's group open up so they could see Doc and his wives approaching. "Roquefell, it's a pleasure to be here. I do hope you'll introduce me around?"

"Of course," David replied. "Ladies, I hope you enjoy this evening. We all have the Silver King to thank for this."

The large man David had motioned toward laughed. "Well, yes, that *is* true. I enjoy the title, but we should do introductions properly. I am the man who had this venue built: Homer Tarbo, and my wife, August Tarbo." He introduced himself and the severe-looking woman beside him.

"He's also the lieutenant governor," David chuckled. "A man who made his wealth in silver, hence the title."

"A pleasure, sir, ma'am," Doc replied as his wives let go of his arms. "I'm Doc Holyday, and these are my wives, Fiala and Sonya."

"Holyday is the owner of the new mine near Deep Gulch, the one you've all heard of," David smiled. "He's also my new business partner."

That got the cold, appraising looks at Doc's wives to become interested looks at Doc.

"Ah, that explains it," Tarbo laughed. "Roquefell said the person he added would be well worth letting a box go. Your mine might be even more profitable than my own."

"You had this fine establishment built?" Doc asked.

"Yes. I always think society needs more art."

"Before we get too involved, we should finish introductions," David cut in.

"Right, right," Tarbo agreed. "I need to circulate, as it is. Holyday, we'll talk again."

"I'll look forward to it," Doc nodded.

CHAPTER TWENTY-FOUR

Dodd was a tall man with a bright smile. Doc shook his hand, glad to be able to meet the governor. "A pleasure, sir," Doc said.

"Pleasure is mine. I've been hoping to meet you."

"And I you. I wanted to thank you for giving Deep Gulch a mayor who listens to the people," Doc replied.

"You do know it's unlikely she'll hold the job after the election, don't you?" Dodd asked with a faint smile. "I know Mr. Suez was on my short list. He'll be eager to throw his hat in against her."

"Dead men can't run for office. Maybe you hadn't heard? Mr. Suez was a kidnapper and murderer."

"He *what*?" Dodd asked, his face going white.

"Had a staff of ten or so at his manor. They were all found dead, buried in the backyard. His end came when he kidnapped a child, we assume to kill her, as well. Luckily for us, Marshal Hickinbotham was in town. He rescued the child and, in the process, Suez and Sheriff Grange died."

"The sheriff died during the rescue? A pity," Dodd said.

"Not really. It turned out that he was a conspirator for Suez."

"Ah... I had thought he was a friend of Goodman?"

"He took bribes from them both."

Dodd rubbed at the bridge of his nose. "I see... Hmm... I'll have to go over my records when I get back to the office tomorrow."

"Probably for the best," Doc agreed. "Nicole won't give you those problems. You have my word on that."

"That would be refreshing right now."

"No one who's sided with me has come away a loser on the deal, Governor. It's all about who you back."

"Rumor has it you're in business with Roquefell."

"Not a rumor. Plain fact," Doc smiled. "A new destination for the state to draw people in. It'll take a few years for it to pay off, but when it's up and running, it'll be worth every penny."

"Does this have something to do with the land you purchased between here and Deep Gulch?"

"Heartwood's Tears," Doc said solemnly. "It'll be a tribute to the tribe that used to call the land home. I've been told no members exist anymore."

"Ah, the Heartwood tribe," Dodd nodded sadly. "Yes... sad days years ago. The Treeheart tribe almost went with them, but I believe a couple of their tribe survived the army's wrath. The few that survived weren't sent off to another reservation, but were given a small plot of land in Deep Gulch as theirs. I believe the leader opened a whorehouse on it."

Doc made a mental note to ask Lia about the death of the tribes. He'd stayed away from it to not bring up memories, but he should probably know more.

"It's a gambling hall now, specializing in a new type of poker," Doc said as evenly as he could. "I'm a partner in the business."

"That makes sense," Dodd nodded. "Ah, here come your wives."

Doc half-turned to see them approaching. Both women wore strained smiles, and Doc's eyes narrowed. "Ladies, is everything okay?"

"It's fine, husband," Sonya said first. "Some minor unpleasantness only. Unlike those who caused it, Fiala and I know how to be civil."

Fiala snorted. "Those... *women*... are nothing more than—"

Doc took her hand gently in his. "You're better than they are. Don't let them drag you down, my love."

"Will you introduce me?" Dodd asked.

"Of course. My wives, Fiala and Sonya Holyday. Ladies, this is Governor Dodd, also mayor of Furden."

"A pleasure, sir," Sonya said, smiling.

"It's an honor," Fiala added.

"I'm new to the territory, Governor. How did the city get its name?" Doc asked to try distancing the problem a bit more.

"It was a major trapping point because of the river when people came through here. It was a rich point for furs for those who could do the job. It started as a joke. When the tent city sprang up, it was called a den of fur, as most used furs to sleep. The name caught on as they are wont to do. I've tried to get the name changed twice, but the voters have rejected both initiatives."

"Ah. Now it has sentimental value to the oldest residents," Doc nodded.

"Yes, I've given up on it," Dodd admitted.

"Ladies and gentlemen," a voice called out from the door to the room, "we are now beginning seating for the VIPs. If you will come this way, ushers will be standing by to lead you to your seats."

David came up alongside Doc as Dodd stepped away from them. "I will be joining you in the box, Doc. It was supposed to be mine, but listing it under your name was the easiest way to arrange this for the evening."

"I'm fine with that," Doc said.

"Good. I was also hoping to get a better chance to speak with your wives. I have met four of them now. Am I mistaken in thinking there is at least one more?"

"Lia," Fiala said. "She's also his wife."

"Lillianna Treeheart, the famed Death Flower," David smiled. "I thought I recognized her at the wedding, but I didn't want to ask during the event."

"She prefers Lia," Doc said.

"I'll keep that in mind. I have no intention of upsetting one of the most feared elves to ever walk the planet. Takes a man with a strong conviction to be her equal."

"That's our husband," Sonya smiled proudly.

"Holyday," David told the usher when they got to the door last.

"Please follow me."

* * *

Doc stretched when intermission came. The silk-lined, velvet-padded seats in the private box were very comfortable, but he was glad to stand again.

"The singer has amazing range," Sonya sighed happily.

"She's famed for it," David agreed. "I believe she chose the pieces tonight just to point out how much she can do. The lounge will be open again for the next half-hour."

"I should mingle again. That's why I'm here," Doc said.

"We'll need to stop to powder our noses again," Fiala said.

"Which neither of you actually do," David murmured. "I have to admit, you both look better than many of the women here who've caked their cheeks with powder. Very refreshing."

"Thank you," Fiala said. "Most of the powder bothers my nose, honestly."

"And dwarves don't usually care for it," Sonya added.

"Maybe you'll start a new trend of using less powder," David said as he led them to the door where an usher was waiting. "Back to the lounge."

"Yes, sir."

"This place is a marvel," Doc said as they walked.

"Thank you," Homer Tarbo said, having overheard Doc as his box door opened. "Enjoying the evening?"

"It's been a delight," Doc smiled.

"Excellent," Tarbo said as he let the other group continue walking, then left his box.

***

Doc was chatting with Tarbo about what it would take to sponsor an opera in a month or two when a cough interrupted them. Tarbo broke off his explanation to give the newcomer a broad smile. "Strongarm, glad you could attend. I missed seeing you earlier. Let me introduce you to Doc Holyday."

"Holyday? From Deep Gulch?" Strongarm asked Doc with a harsh stare.

"The one and only," Doc replied civilly. "I've heard of you, Mr. Strongarm. You're a major player in the city, I'm told."

"I own about a fourth of the property in the city," Strongarm smiled. "I was able to do what my acquaintance Goodman was not. May Apoc be kind to him."

"Well, he was accused of attempted murder and theft before he was killed by the sheriff," Doc said. "Not sure I'd want to call him anything other than an acquaintance, too."

"Was he?" Tarbo asked in shock. "Goodness. Strongarm, weren't you telling me how he would have property I'd be interested in?"

"He did have property you'd have been interested in. I guess his son would, now."

"Doubtful. His son sold it off before leaving Deep Gulch," Doc said. "I bought it all."

"*All* of it?" Strongarm asked pointedly.

"Yes, along with most of what the town confiscated from Suez when he was found to be a murderer. Honestly, I think I own close to ninety percent of Deep Gulch, but that'll be small potatoes compared to the deals I'm working with Roquefell."

"I'd be interested in hearing about those," Tarbo said. "I'll have to make sure to visit your estate. I heard you have the one north of the city by the river."

"Yes."

"I do hope you can rebuild when the river floods," Strongarm smirked slightly.

"Shouldn't be an issue," Doc smiled amiably, playing the part of an unknowing person.

"Hmm... I've heard you are quite the gambler. Is that true?"

"For the right game and stakes. I took a handful of profitable properties off Suez in a poker tournament. I enjoy the thrill of a good bet."

"I've heard about a brand-new type of poker at the Silvered Dreams," Tarbo said. "Haven't visited to see it yet. Would you care to meet there for a few hours of entertainment in the future?"

Doc's smile widened. "Gladly. We can make it an invitation game of say... six others besides us? I'd ask Elder Alaric Ironbeard, Roquefell, and, of course, the owner of Silvered Dreams to sit in."

"I'd ask Strongarm, Dodd, and... hmm... I'd have to consider the last position," Tarbo said. "If you can arrange the time and day with the owner, then pass it along to me."

"Gladly. Ah, I do need to see to something before going back up. Excuse me."

"Enjoy the show," Tarbo called after him.

"Enjoy the night, Holyday," Strongarm said tightly, glaring at his back.

Doc headed for the bathroom, finding Sonya and Fiala in a conversation with a few other women. He slowed as he approached, watching to see if his wives were okay. Fiala giggled, then leaned in to speak softly for a moment. The other women held their fans up as they laughed. Doc relaxed, seeing his wives being accepted by some, at least.

"Doc, did you need us?" Sonya asked, spotting him first.

"Off to see the facilities, dear. Enjoy your conversation," Doc said when he passed them.

"Goodness, he is handsome, isn't he?" one of the women asked. "You've caught quite the prize there."

"I feel the same about them," Doc said, looking back over his shoulder briefly.

"Oh! He heard me?" The woman's face burned enough to be visible around the white powder on her cheeks.

Fiala smiled. "We know how lucky we were for him to choose us."

"Even with it being two of you, he's still a good catch," another woman said.

Doc kept walking, laughing to himself. *What would you say if you knew it was more than just them?* His smile stayed in place as he found the bathroom.

CHAPTER TWENTY-FIVE

Three nights of opera was more than enough for Doc. He hadn't understood that the grand opening of the opera house was a three-day event until the end of the first night. He took Fiala and Sonya with him each night; they dazzled him with new dresses every time.

During the intermissions he made sure to talk with more of the businessmen in the lounge. He doubted he'd do business with most of them, but it was good to at least put names and faces together. Doc did notice that Strongarm stayed away from him the last two days.

Fiala and Sonya had a small circle of other wives to chat with during intermissions. There were even plans to have a couple of them over for tea in the near future, as well as for the two of them to visit other houses.

During those three days, Ayla, Sophia, and Sonya visited the clan elders to get contracts with them, securing the clan to do the work on the railroad all the way to Deep Gulch. They also worked out a contract for the clan to help sculpt the hot springs area, turning the surrounding area into a memorial for the lost tribe and Mother.

* * *

Pushing his empty plate away, Doc sighed happily. "Been a good couple of days."

"Sophia and I are going over to David's again today," Ayla said. "Now that the clan's signed up for the work, we'll be working with him to get the right people to oversee things."

"Speaking of overseeing," Lia said, "I found a half-elf whose mother was one of the last of the remaining Heartwood tribe. I asked her to come out to the estate today."

"I was going to talk to Colin about setting up the poker game, but I can wait until after she gets here," Doc said.

"If it's okay, Sonya and I were going to have tea at the Tarbos' today," Fiala said.

"I'm surprised she asked," Doc said. "She's so quiet and severe-looking. I wasn't sure she was friendly."

"She's a kind soul," Sonya said. "She doesn't care for high society because they've made comments about her appearance. Her husband loves her, but she feels like she causes him trouble. I believe a couple of others will be there, too."

"Sounds good. I'm glad to see that not all of the socialites are going to be a problem for us."

"Voice, I will help the workers again, if that is okay?" Rosa asked, her head resting on his knee.

"Want to use more energy so we can refill you again, hmm?"

"Not only that, but yes," Rosa admitted, earning light laughter from the others.

He stroked her wild tangle of blue-tinged green hair. "Very well, Weed. I know you've had a big hand in the garden becoming what it is."

"The garden will shock the others when they come over," Fiala smiled. "Last night, someone asked what we planned to do with the open front yard we had. It'll be amusing to see her reaction."

"Glad we got that second carriage," Ayla said. "It'll make it easier for us when we all have things to do."

"I'll be happier when the rooms get done and the guards can be here," Harrid said.

"Let's go talk with Simpson and see what he thinks," Doc said as he got up.

Goodbyes were said and kisses were collected as everyone left to get ready for their own business. Doc had Harrid and Rosa behind him when he went out the back door of the manor. He did pause to give Charles, the chef, his compliments on the meal. The basset hound bestial thanked Doc for the kind words before he continued preparing something Doc couldn't identify.

Simpson and his crew were getting things set up for the day and, seeing Doc, Simpson headed his way. "Boss, good morning."

"Good morning, Simpson," Doc greeted him back. "Just coming out to see how things are going."

"Going well," Simpson said, his eyes going to Rosa behind him. "She's been a big help for us. The plumber I brought in was all praise for her. Thank you again."

"Making things easier for Doc is my life," Rosa murmured. "I will be here again most of today if you have need of my talents. Otherwise, I will be assisting Radley with the gardens."

"We should be okay," Simpson said. "It's all above ground at this point for us."

"Speaking of, how are the rooms coming?" Doc asked.

"I'm thinking it'll take about a week for them. I have some new hands starting today. If they work out, we should be able to speed up."

"Just don't cut corners," Doc said. "Quality over speed."

"Yes, sir," Simpson nodded.

"I'll let you get to it," Doc said, shaking Simpson's hand. "I'll be here for a while before heading into the city. If you need me, just let one of the staff know."

"Will do, sir."

Rosa started to go around the house toward the front, giving Doc a bright smile as she went. Doc gave her a smirk, thinking of what he planned to do for her later. He watched her shiver and bite her lip, making him chuckle as he stepped back into the house.

* * *

It was near noon when the half-elf woman Lia had told him about arrived. The hard life she'd endured was etched into her skin; scars and burns dotted her arms, legs, and face. Her flat, hopeless, light blue eyes looked back at Doc and Lia when she was shown into the room.

"Kitanishan Heartwood, welcome to my home here in Furden," Lia said, greeting the other woman. "This is my husband and the shaman of the Treeheart tribe, Doc Holyday."

Suspicion and fear filled the eyes of the woman. "Shaman?"

"He passed the rites to be our shaman," Lia said. "Please, sit. Doc, Kitanishan wasn't born yet when I last visited the Heartwood tribe, but I knew her mother. She would be a cousin to me through marriage to my first husband."

Doc's heart ached for her; she'd seen the worst life could offer. "Miss, welcome to our home. Family, even distantly related, is something to treasure."

"Bitum," Lia addressed the parlor maid standing in the corner, "tea, please. Just bring us the cart."

"Yes, mistress," the mouse bestial bowed, then hurried out.

Kitanishan watched the maid leave, then stared back at Doc as if expecting him to lunge at her. Doc sat farther back in his chair, hoping to put her at ease. "Lilliana said you wished to speak to one related to the Heartwood tribe. Why?" The words were said with a bite.

"Because I was hoping to bring some attention back to the tribe. Lady Luck brought me to this world to bring the light back to it."

"Lady Luck?" Eyes narrowing further, the half-elf was full of suspicion.

The door opened a moment later as Bitum brought the tea trolley into the room. She parked it next to Lia before bowing and leaving.

"Do you take your tea with butter or sugar?" Lia asked as she poured for the three of them.

"Butter. Small bit," Kitanishan said tightly.

With the cups set, she handed them out. Doc conceded that the bitter orange flavor could've used some butter, but he was fine with finishing the cup he had.

"Lady Luck, the goddess who brought me here," Doc finally answered. "I'm the Voice of Luck."

"No! Those stories were lies!" Kitanishan hissed at him. "If they were real, where were you when we had need?!"

"Not on this world yet," Doc said softly. "I wish I had been, but Luck hadn't found me when your tribe needed me."

"Prove your words." The sneer was clear as she stared at Doc.

Doc set his cup down, then sat forward, holding out his hand palm up. "Lady Luck, please help me show your power to this wounded family member. Her belief is gone, but you can help restore it." When he finished talking, he triggered *healing hands*.

Kitanishan's eyes went wide and her breath caught at the display of power. Her mother had told her of shamanistic powers, how they'd reflected nature with the colors of blue, green, and white. Licking her lips, she reached out slowly for his glowing green hand.

Doc let her place her hand in his— he didn't grasp her, just letting her rest her hand on his palm. *Goddess, she needs a lot of help,* Doc thought as Kitanishan's health was reported to him. *Let's start with the worst of it: her lungs.* He coughed gently. "Lia, will you get Rosa? I'll need her help."

The warmth that began suffusing her chest had Kitanishan's eyes beginning to tear. It reminded her of her mother holding her as a child, huddling for warmth against the cold winter. When Lia left the room, she cried in earnest as she recalled the remnants of members of her tribe going into the harsh winter to find food, but never returning.

Doc let his energy flow through the half-elf. He wanted to touch her head, tell her it would be okay, but he knew better than to try. She was wary of him, and Doc didn't blame her, considering what he knew of her physical condition.

Rosa rushed into the room and Kitanishan nearly yanked her hand back, but Doc gently clasped hands with her. "Voice?"

"Rosa, easy. I just need your help for Kitanishan," Doc said softly. "This is Rosa. She's here to help."

Swallowing, Kitanishan started to nod. When she saw the collar on the dryad, her blood went cold. Fear rose in her as Rosa knelt beside Doc. He wasn't a Voice; he was a mage who had tricked her to steal her soul away.

"Calm yourself," Rosa said gently. She rested her head against Doc's knee and his hand gently stroked her hair. "I gave myself to him. He didn't collar me. Mother decreed that I should aid him, and I have. He doesn't treat me as the mages do my sisters. There is only love between us."

Kitanishan's hand trembled in Doc's. What the dryad was saying was impossible, but she could see the love in her and how gently the man was treating her. That and the warmth that continued to flow through her had her confused about what to believe.

Lia entered the room, quietly closing the door behind her. Going to Kitanishan's side, she knelt beside the fearful woman. "*Doc is not human, as you fear. He is half-elven and half-dwarven. Luck gave him this body so he could blend in and do her work. Your fear is understandable, but he is the kindest soul I've ever known. Do you think I would be beside him if it was not so? Do you think I would allow him to collar a dryad who didn't want to walk beside him? Set aside your worry and let the love of Luck show you what we have— a chance to turn back the devouring Darkness,*" Lia told her relative in Elvish.

"*Why not before?*" Kitanishan asked in Elvish as she cried.

"It is not for us to question the gods, child," Rosa said gently. "Be glad he is here at all, and that we have this chance."

"*I am doing my best, but I need help to even have the slimmest chance,*" Doc added in Elvish, causing Kitanishan to jerk slightly and meet his eyes. "*Will you help us?*"

"What must I do?" Kitanishan asked, her mind racing with all the horrible things a human would ask her.

"I need you to help guide the ones who will oversee the memorial of your old home," Doc said as he pushed energy into her, healing every injury and removing the damage to her skin. "The hot springs will become a memorial that will echo over the years to remind people of the Heartwood tribe. I could appoint anyone to do it, but I think someone who loved the area would be best."

"I was only a child... I can't remember it as it was," Kitanishan sniffled.

"I will help you," Rosa said as she slipped from Doc's side to join the other two. She leaned over Kitanishan, gently tilting the half-elf's head back. "Drink and remember, child."

Kitanishan did as Rosa said, letting the dryad feed her the essence needed to manage it.

Doc exhaled as he let his energy go. Sitting back, he picked up his tea and drained it. He'd never have been able to do it all without Rosa's help, but now, Kitanishan was unblemished and fully healed. He wondered how she would take it.

When Rosa broke the kiss, she went back to Doc's side, kneeling beside him again. She nuzzled his leg, her happiness from helping high. Doc stroked her hair as he waited for Kitanishan to refocus.

With a deep exhale and a full-body shudder, Kitanishan sniffled. Blinking, she looked at Lia with sadness in her eyes. "I remember my mother speaking of her brother... how you went to war with him and your wife. The tribe revered your prowess, but feared you would lose yourself in your grief."

Lia bowed her head. "I did for a time. When I came back to myself, I was given a chance to go home. I took it, but when I got there, your tribe was gone and mine was reduced to only me and Jesamin. I was not there when they needed me most."

"She never blamed you for not being there. Mother only said that you knew grief as she did." Kitanishan hugged Lia. "Thank you for seeing me as a full tribe member, but it isn't true. I'm a child of hatred. Mother did her best to make me a child of love."

The words had Doc's hackles go up, as he could only think of one reason that she would call herself a "child of hatred." Rosa touched his leg and gave him a sad nod, but touched her lips with a finger. Exhaling slowly through his nose, Doc nodded back to Rosa. It wasn't his place to ask about what was probably rape.

"If you go to Deep Gulch and speak with Jesamin, she will bring you into our tribe, Kitanishan. It isn't the same, but we welcome all who call themselves elf."

She nodded, then glanced at Doc. "Voice, Shaman… thank you. I will help you as much as I can."

Doc smiled gently. "You're welcome. We'll be having experts work on what the buildings should look like, but you'll be the one to appoint their places at the springs."

Lia shifted away from Kitanishan, retrieving an item before coming back to her side. "Also, you might want to see this now."

Kitanishan took the mirror from her, then blinked at the smooth face looking back at her. Mouth opening in shock, her other hand came up to touch her unblemished face. "What?!"

"Luck can heal old wounds," Doc said softly. "What came before is past. Now, we work on building a future."

She looked away from the mirror at Doc, then bowed her head. "I will join the tribe. The springs will reflect my old tribe. All I can to aid you, Shaman, I will do. I will never be able to repay you." She cleared her throat, then spoke in Elvish again, "*All life must balance. You have given me new life, and I declare that life yours. This balances things, as the tribe declares.*"

Doc shook his head. "I don't need your life, but I won't fight your views. Just do the best you can and that'll be enough. My other wives will be home later, so Ayla will work out a contract and pay with you. You'll be paid enough to never have to fear and worry about your life again."

Kitanishan bowed her head; she had nothing else she could say. This man, her shaman, had taken her and lifted her up. He'd fixed her broken body into a new and healthy one. His wife had accepted her as a tribe member, something even her mother's tribe hadn't done. The dryad spoke of his love for her and that shocked her, but she could see the love the pair had for each other. If she had failed to believe before, she knew belief now.

"Can I speak to others like me? Would they be welcome, too?" Kitanishan asked.

"I'll go with you," Lia said softly. "We'll deal with the contract later."

Doc stood up, giving Lia a kiss and, with Kitanishan's approval, a hug for her. "Be safe. One day, I hope others never have to go through what you did."

"May Luck bless those words to become truth," Kitanishan said before leaving with Lia.

Doc shook his head as he watched them go. When he felt a hand touch his calf, he smiled down at Rosa. Staring into her softly glowing eyes, he nodded. "Upstairs. I can stay for a little while before I go into town."

Rosa kissed his knee. "Thank you, Voice."

CHAPTER TWENTY-SIX

It was early afternoon when Fiala and Sonya returned home. The pair were all smiles as they greeted Doc on the porch.

"Afternoon, husband," Sonya beamed.

"We had a lot of fun," Fiala smiled brightly. "August is bright and funny if you can get her to let her guard down."

"I'm glad you two had a good time," Doc said, kissing both of them. "I'll be heading into town."

"How did your meeting go?" Fiala asked.

"Good. Kitanishan was wary, and for good reason; her life was brutal. By the end of it, she was on board with what we suggested. Lia went with her to talk to other half-elves. She'll be back in time to speak with Ayla about a contract for overseeing the hot springs."

"That's good," Sonya smiled.

"I'll see you for dinner," Doc said. "Rosa will be here with you both. I think she's checking the herbs out back right now."

"See you for dinner... and dessert," Fiala murmured, kissing his cheek when she went past him.

"Sold," Doc chuckled, giving Sonya a wink as he waved to Clyde on the driver's seat. "Silvered Dreams, Clyde."

"Yes, sir," Clyde nodded.

Harrid climbed up beside Clyde as the other driver, Darren, got down. "Thank you."

"Happy to trade off," Darren chuckled. "My brother and I know you're his bodyguard."

Doc got into the carriage. Sitting back, he thought about how to best approach Colin about the invitation-only tournament.

* * *

Doc looked at the sky as he got out of the carriage. Clouds were rolling in from the west, and they looked nasty. "Let's get inside. Clyde, you going to be okay out here?"

"There's a spot for the carriage around back," Clyde said. "I'll go back there. One of the employees will tell me when you're ready for pick up. I have a slicker, if needed."

"We'll try not to take too long," Doc said.

The cage attendants and guards looked their way when they stepped inside. Doc exhaled as Harrid shut the door behind them. Doc went to the check desk, knowing they'd need to at least drop off their weapons.

Harrid unloaded his hardware for the same rabbit bestial who had worked the counter last time. The woman smiled at him, and it was a warm smile, not the professional one she'd used previously. Doc noted it, wondering if Harrid could tell the difference or if he was even interested in women of another race. By the time Harrid was done, one of the guards was waiting for them.

The guard led them toward Colin's office— the main room had moderate business, and the second floor had a dozen people across two tables. Doc noted that one of the tables was hold'em, accounting for nine of the players. The other table was draw, and had only three people.

Colin stood up when they entered his office. "Doc, it's good to see you again."

"Colin, thanks for taking the time. I see you moved the blackjack dealer up here and put him on hold'em."

"Giving him a chance and, honestly, it's been good. The players up here wanted a man on the table. Foolish, if you ask me, but if the players are happy, then they play longer. What can I do for you?"

"I was asked to set up a private poker game and suggested your place. It'd be invitation-only, with eight players for hold'em. You would be one of the players, if you wanted to join in."

"Hmm... I mean, depending on the stakes. Who were you looking at?"

"Myself, Roquefell, Tarbo, Strongarm, Dodd, Elder Alaric Ironbeard, you, and one more that Tarbo was figuring out still."

Colin sat back, looking a bit daunted. "That's a lot of movers and shakers, Doc... Not sure I should be at that game."

"If you don't want the slot, I can see about filling it with another," Doc said. "I figure the game would be a couple thousand, a nice easy game for them. It'd be cash, so anyone can come or go as they want."

Colin looked into the distance for a moment. "I've been thinking over your idea of letting you buy in as a partner and make this a house of worship. I'm thinking it might be easiest just to sell out to you. I really appreciate the offer of the partnership, but the target that'll get painted on with it being a house of worship... I'm not sure I want it on my back."

"I'll let Ayla and Sophia know to come talk to you about the buyout," Doc sighed. "Pity. I really think you'd be fine, and I like spreading around some of the good."

"You'd be the only one with your kind of money who does," Colin snorted.

"Do you want out of the business entirely?"

"What do you mean?"

"I know of a place that'll be building up in the next couple of years, built around relaxing. It'll end up with all sorts of entertainment that keeps the area classy. A well-run gambling hall would work there."

Colin considered it. "Where's it going to be?"

"About halfway between Deep Gulch and here," Doc said. "The property is already bought, and contracts are being signed to build up the road and rail to it. More contracts will be set up to get the buildings built and the whole retreat laid out. I'm talking ground floor entry."

"I'd be pretty set with you taking this place from me..." Colin murmured. "I enjoy being around the people, though. Send them over, and I'll talk to them."

"Works for me," Doc smiled. "Now, what about the game? That's the reason I came today."

Colin laughed. "Comes to set up a private game, and talks me into selling and setting up a new shop. Things just kind of fall into place around you, don't they?"

"Well, I kind of have a lucky life."

"All too true," Colin laughed. "If the numbers are right, we'll get it done. As for the game, sure. Say... two grand as the minimum. This way, they can bring more if they want. I'm sure Strongarm will be doing so, at least."

"Will you close out the second floor in two days for it?"

"Twenty-eighth it is," Colin nodded. "That lets me warn people tonight and tomorrow. Any preference on dealers?"

"One of the girls and the man dealing right now. What's his name?"

"Barney Taxer. His family used to collect tithes a few generations back across the pond."

"Huh... surnames can be a bit odd," Doc chuckled. "Just let the dealers rotate every half-hour to keep them fresh."

"That's the idea. I'll also have a couple of servers to make sure the drinks flow," Colin grinned.

"The more they drink, the worse they play, I hope?"

"Me, too, since I'll be at the table," Colin agreed.

The crash of thunder came with the windows rattling, then the sound of rain pouring down. Doc glanced at the window with a sigh. "Not lucky all the time. That storm sounds terrible, and I'll need to let people know about the game."

"I'll get word sent along to them. Tarbo will be informed that he'll have to let his unknown player know."

"That works for me. Still going to suck getting home in that. I doubt it'll let up quickly. Means the work on my addition is going to stop for a bit."

"Life," Colin nodded sagely.

"As always. It's what happens when you're busy making plans."

The two men said goodbye, with Doc promising to send his wives over to work out the details with him in the next day or two.

Colin watched Doc go with a bemused smile. He'd only talked to Doc because Suez had singled him out during the tournament. Because of that freak chance, Colin was about to become wealthier than he thought he'd ever be, and have the chance to get in on a new venture. With a glance skyward, he said a small prayer to Lady Luck; he felt like he owed it to her.

Harrid thanked the weapon checker as he got all his weapons back, loaded them, and strapped them on. The woman fidgeted, then leaned slightly over the counter and spoke softly to him. Harrid blinked at her for a moment before replying back just as softly. Nodding sadly, the rabbit bestial left him at the counter, going into her cubby.

Doc didn't inquire while they waited for the carriage. When Clyde came around the building, Doc was quick to get inside. "Harrid, in here," he said.

Harrid was glad enough to get into the carriage; he didn't have a slicker to protect him against the rain. "Thank you."

"Rather you didn't catch a cold, not that I'd let you suffer with one," Doc said. The carriage started rolling and Doc looked out the window. "Question for you: why'd you turn her down?"

Harrid jerked, then sighed. "I told her I don't have set days off and, when you do leave town, I'd go with you. I didn't turn her down... just explained the important things to her."

"Ah, got it, and that was enough to make her back off. Sorry to pry. I just noticed her giving you attention and wasn't sure how it'd play out. When she looked dejected, I thought maybe you just flat out refused her."

Harrid hesitated before he spoke slowly, "No... I was dead set on a dwarven woman a year ago. I would've spurned that poor woman then. But... well... your family has shown me that idea is very short-sighted. I'll still keep trying to find a dwarven wife, but... if things happen and someone else approaches me first, maybe it'll be what's meant to be."

"Just not a dryad," Doc said plainly, holding back his laughter.

"Not a dryad," Harrid was quick to agree. "But a bestial would be... good. I'd not turn away a half-dwarf or half-elf, either. Doubt any full elf would ever see me as a catch, honestly. I have too much hair." He touched his beard.

"Got it. Didn't mean to pry that far, but it's good to know."

"Doc, I'm not upset at the question. You should know if I suddenly find someone. This way, maybe things can be arranged, but any woman needs to know what my life is. I'm your guard, Shaman. That's first."

"A tough sell," Doc said softly. "I won't try to stop you. If it comes to a point where you find someone and you want to stay—" He held up a hand when Harrid opened his mouth, forestalling the interruption. "*If*, I said, then talk to me. I consider you a friend, Harrid. You're not just a nameless, faceless body to stand between me and danger. You're a friend first. Have I been doing better, at least?"

Harrid hesitated, then nodded. "You have been, Doc, and I welcome being a friend... but if it comes to it, my life will be spent before yours. That's my duty and my honor."

"Deal. I won't try stupid heroics if it comes to that, but if you still breathe, I'll be trying to heal you."

"That's fair, as long as you're not at risk."

"What do you think of all my plans? You rarely speak up on them."

"There's a lot of good, but chances for terrible. What you did for Kitanishan... that's who you are. You didn't even think about how she'd react to being healed like that, did you?"

"No. I just saw the hurt and wanted to heal it."

"Other men wouldn't be as altruistic, Doc, but you are. I hope you grow and that those who follow you can be even half of what you are. Maybe then, people will see that light can push back the Darkness."

"It's a good hope to have," Doc agreed as the storm raged outside the carriage. "Remind me to make sure all the drivers and guards have easy access to slickers."

"I'll mention it to Ayla," Harrid chuckled. "She'll arrange it."

"Fair enough," Doc laughed. "She handles a lot for me... I worry it might be a bit too much sometimes."

"She would say otherwise. All of them think they should do more for you, Doc. Ayla and Sophia at least feel like they help. Lia and Sonya are focused on being there for the tribes and clans. Rosa is... Rosa. Fiala, though... she's the one I worry about. She pushes herself to fill a role, to be useful. She doesn't see that just being there for you is enough to ease your stress."

Doc stared at the dwarf for a moment. "It's perception like that that helped me see that Posy was the answer when I left Deep Gulch. I've talked with Fiala, and now that she's making friends, I think it's getting better for her."

"I hope so," Harrid said. "I know how much she means to all of you."

"She really does..." Doc murmured, looking out at the storm.

CHAPTER TWENTY-SEVEN

Doc listened to the storm. It had hung around the city for a couple of days and was still going strong. He'd felt bad about going with Ayla and Sophia to meet Colin yesterday, but having the deal completed before the tournament was for the best. Colin was even slated to stay on as operator for a couple of months to make sure his second could step in.

After everything was signed, Doc vetted each person with Rosa's help. Two dealers were let go when Rosa told him how much hatred they harbored for the female dealers. One of them had wanted to cause a scene, but stopped when Harrid stepped forward.

Fiala had a few women over for tea that same day, including a couple of the elders' wives. She explained that it started out strained between the humans and dwarves, but by the time they were done, everyone seemed to be getting along. Sonya agreed with her, telling Doc how Fiala had acted as the intermediary to help both sides find common ground, mostly complaining about their husbands working too much.

With the storm still raging, the family stayed home the following day. Doc had a poker game later, but until he had to leave, they just spent time with each other. Sonya explained she was getting copies of some of the clan's older books. Lia told Doc how she'd spoken to a dozen half-elves in much the same shape as Kitanishan had been. He was going to help them tomorrow before they went off to see Jesamin in Deep Gulch. Ayla and Sophia took the day to relax; they'd been working hard since reaching the city, and the others pampered them in thanks. Rosa flitted from one to the other, doing her best to make them feel relaxed and keep them smiling the entire time.

When it finally came time for him to go, he collected kisses from each of his wives; they'd just finished eating a light meal to keep him tided over during the game. Right before he went out the door, Lia whispered what he would find when he got home. Taking a deep breath, he'd promised to not stay out too late.

* * *

The city streets were nearly empty— no one wanted to be out in the storm if they didn't have to be. Harrid was glad to be inside the carriage with Doc, but felt a little bad that Clyde was out in it by himself.

When the carriage came to a stop, both Doc and Harrid hurried out, giving Clyde a wave. Clyde nodded before getting the carriage rolling to the covered waiting area in the back.

Stepping inside the gambling hall, Doc took off his jacket, which had gotten pretty wet even in that small amount of time between the carriage and door. "Kind of terrible out there," he told the checker.

"Yes, sir. We get a good storm every handful of years. I just hope the river doesn't flood."

Harrid didn't bring everything with him for the game— he'd left the axe at home— but it still took him a moment to get all his other weapons checked. The bestial was efficient with her work, but didn't say anything to him. Harrid took the coldness stoically, though he hadn't meant to upset her. Doc went over to the cage to get his chips while Harrid turned his stuff in, giving Harrid a chance to address the awkwardness.

"I didn't mean to hurt you, miss. Sorry," Harrid mumbled. "I just wanted it to be stated up front."

The woman took his weapons, then glanced at Doc's back before looking at Harrid again. "He'll be busy for a few hours. Would you… care to have a drink, or some food?"

Harrid looked at Doc, then nodded at the rabbit bestial. "Miss, let me tell him, and yes."

A bright smile came to her as she finished up her work. "I'll arrange my relief. See you in the lounge?"

"Yes, ma'am," Harrid said awkwardly.

"I'm Ginger," she whispered.

"Harrid. I'll meet you there shortly."

She handed him his tag, then hurried off.

Harrid took a slow breath, then met Doc by the doors into the hall. "Doc, since you'll be upstairs, do you mind if I have a meal down here?"

Doc's eyebrow went up before he looked at the empty check area, then chuckled. "Take your time. I'll be hoping for you to have a good night."

"Me, too," Harrid said a little tightly. "Do you have any advice?" he asked in a near whisper. "I've not had dinner with a woman like this before."

"Listen to her, ask about her life, find common ground, but above all, just be yourself. She asked you, which means she has interest. Answer her questions honestly, since she probably wants to know more about you."

"This feels more terrifying than when we were ambushed in the alley."

"It can, yeah," Doc agreed. "I'd tell you not to drink too much, but I know I don't have to."

"I'm still on duty, so no. One drink only."

Doc clapped his shoulder. "Luck, Harrid."

"Yes, please," Harrid exhaled a shaky breath.

Doc headed for the stairs, saying a small prayer for his friend's first date.

The guards at the bottom of the stairs gave Doc a nod, stepping aside for him. Doc paused, not going past them. "Everything been okay?"

"Yes, Boss," one of them replied. "A few people are complaining about the second floor being closed, but there are tables downstairs with increased stakes for tonight to offset it."

Doc looked back over the room. It had some business, but it wasn't nearly as busy as he'd expect it to be. *Then again, the storm's been going hard for a couple days,* he thought, chalking the lack of business up to that. "I hope it stays calm."

"Calm would be better than that storm," the other guard snorted the way only a bull bestial could.

"Fair enough. Hopefully, it moves on soon."

"That'd be good. I worry about the river."

"You're the second person to say that," Doc said. "Is anyone else here yet?"

"A couple."

"I'll go be the host, then," Doc said, heading upstairs to see who was there.

David, Alaric, and Colin were chatting at one of the tables, drinks in hand. When Doc came into the room, they raised their glasses to him.

"Well, at least my half of the game is already here," Doc laughed.

"Ah, you brought chips up with you," Colin said. "I have some up here just in case."

"Probably for the best," Doc agreed. "How've you all been?"

"Good, but the storm is getting aggravating," Alaric said.

"It really is. My gardens are going to suffer if this keeps up," David said. "I'm just glad to not be on the river."

"The bestial area in town is going to flood if it doesn't stop," Colin sighed. "It happens every few years, and still Dodd hasn't worked on improving the river to stop the flooding."

"Cost is always an issue," David said. "When it's bestials being displaced, most won't see the cost being worth it. It'd be the same if it was dwarves or elves."

"If it was dwarves, we'd fix it ourselves," Alaric snorted, "like we have for many things."

"So cost and standard bigotry?" Doc asked. "Doesn't it mess up the water for the rest of the city, too?"

"For a couple of days, it means boiling water," Colin nodded.

"Who owns the land right next to the river?" Doc asked.

"Strongarm," David said. "He put up that haphazard shanty town and charges them more than he should for them to live there. As a business model, it works, but from a morally acceptable standpoint, it's repugnant."

"He owns all of it?" Doc asked.

"Just the bestial area. The rest is privately owned or owned by the city for improvements."

"Hmm..." Doc murmured as he looked into the distance. "It might be possible... expensive, but possible... would set a precedent, too."

"Doc?" Colin asked.

"Sorry, just thinking. Tonight might be more than just poker."

"That's similar to the look you had when you went up against Suez," Alaric said.

"I doubt it'll come to that. I'm just going to try making some deals while we play," Doc said.

"Strongarm won't sell," David said. "I've asked him before."

"There are other ways around if he's reluctant," Doc said softly. "We should be improving life for those around us, not just sitting on what we have."

David sat back, looking thoughtful. "You're thinking of philanthropy? Like Frank Benson did when this nation was founded?"

Doc's brow contracted for a second at the name before it clicked for him. "Vaguely, but more than that. I think your family would be known for it if this world were slightly different than it currently is."

David's eye twitched, giving a minute nod when he realized what Doc was saying. "Maybe I can start a trend for my family."

"Hmm... I'm not sure what you have in mind, Shaman. If it's something that would help with your task, the Ironbeard clan will help."

"On that note, there *is* something I can do for the clan. I should've done it for the Oresmelter clan before I left, but I didn't know I could until just before I left." Doc stopped when the door opened and Tarbo and Dodd came into the room. "We'll talk about it later."

"For the best," Alaric nodded,

"Glad you made it. I was concerned, with the weather," Doc greeted the two men.

"It has been a bad few days," Tarbo agreed. Dodd and he still had on their coats, as did everyone but Doc. "Did you not have an umbrella with you?"

"Something I'm missing, but will fix in the near future," Doc shrugged. "Once the others arrive, we can begin. Care for a drink while we wait?"

"Hmm, yes. Cognac would work well, and a cigar, if you have them," Tarbo smiled.

Colin gestured to a woman across the room.

"Same for me," Dodd added.

"Who did you invite, besides Strongarm?" Doc asked as he settled in. "Oh, I should get a drink while I'm at it. The same for me," he raised his voice for the last four words so the waitress could hear him.

"Well, when it comes to wealth, I thought of a single person who has the money and enjoys entertainment," Tarbo said slowly. "He's a bit peculiar, though."

Alaric leaned back. "The soulsmith?"

"Richard Steward," Tarbo nodded. "When I mentioned that Holyday would be here, he was eager to join."

"He wants some soul stones," Doc sighed. "I haven't gotten back to him. Ah, well. I happen to have a few fragments on me, just in case things get serious."

"Good old-fashioned side-bets," Tarbo chuckled. "I'm sure we all have things we can put up."

"Except me," Colin said as the waitress delivered drinks, ashtrays, and cigars. "I don't even own this place anymore. I sold it yesterday."

"You did?" Tarbo asked. "Strongarm didn't tell me. I know he's been after it for a while now."

"He sold it to me," Doc said. "For more than Strongarm's last offer, plus other concessions."

"Oh, that'll tweak his nose," Dodd laughed as he sat down. "This will be entertaining."

The door opened again, and Strongarm came in with Steward. The pair were chatting amiably about how expensive it would be to get soul stones of sufficient size and quality to run a private rail line.

"Welcome," Doc said, standing up. "Glad we all made it with the weather being what it is."

The two men gave Doc their attention as they crossed the room.

"Holyday, I haven't heard back from you," Steward said a little stiffly.

"I've been busy," Doc apologized. "On the plus side, I did bring some soul stones with me just in case there are side-bets."

Steward's eyes gleamed. "Well, then, we should begin at once."

"Side-bets... well, most of us here have property of various kinds we can offer," Strongarm said, looking at Colin. "Even if it is just a single building."

"Actually," Colin chuckled, "I sold this place to Doc yesterday. He nearly doubled your last offer, then threw in a few extra incentives. It was too good to pass up."

Strongarm's lips thinned. "I see. Well, who knows what will happen by the end of tonight?"

"We'll all find out," Doc said amiably, keeping his eyes on Strongarm and Steward. Those two men would be trouble— he was sure of it.

CHAPTER TWENTY-EIGHT

The first dealer for the private game was Barney, the half-elf blackjack dealer who'd been moved to the high stakes table a few days prior. No one said anything about him dealing, but Doc noted the disdain that flashed on Strongarm's face when Barney introduced himself.

Conversation was light to start with, mostly about the rain. Dodd ranted for a good while about the federal government being so slow to accept Coalrud as a full state and not just a territory. David fed him small statements, keeping him going for longer than was really needed. When he finally wound down, silence fell and most of the table was grateful for it.

Collecting the cards after the last hand, Barney stood up. "Gentlemen, I'll be back in a half-hour. My replacement, Padma, will take over for me until then."

No one had seen or paid the bestial attention when she came up behind the majority of them. She gave them a smile as she went around the table to take the dealer's seat.

"Gentlemen, I'm your second dealer for the game," Padma said as she took her seat. "I hope you all have a good game."

"A bestial, much less a woman as a dealer?" Strongarm snorted. "I heard that happens at Holyday's gambling hall down in Deep Gulch. Already twisting this place, too?"

"Now, now, Strongarm," Steward interrupted, "be kind to the poor dear." His smile was kind, but a slight edge to his tone made Doc worry. "I'm sure she'll be perfect. Won't you, darling?"

Padma looked away from Steward. "I'm the best hold'em dealer in the building."

"Your perversions are well-known, Steward," Strongarm snorted.

Steward gave Strongarm a bright smile. "Are they really? I bet not *all* of them are."

"Gentlemen, you're making my dealer uncomfortable," Doc said firmly. "Are we here to play or not?"

"I'll play," Steward said with a twist to his smile.

"Fine," Strongarm snorted.

"Padma, if it's too much, I can see about a new dealer," Doc said gently. "I picked you because you're the best."

Padma exhaled slowly, letting go of her fear and revulsion. Looking up, she scanned the table, her back straight. "I'm fine, sir. I can manage."

"Shuffle up," Doc said.

"Yes, sir," Padma said, making a mess of the cards on the table.

As she got the cards randomized, Doc turned to Dodd. "Dodd, I had a question about the flooding. What's been done to mitigate it in the future? I've taken steps out at my estate to keep it safer, but I have no idea about what the city has done."

Dodd shook his head. "Nothing. I've floated a few ideas, but cost keeps it from happening. It will be bad for the businesses down by the river, but other than those and some homes, most of it has been taken up by... the less fortunate."

"If it happens, we'll just rebuild," Strongarm shrugged. "So the beasts will be inconvenienced? It's not a problem. They know their place."

Doc saw Padma's frown, which vanished a moment after it appeared.

"You'd rather do that than take steps to stop it from happening?" Alaric asked.

"It's cheaper to rebuild than to do major work on the river," Strongarm replied. "I don't really lose much when it happens."

"In the long run, I'd think rebuilding would cost more," David said.

"But each time, there is the chance to re-envision what that section of the city could be," Strongarm countered. "At the moment, it's a shanty town for the beasts. At some point, the city will boom and, when it does, I can rebuild it better."

"Would you be interested in selling it?" Doc asked.

"Not at all," Strongarm smiled. "You ask because you know that it's prime real estate. I'm not going to let that go, not when it'll be worth so much more later."

"If you never fix the potential trouble, it's not worth as much as you think," Doc said. "But that's neither here nor there if you won't sell."

"Ante up, please," Padma said as she dealt.

"If someone funded the river work for the areas owned or held by the city," Doc addressed Dodd, "would you move forward on the project for those parts?"

"Yes," Dodd said. "I want to elevate Furden into the jewel of the west."

"And if we ever get to be a state, I'll be running for our seat," Tarbo said. "I want to make sure we get full state's rights and aren't overlooked like new states normally are."

"I'll have my people look at the numbers," Doc said, "but I'm leaning toward making that happen. I hate to think of what might happen if nothing is done."

"That's very magnanimous of you," Dodd chuckled. "What kind of return are you looking for?"

"Nothing," Doc said as he mucked his cards— they were terrible. "At least not that I know of right now, but something might happen in the future. Honestly, I'd like to see everyone have a better life here. I might not have been born here, but Coalrud feels like my home."

"I know that feeling," David agreed. "It's why I do what I do. I'll be matching your investment in the river project. I think it'll make a statement if the two of us work together to do it."

"That'd work," Doc nodded. "Alaric, would the dwarves give a discount to do the work?"

"Hmm..." Alaric said as he fiddled with his chips. "Raise to fifty. Yes, I think we would. We'd need to see the numbers before committing."

"Of course."

Dodd was grinning when he called Alaric's raise. "If I'd known that tonight was going to be this productive, I'd have called for a private game much earlier."

Tarbo laughed as he folded. "If all business could be done this easily, all business would be done at a poker table."

***

The table lapsed into small talk for the next couple of hours. Colin went out first, then Dodd, followed swiftly by Tarbo and Alaric. At the start of the fourth hour, just David, Steward, Strongarm, and Doc were left at the table.

They paused the game as the four men out left, the rain still pounding down. Doc wondered about the road between the city and his home, reminding himself to talk to Rosa about making it better.

"I still haven't seen these soul stones," Steward grumbled. "I was sure we'd have seen them by now."

"We had people who wouldn't be up for side-bets here," Doc said as he fished out one of the stones from his vest pocket and tossed it across the table. "Here you go. Last tested out above ninety-percent pure."

Steward tossed his cards, freshly dealt and unseen, back to Barney. He pulled a jeweler's loupe and put it up to his eye. The rim glowed a soft gold.

"Tch..." Strongarm clicked his tongue. "Well, he's out of the next couple of hands. Single-minded when soul stone is available."

"This is good... *very* good... as good as the ones I got from you, Strongarm," Steward said.

"Not *as* good, I'm sure," Strongarm snorted.

Doc's face stayed impassive, but he was sure he now knew where the soul stones Goodman stole from him had gone. He had no proof, but it was the only thing that made sense.

"Nearly identical, actually," Steward said. "You said yours came from an auction in Aire, right?"

"Yes. One of my people snapped them up during an auction. Small bits and pieces, but no one wanted them. I knew you'd pay top dollar for them. I made a tidy profit."

"They were almost too small to be useful, but I found a use for them," Steward chuckled. "Ah yes, they did have a use."

Doc didn't care for the creepy smile Steward had as he eyed the soul stone. He was glad Padma wasn't at the table; she'd probably have freaked out, and he wouldn't have blamed her.

"Straight from my mine," Doc said. "Part of the small percentage of stones I can keep. I won't have many of them, as they're being collected by my business for me while I'm away."

"But we could set up a contract for you to sell your percentage to me. I'd even arrange for retrieval," Steward said, putting his loupe back. He rolled the soul stone in his hand gently between two fingers.

"Possibly," Doc agreed, "but in the meantime, I'll sell you that one."

"Done," Steward said quickly, stacking up some chips and sliding them over to Doc. "Good?"

Doc checked the chips, then pursed his lips in thought. Before he could say anything, Steward quickly added another fifty to the stack. Doc chuckled, then kicked the extra chip back to him. "This is fine. After all, kindness now might mean you'll be more disposed to friendly relations later."

"Indeed, I will," Steward grinned and pocketed the stone, then quickly stacked his chips. "I'll be going now. I can put this to use, and don't want to delay it."

"The madam there is going to get upset again," Strongarm snorted.

"She'll make do," Steward waved off the words. "I pay her enough to compensate her."

A shiver ran down Doc's spine at the implication that the soulsmith was doing something to the whores at the house that had bestials. *I shouldn't get involved,* Doc told himself, but the words felt empty.

"Well, if he's done, we might as well call this game," Strongarm sighed, starting to collect his own chips.

"It wasn't much of a last hand," David said, "but a cash game isn't a tournament."

"I'm happy with the game as it was. I more than doubled what I came with," Strongarm laughed.

"Glad you enjoyed it," Doc said, standing up.

"At least *one* of the dealers was good," Strongarm said with a hint of sass.

"Barney's improving," Doc said, deliberately misunderstanding as he patted the half-elf's shoulder. "I thought you did great."

"As did I," David agreed.

Strongarm grimaced that his words were flipped so easily. "Be that as it may, I'm not sure I'll be back again."

"Your call, but we'll probably have Tarbo and Dodd back out at some point."

"Perhaps if they're both here," Strongarm said as he used two chip racks for his haul. "Good night."

Doc let him go; Steward had already left at speed. When the man was gone, Doc took his original money out of his chips, then divided what was left. Taking half of the winnings, he divided it again. "Here you go, Barney," Doc said, giving the man one of the smaller piles.

"Thank you."

"Oh? The game's over?" Padma asked, coming back into the room.

"Yeah, but come collect your tip," Doc said, sliding the other small stack to her. "Take this stack," he tapped the rest of the winnings, "down to the ground floor and split it amongst the others, please. I know some of them would've made money if we'd had the floor open tonight."

Padma hesitated, then bowed her head. "Yes, sir... umm... sir? Thank you."

"You earned it," Doc said as he used a rack to get his original chips ready to go.

"No. Thank you for trying to get the river looked at. My family lives down there... a lot of *us* do. I could see you actually want to help."

Doc gave her a smile. "I'll get it done. If not today, then before the year is out."

Padma just stared at him for a second before she collected the money. "I'll pray to Luck you're right, sir."

"Thank you, Padma."

"We could do something different," David said slowly. "The land on the outskirts of the city heading to your manor is currently owned by the city."

Doc's eyes gleamed. "Oh, yes... that sounds good to me."

Barney was confused as he collected his money and got the table closed up.

"It'd take money and workers, but I think it'd make a real statement about equality," David chuckled.

"I'll need a manager for it, unless you want to head it and I'll take second?"

"Let's do that."

"Sir, is there anything else?" Barney asked.

"No. But, Padma?" he called out before she left the room. "How many are solid workers down where you live?"

"Oh, yes, even better," David laughed.

"Sir?" Padma asked, turning back to them.

"Carpenters, plumbers, builders, how many?"

Padma's brow furrowed. "A lot, sir. We get a lot of the work, but we're labor, not the engineers. The best bestial engineer in the city is already working out at your manor."

"Simpson?"

"Yes, sir."

"I'll go through him, then," Doc grinned. "Hope is coming, Padma. Luck will provide. Just start letting your friends know that."

"Yes, sir," Padma said, confused.

"We'll need Ayla and Sophia to set up a trust to handle the philanthropy," David said, "and we'll need a name."

"Luck's Providence?" Doc suggested.

David's lips tugged upward. "I think that will work."

"But for now, home," Doc yawned. "Not looking forward to the rain."

"Small moments of suffering make the bright spots brighter," David said.

"Very philosophical."

"I try at times."

* * *

When Doc got downstairs, he found Harrid talking to Ginger in the lounge. The two sat side by side, chatting quietly and smiling softly. Doc hesitated— he didn't want to interrupt what was clearly a good night.

Ginger saw him first and shot to her feet. "Sir?"

Doc sighed internally, giving her a nod. "Sorry to interrupt. I'm going to steal my bodyguard back."

"Oh, uh...! We were—!" Ginger started to say, but cut off when Doc raised his hand.

"I'm not upset. I was going to sneak off for a little longer, but you spotted me. We'll both be back for business in the future, so don't worry. I'll even see about staying home now and again so he can have a day off."

Ginger's face flushed, but she smiled. "That would be... nice."

Harrid was stone-faced as he got to his feet. "I'm ready, Shaman."

"Let's get our things. Maybe by then, Clyde will be around with the carriage," Doc said.

* * *

Doc stayed quiet until they were inside the carriage and heading home. Once they were moving, he said, "It looked like you were having a good time."

"She is... a good woman," Harrid answered softly. "We have a lot in common, it turns out."

"Sounds promising."

"Both of us are orphans. She had an uncle to take her in. He died a year ago."

"Okay, sounds terrible," Doc said.

"Both of us love weapons, and she... said I was handsome."

Doc grinned. "I'd say you have a good start."

The carriage suddenly slid and Clyde cursed. Doc grabbed the seat and, a second later, everything settled out.

"Clyde?!" Doc called out.

"Road's shit!" Clyde yelled back. "We're fine."

"Got to fix that..." Doc exhaled. "We'll find time for you to talk to her again, okay?"

Harrid nodded. "Thank you, Doc."

"Anything for a friend."

CHAPTER TWENTY-NINE

"That's how the game went," Doc finished explaining when breakfast ended. "I have a couple of things on deck, but I can't get to them all right away. Ayla, Sophia, I'm pressing you into even more work again with David."

"What're we setting up?" Ayla asked.

"Luck's Providence: an organization for philanthropic deeds. David and I will be funding it to start doing good things. First, we're buying the land just outside the city— on this side of it— to set up housing for the bestials. We're planning quality homes. They might not be the best, but they'll be good, solid quality. I want them set up and sold but with a contract that says, if they sell, we get the first chance to buy the houses back. I'll let you work out the numbers for them buying from us. We'll take nothing down and let them float the deed for thirty years if they can make the payments, with say... two-percent interest."

"Doc, that's almost giving them away," Ayla said softly before she nodded.

"That's the point if it's philanthropy. We're not looking to make money on it. The interest is just to keep them invested and help pay for the general upkeep of the area."

"What about where they currently live? And just bestials?" Lia asked.

"*Anyone* who is looked down on," Doc clarified. "Bestials, half-bloods, dwarves, elves, gnomes, and so on."

"That'll get a lot of hate back if we exclude humans," Sophia said. "We can mitigate that if we have them sign a civility clause. If they cause trouble with their neighbors, we can force them out. They'll be renting until they've paid enough to own it that way."

Doc nodded. "I don't want humans to hate Luck. That won't work out. We can favor the others, but still accept humans. We'd need to staff deputies for the area to make sure people behave themselves."

"Which means you'll need the sheriff to sign off," Fiala said.

"Once we get it running, I'll approach him with money to build a substation there and staff it," Doc grimaced. "I can play into staffing it with 'lessers,' as I'm sure he'll be happy to let his bigotry show for that. Sophia, do me a favor and check the laws on when and where private guards are allowed, and how they interact with lawmen."

"Thinking of setting up a private force for the area?" Fiala asked.

"It might be for the best. I don't trust the sheriff, but at least he isn't Grange," Doc said. "I have some other things I want to do, too. I want to send a letter to Posy and ask her to help the dwarves of the Oresmelter clan like I'm going to help the Ironbeards. I didn't think of it before I left there, and I think she can do it, if slowly."

"Do what?" Sonya asked.

"Increase the fertility of any woman who wants it," Doc said.

"Oh…" Sonya whispered, clearly shocked. "Because you did it for Gretchen and the others the night before we left…"

"Yeah. I should've thought about it then, but I didn't."

"That would create a boom of babies for the clans," Harrid said. "You would be celebrated widely, Shaman."

"A big step toward getting the clans behind me." His gaze shifted to meet Lia's eyes. "The same for any tribes we meet."

"That would be a big step toward showing that you want to help," Lia nodded. "You don't need to do that for the half-elves. They're as fertile as humans are."

"Today, I'm going with you to meet the half-elves who are leaving for Deep Gulch," Doc said. "Rosa will be needed for this. Before we leave, I need to speak to Simpson about heading up the new project. I want to warn him ahead of time. We'll be hiring as many of the disenfranchised who can do the work as possible."

"All about building them up," Sophia smiled. "I'll ensure the contracts are written correctly after we get the new company set up with David."

"Doc, how sure of him are you?" Lia asked softly. "We've been tying up a lot with him."

"I'm sure he wants his old family beliefs to come back. He wants the god or goddess of trade to be here again," Doc told her. "If that happens, I think he'll be even more indebted."

"Very well. You also need a small office added to the Silvered Dreams," Ayla said. "I'll ask Simpson to do that as soon as the rooms for the guards are done. Then, he can come back here to finish the stables."

"I need to really start making a name for myself."

"We've taken on a lot for Luck's Holdings," Sophia said. "We still need to vet people to oversee whatever we leave behind here."

"Lots to do," Doc agreed. "Fiala, Sonya, are you having tea again today?"

"They're coming here," Fiala smiled. "They might still be here when you return. If so, please stop in?"

"I will," Doc said as he got up. "Before I start my day... kisses?"

His wives beamed, and Harrid slipped out the door.

* * *

Simpson and crew were working hard when Doc came out with Rosa and Harrid in tow. Doc was glad for the umbrella his wives had arranged for him. It wasn't pouring, but the drizzle was persistent.

Seeing them, Simpson met them short of the worksite, his rain slicker shedding the water. "Doc, how can I help you?"

"My wives are going to work on some contracts with you," Doc said. "We'll be buying land and need good, serviceable homes built. We don't need anything fancy; just good, solid houses. There'll be a lot of them. That'll likely keep you tied up until the hot spring job is ready. Are you interested?"

Simpson blinked slowly at Doc for a long few moments before shaking his head. "Yeah, I'm sure I'll sign on. But why? Why me and for what?"

"Getting better homes for the bestials, half-elves, and the rest who have to live in the slums that Strongarm currently owns. It'll be away from the river, as well."

"The river is close to flooding today," Simpson said tightly. "If this storm doesn't stop soon…"

"Which is one of the reasons why."

"I'll sign."

"We'll want you to get the people to help, as you'll be the foreman. Hire as many of those who will live there who can do the work as possible, but make sure you get the best you can. I want these houses to survive for decades."

"Yes, sir," Simpson smiled. "I wasn't sure about you when we first started, but I'm glad to have met you."

"Same for me, Simpson. You do good work. Should you be working in this weather, though?"

"We'll be fine, Doc. I have them doing work inside to keep them as out of it as possible. We want to get it done, too."

"Speaking of," Doc sighed, "when you finish the suites, but before you finish the stables, I have a small remodel job I need done with speed."

"What?"

"Silvered Dreams. The front lounge needs to be cut in half so I can have an office. I'll be meeting people there. Nothing big— just cut it off and make it as soundproof as you can."

"I'll get it done," Simpson said.

"Thanks. See you later."

The two men shook hands before separating. When Doc made it to the front of the manor, Clyde had the carriage waiting and Lia was already inside. Doc gave Clyde a wave before he climbed in with Rosa behind him. Harrid had borrowed a rain slicker from one of the other drivers, so he sat with Clyde on the bench.

"He agreed?" Lia asked as the carriage got rolling.

"To everything," Doc said.

"He's very eager for the work and was silently praising Doc," Rosa added. "The rumor that Doc has healed people and might be someone who truly cares for the bestials is spreading in their community."

"Good," Lia smiled.

"Ready to help the road, Weed?" Doc asked.

Rosa shivered as she shifted to kneel. "I'll do my best, Voice. You'll keep me recharged as we go?"

"We will," Lia said, taking Rosa's hand in hers. "Sip from me while he fills you with power, but focus on your work."

"As you decree, mistress," Rosa moaned as she watched Doc get himself ready for her.

* * *

Doc felt a touch faint when the carriage rolled to a stop. Lia and Rosa had coaxed him into filling Rosa time and again, and Doc and Lia both gave her blood to help. The road between his manor and the city was in much better condition by the time they'd reached the city.

"Catch your breath," Lia whispered to him. "I'll go make sure they're ready. Weed, you're with me."

"Yes, mistress," Rosa said, going with her.

Doc took a moment to check his status, nodding at his numbers. He was full up on energy thanks to Rosa, but his vitality was down a little, as was his health from the blood loss. He'd be fine, and he wasn't worried about replacing the deficit immediately.

Harrid glanced in the door. "Doc?"

"Just getting my head on straight," Doc replied. "When Lia says it's good, we can go in."

"You might want to come out before that," Harrid said, looking to the side.

With a grunt, Doc stepped out. Seeing where Harrid was looking, he glanced over to see the river lapping just over its banks— it was clear that it was going to start flooding. He saw a dozen people with sandbags trying to set up a makeshift containment.

"Fuck..." Doc said.

"Figured you'd want to know."

"I already have healing to do," Doc murmured. "Rosa can help, but..."

"But?" Harrid asked.

"I'm not a cold enough bastard at times. The best thing to make my point would be to do nothing."

"Because it would flood and show what we were talking about with the others. The other side is that everyone who lives here will be badly affected."

"Like I said, I'm not a cold enough bastard," Doc sighed. "Healing first, and then we'll see what we can do."

"Voice, Lia says it's ready," Rosa called to him from the doorway. She looked at him quizzically, then at the river. Hurrying to his side, she kept her voice low as she murmured, "I can help after, but I might not be able to do enough without strain."

"Worry about that after healing," Doc told her. "If we do anything, it'll be better than doing nothing."

"True," Rosa said as she touched his hand. "I'm here."

He gave her a soft smile. "I know. Thank you, my precious Weed."

Rosa shivered, then fell into step behind him when he headed for the door.

CHAPTER THIRTY

Close to two dozen people crowded the living space of the home. All of them, except Lia, were half-elven. Out of those with mixed blood, only one didn't look like they'd been abused— Kitanishan— and only because Doc had already healed her. His heart ached for these people who'd faced hardships solely based on who their parents were.

"Ladies and gentlemen," Doc addressed them gently, "my name is Doc Holyday. I'm the shaman of the Treeheart tribe, and married to Lia." He rested his hand lightly on her shoulder for a second. "I've been told you all want to go see Jesamin, the leader of the tribe, to join. Is this true?"

The others nodded, but one of them spoke up, "We were told you could heal us... like Kitanishan. Is that true, sir?"

"I can and will. In return, all that I ask is that you say a small prayer to Lady Luck. It's through her that the healing comes; I'm merely a conduit of her power. While I work, will you tell me about what life has been like here in this section of the city? I have plans to make life better for the people who live here, but the more I know, the better."

"Sit here, Doc," Lia said, guiding him to a chair.

The chair itself had clearly seen much better days. Doc would've guessed it to have been tossed from a business that thought it near worthless. It'd been given a coat of stain since then to improve its appearance, but even that had worn thin, which made it look even worse.

Rosa knelt beside him the moment he sat. All the half-elves glanced from him to her, then back. Doc stroked her hair softly, then smiled at the assembled people.

Kitanishan cleared her throat. "Evard," she called to one of the men, motioning toward Doc.

The man who stepped forward limped heavily as he came to a stop in front of Doc. While his hope was bright, Doc caught the undercurrent of disdain in the man's eyes. "I'm ready."

Doc looked up at Evard. "What do you dislike? Me?"

Evard's eyes went wide and he stammered, "Uh…! No, sir…! I…!"

"You see me as human," Doc said sadly. "I don't blame you for having harsh feelings for those who hurt you. It's natural. I'm not what you think or fear, Evard. I'm the Voice of Luck, the shaman of your soon-to-be tribe. Today is the start of a whole new life for you. Don't let the old hate and pain hold you down, nor let it make you into that which you hated."

Evard's gaze darted around; he felt uncomfortable being the center of attention. He looked at Rosa watching him with sorrow. His heart clenched that a nature spirit— a collared nature spirit— could feel sorrow for him. It made him take a ragged breath to stop the tears he felt forming.

"Lady, Evard comes to you with pain. His body has been abused, but so has his mind and, worse, his soul. Please help him heal from what has come before. The tribe will welcome him and soothe the old pains, but first, he needs to see your power to know that this is the path he can choose to walk with you." Doc's hands blazed with green light as he held one out to Evard, the other resting on Rosa's hair. "Just take my hand and let the goddess heal your body."

Tears did fall, but Evard didn't care. He'd either be beaten for being weak again or the shaman would be proven right. He grasped

Doc's hand tightly with both of his, but pain didn't come. Instead, a calming warmth infused his body. He felt distant memories of a soft voice singing in Elvish as he was cradled to his mother's chest. She'd died at his father's hands in a drunken rage decades ago, and he'd forgotten the song and the warmth of her love.

Doc's sorrow for Evard was clear to the others while he worked. He started at Evard's feet, healing the half-elf's years of injuries. The worst was the thrice-broken knee cap, but Doc made it as good as new. He erased the many scars as he went, the last being the ones marring Evard's face.

The others in the room gasped when his scars faded away, and murmured conversations sprang up as Doc let the energy fade. Wide eyes full of wonder and hope stared at Doc when he sat back.

"Evard?" Doc asked the crying man.

Sniffling, Evard wiped the tears away. "Sir?"

"You're healed."

Evard blinked at him for a long moment, then looked at the others. Seeing their looks, he touched his face with trembling fingers — the ridges of his scars were no longer there. Only unblemished skin met his questing digits. After a moment, he walked into the gathering. They each touched him, feeling his skin for themselves, and the conversation became more animated.

"Kitanishan, who's next?" Doc asked with a smile.

* * *

Rosa was just turning white-haired when they finished healing the half-elves. She was well under half her energy from all they had done. Every single half-elf was near perfect, and Doc had learned a couple of things he didn't know. He couldn't replace lost extremities; one half-elf had been a little disappointed that they didn't have their pinky fingers back, but was still very happy to be healed otherwise. Doc had also been unable to regrow the tips of another's ears, but he'd removed the worst of her scarring, giving her almost human ears.

"We leave tomorrow, even if the rain continues," Kitanishan said, addressing the crowd. "I have a letter from Lia for the tribal elder. It promises us jobs, honest work at good wages. Before we go, we should thank our shaman."

Doc held up a hand to stop them. "No. Thank Luck. She's the one who made this possible. If you want to do more, offer a little blood to Rosa. As you can see, she did a lot for you all."

Rosa's smile was bright. "I will take only a little if you offer, just enough to help rebalance me. You will have a small scar to remember today by from doing so."

Evard was the first to step forward. He pushed his sleeve up, exposing his forearm. "Dryad, please take from me in thanks."

Others started to do the same, but Lia stopped them. "One at a time. This way, she can do so with care, the way it should be done."

In time, the crowd was gone, leaving just Harrid, Lia, Rosa, Kitanishan, and Doc in the home. Kitanishan knelt beside Rosa, offering her own arm to the dryad. Rosa smiled and took a little blood from her.

"Will the elder accept us so easily?" Kitanishan asked Lia, clearly having a little fear on the subject.

"She will," Lia smiled. "We hope to send other elves to the tribe, but we'll only send those that will accept you. If the tribe is ever to rebuild, we'll accept all who want to join, as long as they don't cause discord."

"I was worried when you came to me dressed in your leathers. I feared that you would take those who wanted revenge and the killing would begin again."

"That's not the way forward with my husband," Lia said softly. "I only wear my guns now to protect my family, not for war. Now, you'll be given the chance that you always should've had."

"What about Heather?" Doc asked Lia.

"It's in the letter," Lia told him. "It asks Jesamin to talk to her."

"Good. I'm going to ask her if she'll come up to the capital for a few days to play her music at the opera house."

"That'll cause a stir," Lia nodded slowly. "After we've made moves, or before?"

"After. Once people begin to question why we're doing what we do, then we'll show them culture."

"I think she'll be glad to do that."

Rosa pulled back from Kitanishan. "Done."

"Thank you, Dryad."

"Doc, are we going to help?" Harrid asked. "I looked outside. The river's getting worse."

Doc stood up slowly. "Some, yes. Rosa, what do you think?"

"I can only do a little if you want to cover a wider area, Voice. Deepening the channel or raising the banks would be the easiest, but both will still be taxing."

"We can't alter the banks. I'm sure Strongarm would throw a fit and try starting shit... deepening the channel would be best. We just need to start the rumor that it was our doing that kept the river from flooding so badly."

"We'll walk the bank," Lia said. "Those who are trying to stop it will see us and clearly see the drop in water level."

Doc frowned as he thought over the idea for a moment longer. "What will that mean down from where we start? Will it suddenly surge more?"

"Yes. More volume into a small channel." Rosa looked thoughtful. "Anything we do will cause the river to surge farther down."

Doc exhaled slowly. He wanted to help, but if it became known that the better section of town had flooded because of him, it might make things even harder to deal with later. He was stuck between hard roads: either he helped now and reaped problems later, or he did nothing and let the suffering continue.

"Doc?" Lia asked softly, touching his shoulder.

"I want to help make things better for them now..." Doc whispered. "Doing that might alienate the people I'll need later. Doing nothing will make the path later easier, but at the cost of my wanting to help now."

"Ask Luck?" Harrid suggested.

Doc snorted as he nodded. "When faced with a tough choice, it isn't wrong to ask those who are there to help." He dug out a coin, looking at the golden twenty-dollar coin longer than he had previously. In doing so, he found differences he hadn't noted before. The bird wasn't a bald eagle, but a turkey. Doc's lips twitched at the old story of Benjamin Franklin wanting the turkey as the national bird; it was a myth that had no real basis in fact, but it seemed to have been fact here.

"Heads, I help. Tails, I don't." Doc said the words, the second part tugging at his heart. He snapped the coin up, but Lia caught it before he could catch it. She put the coin on the back of her hand to show it to him.

"It would've hurt you not to help, Doc. Even Luck knew that. A hard path later is better than your heart hurting now," Lia said. The coin showed heads up on her hand.

"True enough," Doc said. "Rosa, are you ready?"

"Always to help you, Voice."

"Harrid, we'll be walking a bit."

"Take this umbrella," Kitanishan said, hurrying to them with the item in hand.

"We'll return it before we head home," Doc said. "You might need it tomorrow."

"Thank you, Shaman." Kitanishan bowed her head.

CHAPTER THIRTY-ONE

The drizzle continued as the five of them left the home. Kitanishan had put on a rain slicker so she was as protected as Harrid, but Rosa walked in the rain with a bright smile on her lips. She reveled in the feeling of it cascading over her body, though she was a little sad that she had to wear the sundress, which was quickly sticking to her curves. Doc held the umbrella for both him and Lia.

The bestials who were stacking up the sandbags along the bank, standing in ankle-deep water to do so, were shocked that others were approaching. They recognized Rosa as a dryad before anyone else, and they moved back from her.

"She won't hurt you," Doc said. "We're here to help as much as we can, but it won't be as much as we'd like."

"Are you... Holyday?" one of them asked, stepping forward to get a better look at the group.

"I prefer to be called Doc," Doc smiled, "but yes, my last name is Holyday."

"What're you doing down here and in this weather?" another bestial asked suspiciously as he went to grab a sandbag, having snapped out of his shock.

"I was meeting with a group of people moving to Deep Gulch. I saw the problem you're having and wanted to help. Rosa, go ahead."

Rosa went to the edge of the sandbags, letting the water soak into her bare feet. With a smile, she focused on the river and how to best stop it from flooding.

"What's she doing?"

"She'll either deepen the river so it has more room to flow or she'll raise the bank so it'll have to rise more to flood," Doc explained. "Neither is the best solution, but it'll work for now."

"Why?" the suspicious bestial asked.

Doc gave the bestial a questioning look. The man's squat form, which included a blocky head, had Doc trying to place what kind of bestial he was. "Because it's the right thing to do. Is this the worst spot?"

With a grunt, the man dropped his sandbag, then turned to face Doc. When he spoke again, Doc noticed the man had mini-tusks when he talked, making him a hippopotamus bestial. "This whole area is lower banked than farther up or downstream."

"Will you show us the worst spots?" Doc asked, not fazed by the man being suspicious and disgruntled with them. "Rosa can only do so much, so we'd like to be as helpful as possible."

"If Steve won't, I will," the other bestial who'd spoken first said.

"I'll do it," Steve, the hippo bestial, grunted. "This is the lowest spot of the river in the city."

Rosa exhaled as she let her nature connect to the river. Her mind expanded to touch up and down the stream as she let herself root into the dirt to better connect. The bestial was right— this *was* the lowest spot in the city. She called on Mother to raise the banks to make it even with other areas.

The ground trembled slightly, and the bestials working with the sandbags shivered at the idea of an earthquake during a flood. But it was a gentle shake, like a cat shifting slightly while it slept. The man who'd just been placing a bag gasped as he watched the bank rise. Dropping it, he stumbled backward, falling into the pooled water behind him.

"The bank!" the man shouted as he stared at the shifting earth. The other bestials moved closer to watch.

"Is that... rock?" Steve asked with a touch of awe.

"Bedrock, probably," Doc said. "Have to make sure it can stand up to the river. Just dirt and clay wouldn't survive very long."

Rosa slowly let her connection fade, her feet unrooting. "The bank is raised to match the rest of this area. I also dug the river down a half-foot. Unless the storm rages again, it will not flood here. The bags can be used to help elsewhere."

"You heard her," Doc said. "It's your choice."

The bestials looked at the river which was far from flooding now, to Rosa, and then finally to Doc. They bowed their heads, murmuring their thanks.

"Thank Lady Luck, my goddess; she's why this is possible at all," Doc said. "Steve, ready to show us to the next spot?"

Steve looked back at the river, then at Doc again. "Sir...I'll lead, if you'll help again."

"Not too much, but we'll do what we can," Doc said as he shifted to Rosa's side. "Are you okay?"

"Two, maybe three more... that will be all I can do today, Voice. I'm sorry."

"Shh," Doc whispered, stroking her wet hair. "You like standing in the rain?"

"Nature always soothes me and makes me happy," Rosa replied. "I'm sorry I'm looking less than your wives wish me to, but this makes me happy."

Doc looked at the sundress plastered to her skin. Rosa shivered while she watched his thoughts, biting her lip as her eyes started to glow. Doc chuckled softly. "Later. I promise."

"Thank you, Voice," Rosa said huskily. "I will earn it."

Lia snickered lightly. "I'll make sure you do. Now come on. Work first."

* * *

They walked the bank with Steve as their guide. Kitanishan talked with those who approached her to ask what was happening. Steve told the bestials who were trying to sandbag the spots they'd worried about how Rosa had helped farther downstream. That led into Rosa slightly raising the bank in a few more areas.

Doc listened to the people around them, a smile touching his lips at the hope in their voices. Lia squeezed his hand, hearing even more than he did. Talk of them walking around in the rain and trying to help was spreading like wildfire, a wildfire that the rain could not dim. By tomorrow, word of Doc being here would've spread to everyone in the area. The name Lady Luck was second only to Doc's name.

When Rosa was white of hair and looked tired, Doc called it off. Clyde had been trailing them a street over and brought the carriage to them. Lia and Rosa got in first, and Harrid climbed up next to Clyde. Doc handed the umbrella off to Kitanishan with his thanks.

Before he climbed into the carriage, Doc turned to Steve and the other bestials who had tagged along. "I had no right to do that, and the man who owns this area might cause problems for me because I did... but I know how bad things have been for you. Give me time and I'll give you a hand up. My goddess told me to bring light back to the world, and that's what I am doing. Let your hope shine and, when the time comes, remember that it was Lady Luck who helped."

Steve watched Doc get into the carriage. He'd heard of Holyday; the man had come into town, bought a fancy house, then hired staff. It had been mostly bestials, and those who'd been hired told their family and friends how nice this man was. Steve figured it was a mask — humans only used bestials. They didn't care for them. Yet... today, Doc had been there, having his dryad help them. It would gain him nothing, and it might even cause him trouble. That made Steve question his assumptions about Doc.

Doc pulled Rosa to him, not caring if her wet dress soaked his suit. He kissed her softly, but passionately. She'd done so much for him today and he wanted her to know his appreciation. Rosa surrendered to him, diving deep into his mind and reveling in his thoughts, eager for them.

Lia watched the pair, making plans to properly thank Rosa while giving Doc more love. He'd briefly thought about not helping, thinking of the trouble it would cause, but Lia had known he would help; it was who he was. He tried to hold back to make things easier, but he couldn't stand seeing people pushed down. Her love of him grew to new heights every day, and she found that wonderful.

"Weed, stop," Lia said gently. "You'll ruin his clothing."

Rosa groaned, but she pulled back from him. "As you command, mistress."

"Uh, I think one ruined suit—" Doc started.

"Shh," Lia chuckled. "Rosa, take the dress off, then kneel for him. That'll do what you both want for now."

Rosa was quick to do as she was told, and Doc chuckled as he worked to get himself ready for her, too.

"See? I'm helping everyone *and* also not letting you ruin a perfectly good suit," Lia smiled. "Dear husband, hands flat on the seat. You don't get to control her."

Doc exhaled roughly as he did what Lia said— he loved his beautiful elven wife taking control. His breath caught when Lia snagged Rosa by her messy hair before she could take Doc the way they all wanted.

"Weed, I will control you, for you." She trailed a kiss along Rosa's neck. "For him." More kisses followed. "And me." With those last two words, she pushed Rosa's head forward.

The storm wasn't loud, not nearly loud enough to stop the sounds inside the carriage from reaching Clyde's and Harrid's ears. The two men pointedly didn't look at each other.

Clyde coughed, wanting to help muffle the noise from the carriage. "So... what happened today?"

"Helping people, as he does," Harrid said, understanding the reason Clyde asked. "First, it was healing the half-elves who will go join Lia's tribe."

"Half-elves? Being accepted into a tribe?" Clyde asked, surprised.

"Yes. Doc helps make things better," Harrid smiled. "We saw the river before we went to help, and Doc couldn't not help the bestials, too. So, after the healing was done, we went to help stop the flooding that was already starting."

"Ah, that explains why you motioned for me to follow, but at a distance," Clyde nodded. "I was unsure, since you all started walking."

"That's why Rosa is white of hair... and why they're doing *that*," Harrid grunted.

"So dryads really do feed off...?" Clyde trailed off.

"Blood, semen, and, from what Rosa has said, connecting to nature, though the last one takes far longer. She was very happy about the rain, hence her dress being soaked to the skin."

"Huh. I always thought dryads were just murderous woodfolk. I've had to change that since I've met Rosa."

"From the bits and pieces that I've heard, it was more than just killing," Harrid explained. "The energy they took would get passed to Mother to help keep her able to resist the Darkness longer."

"So those old myths are true?" Clyde asked.

"Dwarves and elves still have stories and songs about it. I'm sure humanity and bestials did, too... before Apoc."

"Because Apoc is the Darkness. I've heard that much from being around the family, and honestly, it explains so much."

"Which means we'll have more confrontations in the future."

"But he's got us, and even more help coming soon," Clyde said with a hint of pride. "We'll help keep him safe."

"Him and his wives," Harrid agreed. "I fear what he'll do if any of his wives are harmed. He's a calm man who loves those around him. There's an old saying: 'When true love dies and ruin comes, a good man goes to war. Darkness will run and blood will become the tide when a good man goes to war. The night will fall and the sun will burn bright when a good man goes to war.'"

"Never heard that... makes me shiver in dread," Clyde said.

"It's an old saying that Sonya found when she was studying about shamans," Harrid agreed. "She's told the others, but none of them have told him. None of them want it to be prophecy."

"Yeah... I can see why."

CHAPTER THIRTY-TWO

The drizzle continued into the next day. Ayla and Sophia went to David's to set up the non-profit, and Doc gave Harrid the day off, promising to stay home. Harrid thanked him as he took the day to go see Ginger.

Doc spent time at home with Fiala, Sonya, Lia, and Rosa. Most of that was used getting Rosa energy so he could do what he wanted to for the dwarves. Outside of those intimate moments, Doc talked with each of them, trading stories of his past for stories of theirs.

When Ayla and Sophia got home, he focused on spending time with them. They'd gotten the new organization set up, transferring funds from his account and David's so they could buy the property and begin work. They would be meeting with a couple of people the next day to see if any of them could handle running the many things Doc had started. He promised to go with them for that, as he wanted to make sure the people he was handing so much to were honest.

* * *

"We're busy today," Doc said once breakfast had ended.

"All of us are," Fiala agreed. "I'm glad it finally stopped raining. That was a terrible storm."

"Hopefully, what we did helped stop the worst of the flooding..."

"Things will be a mess for a few days. The mud needs time to harden again," Lia said.

"You're coming with me and Sophia first, Doc?" Ayla asked.

"Yeah. Meeting the people, then off to the clan."

"Lia and I will be having tea with some of the ladies here while you're all out," Fiala said. "None of the clan this time, though, since you'll be seeing them."

"How's Tarbo's wife?" Doc asked.

"Good. She's really opened up."

"Having her friendly with us will help with Tarbo later," Sophia said. "Depending on how long things take, we might be back for part of the tea, too."

"That would be nice," Fiala smiled.

"Things should be quiet for a little while after today. Until we start building things, it should be good..." Doc said, then paused. "There was something that bothered me at the poker game. The soulsmith's comment led me to believe he's doing something to the bestial women that work at one of the whorehouses in the city."

"And you want to go check," Lia said.

"I kind of do," Doc admitted. "Not today, but maybe in the near future?"

"Just be careful?" Fiala asked.

"I will be. I'm mentioning it now so you all know that I'll be going there and checking things out. It might start rumors."

"We can work around it if people ask," Ayla said. "Your care for bestials is becoming known, so you're just checking in on an establishment that has them to see how they're being treated."

Doc paused, a smile crossing his face. "I... can probably use that when I visit. I'll take things with me, just in case. I'll also bring Rosa. She'll be able to tell me if they're okay."

"Gladly, Voice," Rosa said from beside his seat.

"Where are we meeting them?" Doc asked as he got to his feet.

"David's," Sophia said, "since he's the one who invited them to speak to us. We'll take both carriages. This way, you, Sonya, and Rosa can go on to the clan afterward."

Doc collected kisses from Lia and Fiala, telling them to have fun with their guests. They murmured their well wishes for him back, then did the same to the wives who were going with him.

* * *

Doc didn't ask Rosa to fix the road out to David's— he knew they would have a lot to do with the dwarves later— though he wanted to ask her at a later date to try it.

"So are we final approval or full interviews?" Doc asked as the carriage drew closer to their destination.

"I think we're more the final step. David wouldn't suggest them if they couldn't do the job," Ayla said. "I doubt he would take it wrong if you asked a question or two, though."

"I'll let you and Sophia ask questions," Doc chuckled. "I'm not business-minded. I'll just ask how they feel about working with others. Rosa, tap my leg if the person we're speaking to isn't to be trusted for some reason, okay?"

"Yes, Doc."

"We should be good for making this relatively painless for everyone involved, then."

"Someone to oversee Luck's Providence, someone to handle the business side of Heartwood's Tears once that starts, and someone to help facilitate Lucky Claims," Ayla listed off. "It's a lot of people to hire, honestly. They'll handle filling out the people under them."

"It all comes down to if you trust David to have the right people to pick their helpers," Sophia said.

"Micromanaging is a pain, so yeah, we have to show trust in our partners," Doc said. "Did we mention the bank manager's 'ties' with Goodman to David?"

"We did. David is looking for someone to switch him out with. That position is on par to what we're asking people to do for us today, so his pool of people is low," Ayla said. "Outside of me almost being..." She cleared her throat. "He does the job and hasn't broken trust. Not yet, at least... but the fact he'd consider it was a black mark with David."

"Guess we stay back, then," Doc exhaled slowly. "Life is complicated."

"But good," Sophia smiled brightly.

"Agreed."

* * *

David greeted them in the parlor. "Glad you could make it out today. This will make things easier to manage."

Doc nodded. "I'm not really the manager type. Luckily for me, my wives have found good people to handle what we need."

"Lucky for you," David said with a small laugh.

"I thank her every day."

David got them seated with drinks before he sat. "It is good to see you today, as well, Sonya."

"Thank you," Sonya smiled. "I'm here because he has business with the clan after this."

"Ah, that makes sense. You and the others are welcome over at any time. I'd just ask for a little warning so my staff can have things prepared."

"I'll let the others know."

"We appreciate the offer," Doc agreed with Sonya. "Since I do have business after this, we should get started."

"Did you want them in here one at a time, or all together?"

"Might as well see them together," Doc said. "Not like we're doing a full vetting; we're just doing enough to verify a few things."

David smiled. "Glad to see you trust my judgment."

"Your judgment has proven that you know solid people. The only stumbles were Goodman— who was minor to you with where he'd been and what he'd been doing until I showed up— and perhaps your bank manager here."

"He's good at his job, but Buchon gained a black mark. Ayla told me about his hopes to have her when she worked for Goodman and about his lusting after your dryad. However, we'll be taking a large chunk of my qualified people today and shifting them into our joint ventures."

"You're still sold on my plans?" Doc asked.

"Very. I have no reason to not trust in Luck."

"Excellent. Bring them in. Ayla and Sophia will ask most of the job-related questions. I'm just here for character questions."

"Very well," David motioned to the butler, who left the room.

* * *

Doc was happy with Sonya resting beside him as they were taken into the city. "That went faster than I thought it would."

"They were all honest in their answers," Rosa murmured, leaning against Doc's other side. "They were eager to prove their worth to both you and David. Two of them heard about what you did with the river."

"Partial bestials with family still in the slums..." Doc nodded sadly. "Well, they won't have to be there for much longer... it'll be longer for the others, though."

"You already have them working on changing that," Sonya said, patting his thigh. "Honestly, Doc, you do so much for everyone around you. I knew you were a good man when you saved me, but you just keep proving it again and again."

"I'm just doing what Luck would have of me."

"No, I don't believe that. You could do half or less and still say the same. Your heart yearns to make life better for all you meet. If I weren't already madly in love with you, I'd be falling for you every day."

Doc's lips twitched. "Glad I stopped fighting you."

"So am I."

They lapsed into a comfortable silence, just enjoying the closeness as the carriage carried them closer to the clan hall.

* * *

Arriving at the hall, they were allowed into the elder's chambers without trouble. The three older men waited for them, their curiosity plainly visible.

"Elders," Doc said softly, "I am ready to be announced as your shaman."

"We had been waiting for you to come," Alaric said. "The eldest of the clan will be summoned so we can announce it."

"Please invite all the women who would also like to have a child," Doc said.

The eldest of the three, Elder Itoniv, stared at Doc with a piercing gaze. "Why do you require them?"

"I will explain it when they are assembled, Elder," Doc said simply. "If you want me as the shaman, you'll need to trust me."

"We will manage it," Elder Werner said. "That will take longer, however."

"We'll wait," Doc said. "If you can have us escorted to where this meeting will take place?"

"I will take you," Alaric said, standing up. "Itoniv and Werner will arrange for them to attend."

The other two got to their feet, as well.

Alaric led Doc to what looked like the feasting hall where he'd had his wedding receptions in Deep Gulch. Tables took up most of the room, and the elder guided Doc and his wives to the table that clearly was special, being a rectangle, slightly removed from the others, and facing the round tables.

"We will join you at this table. Please," Alaric said, motioning to the seats. "Do you require a drink?"

Doc and Sonya both asked for something, and Rosa just knelt between the pair after they took their seats.

Once Alaric was back, he took the seat next to Doc. "I do not believe you are looking to add one of the clan to your family, but my fellow elders probably worried about that when you asked for the women to be brought forward."

"I don't want just the single women, but any woman who is interested in having a child," Doc said. "And no, I will not be adding a wife, nor sleeping with them."

Alaric looked thoughtful. "Hmm... I should go verify that they are bringing even the married women, then. Excuse me."

It took nearly an hour, but people finally began to fill the room. Doc watched the crowd gather— it was half elderly dwarves of both sexes. Of the women that were there, half had barely reached their majority while the others were graying matrons.

The three elders entered last, and the guards shut the doors behind them. When the elders sat with Doc, the assembled crowd fell silent.

"Clan, we brought you here for a reason: to meet our shaman. This is Shaman Holyday, the shaman for Oresmelter clan in Deep Gulch, and now, our shaman," Alaric announced. "He asked for half of you to be here, but has not yet told us why."

Doc stood when Alaric sat. "Ladies and gentlemen, it is an honor to become the shaman for your clan. I know some of you are not impressed with me; I can see it plainly. A few of you likely disagree with the ruling I made about women working, as well."

Some of the elders nodded, but most of the young women shook their heads. One of them even got to her feet. "No, Shaman. We love that ruling, and we thank you for it. I now have over thirty men asking to court me."

A ripple of mutters went through the crowd and Doc held up his hand. "Wait. Maybe some of you didn't understand how this has affected the younger members of the clan. Ladies, those of you who are working now or finding work, has this ruling been beneficial to you?"

"It has," the same young female dwarf replied, "for all of us." She motioned to the others who stood up, and they represented a third of the assembled clan members. "We have seen more men approach us since the ruling. Elders and longbeards, every single one of us has had double the interest we've had before. How could we see this as anything but the blessing it is? We are not turning men away to only work. We are going to work and raise a family, just as our ancestors did in ages past."

Her impassioned speech caused more commotion among the older clan members, who seemed roughly split on the idea. Doc let them continue for a minute before he clapped his hands together.

"Before we get too distracted by what was said, thank you. Thank you for letting me become your shaman. I know you all worry about the future of the clan and of dwarfdom in general. I recently realized that I could help alleviate those fears even more, which is why I asked all the women who want to have children to attend."

The room went silent as everyone was focused on him. Some looked on with bright hope, but a few looked at him with suspicion or disdain.

"Just before I left Deep Gulch, I found that I could, with help from my goddess, Lady Luck, make a woman more fertile. It would be nearly certain for the person I helped to conceive a child. I want this to be my first act as your shaman, to help the clan grow stronger."

"How?" Itoniv asked tightly. "Some of these women are married, so you know, Shaman."

"You think I mean to dishonor them?" Doc asked coldly. "I am not a man who sleeps with other's wives, sir."

Itoniv hesitated, clearly taken aback by Doc's flat refusal.

"Shaman," Werner said slowly, "we did not think that was what you had in mind, but we do worry about what it might entail."

"Lady Luck, the Ironbeard clan needs your aid. Children are hard for them to have. Please, show your blessings to them," Doc intoned, letting his magic coat his hands. He sat down, using his left hand to stroke Rosa's hair. "All they need to do is take my hand. If they will come forward and take my hand for a minute each, I will be the conduit for my goddess' blessing. I can also heal any injuries or illnesses you have, though that will take longer and more energy."

The woman who had spoken up hurried forward, clasping his hand before anyone could object. "Please, Shaman? When I choose my husband, I want to make sure I'm ready for children."

When her hand met Doc's, he smiled gently. "Admirable. You're in good health, too. You tweaked your right knee yesterday."

"I did," she breathed out in wonder as warmth suffused her.

"It's healed, and now you'll be able to have children without worry. The downside is that you might have many children if you aren't careful."

"*Many*?" she asked breathlessly with hopeful eyes. "Three?"

"Possibly as many as six," Doc clarified, "with a chance for twins."

She pulled Doc's hand up, kissing his knuckles. "Thank you, Shaman."

Doc lurched forward, as he hadn't expected the yank on his arm. "You're welcome," he chuckled.

She let go of his hand, stepping back and wiping at her face. "I need to go pick one of them. Excuse me. I will not let Luck's blessing be delayed!"

"Stop!" Doc nearly shouted in worry.

The woman paused, looking worried. "Shaman?"

"Don't rush your choice. It will not fade quickly, so you have time to decide. Please take the time to find the right husband for you."

The young dwarf exhaled slowly, then nodded. "Very well, Shaman. I'll go talk with my mother so she can help advise me on my choice."

"That's a good idea. Best of luck, miss."

"Adalni Striker, Shaman."

"May Luck guide you, Adalni."

She bowed her head, then left the room with firm steps. By the time she was gone, another of the younger women was at Doc's table.

CHAPTER THIRTY-THREE

A little over a week flew by for Doc. He didn't have anything actionable to move on, so he spent most of his time at home. He even stepped in during a couple of the teas Fiala hosted, surprising the women that he wanted to sit with them.

Ayla and Sophia got all the paperwork in order for the many things Doc had started. Their new workers were up to speed, and had been handed off what they could. The property just outside of the city was purchased by Luck's Providence the day prior, and Doc planned to visit the area, marking out roads and plots.

Doc and Sonya visited the clan twice more so that the women who hadn't come originally could also be made more fertile. The whole clan was buzzing with excitement— there was a lot of praise going to Doc for his help, and some to the elders for accepting him as shaman.

The suites attached to the stables were finally completed, so Simpson had two of his men begin work on the office inside the Silvered Dreams for Doc while the rest worked on the stables. The elephant bestial guards came out to the manor and thanked Doc for their new homes, which were better than what they'd had previously.

In the bestial section of town, Doc's name was being spoken of with wonder. The river had spared them the flood, but a couple of city buildings downriver had had issues. The fact that he'd walked in the rain to help was well-known among those who lived near the river. A newer rumor of better homes being offered soon was starting up, but many couldn't believe it.

Doc had put off going to the whorehouse over the last week, but that was needling his conscience. With things to do coming up again, he knew he'd have to do something about it soon. Strongarm hadn't raised a fuss over the lack of flooding, but when the new houses started being built and the bestials left, Doc was sure he'd have another fight on his hands.

* * *

"I'm going to head to the Iniquitous Den today," Doc said. "I've already put it off longer than I'd originally intended to."

"Fiala and I are going to the clan to have tea with the elder's wives," Sonya smiled.

"I've got an appointment to speak to the best lawyer in the city," Sophia said. "I want to bounce ideas off him. David uses him, so it should be fine to ask the questions I've had in mind."

"And I'll be going with her," Ayla added. "We've reached a point where we have time to ensure everything lines up neatly."

"You're taking Rosa with you, Doc?" Lia asked, and he nodded. "I'll stay here and talk with the new guards, then. I should make sure they're up to snuff on their new guns."

"We're all going to be busy again," Doc said as he got up. "It was a nice slow period, at least."

"Slow for you," Ayla chuckled.

Doc paused, then nodded. "Sophia, Ayla, tonight, we're going into the city. Me and you two."

"Doc, I didn't mean—"

"No, you didn't, but you raised a good point," Doc cut her off gently. "Tonight, I'm taking you into town on a date. You both deserve it."

"I approve," Sonya smiled.

"Me, too," Fiala nodded.

"Hmm... I'll take a date after them, then," Lia smirked, "as I'll be the only one who hasn't had one."

"Fully approved," Doc said, looking at Lia. "I'll think of something you'll enjoy for that."

"I look forward to it."

Taking a minute to look over his wives, Doc smiled a little guiltily. "Ladies, please remember the rules. If you feel like things are even a little off, talk to me? I've never been in a long relationship before, and ours is even more complicated than most. I never want any of you feeling left out, hurt, or neglected."

"None of us do," Ayla said, looking down. "I was trying to joke that Sophia and I have been working a lot, was all."

"But we *will* take the date," Sophia jumped in. "We haven't felt overworked or neglected, Doc, but we'd all love time out with you. We didn't begrudge Fiala and Sonya for the opera. The fact that they got to enjoy that with you made all of us happy."

"Voice," Rosa said, touching his leg, kneeling beside his chair where he was standing, "you're overthinking. They speak true to you. Your mind is the one thinking things are going wrong, not theirs."

Doc looked down at her, staring into her emerald eyes. His worry and fear ebbed away. "Okay. Sorry," he added, looking at the others. "My greatest fear is that this will all fall apart... but I'll do even better than I have been."

His wives converged on him, holding him, kissing him, and murmuring their love. The moment strengthened his resolve to make sure his wives knew how much he loved them in return.

That thought came up against the fact that he was about to visit a whorehouse and jarred him. "Umm... maybe I should change my plans for today."

Lia laughed when she caught what he was thinking. "No, Doc. We know you're going there to check on the women, not to get your needs cared for. We all take more than ample care of you; we know that. Not one of us thinks otherwise, do we?"

The others laughed along with Lia, agreeing they knew he wasn't going for sex.

"Doc, if you do need to take one of them to a room, we understand," Sonya added. "Even if you want to keep it as a ruse and need to do some things, we're okay with it."

"Just make sure to take the right precautions," Fiala said.

"Don't linger on the act," Sophia added. "That's all I ask."

"I'm with Sophia," Ayla said.

Lia's lips twitched. "He can have Rosa do anything and mostly watch."

"Good plan," Doc told Lia. "I'll do that if it's needed. Rosa would love to do what I need her to."

"Yes!" Rosa agreed eagerly.

"That makes it easier for me," Doc smiled. "Okay, I'll see you all later."

Harrid was glad the family had come to an agreement— he feared that moments like these would hurt them. He was the first one out of the room, leading Doc and Rosa toward the front door.

* * *

The weather had cleared up over the last week. The massive storm was gone with only a few cloudy days, but now, it was back to sunny and hot. The carriage at least provided shade, but Doc wished he was in one of his favorite book series where the MC had made air-conditioned cars.

Then again, that poor bastard had wives die on him, Doc thought. *I'll deal with the unpleasantness as long as my wives stay healthy.*

"It's odd, Doc," Rosa said softly from beside him. "There are times you often think of movies or books and compare them to our lives here. I know how much you love what we have, so I'm confused when those moments happen."

"Grass is always greener," Doc shrugged. "You caught my last thought?"

"Yes, about the man who could heal and shape things. He's nebulous in your thoughts... more a rough outline of a man than a real person."

"His face is whatever face I give him because he's a book character, and it changes over time. I'm not surprised he's a bit blurry... but yeah, I loved that series. Reminds me a lot of our life, because of the large family."

"You can heal as he could," Rosa said slowly, "but you always think of him as a crafter. You wish you could make things like he did."

"Especially at times like today, when it's hot. Air-conditioning would be great right now." He pulled out his handkerchief and dabbed his brow where sweat had formed.

Rosa shifted away from him.

"Nope," Doc said, pulling her right back to his side. "I prefer you here. Even when it's uncomfortably warm, you being beside me makes me happy."

Rosa beamed as she read his mind. "I would like all of that, Voice, but all I require is you."

"Hard to surprise you because you read my mind, Weed. I want to do something for you too, though. You *are* one of my wives, even if the world doesn't know it."

"I would take the ribbons or jewelry. They would mark me as yours, which makes me even happier."

"I'll work on it, then, Rosa," Doc murmured, kissing her gently. When he leaned back again, he stared into her eyes. "I love the sex, don't get me wrong, but I want you to have other affection, too."

Rosa's eyes glowed lightly. "I will accept anything or everything you wish, Voice. Just being here beside you, constantly able to help, is all I wish for. Well... and to be filled by you."

Doc chuckled at her honesty. He kissed her again— gently, tenderly, letting all of his love for her fill his thoughts.

Rosa moaned into the kiss, allowing his love to flood her mind. This is what she craved, being the center of his thoughts. She would never tell him how she worked to be the best of his women. The weed would tower over the flowers and be loved for it.

Doc could never fully tell Rosa how much she meant to him.

She'd given her life to him, literally begging him to collar her. Then, she gave everything she had, again and again, to make his life easier, to help him with his goal. His love for her was equal to the others, and if he was honest with himself, he felt that he leaned on her even more than the others, even more than Ayla and Sophia who strove every day to help. When the carriage slowed, Doc finally broke the kiss.

"Anything you need," Rosa murmured. "I will never fail you, Doc. I want to help you, all on my own, not because Mother wants me to. I will cling to life with every ounce of strength I have because my death would hurt you, but even then, I would give my life for yours."

Doc touched her cheek gently. "I know, which is why I will guard you as zealously as I can."

Rosa's eyes closed and she soaked in his love. Life was as close to perfect as it could be for her, and she reveled in it.

CHAPTER THIRTY-FOUR

The Iniquitous Den looked more like a small apartment complex than a whorehouse. The biggest difference was that there were no windows on the first floor. The brick building climbed four stories tall; the second story had odd wide but narrow windows which Doc wondered about, but floors three and four had normal windows spaced out far enough that Doc figured it was one per room.

Harrid followed Doc and Rosa up the three wide stairs from the street to the awning that shaded the front door. The large door had a heart with the initials "ID" set firmly in the middle. It was the only sign that this was the place Doc intended to go.

Entering the establishment, Doc nodded slowly, as the lobby held more signs of it being upscale. An ornate silver chandelier hung in the room, giving light to the rich white oak furniture. A young woman sat behind a counter, wearing a professional smile when she saw them enter. Curiosity filled her gaze while she waited for Doc to approach.

"Can I help you, sir?" the receptionist asked as she brushed her long black hair behind her back.

"Perhaps," Doc said. "I've heard this is a place for some... unusual entertainment."

"We excel in things most others don't wish to know about," the receptionist replied. "We don't normally allow for groups, though." Her gaze went to Rosa and Harrid before returning to Doc.

"Ah, my pet has to be beside me, and my bodyguard is, of course, just here to do his job."

"We have a room for guards to relax while they wait for their employers," the woman smiled. "Unless you are paying for him to enjoy the entertainment?"

Doc glanced back at Harrid, who shook his head. "He'll use the provided room."

She motioned to her right where a door was set in the middle of the side wall. "Through there is the lounge. The staff will help see to his food and drink needs."

Harrid nodded, staying silent as he headed for the door.

When Harrid was out of the room, Doc turned back to the receptionist. "Now, what about me and my pet?"

"We've never had a mage bring his dryad along," the receptionist said slowly. "I'd have to charge you more because of it. She isn't allowed to harm the staff, either."

"She won't hurt them. I don't allow her to," Doc said.

"We offer a simple hourly rate model, depending on how many of the girls you want to engage. Do you plan to spend time with two or more at the same time?"

"Not at the same time," Doc smiled. "Not this time, at least. I'd rather sample each of them a little to see if any pique my interest."

"Ah, we do allow that, but many find that just one or two is all they need. How long are you planning on staying with us?"

"A couple of hours, maybe. Perhaps longer."

"We'll have to charge you the base hourly rate, unless you'd like to join our exclusive club?"

"Can you explain what that entails?"

"Our hourly rate for any non-member is fifty dollars. Our members pay a once-yearly fee of only ten thousand dollars. I know it sounds high, but we do not put limits on how often you visit or how many of the staff you engage at a time. We are also more flexible about any special needs you may have. What most of our members love is being able to reserve a specific staff member for a set day and time, helping them get what they need during their busy schedules."

Doc's lips pursed as he debated if he really needed to become a member or not.

"Our members also have a private lounge and can use the back entrance so they can come and go without being seen on the street," she added in a whisper as if that might help him decide. "Some find that bit of secrecy helps them."

"Would I need to pay extra as a member for my pet to be with me?"

Smile blooming brighter, she shook her head. "No, sir. As I said, members have special needs that we can be flexible with."

It was a big expenditure, but he had the money to spare, and it would help ease any restrictions he might encounter otherwise. Doc pulled out his checkbook. "You'll take a check?"

"We will, indeed," the receptionist beamed. "I'll also need you to fill out the paperwork"

Doc slowed as he drew his pen out from his suit pocket. "Paperwork?"

"Yes, sir. It's just your name, the fact that you are signing up for membership to the Den's club, and your signature. We seal it and give you a membership number. The number is so you can access the private lounge and entrance if you lose your token."

Doc nodded slowly— it wasn't like he was afraid that the news of his visiting the business would get out. He signed the paperwork and the check. The moment he did, the receptionist unlocked a small box, then pulled out a small golden heart with "ID" engraved on one side and "42" on the other. He smirked at the number as he pocketed the token. It was solid gold and weighed at least three ounces.

"There you go, Mr. Holyday. The door to your right is the normal lounge. The second door to the private lounge is on the far side of that room. There is also a separate bodyguard's room off the private lounge."

"Thank you, Miss...?"

"Pearl, sir. Just call me Pearl."

"Thank you, Pearl," Doc smiled. "Have a good day."

"You, as well, sir."

Rosa followed him silently, her head bowed while she thought over what she was learning already.

Entering the lounge, Doc slowed. The wide and narrow windows he'd seen outside that he'd thought were on the second floor turned out to be ceiling-level windows in the lounge. The light from them illuminated the room, with one of the three silver chandeliers lit to make up the difference. The same white oak was used for the furnishings in the lounge. One wall had a bar with a smiling cat bestial behind it. Three other bestial women sat around other parts of the room, with one of them speaking quietly with an older gentleman in a corner.

The two unoccupied bestial women gave Doc bright smiles, but didn't go to him. They watched Doc with interest, and one of them shivered when she saw Rosa trailing him. Doc went to the bartender to get a drink first. The woman behind the bar wore a slinky, short, black dress that clung to her figure. "Your best cognac, please."

"Of course, sir," the bartender purred at him. When she turned around to get his drink, Doc was given a view of the wide slit in the back of her dress that allowed her gently flicking tail to move freely. When she turned back around, she gave him a wink. "One cognac for a discerning gentleman."

"Thank you." Doc stayed at the bar for a moment. He placed a ten-dollar coin on it as he spoke, "I'd be grateful if you'd explain what I should know."

Smile brightening, the bartender made the coin vanish as she leaned against the bar. "Depends. Are you a member?"

Doc flashed her the golden heart token he had. "I am."

Her smile grew even wider. "Well, then, sir, the only thing you need to know is that all the women who aren't already with another are free to you. They will not approach you; this way, you don't feel pressured. If you decide to do more than just talk, let your chosen one know and she'll take you up to her room."

"If I just want to talk?" Doc asked, sipping the cognac she'd given him.

"You may do that here, or even in her room," the bartender winked. "We know that a few prefer privacy for some conversations."

"Would any of them balk at my pet being brought along?" Doc asked casually.

The bartender gave Rosa a long look, her eyebrows going up. "A dryad?"

"Mine," Doc said. Rosa lifted her chin more, showing the collar off.

"None of those employed here will turn you away," the bartender said, but her eyes flickered to one of the women in the room briefly. "Members, even more so, are known for their special needs."

Doc nodded, catching sight of a single stud earring in the bartender's ear— it was a soul stone mounted in silver. He wondered about it, but didn't want to push on it, not right now.

"Is the private lounge like this?" Doc asked.

"It's smaller, more intimate, but it has a bar and some of the staff waiting. The women there are more... open."

"Ah. So it would be better to speak with them if I want my pet to join?"

The bartender hesitated, then nodded. "Probably, sir. I can ask the private staff when I serve the bar tomorrow. I normally tend that bar in the evenings, but was moved here this morning."

"A reason to visit again in the evenings," Doc gave her a warm smile.

"I'm not normally on the menu," the bartender cautioned him.

"A friendly face and good conversation is all I meant. I don't chase or press for companionship. If someone isn't interested, it's better to walk away."

She didn't reply, but there was briefly a hint of gratitude in her eyes.

Doc looked back over the room, letting him see one staff member look away from him. He made a note that she was sitting in the same direction where the bartender had looked earlier. The other woman in the room, though, gave him a bright smile and wink.

"Thank you." Picking his drink up, he headed for the woman who'd winked at him.

The fox bestial straightened. Her green dress was just as slinky, short, and tight as the bartender's. The clothing accented each woman's attributes, making it easy to see their curves. Her orange-red furred ears matched her hair and tail. Add in her red irises and vertical pupils, and she was a lot of fox.

"Excuse me, miss, is this seat taken?" Doc asked.

"Call me Ruby, and no, sir, but I hope you take it."

"You can call me Doc. This is my pet, Weed."

Ruby looked at Rosa for a moment. "Never seen a dryad before. I saw the collar. Are you a mage, sir?"

"Not a mage," Doc chuckled, "but I caught her, and I'm not about to sell her now."

"Ohhh. I hear dryad hunting is dangerous," Ruby murmured, sitting forward to allow a better view of her cleavage. "Is she tame?"

"Entirely. My word is her command. Weed, tell her."

"Doc's word is my law. His happiness is my only wish," Rosa said obediently.

"Hmm... You have to keep her with you, don't you?"

"Yes, but I also wanted her here for other reasons," Doc smiled at Ruby. "Tell me, how did a fox bestial of your beauty end up here?"

Ruby giggled. "No need for flattery, sir. The honest truth is that I auditioned for the job and was thrilled to have it. The madam doesn't take just anyone on. We have to be open and willing to do many things." Her eyes went back to Rosa. "*Many* things."

"Oh? Would that include trying a woodfolk?" Doc asked quietly.

"If that's what you want... sir?" Ruby licked her lips hopefully.

"Shall we go upstairs?" Doc asked, looking toward the spiraling staircase in one corner of the room.

"Yes." Ruby stood and extended her hand to him. "If you'll come with me, sir?"

Doc got to his feet, giving her his hand. "Lead us, Ruby. Weed, attend."

"As you wish, Master," Rosa said huskily, her eyes glowing lightly.

CHAPTER THIRTY-FIVE

They were taken to what Doc had thought was the third floor from outside, but was really the second floor. Doorways lined the hall, each bearing a nameplate. Doc's lips pursed when he realized all of the names were gems.

Not their real names, then. That makes sense if the madam is trying to keep them safe, Doc thought. *Unless the madam here is as lucky as Lia was in always getting flower names...?*

Ruby paused next to her door, giving him a wink before opening it. "Here we are, sir. Please come in and make yourself comfortable."

Doc followed her in. Her room was a suite, with a front room and a closed door that probably led to a bedroom. The curtains were open, allowing light in and illuminating a room of rich furniture and silver lanterns attached to the walls.

"Cozy place," Doc said as he took a seat in a padded chair, Rosa kneeling beside him.

"Thank you. The madam has given us many luxuries so that we may entertain our guests in a suitable environment. Would you mind if I changed into something more... comfortable?"

"I doubt that dress is uncomfortable," Doc chuckled, "but go ahead. Let's see what you have in mind."

"I'll be right back," Ruby smiled brightly.

When she slipped into her bedroom, Doc looked down at Rosa. "Go ahead."

"She really does want to try a dryad," Rosa smiled. "As for her, the staff is happy enough to endure the things they have to. It means they get the luxury you see here, and many of them go a day or more without seeing a customer."

"The bartender?"

"She was hired to just serve the bar, but she was talked into doing more for select clientele. Steward had her the other night. She very much dislikes him, but her new contract doesn't give her the choice to decline if a member asks. Her thoughts on what happened are unclear, but she's afraid of another man like him asking for her."

"Got it. You'll be having some fun, but I'll mostly be watching."

Rosa's eyes began to glow. "Yes, Voice."

"I'll be trying to steer her thoughts during your acts, so keep focused on her."

"As you require," Rosa murmured, nuzzling his leg.

The bedroom door clicked open, getting Doc's attention. Ruby stood against the frame in a red silk negligee. It covered all of the important parts, but it also showed a lot of skin. With her hair and eyes also being red, the new outfit really helped sell her name.

"That's quite an entrance," Doc murmured. "You might call it flattery, but I still say you're beautiful."

Ruby's smile grew as she stepped away from the door. "A gentleman like you saying that always makes me happy. Did you still want to... talk?"

"I think tongues and lips are going to be involved quite a bit," Doc chuckled. "You did want to know what a dryad could do, didn't you?"

Ruby's eyes went to Rosa, whose eyes were still glowing. "Oh...! Her eyes... how beautiful."

"Like emeralds that have caught the sun," Doc agreed. "They do that when she gets excited. She loves making women cry out in pleasure. I should warn you: her tongue will ruin you for other women."

Ruby's eyes gleamed with excitement. "We'll have to see about that. But what of you, sir? Do you not wish to," she let a hand trail up her curves until she was squeezing one breast lightly, "sample me yourself?"

"I'd like to watch. I'm sure it's far from the strangest request you've had."

Ruby's eyelid twitched as something clearly came to mind, but she gave Doc a warm smile. "Far from it. I've enjoyed the few times I've put on a show for a gentleman, though that's normally just me or another of the girls here."

"I'm glad I'm not making you uncomfortable," Doc said honestly. "If someone involved isn't enjoying it, then it's just wrong."

Ruby was clearly surprised at his words, but also quite pleased. She started toward him. "That's a wonderful thing to hear, sir. Are you sure I can't help make you more comfortable, at least?"

Doc held up a hand to stop her. "Maybe in a bit. Why don't you recline on that divan? I'll send my pet over to you."

Ruby licked her lips before walking away from him, her bushy red tail swaying side-to-side. Looking back over her shoulder, she caught him watching it. Ruby gave him a wink and lifted her tail so he could see her panty-clad ass better.

"I have a feeling you prefer having a man behind you the most," Doc murmured as he lifted his gaze to hers. "More comfortable with your tail, I'd bet."

"Y-yes," Ruby whispered, shocked that he knew that. "Most people don't consider how our tails can cause... discomfort."

"Weed, you're on the bottom. She'll ride your face," Doc said. "Ruby, let her recline. This way, you can face me. I want to watch your face as she shows you what dryads can really do."

There was a momentary flicker of worry, but it was erased by lust. "Wonderful. It might be even better if you gave me a peek in return, sir."

She's persistent, Doc chuckled internally. *Reminds me of Fiala that first day I met her.* Doc put on a thoughtful expression before he stood up. "Maybe a little more comfort right now, but not what you're truly hoping for."

Rosa lay on the divan, eager for what was to come. She knew it was exciting for Ruby, and that Doc would reward her with all he had later. Ruby slipped her silk panties free, flipping them at Doc as she positioned herself above the dryad.

"If you want a scent of how excited I am before she even starts..." Ruby said huskily, staring at Doc as she lowered her damp sex to Rosa's waiting mouth.

Doc had slipped his jacket off and removed his tie before he caught the underwear. Taking a seat, he draped the silk over his shoulder as he watched the pair. "Slowly, Weed, slowly. Let her know your full range."

Rosa let out a muffled reply as she began to please the fox bestial above her. Doc had already gotten Ruby to show her more than he'd want to know about, so Rosa filed those thoughts away for after.

Ruby's eyelids twitched when Rosa licked her. The dryad was hitting all the right spots after a few seconds. She locked eyes with Doc as she moaned and ground her sex against Rosa's mouth. "Goodness... she's... mhmm...! Just like that!"

Doc chuckled and leaned back in his seat, crossing his legs as he watched the bestial with Rosa. He had a growing problem, but he had plans for how to deal with that. He waited until he saw Ruby's eyes go wide before asking, "Push into you with her tongue, did she?"

"Oh...yes...! So good!" Ruby moaned, her eyes closing as she lost herself to the pleasure. No one, man nor woman, had ever given her so much ecstasy.

"Just wait. You still have a bit more to learn about dryads," Doc said softly. "How do you deal with minor pains?"

Ruby's brain was buzzing with pleasure, but the question almost pulled her from it. She'd been asked about pain before with another member and the memories haunted her. Before she could say anything, she gasped, her eyes shooting open as Rosa's tongue went deeper.

"There she goes," Doc murmured. "I'd guess you have about half of what she can give."

"Half...?" The word was a trailed-off question as she bucked against Rosa's face. "More...! Give me more!"

"She will in a moment," Doc said softly. "Would you give a tiny bit back to her?"

"Yes, anything! Just more!" Ruby moaned out, feeling Rosa's tongue doing things she'd never felt before.

"She'll take a tiny amount of blood, but the wounds will heal before we leave. Are you sure you're okay with that?"

"Yes!" Ruby cried as Rosa pushed her tongue farther in.

"Weed, a tiny sip only. We don't want to harm her," Doc said.

Ruby didn't even react to the tendril pushing into her hips where Rosa held the bestial down to her mouth. She was dimly aware of it, but it didn't matter compared to the pleasure. If this is what Doc had meant by pain, she'd gladly endure it a dozen times over for what she was receiving.

"Now, Weed. Give her everything now," Doc growled.

Rosa did as commanded. Ruby's mouth fell open and her eyes rolled back as she rode the swirling tongue inside of her. She would never have thought she'd feel what she did in that moment. After a minute, Ruby shuddered violently as she came, then again and again, and kept orgasming until she went limp.

"Enough, Weed," Doc chuckled as he crossed to help ease Ruby off Rosa. "I've got her."

Rosa's eyes blazed when she met Doc's eyes. "Please, Voice..." she whimpered, her legs scissoring open and closed.

Doc put Ruby in the chair he'd been in. With her settled, he triggered *healing hands* to check her. Frowning when his magic told him what was wrong, he exhaled a rough breath. She'd been cut into repeatedly, then healed, but not the way Doc would manage it. What was more, she held small chunks of soul stone where she'd been cut before. There were tiny fragments— a quarter the size of a pea— deep inside her.

Rosa was at his side in an instant, the sex forgotten. "The stones are active... they are tied to her."

"What does that mean?" Doc asked.

"A mage once did it to a sister of mine," Rosa whispered in horror. "With the right control stone, he could move her like a puppet. Her arms and legs are embedded, so she would not be able to fight back... which goes with her thoughts of how Steward has hurt her. When you asked about pain, there was a brief memory of him fucking her with a bloody knife in hand."

"We can remove them, can't we?" Doc asked.

"Only if you want to cripple her," Rosa sniffled. "It would pull parts of her soul out if you did."

Doc knelt beside the unaware bestial, anger and sadness warring in him. "That's why he wanted my stones."

"These are old... months old, at least."

Doc exhaled slowly, recalling giving Steward the stones the other day. "But he has more now. He can do this again."

Rosa watched him with worry. "He can. You'd need to touch each of them to see who has or hasn't been implanted similarly."

Doc's hands clenched as he considered his options. After a moment, he shook his head; he needed to talk to his wives. The city had just gotten much uglier, and he would move to fix what he could, though it might not be as fast as he wanted.

"Voice," Rosa said softly, "all of us will be with you, no matter which of those options you take. For today, we need to leave without letting it be known that you know."

Doc exhaled slowly. "Right now, she's doing what she wants, right?"

"Yes. She wants to have you and me. That is not being forced on her," Rosa assured him.

"Hmm..." Ruby exhaled a languid sigh of happiness. "Dryads are the best..."

"They really are," Doc agreed. "Are you okay?"

One red eye opened to meet his, a happy smile filling Ruby's face.

"Oh, yes. I'd love to do more. I'd be happy to return the favor as you get behind me."

"Today, I was going to fill my dryad. She needs the cum to stay healthy," Doc said.

Ruby sat up, leaning in toward him. "If that's the case, what if I return the favor to her, and you can have her mouth?"

That would be for the best if I'm not going to actually fuck her, Doc thought. He smiled at Ruby. "Perfect."

CHAPTER THIRTY-SIX

Doc came downstairs with Rosa beside him; Ruby was asleep in her bed. The time with her had been more convoluted than Doc thought it would be, but he'd done that to himself by not having sex with her. He'd only played with Rosa while she played with Ruby. By the very end of it, Rosa pushed Ruby hard enough that she passed out again.

The lounge had two customers chatting with staff members. One of them was the man who'd been in the lounge when Doc had gone upstairs. The other was, surprisingly to Doc, Sheriff Franklin Donadin. The sheriff was chatting up not a bestial, but an elf. Doc's steps slowed when he reached the ground floor; he hadn't expected an elf to be part of the staff.

Franklin glanced up, his eyes going a little wide to see Doc there. He said something to the elf before he stood up, advancing on Doc. "Holyday, didn't expect you to be a guest here."

Doc chuckled. "I could say the same, Sheriff."

"I stop in once a week to... make sure business is good," Franklin said slowly.

"Ah, a perk, no doubt," Doc said knowingly, nodding as if he understood. His gaze went to the blond elf Franklin had been talking with. "Didn't know the establishment had an elf."

Franklin looked back at the woman before chuckling. "Her name is Citrine. She's... docile."

Doc's eye twitched, but he was impassive when Franklin turned back to him. "Maybe I'll make her acquaintance next time."

"She's fun if you get her ears," Franklin chuckled. "Not sure you've ever been with an elf, but trust me on that."

"I'll keep it in mind. I won't interrupt your time with her."

"We should talk again in the near future."

"I'll make a point of it, Sheriff," Doc said, shaking the man's hand. "Have a good day."

"Oh, I will," Franklin laughed as he went back to Citrine.

Doc walked away with Rosa. She managed to walk evenly even as she felt Franklin's eyes raking over her back. She caught the look of shock on Citrine's face before it went to sorrow and anger, then smoothed over.

Pearl gave him a bright smile when he came out of the lounge. "If you give us a moment, we'll tell your guard and driver that you're ready."

"Ah, another question. Is my driver able to relax, as well?" Doc asked, as that hadn't been mentioned before.

"There's a yard for them where shade and refreshments are offered. They don't come inside like the guards."

"Good to know. I won't feel bad for him, then."

"We hope to see you again, Mr. Holyday," Pearl beamed.

"I do believe I'll be back, but I'll likely be coming in through the back."

"Understandable. We understand the need for discretion. If you want, we can send your driver and guard around back."

"I came in through the front today, so I might as well leave the same way."

"Very well, sir. Please have a good day. Your carriage should be arriving in just a moment."

The side door opened and Harrid came out, his face impassive. "Ready to go, sir?"

"Yes. Lead me out."

Harrid nodded brusquely, opening the door for Doc to leave.

Pearl watched Doc go, her lips pursed in thought. The madam had been informed of the new member when he'd paid, and she'd seemed very interested in him. Pearl wouldn't put it past her to say hello to him when he next visited.

* * *

Clyde was coming around the building when Doc stepped outside. He'd been given good food and drink while he waited, so he was happy with the day. He *was* curious about why a man with five wives was visiting a whorehouse, but he wasn't about to ask.

"Did you learn what you wanted to?" Harrid murmured.

"More than I feared," Doc replied a bit tightly. "I'll explain it later, but I'll be coming back to see the other women to find out how pervasive the problem is. As to who, *that* I already know."

"Home?" Harrid asked.

"No, to the new property. We can begin work there for a few hours. I need to do something, even if that's just watching Rosa change the ground, but take us to the opera house first, please. I have a date tonight, even with what I know."

Clyde came to a stop in front of the stairs, nodding to the group. Their expressions told him that something was wrong, and he waffled on the idea of asking. Doc had helped him enough that he felt like he should do more, but he wasn't sure if he should even offer.

When Harrid climbed up beside him, Clyde nodded. "He looked... grim. Odd for a man coming out of the Den."

Harrid grunted. "He didn't go in for what most people go in for. If you really want to poke into that, you need to talk to him about it. He'll be coming back a few more times, at least."

Clyde stayed quiet for a few minutes as he paid attention to the road. "I thought the women there were clean and in good health."

"Far as I know, they are. Clyde… if you want to know, you need to talk to him, but knowing means buying into something bigger than you probably think."

"Because he's a Voice to Lady Luck?" Clyde asked.

"To start with."

Silence lapsed for a while again.

"He wants to go to the opera house first, then to the new property," Harrid coughed. "Forgot to say. Sorry."

"We're heading that way as it is, so it's fine," Clyde replied. "You know the full truth?"

"I'm his bodyguard. I have to if I'm going to do my job."

"I'm contracted with him, but that's different. I know he gave me my life back by fixing my leg. I could never explain the relief of the pain being gone. I've seen him time and again help people who he has no need or reason to help, too. The river, for instance…" Clyde trailed off, clearly thinking. "Elves, dwarves, or bestials, he really doesn't care about their heritage… can't think of a man more altruistic than him."

"Doubt another will ever be like he is," Harrid grunted.

The badger bestial nodded slowly. "I'll be asking. If I can help him in some way to make life better for others, it'd be selfish of me to do nothing."

"The funny part is he doesn't mind if you're selfish," Harrid snorted. "He understands the idea that people are out for themselves first. He'll never say a word against it, even as he gives and gives to others."

"Seeing him push the way he does for people… it feels bad to do nothing."

"I know."

"He's going to change the city, or maybe even the territory if he can keep doing what he has."

"The world," Harrid said softly. "He'll change the world, even if that means he has to do it one city at a time."

Clyde fell silent again as he thought about that. He hadn't really understood the scope of what Doc wanted. Hearing it from Harrid had him consider what he could do to help that lofty goal.

* * *

Doc stood beside Rosa as she worked on the new property. She was only making solid roads, laid out in a uniform grid. It would be easier for Simpson to get the supplies in that way, and also clearly marked out each spot for a home to be built.

"Doc, can we talk?"

"Always, Clyde. What's on your mind?"

Setting the brake, the bestial got down from the carriage. "I wanted to thank you."

"You're welcome?"

"Didn't mean me, specifically," Clyde said. "Wanted to thank you for what you're doing."

Doc looked at the property that Rosa was working on. "You're welcome," he said softly. "It's a step in the right direction. I'm going to make some enemies doing it, but I'll deal with them when I have to."

"You also helped in the city with the flooding."

"It should've been done before I even got here," Doc grimaced. "Stupid and shortsighted to not do anything about it."

"That was after you helped the half-elves, too... You just keep giving to others. I wanted to thank you for doing what you do."

"It's my task, but I want to do it beyond that, too."

"I'm just a driver," Clyde said. "I'm not a lot of help, but—"

"No," Doc cut the badger bestial off. Turning to Clyde, Doc shook his head. "You arranged for the other carriage, and the drivers and shotgun men for it. It was you who helped me find the right people for the manor guard. You've done a lot to help, Clyde. Thank *you*."

Clyde blinked at him for a second, taken aback by Doc's clear appreciation. "Oh... umm. You're welcome." A moment of silence fell between them until Clyde tried again, "I was going to ask... can I help more?"

"Keep my wives safe when you take them out," Doc said softly. "That's a big worry for me. If I can think of anything else you can do, or if you think of something, I'm here. Bring it to me, Harrid, or one of my wives."

"Okay. I will." Clyde nodded. He wanted to try expressing it more, but thought it best to stop there for now.

"Doc, Clyde wants to be a part of the core," Rosa said, having been watching the driver from the corner of her eye. "He doesn't know how to ask to be brought in on the full story."

Clyde jerked, his eyes widening as he stared at Rosa.

Doc chuckled. "You just scared him, Weed."

"She...! H-how...?" Clyde stammered.

"Dryads have a limited telepathic ability," Doc said. "You want in on one of our bigger secrets? There's a reason she's with me almost all the time."

"She's saved his life by doing what she does," Harrid added from the shade beside the carriage. "If you ask her to stop, she will."

Clyde's mind raced through all the things he never wanted anyone to know. "Can you read *all* my thoughts?"

"Just what's on the surface," Rosa murmured. "None of that matters to Doc. Most of what you fear isn't a concern for any of us, though the way some of the bank staff treats the non-human wagon teams is a concern that David should be told."

Clyde shifted in place, clearly unnerved.

"Rosa, stop," Doc said softly. "Clyde, I'm sorry."

Exhaling a held breath, Clyde swallowed. "It's okay. Just give me a minute."

Rosa went back to focusing on her task.

"That was a lot to take in..." he said after a moment. "Rosa, please don't do that often?"

"I will do it as rarely as I do with Harrid."

"We have to trust her on that. There's no way of knowing if she is or not," Harrid said.

"Okay," Clyde nodded.

"What was that about the wagon teams?" Doc asked. "If you want to tell me, that is, Clyde?"

"Same old song and dance," Clyde shrugged. "Most of the teams are bestial. We do the work cheaper than a human would, yet even then, some in the bank look down on us, even though it's *our* lives guarding the money. Outright blatant bigotry isn't usual, but small things can add up. Most leads are human, though, much like the foremen used for mines."

"Got it," Doc sighed. "I can pass it along to David."

"Won't change anything for the better. The people who discriminate will think one of the workers talked. The only thing to do would be to change who's in charge of the teams."

Doc thought about someone he knew that might work. "Did you know Rondle?"

"He was part of my team for a few months before the shooting."

"Would he be able to manage it correctly?"

"If he's the same as he was, yes."

"I think I have a plan. It'll change things up more than I expected, and I'll have to ask for permission from a friend first," Doc said. "I don't want her to be unhappy."

Rosa's lips ticked up as she looked at Doc. "Heather would if you asked."

"I'll send a letter to her when I get Posy's sent, which I still need to do."

"Should we head home, then?" Harrid asked, having seen Rosa's hair color dull.

Doc noticed that same thing. "Yeah. That's enough for today, Weed."

"As you command, Voice," Rosa murmured with a smile.

"Clyde, welcome to the start of what we keep from others," Doc said. "Give it some time and, if you still want in, I'll tell you more."

"Yes, sir," Clyde said, moving to get back onto the carriage.

CHAPTER THIRTY-SEVEN

Doc set aside the letters to Nicole, Heather, and Posy. A smile came to him when he thought about Posy's exhilaration to get one from him. He could easily imagine her bouncing up and down, waving the letter as she excitedly told Daf that she'd gotten it. It'd been a month since he'd left, and it'd be at least a week before she got the letter, but he wondered how she was doing. He was sure she'd write him back, and he looked forward to it.

His letter to Heather covered a few things, like his request to have her come up and put on a show or two at the new opera hall. It also touched on the fact that he was thinking of asking David to bring Rondle back to deal with bank wagon problems. Along with that, he asked how she'd feel about moving to Furden with Peabody so he could take on the bank. If she didn't want to leave, he'd only ask David to bring Rondle back.

Nicole's letter was more straightforward than the other two: he just asked how she was doing as mayor, and if she needed anything from him. He caught her up on what they'd been doing from a business standpoint, as well. He smiled when he thought about how she was probably really happy to not have to manage everything that he'd set up in Furden.

"Husband, it's time for lunch," Lia said, coming into the office. "Did you get them all written?"

"All done," Doc nodded as he sealed the envelopes. "I'll take them down to post tomorrow."

"Can you take mine with you?" Lia asked. "I sent a special dispatch to Jesamin so she knows the elves are coming. I wanted to tell her more, so I have a letter for both her and Cassia. Sonya also has a letter for her parents, and Sophia has one for her mother."

"I'll take them all," Doc smiled and stood up. "There's a lot to discuss on my end, and I'm sure Ayla and Sophia have stuff, too."

"Undoubtedly," Lia murmured as Doc crossed the room to her. "Before we go, I want a kiss."

Doc slipped his arms around her waist, drawing her closer. "As my beautiful wife desires."

Lia kissed him passionately, pressing into him and pushing him against the wall. Her leg hitched up against his side as she forced her tongue into his mouth demandingly. She reveled in the fact that Doc never fought her need to lead these moments.

Doc accepted her love as she needed. He wasn't opposed to being the one to submit to his lover if that's what brought her the most joy. The fact that his wives were so different from each other, with their different levels of wants and needs, brought him untold joy in turn.

Lia broke the kiss suddenly, stepping back from him. "Thank you, Doc."

Letting out a shuddering breath, Doc grinned. "Anytime."

Lia stepped forward again, but only took his hand. "Come on. It really is time for food."

"I'm right behind you."

"I enjoy you there sometimes," Lia smirked over her shoulder.

Doc laughed as he trailed her toward the dining room, his heart light.

Everyone was already gathered at the table. Doc didn't go to sit right away; instead, he went around the table, kissing each of his wives. Finally taking his seat, he gave them all a bright smile. "Should we wait until after we eat?"

"Probably for the best," Fiala said. "I know that Charles was working on this for hours."

"Okay," Doc agreed as the food was brought into the room.

* * *

With the meal done and the table cleared, the family retired to the parlor to discuss their days in comfort. Harrid took the chair by the door; this way, he could leave if needed. Doc found himself book-ended by Ayla and Sophia. Lia, Fiala, and Sonya had the couch across from them, and Rosa leaned against Fiala's legs.

"I'll start," Doc said softly. "I spent too much money to become a member of the Iniquitous Den..."

His wives were appalled at what he told them, and Lia was shocked to hear an elf was working in the whorehouse. None of them were really surprised to hear that the sheriff was getting free service there.

"The soulsmith needs to be dealt with," Lia said tightly. "He's taking away their free will."

"Agreed, but the problem is that if I move too early, he'll know and will be a clear enemy," Doc sighed. "I can't exactly remove the soul stones."

"It would rip part of their soul out if he did," Rosa explained. "They would be... not themselves. Lesser."

"Which gives only one option in the long run: we have to remove him and whatever he controls them with," Fiala said. "I take it that removing the item he uses to control them wouldn't work because he'd just make a new one?"

"Very likely," Lia nodded.

"We need to see how many of the women have been... implanted." Ayla shivered at the thought of what'd happened to them. She knew Goodman would've done similar to her if he'd had the chance.

"And if the madam knows..." Sophia added. "If she knows and does nothing..."

"Then she gets added to the list," Doc said tightly. "If she doesn't know, then I'll have to see about how to bring her in without tipping too much of what I can do."

"This is going to be a long-term project, sadly," Sonya said. "That means more of them will be hurt before we can implement a solution. We have to accept that."

Doc grimaced, then nodded. "Yes, but once he's been handled, they'll be free of control again. No one else but us would know that they're implanted."

The others agreed to the idea of a slow move to find out how many of the women there had been violated.

"I'm going to have to get closer to Steward, too," Doc said. "It'll be the only way to get him to tell me how he does what he's doing. That'll be hard to do, but I'll walk that path to help those women."

"It explains why he wants the soul stones so badly," Sonya said. "Be careful about giving him more."

"I'll be very careful. That's everything I had."

"Clyde?" Harrid reminded Doc.

"Right. Thank you, Harrid. Clyde was asking if he could do more to help us." Doc explained the conversation he'd had with Clyde. "He knows more now than he did, but we'll have to see if we want to tell him more."

"I think he'll be loyal," Ayla said, "but giving it some time is fine."

Sophia nodded. "I agree with Ayla. Was that everything for you, Doc?"

"Yeah."

"Before you two start," Sonya cut in, "Doc, the clan is ecstatically happy with you. Some of the older wives— who are still young enough that having another child would not put them in danger— are going to be asking to see you soon."

Doc nodded. "I'll check their health when I make them fertile, just to be sure."

"That was all," Sonya smiled at Ayla and Sophia. "Go ahead."

"Thank you, Sonya. That's wonderful news," Ayla said. "Sophia did most of the questioning, so go ahead, Sophia."

"Very well. Doc, you can hire a private security team for the land you own. The sheriff will still have the right to take over any investigation of a crime, but having a small peacekeeping team is fine. I have all the legal citations to make it stick."

"That would make us better able to enforce the rule about peacefulness..." Doc murmured.

"We've also found laws to help with the philanthropy you want to do," Sophia smiled. "It affects the taxes due for the land used in those endeavors."

"A bonus," Doc chuckled.

"The Silvered Dreams has been set as your house of worship. Ayla and I were thinking you might want to change the name, though."

"Oh?"

"Ayla?" Sophia asked.

"Either the Silvered Lily, to tie back to Lia's; Lucky Silver; or Silvered Luck," Ayla said.

"The Silver Lily," Doc said. "A little more of a tweak, but I like it. We can see about getting the poker chips and signage changed over. We might want to run with that naming scheme for each new house of worship, too."

"We'll start drawing up the contracts to get it done," Sophia smiled. "And we'll come up with more names to play off the Lily theme, for the future."

"Thank you."

"It's our pleasure," Ayla smiled. "I think that covers everything."

"Then it's time for you three to get ready for your date," Fiala grinned.

"Have a good night," Sonya smiled.

"We'll be here when you get home," Lia chuckled. "No need to rush back, but we'll be ready for you."

"I want to take a quick bath first before changing," Ayla said, standing up. "Sophia?"

"Might be for the best," Sophia agreed. "Are we going to wear what we discussed?"

"Of course."

Doc watched his wives with a smile. "Secrets, hmm? I won't pry, but I'm intrigued already."

"Good," Ayla beamed. "Say... an hour to leave?"

"I'll let Clyde know," Harrid said, slipping out of the room.

Doc watched Harrid and his two wives go. He was about to get up himself when Fiala took the space next to him. "Fiala?"

"I just wanted a cuddle for a bit."

"Me, too," Sonya said, taking his other side.

"Me, three, but where should I sit?" Lia smirked as she moved over to them. "Hmm... this looks good." She took Doc's lap, wiggling against him. "Comfortable."

Rosa sprawled on the floor at their feet, her eyes glowing as she touched all of them.

"Just cuddles?" Doc asked with a sardonic grin.

"Yes," Lia whispered. "We wouldn't ruin our wives' date night."

"Mean," Doc chuckled, his arms wrapping around Lia's waist. "But that's fine. I can deal with it."

"Doc, when you do go back, talk with the elf, please?" Lia murmured. "Make sure she's there of her own free will."

"I will, Lia," Doc agreed. "If she isn't, then I'll do all I can to help her."

"Thank you," Lia said as she rested her head against his shoulder.

Fiala and Sonya snuggled in against the pair. Both of them were a little worried about what might happen in the future, but they were already thinking of ways they might be able to help, too.

CHAPTER THIRTY-EIGHT

Doc smiled as he climbed into the carriage behind his wives. Doc had given Harrid the night off so he could go see Ginger. The dwarf argued a little, but Doc explained that having Harrid along on his date would be... wrong. They'd only be going to dinner, then catching the play that night at the opera house.

Taking his seat across from the two women, he smiled at them, letting his eyes take in their dresses again. Sophia had gone with a sapphire blue dress; it was demurely cut, but hugged her figure and stopped just above her knees. The blue helped her orange eyes stand out vividly. Ayla had gone with a red dress that gave a sharp contrast to Sophia's blue, helping them stand out even more. Ayla's dress was a bit more daring, showing off a hint of cleavage. The ankle-length gown had slits that went just above her knee, so her legs flashed into view with each step.

"I'll say it again," Doc said, "you both look fabulous tonight."

"You look quite handsome, yourself," Sophia smiled. "Did Fiala help you pick out your suit?"

"Yes. I figured out why when I saw your dresses," Doc chuckled.

"The blue suit and red tie work well together," Ayla smiled. "It helps tie our dresses in with you."

"I think that's why she helped me."

"You still haven't told us anything about what we're going to be doing tonight," Sophia said. "Just that we should dress up."

"Makes me wonder what he has in mind," Ayla agreed with Sophia. "Dinner, we know, but not what he's planning after that."

"I'll tell you, if you want," Doc offered. "I just thought a little surprise might make it more fun, though."

"I don't mind a surprise," Sophia said.

"I can wait..." Ayla murmured. "Why did you sit across from us instead of between us?"

"To make sure we arrive in unrumpled clothing," Doc chuckled. "I'd have been too tempted to snuggle you both into me."

"You'll sit closer to us later, right?" Ayla asked, batting her lashes at him.

"After dinner and the show."

"Oh!" Sophia said with a bright smile. "The play?"

Doc blinked at her, then snorted. "You're quick, Sophia. You've guessed it."

"I'm still surprised. I didn't think you had time to arrange for us to attend."

"After the Den, I had Clyde take me there to get tickets before we went to the property."

"That's very sweet," Ayla smiled softly. "You wanted to see it, too, Sophia."

"Yes. It came out seven years ago, but I've never had the chance to see it. I've read the reviews. It's a comedy piece by a newer playwright, Howard Bronson." She paused, then began to giggle. "Oh, goodness, this will be entertaining."

"Why?" Ayla asked for her and Doc.

"*Seven Pistols* is based around a man courting multiple women," Sophia explained.

Ayla giggled with her, and Doc joined in with a chuckle.

"I'm guessing a comedy of errors, then," Doc snorted.

"Best to see it," Sophia grinned.

"Considering our family, it should be entertaining for many reasons," Ayla added.

Doc had to agree with her. Sitting back, he thought of the opera house and wondered if they might run into people they knew.

* * *

Dinner was at the Palace Hotel's restaurant. Doc knew the chef there was talented, and he hadn't had a chance to ask around after other places of equal quality. Darren opened the door for them, stepping aside when he did.

Doc got out first, then helped his wives down. "Thank you," Doc told the half-dwarf driver-guard. "You should have time for dinner, yourself."

"We'll be fine, sir," Darren said. "William and I brought food with us. This way, we're ready to go the instant you are."

Doc glanced at William, the younger of the brothers. "Thank you again."

"Glad to help, sir."

Offering his arms to the two women, Doc led his wives to the front door. The doorman was quick to let them in. The restaurant was away from the front desk, making it easy for the staff to know that they were there for food and not a room.

The maître d' smiled politely as they approached. "Mr. Holyday, it is a pleasure to see you again. Table for three?"

"Indeed. Something out of the way, if possible."

"Of course, sir. Give me just a moment to make sure things are in order."

Doc nodded. He wasn't in a hurry— he'd made sure they had plenty of time before the opera house opened. While they waited, Sophia looked behind them, then Ayla did, too. Both of them turning to look back got Doc to do so.

Volenite, the manager of the Palace, was coming their way with a bright smile. "Mr. Holyday, I was just about to leave for the day when I saw you. Can I be of assistance before I go?"

"We're just having dinner," Doc said as his wives let go of his arms so he could shake the man's hand. "You're perfectly fine to go home and enjoy the night."

"Ah, of course. If you do need anything, my staff here can take care of it. Anything at all will be handled. Mr. Roquefell has informed us— and I believe all of his properties— that you are to be given the very best we can offer."

"I'll have to thank him and let him know how wonderful the evening was later."

"I don't want to intrude further," Volenite said. "Enjoy your evening."

Doc said his goodbyes and was just turning back to the front when the maître d' came back. He thanked them for waiting before leading the three of them into the dining room. There were only three other tables in use, leaving most of the room open, but they were brought to a secluded table in the back of the restaurant. Thanking the maître d', Doc sat his wives before taking his own seat.

"Your server tonight will be Pierre," the maître d' said as he presented them their menus. "I can say that he will give you the best service we can provide this evening. The chef was working on a specialty tonight, as well: a delightful lemon pepper trout caught fresh this morning. The plate is finished with a medley of steamed vegetables in a light lemon drizzle and some wild rice. If you opt for the chef's special, I would recommend a wonderful white wine from western Gaul to accompany it. But please, take a moment to look over the menu and Pierre will be with you shortly."

They gave their menus a quick glance, scanning them as Pierre arrived with the water to fill their glasses. "Good evening, ladies and gentleman. I'm your waiter tonight, Pierre. Did you have any questions that I could answer for you?"

The trio exchanged looks, then set their menus down. "No. I think we're good, actually," Doc said. "Ladies, you're interested in the chef's special tonight, right?" When they both agreed, he smiled. "We'd like three of his creations. Also, please have him select an appetizer to accent the meal. The maître d' mentioned a white wine from western

Gaul to accompany it, so we'll take at least one bottle of that to start with."

Pierre was all smiles as he collected their menus. "Very well, sir. I will inform the chef and sommelier."

As Pierre left, Doc put his hands out, taking theirs in his. Looking from one to the other, he smiled at them. "Ladies, I love you both very much. I'm delighted we get tonight, and I'll try to make sure we have other opportunities for more nights like this evening."

"We'd love that," Sophia beamed at him.

"We would," Ayla agreed. "I'm glad my joke brought us here, even if it wasn't intended to."

* * *

The meal was excellent. Doc praised the chef, server, sommelier, and maître d' for the service. The four men preened at the praise, thanking them for coming.

Doc noticed that the dining room had a dozen tables in use by the time they left; the brothers were ready for them when they came outside.

The opera house was busy when they arrived. Doc had arranged things earlier, so instead of waiting to get in, the guard on the door waved them forward, ahead of the line. Doc thanked the man, slipping him a five-dollar coin when he went by.

When the usher saw them enter, he smiled and came up to them. "Mr. Holyday, welcome back, sir." The words were professional, but it was clear he was confused by the women with Doc.

"Thank you," Doc replied, recalling him as the same usher who'd helped him when he'd brought Fiala and Sonya. "I didn't get your name last time."

"Kyle, sir."

"Kyle, thank you for seeing to me and my wives again. I think the play begins soon, so take us to our box, please."

"Right away, sir," Kyle said professionally, clearly shocked to hear that these two were also Doc's wives.

As they took their seats in the box, Doc asked Kyle to arrange for some wine for them.

The moment the door shut, Ayla turned to Doc. "Well, the cat's out now."

"Intermission is when it will really come out," Sophia said.

"Doesn't matter," Doc said. "All that matters is I have my beautiful wives beside me. I'm sorry that I didn't think that our date might be marred slightly by what some people might do or say later."

"No," Ayla said, touching his hand. "We'll cherish tonight regardless of what happens."

"We will," Sophia agreed, touching his other hand. "Nothing said by anyone will dim the fact that you set up this night for us to enjoy. Some people might even find it amusing, considering the play."

Ayla snickered. "We'll show them multiple partners can be a joy, not a comedy."

Doc's chest warmed, and he leaned over to kiss both of them. "We will, indeed."

* * *

The intermission came right as the story turned from the main character courting seven women to all of them finding out. It gave the audience a chance to theorize what would happen in the last couple of acts, and how badly the lead had erred in trying to be with seven women.

Doc had Kyle lead them down to the VIP lounge. Before they mingled, the trio paused to use the bathrooms. Doc was waiting for his wives when Dodd approached him.

"Mr. Holyday, glad to see you out for the opening night of the play," Dodd greeted him.

"Governor, it's a pleasure to see you again."

"Are you enjoying the show? I asked for them to pause on their way to Golden Bay to put on three showings."

"It is amusing," Doc chuckled.

"As a man with multiple wives, I'm sure it has a different humor," Dodd laughed.

"You could say that," Doc chuckled as he saw Ayla and Sophia coming his way. "Ladies, let me introduce you to Governor Nathanial Dodd. He's also the mayor of Furden."

"A pleasure," Ayla smiled, greeting him. "We've heard a lot about you from Mr. Roquefell."

"He has nothing but praise for you, sir," Sophia added.

"Governor, these are my wives, Ayla and Sophia."

Dodd froze for a moment, the shock clear on his face before he was able to smile. "Ladies, a pleasure. Does this mean you have four wives, Holyday?"

"Five," Doc smiled. "The only one you haven't met is Lia."

Dodd shook his head, then laughed. "This play must seem most peculiar to you."

"No, I understand it, and the lead made many mistakes in his ill-advised idea of courting those women. The biggest keys to having multiple partners are communication, trust, and honesty. He wasn't trying to do any of that: he was keeping secrets and lying to them all. I can see the humor in it. I do find it funny, but also sad that people think that's how having multiple partners works."

"Yes, I can see that," Dodd said slowly. "Shall I introduce you and your wives around?"

Doc grinned. "You want to see others' faces when they hear, you mean?"

It was clear Doc had caught Dodd out with his flat estimation.

"By all means," Ayla snickered. "There's nothing wrong in letting others experience the shock, as well."

"We knew it would happen. It's not as if we've tried to hide our relationship," Sophia smiled. "We all would've come for the opera, but between work and how small the private boxes are, it wouldn't have worked."

"I'll do my best to guide you, then," Dodd chuckled. "Oh, this will be entertaining."

CHAPTER THIRTY-NINE

Doc blinked slowly as he woke. The first thing he saw was Rosa kneeling beside the bed, watching him. Chuckling, he met her eyes, a warm smile coming to his lips. "Creepy Weed."

"I'm glad you accept me watching you, Voice. Your dreams were conflicted over the Iniquitous Den."

"Yeah... I think that's the first big step I'm going to take in the city."

"Not the housing project?"

"Well, technically, *that's* the first, but the Den will probably be done before the houses are."

"That depends on how quickly you move on the Den."

"It won't be fast, but I need to go back over the next few days and check different women. I need to see how far and wide the rot is, and maybe meet the madam if I can swing it. You'll need to be with me, Weed."

Rosa's eyes started to glow. "Oh, yes, please."

"Down, girl," Doc chuckled. "We'll also begin to offer healing today at the Silver Lily."

"Which gives us even more reason to go to the Den," Rosa murmured, staring at him with glowing eyes.

"It does," Doc agreed. He leaned over the side of the bed and Rosa surged up to kiss him.

Doc kissed her, but broke it before she got carried away. Rosa whined and sat back, her eyes bright as she watched his mind.

"Yes, Doc," Rosa murmured, lowering her gaze.

Reaching out, he stroked her silky tangle of blue-tinged green hair. "Good, Weed. You'll get plenty later, I promise. Have to if we're going to keep working on the land, too."

"Yes, Voice. I just want to do it all for you as quickly as I can."

"Thank you for that, but we can't rush some things." Doc pushed the blankets off. "It should be time to get up. The others always wake up before me."

The bedroom door opened, admitting Sophia. She gave him a smile upon seeing him still in bed, naked, and with the blankets off of him. "Doc, it's my morning to get you for breakfast," Sophia said and began unbuttoning her dress.

Rosa's eyes glowed even brighter.

Doc gave his lawyer a smirk. "Ah. We're settling back into routine?"

"We'd like to," Sophia said as her dress slid off her shoulders.

"I won't turn any of you away." He patted the bed. "Come here, my sweet wife. I want to feast on you first this morning."

Sophia beamed as she walked around the bed toward him. She paused at Rosa, stroking the dryad's hair. "Gladly, husband. Maybe we should let our dear helper here get you ready for me while you do that."

"Thank you, mistress," Rosa said huskily.

"As you wish," Doc smiled as he helped Sophia into bed.

* * *

Doc was glad they'd hired the chef. Fiala had become a good cook before they left Deep Gulch, but Charles was an artist in the kitchen. Their breakfast that morning was delicious.

"I'll be dropping the letters off on my way to the Silver Lily," Doc told them when they discussed plans for the day. "After spending some time healing, I'll be taking Rosa over to the Iniquitous Den to recharge her, but mostly so I can check on a different woman."

"Doc, I'm curious... why did you refrain from sleeping with the woman you chose first?" Fiala asked.

"Didn't feel right," Doc replied. "Honestly, I don't think casual lovers are going to be a thing now. With Lotus and Jasmine, I knew them before our family grew so large. Gretchen and Jesamin were so I could leave children behind. I'm not saying we won't ever have another who joins us for a night, but if we do, they'll be with more than just me and Rosa. I'll be using Rosa for this and, at the most, maybe receive oral at the Den to throw off suspicion, but that's it."

"He loves you all, and it feels to him like cheating since they are completely unknown to you," Rosa added.

Doc frowned for a second, then nodded. "Actually, that's correct. Thank you, Weed."

"I wish to help, Voice."

His wives were smiling at him, their love for him burning brighter. They'd given him permission, but the fact that he'd rather not because he loved them so much touched all of them.

"Anyway," Doc exhaled, looking at the table, "after that, Rosa and I will swing by the housing project to work on the ground. I'm probably going to run this schedule for a while, at least until we know how many women at the Den are being controlled."

"That makes sense," Lia said. "You'll speak with the elf today?"

"That's my plan," Doc nodded.

"I'm going to be home, but if you need me to help with her, let me know."

"I will, Lia."

"Sonya and I will just be staying home," Fiala said. "No tea today. We're going to observe the staff to better understand all their tasks."

"Solid plan."

"The clan is in high spirits," Sonya added. "You helping them have more children has really solidified them behind you. Elder Alaric's wife was wondering if she was young enough to have another child safely."

"No idea. I could check her? When you see her next, tell her to come by the Silver Lily."

"If the church hears about you helping the dwarves have more children, they'll move against you quicker and with more force," Sophia said softly. "We might want to caution the dwarves about letting the news out."

"Yes," Ayla nodded. "We can swing by there on the way to get the name change for the Silver Lily."

"Oh, can you pass word to Iona for me, then?" Sonya asked.

"We will."

"Sounds like we all have our plans set," Doc smiled.

* * *

Doc had Harrid ride in the carriage with them on the way to the post office.

"How did your date go?" Doc asked as they left the manor.

Harrid shifted in his seat. "I think it went well."

"You think?" Doc asked.

"I met her after she finished work. She went home to change and we met at a bestial tavern. Since I was there before her, I got some hard looks. When Ginger arrived, some of those looks got angry, but they left us alone. The food and drink were passable, but not great. We talked about weapons, since we both have a passion for them."

"Having a common interest is good."

"As the night wore on, the clientele started getting louder, rougher, and cruder," Harrid went on. "A few of the regulars came over to pester Ginger. She brushed them off, but it was obviously starting to get on her nerves, so I suggested we go for a walk."

"It was a beautiful night," Doc smiled, thinking back to his own evening out with his wives.

"It was good. The walk was not as wonderful as I would've liked. We walked through the area by the river." Harrid went quiet for a moment. "Doc, what you're going to do for them... I don't know if you understand how much better their lives will be."

"I have an edge of it, but that's all. I've never dealt with the prejudice they deal with, but with the living conditions being well below normal... I know how that goes. I've lived in similar situations before."

"Even with the constant reminders, we had a good walk," Harrid nodded. "If you can turn the river into the park things you've mentioned before... I can only imagine how the walk would've been."

"Pretty magical," Doc smiled. "We'll have to see how Strongarm reacts first before I try pressuring him."

"We walked for a while before doubling back to her house." Harrid trailed off at the end, a faint hint of red visible above his beard.

"Kissed her good night and promised to see her again?" Doc asked when Harrid let the silence stretch.

"Yeah," Harrid muttered. "She... ah..." He trailed off again.

"Asked you in, but you declined," Rosa offered softly.

Harrid grimaced, then nodded.

"Because you wanted to be a gentleman?" Doc asked.

"Partially," Harrid muttered.

"Ah," Doc said, thinking he understood. "Harrid, word of advice? Those moments handle themselves. Just be honest with her and, even if you're both in the same place of uncertainty, you'll find your way together. If you're worried about not knowing how, we can see about you learning later today at the Den."

Harrid's head jerked up as the red crept well into his face. "No! I mean... no thank you, Doc."

"Probably the right choice. First times can be special," Doc said softly. "You do realize she might not be... unexperienced, right?"

Harrid nodded. "Yes. The way she kissed me..."

"Kissing is just kissing in some cases. She might not have gotten past first base, either."

"What?" Harrid asked, puzzled.

"Huh? Is baseball not a thing here?"

"Baseball...? You mean rounders?" Harrid asked.

"Yes," Rosa said, checking both men's minds. "Doc's is the evolution of that game on his old world."

"Off track," Doc said. "Baseball got a lot of references for dating. First base was kissing, second was making out, third was heavy making out— including oral most of the time— and of course, home means you went all the way."

Harrid just stared at Doc for a long moment.

"Blue-screened him," Doc snorted. "Anyway, she might be more experienced or might've only just kissed people before."

Shaking his head, Harrid exhaled as he tried to get his mind back on track. "I know, but I worry."

"Perfectly normal," Doc told him. "Did you have a good time?"

"Yes."

"Would you want to do it again?"

"Yes."

"That's all that matters. Ask her out again, enjoy the night, and if things go that way, it'll be up to you. You know she might be just as worried, right?"

Harrid's brow furrowed. "Why?"

"Because you turned her down," Doc said softly. "Take a minute and imagine if you asked her in and she refused."

Harrid sat silently for a moment, then hung his head. "Oh..."

"We'll be seeing her today," Doc said softly. "Just ask her out again. Tell me and I'll make sure to take Lia out that same night."

Harrid met Doc's eyes, then bowed his head. "Thank you, Doc."

"Friends help friends," Doc chuckled. "Besides, I've been there. The only difference is that your days off are wonky as hell because of me. If you want to court her, I'll help as much as I can."

"Thank you. I won't ask often. She understood that my days off are few and fleeting, but knowing that you'll help me make days so I can be with her... Thank you."

Doc smiled. "Just do it right. Make sure she knows that you'll be going with me, too."

"I made it very clear, but will do so again."

The carriage slowed and Doc glanced out the window. "Damn... didn't realize we were here already." He looked at the tall pole with lines running off it, then down the row of them until they disappeared behind buildings. "Telegraph? Fuck me... I forgot all about it."

Rosa watched his thoughts, her eyes widening when she saw what he was thinking.

"Doc?" Harrid asked as he got out.

Stepping out of the carriage, Doc saw the railroad line running parallel to the telegraph and nodded. "Yes, of course! The phone... when did it get patented...?"

Rosa got out behind him with her head bowed, her eyes watching everyone around them.

"We can get in on the ground floor...!" Doc breathed out, eyes starting to gleam with ideas.

"Uh... Doc?" Harrid coughed.

Jerked from his thoughts, Doc looked at Harrid, then grinned widely. "Today just started a whole new business venture. I'm going to have to thank Ayla and Sophia all over again. David is going to buy in. I *know* he will."

Harrid just waited, as Doc was clearly still half-lost in thought.

Rosa touched Doc's arm lightly. "Doc, the letters."

"Right. One thing at a time. Remind me to talk with Ayla and Sophia later, Rosa."

"I will, Doc."

Doc started for the post office, his mind still running at full tilt over how to take a giant step forward in influencing the country—the one who controlled communication could control the world.

CHAPTER FORTY

The post office was far from what Doc thought of as post offices. There was just a front room with a handful of counters, with only two of them staffed. No post office boxes was the biggest jolt— he was used to them being there from his old world.

Both tellers straightened up when Doc entered, professional smiles on their faces. One of them lost their smile when they saw Rosa trailing him. The smile fading from the one made Doc go to the other teller.

That man smiled broader, showing slightly enlarged front teeth. His two furred ears twitched when Doc came to a stop in front of him. "Good morning, sir. How can we at Emerita Union help you?"

Doc saw the flick of a hairless tail behind the worker. "Good morning," he greeted the rat bestial. "I have letters to send to Deep Gulch. I'd use the telegraph, but you don't have a line down there yet, do you?"

"No sir. The line follows the rail," the employee replied. "I'll need to weigh the letters to find the postage required."

Doc pulled them from his jacket pocket. "Here you go...?" He trailed off, prompting the man for a name.

"Simon, sir," the bestial answered as he collected the letters. "One moment."

Doc nodded as Simon slipped through the door behind the counter. Taking in the work area he could see, there was no hint of telegraph machinery or other postal work. *Must be through the door,* Doc thought while he waited.

Simon came back a moment later with the letters. "None of them cost more than five pennies by themselves. In total, you're looking at thirty-five cents."

Doc pulled out the required money, passing it over. "How long will it take before it ships out?"

"The coach runs twice a month on a loop," Simon explained. "Should be back here tomorrow, then it'll leave two days after that."

"What's the cost of the telegraph?" Doc asked.

"It's a dollar for up to two hundred and fifty words, sir. If you need more than that, you'd have to send a second telegraph."

"What's the drop rate?" Doc asked.

"What?"

"We all know that the longer a message travels, the more prone it is to degradation," Doc said. "What's the drop rate from clear message to garbled?"

Simon blinked at him in shock— customers didn't ask those kinds of questions. Most of them were not even aware that messages could degrade. "Depends on how many junctions it passes through, sir."

"Because it has to be received and re-transcribed to keep going," Doc smiled.

"Yes, sir."

"What's the rate of drop, then?" Doc asked. "Let's call it... two junctions, if I send a hundred words."

"I'm not a technician myself, but my cousin says that a hundred words might lose two or three at each junction on average. He'd be shocked to know a customer even knew to ask."

The human teller coughed loudly. "These aren't things that should be explained, Simon."

Simon ducked his head. "Sorry, Fred."

"Answering questions isn't something you should do?" Doc asked with a crooked smile. "How very forthright of the company."

Fred gave Doc a long look. "Sir, no company wants its problems told to one and all. Last I heard, the company was always looking to improve things."

"That'd be a first," Doc chuckled. "Most look at the bottom line only. I'll leave it be, Fred. This is a full branch of Emerita Union, right?"

"Yes, sir. We aren't an offshoot," Fred said stiffly.

"Can't buy it out, then," Doc sighed. "Pity. Ah well. There are ways to work around these things. Have a good day."

As they went to leave, Fred whispered to Simon in an angry voice, "Never do that again, rat. Understand?"

"Yes, sir..." Simon whispered back.

"I'm going to talk to the manager. You and your cousin should know better."

Rosa's lips pursed as she followed Doc; he'd find that exchange very informative.

As soon as they were back in the coach, Rosa leaned against Doc. "Voice, Simon and his cousin are getting in trouble. Fred is angry with him and plans to tell the manager."

Doc nodded. "Yeah, that's my fault. I'll fix that soon. For what I'm planning, I'd need a technician for the telegraph. Simon can run the office at Heartwood's Tears once it gets built."

"You always do that, taking someone and raising them up," Harrid said approvingly.

"In this case, it'll be my fault they get in trouble, possibly fired. I'll fix it. Besides, I'd need someone to handle the telegraph anyway, so it'll work out."

"You're really going to get involved in that business?"

"The telegraph is the precursor to the telephone," Doc smiled. "The telephone changed the world even more than the telegraph did. That's my next big push."

"Don't you have enough already?" Harrid asked with a hint of concern.

Doc sighed, but he nodded. "I'll make it up to Ayla and Sophia, but this is the best time to get involved. Either the telephone is already started or will be soon. We'll have the money once we lock up the mines we're interested in having. Hell, we can probably buy out Emerita Union with that kind of money, or at least controlling interest. David will have something to take care of, as I'll be handing it off to him to run."

"Tying him to you more firmly," Rosa smiled.

"Which we want," Doc murmured, kissing her head. "Ready for healing?"

Rosa shivered. "Yes, Voice."

Harrid stayed quiet, but he thought over what Doc was saying and tried to see the pieces that Doc saw. If he could see the puzzle, he might be able to help more.

***

Arriving at the soon-to-be Silver Lily, Doc led Harrid and Rosa inside. Doc glanced at Harrid, then Ginger, before giving the rabbit bestial a smile. Ginger gave him a nod in return, straightening up when he came her way. "Just going to check my hat with you," Doc said, taking his bowler off.

"Yes, sir."

"Harrid, you're guarding me, so keep your gear," Doc said. "I'll be in my new office for a little while before seeing anyone, so you have a moment."

Rosa followed Doc with her head down, but a smile on her lips. She'd caught Ginger's thoughts before she'd left.

Harrid watched Doc go, knowing why he'd checked his hat. With a slow breath, he moved to the counter. Ginger was smiling at him, but there was clear worry visible on her face. "Ginger... uh... good morning," Harrid started awkwardly.

"Yes, it is, Harrid. I hope you're well today?"

"Yes. Umm... I was hoping..." Harrid stumbled, slowly trailing off as he felt his face flush. "If you might be okay with another date?"

The relief in Ginger's eyes was clear to him, and her smile grew wider. "I'd love that. I worried that maybe..." She trailed off, looking away. She fidgeted as her cheeks also began to redden. "I was forward, and I apologize."

"No," Harrid said softly, lowering his voice. "I... panicked... It wasn't you."

Ginger looked into his eyes for a long moment before giving him a secretive smile. "I worried *you*?"

"We can talk about it when we go out again, if that's okay?"

"I'm off in three days. Would you be available then?" Ginger asked, then felt foolish for asking for his day; she knew how busy he was.

"Let me talk to Doc. He mentioned going on a date with his wives. I'll see if we can arrange it."

Ginger's eyes went to the door into the gambling hall, then back to Harrid. She lowered her voice even more, "Is it true, then, that he has multiple wives? The rumor going around says he has a dozen."

Harrid's lips twitched. "Not a dozen, but he does have five. I'm sure him taking them to the opera and the play spread that around faster."

"My friend works at the opera house. She said she met four of them. The matrons of the wealthy houses were disparaging them behind their backs. Not all of them, but more than a few. One even mentioned going to tell the preachers, saying it was revolting... more so because... none of them are human." The last five words were even softer.

"He's married to a dwarf from my clan, an elf from the tribe of the same town, two bestials— one of which is a Sagesse—, and a half-elf," Harrid replied. "He doesn't care about heritage. He only cares about who the person is."

"That's... hard to believe," Ginger whispered. "But you trust him, so I will, too."

"Do you know anyone who's injured?" Harrid asked suddenly.

"My neighbor hurt herself yesterday. She was rushing to get out of the way of an idiot on a horse and twisted her ankle."

"Go get her. Bring her to see Doc."

"Can he really heal?" Ginger asked with wide eyes.

"Yes. He's saved my life multiple times."

"Uh, I have to get someone to cover for me."

"He'll be here for at least a few hours," Harrid said. "I'll have an answer for you soon about our date, too."

"I'll look forward to hearing about it," Ginger said, then hurried out of her office to get a replacement for her.

Harrid went to the new office, which took up half the previous lounge area. Knocking once, Harrid then went in. "Doc, do you have a moment?"

"Of course. What did she say?" Doc grinned.

"I think you were right. She was worried that she was too forward. She has the day off three days from today. If that's okay, I can tell her before we leave."

"Done and done," Doc chuckled. "I'll arrange for my date with Lia that same day. See? Told you I'd make this work."

Harrid exhaled slowly. "Thank you, Doc. Uh… she's going to get her neighbor who sprained her ankle yesterday. I told her to bring the woman here for you to see."

"Perfect. I figure the first couple of days will be slow, but this will help spread things. I'll have to post a sign letting people know when I'll be in or out," Doc said. "Should post it in the front room so everyone knows."

"Might be best," Harrid agreed.

"We'll likely have Alaric's wife, Iona, here today, but I'm not sure if we'll see anyone else," Doc said. "Around noon, we're going to the Den, so be ready for that. Though if you want to stay here and have lunch with Ginger…"

Harrid hesitated, then shook his head. "If you get people mad there, you might need me."

"Shouldn't happen today, but going forward, yes," Doc agreed.

"It's why I was offering today. I know I'm playing fast and loose again, but I'm also hoping to see my friend find a relationship."

"I appreciate it, Doc, but my first priority is your safety."

"Yeah, okay. Not going to fight it. Just make sure to enjoy your next date. You'll have the whole day off, so use it wisely."

Harrid nodded slowly. "I... should make plans."

"Clyde knows the city," Doc suggested. "Maybe he'd have advice?"

"I'll ask him later," Harrid said. "For now, I'll be posted outside your door."

"Let's hope for a good day."

"Luck willing."

CHAPTER FORTY-ONE

The older mink bestial thanked him profusely for helping with her ankle. Ginger was staring at him with wide eyes, having asked to be in the room during the healing. Doc knew it was because the younger woman was protective of her friend; he appreciated her being cautious, but respectful.

"Ginger, did you want me to check you, too?" Doc asked as the older woman was leaving.

"I'm not injured, sir."

"Maybe not that you're aware of, but the choice is yours."

Ginger looked at the still open door where Harrid was looking back at her. With a nod, Ginger went to take the seat her friend had used. "Very well, sir."

"Lady, please give your blessing to Ginger," Doc murmured as he triggered his spell. He gently took Ginger's offered hand in his.

Slight infection in her left ear? That'll be easy to knock out. She has two teeth going bad. I haven't tried teeth before, so I'll give that a go. Scar tissue inside her...? What the fuck...?! Doc's mental ability to process injuries jarred to a halt.

Ginger had been watching Doc's face, seeing the care and compassion, but it suddenly became hard, cold, and angry. "S-sir?"

Harrid came into the room. He was sure Doc wasn't upset with Ginger, meaning he'd found something that made him mad. Harrid's lips went thin— if someone had hurt Ginger, he wanted to know.

Hearing the worry in her tone, Doc blinked as he met Ginger's uncertain gaze, the anger falling away. "Ginger, I'm sorry. You have a few problems. The most minor is a mild infection in your left ear; that's easily handled. There are two teeth— your back left molars— that are going bad. I've never tried to work on teeth, but I'm going to see if I can fix them." He paused as he tried to approach the next one with care. "What caused me concern was more personal. Harrid, you should step out. The last one is delicate."

Ginger's heart sped up as her eyes began to water. She was sure she knew what Doc was going to say. "Please?" Ginger sniffled, not wanting Harrid to hear about her trauma.

Harrid met her gaze for a moment, his worry for her obvious. "If that's what you want, Ginger."

She saw the concern he had and her heart twisted. She'd chased him, but she should've known better. She'd even tried to invite him into her home the other day like a fool. She'd been so happy to have a good man interested in her that she'd forgotten about what Doc had obviously found.

When Harrid stepped out, Doc exhaled slowly. "Ginger, what happened?"

Hiccupping, Ginger began to sob a little harder as old trauma rose up to plague her. "I was... barely an adult... some men came through the bestial area... they grabbed any woman they wanted..."

Rosa slid from Doc's side to Ginger's, knowing what Doc would want. "I can maybe help with those memories, but you'd need to focus intently on them."

Ginger's puffy, teary eyes met Rosa's. "What?"

"I can help with trauma. It's better if it's fresh, but if you can hold the memories tightly, I can dull them," Rosa whispered. "Do you want that?"

"But it won't fix what they did... the file...!" Arms wrapping around herself, Ginger rocked in place.

"I can fix the physical trauma," Doc said, letting go of her hand when she pulled away to wrap her arms around herself. He moved so he could kneel beside her, opposite Rosa. "It'll be gone as if it never happened. Luck will see to that. If you want, Rosa will help you so the memories dim and stop plaguing you."

No one could help her; no one should help her. *Trash, useless filth! Barely even worth our time to torment,* a dark sneering voice echoed in her head. *Maybe we can widen you up with a file? If nothing else, your screams will be fun.* Ginger jerked back when two glowing emerald eyes filled her vision.

"Do not listen to the lies of evil men, child," Rosa whispered, forcing Ginger to focus on her. "Do not let them continue to hurt you. Do you want to be free of them?"

"Yes..." The word was barely audible, but it was said.

"Close your eyes, tilt your head back, and when I give you a drink, swallow. Hold on to the memories. Let them hurt you one last time, and then they will never touch you again," Rosa whispered as she stood over Ginger.

When Rosa moved, Ginger's head tilted back to follow the dryad's glowing eyes before she slowly closed hers. Rosa leaned down as Ginger's mouth opened slightly— she didn't kiss the other woman. She just let a few drops of amber drip from her to the bestial.

While she did that, Doc touched Ginger's knee, pushing healing into her and focusing on the trauma. The scars faded away, leaving behind the flesh that should be in their place. Doc had no idea how she'd survived the ordeal or even managed to have a semblance of a regular life.

Rosa dove into Ginger's mind as the memories went past, making sure to memorize the men who were involved— both Doc and Harrid would want to know who had committed those atrocities to this woman. In the meantime, her nectar worked to nearly erase the memories of pain and torment.

Doc reached over Ginger to touch Rosa's wrist, pulling energy as he finished healing the infection in Ginger's ear. He finally turned his attention to her teeth, worried about how bad it would be. His fear, however, was unfounded. Her teeth healed just as quickly as the slight infection had. Finally finished, he leaned back, waiting for Rosa to be done.

Rosa exhaled a shaky breath, then smiled softly down at Ginger. "All done, child. No more trauma for you."

Ginger blinked dully up at Rosa with a soft smile on her lips. "Thank you."

"You're healed. No trace of any injury remains," Doc added.

Looking away from Rosa, Ginger frowned for a moment as something tried to come to mind, but slipped away. The memory of them asking to heal her of old wounds came back, and she looked at them confusedly. "What...? I... did you...?"

"What happened in the past is gone," Doc said. "What you tell Harrid, if he asks, is up to you."

"I know what happened, but the memories are... missing," Ginger whispered.

"Keep that to yourself, please?" Doc asked her.

"Yes, of course... I can tell Harrid, though?"

"Yes."

Ginger looked at Rosa, who went back to kneel at Doc's feet. "Thank you, dryad."

"Rosa," Doc said softly. "Her name is Rosa."

"Thank you, Rosa. It's been years... I know there was an attack on me, but nothing after that until I saw the alchemist to stop the bleeding." She shivered at that memory. "I feel better, though."

"You're free to go," Doc said. "If you want to take the rest of the day off, just talk to whoever took over for you."

Ginger nodded, standing up. "Thank you, sir."

"Call me Doc," Doc told her. "Have a good day."

The moment she left, Doc expected Harrid, but he didn't come in. Rosa pressed into his leg so he focused on her. "Talk to me, Weed."

"She was sexually abused by the men, and they used implements on her afterward," Rosa said. "I nearly erased the memories, but didn't completely. She'll know they are there, but can't touch them."

"Who were they?" Doc asked, anger tingeing his voice.

"I do not know, but I memorized their faces so, if I see them, I can tell you."

A crisp knock came on the door a moment before it opened for Harrid. He stepped inside and shut it behind him. "Doc, what can you tell me?"

"Only what I have so far," Doc said softly. "It's up to her to share with you, Harrid."

Harrid grimaced, but nodded. "That... is fair."

"She was traumatized years in the past," Rosa whispered. "The rest is her story."

"Who was it?" Harrid asked tightly.

"We haven't met them, but Rosa will tell us if we meet them," Doc said. "For now, just give her time to tell you herself."

"If we do meet them, Doc, I'll want to hurt them."

"I probably won't stop you, but I'd rather not have my bodyguard arrested. Time and place, but I'll condone retribution."

Harrid took a deep breath, deflating a little as he exhaled. "Thank you. I don't know why I got so angry."

"Because you care about her," Doc smiled. "It's natural when you care for someone. As for her injuries... you really don't want to know. Trust me on that."

"That makes me angrier at these nameless men, but very well."

"I'm going to rest until Iona Ironbeard gets here, someone else shows up for healing, or when it's noon," Doc said.

"Understood, Doc," Harrid said, slipping back out the door.

Doc looked at the door, then at Rosa. A small smile crossed his face as her eyes began to glow. "Yes, you were a very good Weed. Go lock the door, then meet me at my desk."

"As you command, Voice," Rosa replied huskily as she scampered off to obey.

* * *

Rosa was just unlocking the door when there was a knock. She opened it, revealing Harrid and an older female dwarf wearing a finely made dress. Bowing her head, Rosa stepped aside for them.

"Doc, Mrs. Iona Ironbeard to see you," Harrid announced.

Doc stood up; he'd met Iona at one of Fiala's tea parties before. "Iona, a pleasure. Please, come in."

The matronly dwarf came into the room with a bright smile. "Shaman, thank you for seeing me."

"No need to be so formal, Iona. I'd like you to see me as a friend, not just as the shaman."

"Which is gratifying, as I'm not sure if you *can* help," Iona said as Harrid shut the door behind her. She glanced back at Rosa. "Your dryad has been there to help you for everyone else. Rumor says she is how you are able to do so much."

"Dryads hold a massive amount of energy," Doc explained as he joined Iona in the small sitting area where he healed. "Rosa has been with me for a while now, and has made many things possible."

"Maybe that's why the elven shamans always seemed to have more energy than ours," Iona sighed. "Just stories, of course. I'm not that old," she added.

"You barely look a day over fifty," Doc said, having heard she was closer to a hundred.

"I do try." Iona touched her hair with a smile. She exhaled, turning serious. "Am I still young enough for another child, Shaman?"

Doc extended his hand. "Lady, Iona comes to you to see if she might have another child with her husband. Please help me see if she might know the blessing of motherhood again."

Iona placed her hand into his green glowing hands, clearly hopeful and worried.

Everything looks okay. She has viable eggs and just recently had a cycle. Nothing to say she couldn't. She seems as healthy as anyone else I've seen in the clan. Let's just make those eggs more fertile to help her, Doc thought as he smiled at Iona.

When Doc let go of her hand, Iona's heart was hammering in her chest. She wasn't sure what had happened, but she'd felt the warmth that infused her. Memories of her husband holding her after having their first child had come to her unbidden.

"Iona, you're as healthy as a woman half your age," Doc said softly. "I've done what I could for you. I wouldn't be surprised if you catch in the next two months."

Iona swallowed the lump in her throat, choking back the tears that threatened to spill. "Thank you, Shaman."

"For a friend, it was a pleasure. As the shaman, it was my duty. May your child grow to be as wise as you and your husband."

Pulling a handkerchief from her sleeve, Iona dabbed at her eyes, stopping the tears from getting far. "If anyone ever speaks against you, they will find the displeasure of the entire clan brought against them. Not only do you show your kindness, but you are also helping us grow again. First with the business you bring, and now with expanding the clan. My husband will never speak against you unless it truly endangers the clan, Shaman."

Doc rose when she did. "He should speak against me when he feels the need. I don't want to control, only to help. I welcome dissenting opinions; they help us examine a problem and find better ways of doing things."

"So wise," Iona sniffled, finally able to suppress her tears. She dabbed her face again, then pushed the handkerchief back into her sleeve. "May you be as blessed as you make the clan, Shaman."

"I am every day," Doc said, leading her to the door. "I wish you a good night. I'm sure your husband will be very happy."

Iona laughed as Doc opened the door for her. "Oh, he will be busy all day now. Good day." She swept away like a grand dame, but with the eagerness of a young maiden.

Harrid smiled after her. "You do great things for the clans, Doc."

"I hope so, Harrid. If no one else shows up, we'll be off to the Den at noon."

"Understood."

CHAPTER FORTY-TWO

Doc only saw to one other bestial who'd spoken with Ginger's friend. The weasel bestial had an infected foot from stepping on a rusted piece of metal. While Doc healed him, the man explained he'd cut his foot when hurrying away from someone he owed money.

With just four people taken care of, Doc left for the day. He stopped in briefly to ask Colin to arrange for a sign near the front room, posting what day and hours Doc expected to be in next.

It was just after noon when Clyde pulled the carriage up to the back entrance of the Iniquitous Den. Harrid opened the door of the carriage for Doc and Rosa to step out. The private entrance was in a walled-off area, giving the people leaving their carriages privacy from passersby seeing them.

Doc went up to the door that had no way to open from the outside. Knocking on it firmly, he waited. The small viewing port in the door slid open, and Doc could see bright yellow eyes looking out at him. "I'd like entrance, please, but I don't know how this works."

"Token?" the woman asked.

"Ah." Doc pulled the golden heart out of his pocket, showing it to her.

The panel slid shut and the door opened. The wolf bestial on the inside bowed her head to Doc. "Welcome back, sir." Her tail was still and her ears were canted forward as she waited for him to enter.

The room was obviously just a greeting room. It only held a chair and table near the door for the woman to wait for someone to arrive. Doc was surprised to see a knitting project on the table, but that made him smile.

"Your guard goes through that door to wait," the wolf bestial told Doc. Her eyes went to Rosa. She'd obviously heard of a patron with a dryad, as she didn't react. "Otherwise, your door is right here." She motioned to the second door in the room.

"Thank you, Miss...?" Doc trailed off to get her name.

"I'm Heliodor, sir. If you return tomorrow, I'll be in the lounge."

"You take turns with the door?"

"Yes, sir. Madam thought it would be a good way for us to meet the important members."

The name finally registered, as he'd heard the names of some of the others. "Golden beryl," Doc smiled. "I can see it with your eyes."

The woman's tail wagged slightly. "No one has known the meaning before."

"I own a mine or two," Doc told her. "I'm sure we'll be speaking in the future."

"I'd like that, sir," Heliodor smiled brightly, her tail wagging a little faster.

"Harrid, probably be a while."

"Yes, sir," Harrid replied, going toward the door he'd been pointed to.

As Harrid left the room, but before Doc could, Heliodor cleared her throat gently. "Sir... Ruby might have said that your companion there joins you. Is that true?"

Doc paused by the door into the lounge, looking back at her. "Rosa does join me. In fact, she'll be the focus of any time I have with an employee here. Should I exclude you from the list?"

"No, sir. Ruby was... very happy afterward. I am a bit hopeful, truth be told."

"Perhaps the next time, then."

"I hope so, sir. You can always request one or more of us by name with the bartender, as well. Ruby and I get along rather well, for instance."

Rosa's eyes glowed brightly for a moment, but as she was facing mostly away from Heliodor, the wolf bestial didn't see it.

"Very tempting," Doc chuckled. "Not today, but I'll remember it in the future. I hope you have a pleasant day, miss."

"You, too, sir." Heliodor curtsied to him.

Stepping into the members' only lounge had Doc whistle softly. This lounge was a third the size of the other, but was furnished differently. Instead of white oak and silver, this one had dark oak with golden fixtures.

The bartender behind the bar was a brightly smiling woman. Her black, rounded, furred ears flicked when he approached. "Afternoon, sir. What can I get you?"

Doc gave her a return smile. "Your best cognac, please."

"Of course, sir." The bartender turned around to get his drink. She wasn't thin like most of the other women in the Den. In fact, she was thicker in all areas.

I'd bet she's a panda, Doc thought as he looked over the room. There was only one other woman in the lounge. Her broad flat tail clearly meant she was a beaver bestial. Her eyes were bright as she gave him a once over, then a wink. A dozen bad lines about wood in relation to the young woman flashed through his mind, and he shut them all down.

"Here you go, sir," the bartender said.

"Thank you, Miss..."

"Onyx, sir. I'm the morning bartender for the private lounge."

"Thank you, Onyx. Is Citrine available?"

"I'll ask, sir. Please give me a moment."

"Of course," Doc said as he led Rosa toward a table off to the side.

The beaver bestial looked away, clearly sad that he didn't come over to her.

Rosa spoke softly as she knelt beside Doc's chair, "All of them heard about us from Ruby, who appears to be a gossip. Ruby was very effusive in her praise of our skills, if sad that you personally didn't sample her."

"That explains it," Doc murmured while taking a sip of his drink.

"The biggest points are that you didn't hurt or degrade her at all. From what I can get, the members are prone to one or both. The women are regularly seen by a doctor or alchemist to remove signs of their trauma, or as much as they can."

Onyx came their way a moment later. "Sir, Citrine will be with you shortly."

"Thank you, Onyx. A question about decorum here, if you don't mind. Tipping?"

"We are allowed to accept tips, sir."

Doc fished out a five-dollar coin, handing it to her. "Thank you again. I appreciate your time."

Onyx blinked briefly, but her smile was bright as she took the tip. "I'll make sure you always have the best I can give sir."

"I'm sure I'll be well cared for in the mornings, then," Doc chuckled. "Who's the evening bartender?"

"That would be Snowflake, sir."

"Obsidian?" Doc asked.

"Yes, sir, but she goes by just Snowflake."

"I'll keep that in mind. Thank you."

"Anything you need, sir," Onyx said with a hint of suggestion before she walked away.

Doc watched her go. He had to admit that he did like the way she filled out her dress. Some people might look down on a padded figure, but Doc had always enjoyed the softness.

Rosa shifted when she caught sight of Citrine entering the room. That got Doc's attention, and he looked over as the elf slowed upon seeing them. Citrine's face became an impassive mask by the time she'd reached them.

"You asked for me, sir?" Citrine's voice was far removed from Lia's.

"Please, sit," Doc said, motioning to the other chair.

Citrine's eyes flickered to Rosa staring at her before she slowly sat down. "What can I do for you, mage?" The words were calm, but Doc wasn't fooled by the tone.

"I'm not a mage," Doc said softly.

Brow furrowing, the elf's lips pursed. She caught sight of Rosa's nod and leaned back. "I apologize, then, sir."

"I'd like to talk with you in private, if possible? My wife, Lillianna Treeheart, thought we should."

"*Death Flower?*" she whispered in Elvish.

"*She was known as that,*" Doc agreed, speaking Elvish back to her.

Citrine's eyes went wide for a moment before she stood. "Please, sir, follow me."

"Gladly," Doc smiled broadly.

The stairs in the private lounge still took them up to the rooms above. Citrine's room was the same as Ruby's suite, though the décor was different. Bison were clearly special to the elf from what Doc saw.

The moment the door shut behind them, Rosa snagged Citrine's hand. "Child, I am not bound as you think. Do not hate the Voice for my being collared. I gave my neck to him."

Citrine's eyes went wide, but then narrowed. "He could make you say that."

"True," Doc agreed. "She's collared. How can you trust anything she says, right?"

"Correct, but..." Citrine hesitated. "She called you something."

"Voice," Rosa said as she moved to kneel next to a chair. "He is Luck's Voice, child."

Doc took the chair next to where Rosa knelt. "Lady Luck sent me here, Citrine. If Rosa was willing to say as much as she has, I know it's safe to do so."

"Because they can peer into one's soul," Citrine said softly. "I thought that secret was unknown to others not of the tribes."

"It is," Rosa replied, "but it's your minds, not your souls. Doc, she is here of her own will, but not of her own will."

"That's not clear," Doc sighed. "Citrine, my wife, Lia, asked me to verify that you're working here because you want to."

"*I follow until balance is restored,*" Citrine said in Elvish.

"Fuck... The madam holds your oath?"

"She saved me from death at the hands of the government for my tribe's uprising."

"Which tribe?" Doc asked.

"Raven. My tribe was Ravenfoot. We are from the north. Many tribes come from Raven. Our government calls our home Sikahno." The last word was a sneer.

"Land of Black?" Doc asked, knowing the word was twisted.

"They can't pronounce it correctly," Citrine snorted. "Before that, they called it Monhom."

Doc was quiet for a moment before he placed it all. *Montana*, he told himself. *She's Blackfoot, or similar.* "I see. So you work here because of the oath."

"Yes."

Doc sat forward. "Lady Luck, please show your power to Citrine so she can know that we speak true to her," Doc said before he triggered *healing hands*. "Might I check your health?"

"It will not hurt. He only wants to see if you've been injured," Rosa said as she leaned against Doc's legs.

Citrine hesitated, but put her hand in Doc's. The warmth that flowed into her almost made her cry. The memory of her mother singing of the gods came back to her, and how she would sing along to praise Mother, wishing for the Voices to return to drive the humans back. It was so very different from when Steward pushed his energy at her.

Doc shuddered when he felt the soul stones implanted in her. Four of them were in her shoulders and hips, which would control her enough for the soulsmith. On top of that, old wounds and scars dotted her body.

"I can't undo some of what's wrong, but I can do a lot," Doc said thickly. "Are you okay with me healing what I can?"

"Please?" Citrine hiccupped as the memory washed through her. The warmth surged, and Citrine began to cry.

Rosa touched her knee. "Yes, child. Mother felt much the same way until Doc came. He is but one against the Darkness, but he has his wives and plans. Rejoice that we have a chance to begin the return of what was."

"I will... oh, Mother, I will."

Doc let the energy fade, his other hand touching Rosa's so he could pull energy from her to refill. "I can't undo what Steward did. I'm sorry, Citrine."

It took a moment for her to calm again. When she finished wiping her eyes, she shook her head. "No. He perverted Mother's will. I'm a puppet whenever he wants it. If I'd known then, I would've fought him, even if it broke my oath and damned me in my clan's eyes. But I didn't know until he came back after that... then, he controlled my limbs and laughed at me."

"We'll work to fix it," Doc whispered. "I won't allow it to stand. Do you know how many others are also... controlled?"

"No, but he has seen many of us. We can't refuse... not him. Madam has said that he's the most important customer. He supersedes all others."

"That seals it for her, then," Doc said grimly. "I should speak with her to make sure, but I'm pretty sure she's an accomplice."

Citrine grimaced.

"Citrine can't speak against the madam, but you will be unhappy when you do speak with her, Doc. Mostly unhappy," Rosa said as she sat up. "You can buy Citrine. Madam offered to sell her to the soulsmith last month."

"She perverts the oath!" Citrine snarled.

"Because you shouldn't be sold like cattle," Doc agreed. "Would you object if I did, though? If you do, I won't."

"She is conflicted," Rosa said as the silence stretched in the room. "Being free of this life is her deepest wish, but buying an oath is... abhorrent to the ideal of the oath."

"It's your choice. You would be freed," Doc said.

"Free from this, but her oath would be to Doc, instead," Rosa said. "He will never touch you in that way. He has his wives and me for that. You would be placed as a guard to the home here. His family is important to him and to his mission."

Doc was about to object, but then he recalled how the oaths worked. "Rosa's right."

Citrine bit her lip hard, hard enough to bleed. "But the oath…"

Doc reached out, touching her knee. His hand glowed as he healed her lip. "Was a sham used to control you. If she believed in them, you would never be sold."

The warmth touched her again and she exhaled slowly. "I'll agree… but why were you here before? Ruby spoke of your time with her." Citrine's brow furrowed. "Wait, you didn't… lay with her. Only Rosa did."

"I came to check on those who worked here. I… erred. Before I knew what was happening here, I sold soul stones to Steward. His comment had me worry about everyone who worked here. Now, I know why I should've worried."

"Even Voices can err," Citrine snorted softly. "If they couldn't, we'd never be so far in the night now."

"I'm looking for ways to fix what is," Doc said gently. "I'm not sure how yet, but first, I need to see how far the problem goes."

"*Death Flower* knows you are here?"

"Yes. All of them encouraged me to visit and find the extent of the problem. Rosa will do the sexual acts, with me only using her when I need. This way, appearances are kept up."

Citrine looked at Rosa, who nodded eagerly. "I see. Very well, Voice. Should I take her into my room now?"

Rosa's eyes blazed, and Doc laughed. "Yeah, go ahead. Enjoy yourselves. I'll just wait here."

CHAPTER FORTY-THREE

Doc gave Rosa a crooked smile. "You certainly enjoyed them both."

"I did. Thank you, Voice," Rosa murmured, her eyes glowing as she cuddled him. "I was surprised you opted to go back down for another after Citrine."

"I'm considering doubling up just to check all of them more quickly. It was good to find out Quartz isn't embedded... Those aren't their real names, are they?"

"Quartz is not the beaver bestial's birthname. She is new, too. Barely here two months, which might be why she hasn't seen Steward yet. Ruby, Onyx, and Citrine were all called that at birth. Heliodor didn't think of another name when you spoke to her, so maybe her as well."

"Hmm... like the Lily, but not, then," Doc murmured.

"When word gets around from Citrine and Quartz, you will have even more of them interested in you," Rosa smiled. "I will be ready to help as much as you need me to."

Doc laughed lightly as he stroked her hair. "I'm sure you will."

"Onyx was hoping you'd stay until she was off shift. She might not see customers often, but she was entertaining thoughts when you came down for Quartz."

"Luck must've turned my pheromones up to eleven," Doc snorted. "Never had women so interested in me until I came to this world."

"Handsome, smart, kind, *and* powerful," Rosa ticked the points off one by one. "Yes, it is hard to understand why they would be interested, especially when one of their own has gone on at length about how amazing their orgasms were with us."

"Point, you bratty Weed," Doc laughed, kissing her tangled thatch of hair.

"You often fail to see yourself as you should, Doc," Rosa said softly. "It is good to know your ego is not inflated, but you devalue yourself so much."

"Forty years of being told I'm shit is hard to kick in less than a year," Doc shrugged. "With my wives constantly around to tell me otherwise, I'm sure I'll come around in time."

"I'm sure you will, Voice."

The carriage slowed, and Rosa sighed as she shifted off of him. Doc pulled her back to his side, snuggling her until the carriage stopped completely. Rosa giggled, her core warming at how affectionate Doc was with her.

When Harrid opened the door, Doc let Rosa go so he could get out. The land was slowly coming along, but the biggest difference was the crew working on the first house. Doc helped Rosa out before he headed over to where Simpson was.

"How's it going?" Doc asked the foreman.

"Good," Simpson grinned. "I split my old crew into two so there are experienced people to guide the new ones both here and at the stables on your property. Between the two, this has the chance of being trickier, so I'm mostly going to be out here."

"That works for me. Rosa will be continuing to work the land off that way," Doc told Simpson, pointing. "We'll be here for an hour, maybe, and then we'll be heading home."

"Yes, sir. Umm, I had a question, if you don't mind?"

"Go ahead."

"Why just homes, sir?"

"Huh?"

"You've slated all of this for houses. It's amazing, don't get me wrong, but why just that?"

Doc frowned, then slowly began to nod. "Good point. We should have a couple of small businesses in so the residents have things on hand that they would need."

"If you're willing to let me, I can mark out spots to make them spaced out," Simpson offered.

"Let me get an expert. I should add in the sheriff substation that I'll have to allow, and one or two other things, like maybe a clinic..." Doc murmured. "I'll have to see who in town can do the planning."

"McKenzie could, sir, if you're okay with a Hibernian handling it. He doesn't get a lot of work with his heritage, but he's good people. Smart, understands how things should be laid out... doesn't have schooling, though."

Doc wanted to ask about what a Hibernian was, but just nodded. "Let Clyde know where to find him. I'll see about swinging by there tomorrow."

"If you tell him I sent you along, he'll mellow some. McKenzie can be... rough around the edges."

Doc took the fact the bull bestial was calling someone else "rough around the edges" with a nod. "I'll keep that in mind. I'll wrangle Rosa and go talk to him now."

"He might already be at the pub," Simpson said slowly, looking at the late afternoon sky.

"Even easier to talk to him, then," Doc grinned. "I can buy him a drink."

"Sir, that's not a good idea," Simpson said earnestly. "He drinks down at the Green Cup. It's not... friendly... to certain people. Fights are common as the evening wears long."

"I'll go handle it now before it gets too late," Doc said. "I've been in bad places before. This should be fine."

Simpson deflated some, just nodding. "Yes, sir."

Doc went to get Rosa, who was a hundred yards away, rooted into the ground while she worked. Simpson walked over to Clyde and Harrid with slow steps; he had a bad feeling about what he was doing, but Doc was the boss.

"Rosa, we're changing plans. We're going to talk to a planner," Doc told her. "Finish up what you're doing, please."

Rosa pulled her tendrils back into her feet, letting her energy retract to her core. "I'm ready, Voice. Why the change?"

"Simpson pointed out that this should be more than just houses. Taverns, a sheriff's office, and the like should be here, too. I'd rather have someone who knows how to lay things out do that work for me. We're off to see a McKenzie."

"McKenzie... a Hibernian?" Rosa asked.

"Yes." Doc lowered his voice, "Can you explain that?"

"They are from an island near Avalon. Those closest to their ancient line are a mix of elven and bestial, but over the last few hundred years, humanity has added a lot to their stock. Because of their ancient bloodlines, most Hibernians are seen as lesser than elf or bestial."

"Irish," Doc murmured. "I knew I'd heard the name before. Caesar called Ireland 'Hibernia.' The Irish were also second-class citizens in America for generations."

"Many of them came to these shores during their great famine," Rosa said as she finally finished freeing herself from the earth.

"The Great Potato Famine," Doc sighed. "Yeah, I have an idea about it."

"Mother was very distraught about it," Rosa whispered. "It wasn't natural. I'm not sure any dryads are still alive on the island. They were all culled on Avalon."

Doc grimaced. "I'm sure the church was only too glad to do that... Come on."

Harrid was looking grim when Doc approached the carriage. "Doc, this is a bad idea. It'd be best to wait until tomorrow."

"Harrid's right," Clyde added. "The Green Cup is not a good place for any people not from Hibernia... they usually only welcome the occasional bestial who can keep up with them."

"I'm pretty sure I know the people," Doc said softly. "To make friends with them will take me being able to keep up with them. I can manage that."

"Sir, if they see her with you..." Clyde shook his head. "They won't give you the chance. It's not unknown for a Hibernian to attack a mage who has a dryad with them."

"Please, Doc, don't do this," Harrid said simply.

Doc exhaled, but he nodded. "Very well... We'll be going to see McKenzie tomorrow after breakfast, instead."

"Thank you."

"Wasn't looking forward to the trouble that would happen if you stepped into the tavern with her," Clyde agreed.

"Guess we're changing the change, Rosa," Doc said. "Go ahead and do what you were doing. We'll go home after that to catch up with the others."

"As you will it, Voice," Rosa said before drifting back to where she'd been.

Doc watched her go, then glanced at Clyde, who quickly averted his eyes. "Simpson told you, and I guess explained why it was a bad idea."

"He told me the Green Cup and I knew," Clyde said, "but he did explain the potential trouble to Harrid."

"It would be foolish to walk into danger so readily," Harrid grunted.

"I can see your point," Doc said. "I just didn't see it as dangerous. I've been in bad bars before. I didn't know about dryads being a hot point for them, but it makes sense depending on how their history went."

"Thank you for listening. I thought you would dig in."

Doc gave Harrid a twisted grin. "I'm trying to listen to my bodyguard more."

"Gratifying."

"You're doing a lot, Doc," Clyde said. "Hate to see it tragically cut short."

"So would I," Doc agreed, giving the badger bestial a long look.

"You'd been wondering about things, Clyde. I won't tell you everything right now, but if you want to hear some about what's going on and why, now would be a good time."

"Here, sir?"

"Inside the carriage would dampen the sound," Doc said.

"Very well." Clyde double-checked the brake. "Harrid, do you mind sitting up here? Just in case."

"Sure," Harrid said, getting onto the driver's bench as Clyde slipped down.

Doc let Clyde get comfortable before he began, "You know that Rosa is with me, and I'm sure you've heard mention that she let me collar her."

"Yes, sir."

"That's because I have a job to do that she fully supports. You've seen what I'm doing, how I want to help raise everyone up to be equal."

"It's humbling to see a human do that, Doc. Honestly never thought I'd see it."

"Yeah..." Doc mumbled, not touching the human line. "My goal is to bring light back to the world. Everything is dim and darkening. Have you heard the old stories or songs of the Darkness?"

Clyde sat back. "Legends that the vast Darkness encroaches on worlds before snuffing them out."

"It's not just a legend; it's real. The light of this world has been throttled back to the brink."

"Dryads worship Mother... the planet itself," Clyde said slowly. "She's dying?"

"Slowly being robbed of life. She's not dead yet and, Luck willing, she'll not get to that point."

"Sir... Doc, did... a goddess send you to help us?"

Doc's lips turned up. "Lady Luck. She sent me to try to save the world."

"I wasn't sure, but that's what I had thought. I know you praised her, thanked her for everything you can do." Clyde's eyes held wonder. "An actual goddess sent you to help the world..."

"The church will come for me, Clyde. You saw McIan. I think he was far from the worst."

Clyde exhaled, his eyes focusing back on Doc. "Doc, I want to help. I know Luck and you gave me my knee back. I've seen the good you do. None of your wives or friends have *ever* said a word against you, not even when you aren't there. I'm sure you want to be sure, so I'll wait, but I have your back, Doc."

Doc studied Clyde for a moment before he smiled. "Okay. We won't try to hide as much from you, but you can clearly see why we hold things back."

"For good damned reason," Clyde nodded. "As little or as much as you're comfortable with. Against the church, country, or world, sir... I don't have family besides a sister and her kids who I haven't seen in a decade, so they won't have ties to pull on to sway me."

Doc extended his hand, letting the green energy of his spell flare to life. "Give me your hand, please."

Clyde did so without hesitation.

Doc eased the tight muscles in Clyde's back, then released him. "Okay."

"Uh... what was that for?"

"I can sense the Darkness if it preys on a person. You're fine, but I also eased your back pain."

Clyde nodded slowly. "I see. You have to touch them with your energy for that?"

"Yes. If not, it'd be so much easier to know who was potentially against us."

"That would be useful. Life doesn't give us many easy roads, though."

"Hard roads have to be walked," Doc said softly, "but with friends and family, even tough roads feel easier."

"I can agree to that," Clyde grinned.

CHAPTER FORTY-FOUR

"I missed talking about things last night," Doc said when breakfast was over. "You know I'm going to see McKenzie after healing, but before I go back to the Iniquitous Den. However, there's another major project I want to start, as well."

Ayla and Sophia exchanged a look, but waited to hear what he had to say.

"Rope David into this with us. Telegraphy is up and running, but we need to loop it everywhere we have projects. More than that, a new device should be starting up this year or next, if it's not out already. It's called the telephone, and it has a few parts to it. David should have the connections to find them all and get us in on it before it becomes what it should."

"What does it do?" Sonya asked.

"Transmits voices over lines like the telegraph. To start with, it'll be limited to inside a city, but it'll grow to be able to call someone across the country. Eventually, it'll overtake the telegraph. It's a long-term play, but it'll pay off. We want to get in early and get enough control that we can take it over after it's solidly in place."

"The one who controls communication can dictate what's said," Sophia said sagely.

"Exactly," Doc grinned.

"We'll set up to talk to him and get it started," Ayla said. "This sounds like we'll have him doing most of the work. It'll require his connections to run it all down."

"It will. He'll understand the reasoning."

"If he doesn't agree, then what?"

"I'd be shocked, but if he doesn't, I'll have to find a different route. Telephones in my world took over and became the key to all communication for long distances, including what came after them still being based off the idea."

"It might not be as popular here, though," Fiala said softly. "You've said there are differences between here and there."

"Slight, mostly, but there are. I doubt the telephone would be one of those differences. It's too useful."

"We'll arrange a meeting and get it started," Sophia said. "The Ironbeard clan is starting to gather the items needed to lay track to the hot springs."

Doc grinned. "Good. It'll take longer than I think that we'll be in the city, but things in motion are good."

"We've started a lot," Ayla said softly. "I just pray that everything works."

"Have faith in Luck," Lia smiled at Ayla. "Some of it might fall apart, but with what we have in the air, it should be fine in the long run."

"Lia," Doc said softly, "our date is in two days. I have it planned in my head, so I'll make sure things are set up for it. Harrid will also be having a date that night."

All of the women looked at Harrid, who looked away from them.

"That's good, Harrid," Sonya said. "I encourage you. You'll be good for her."

"She's had pain in the past. Not sure if me only being with her for a short while is a good thing..." Harrid mumbled, clearly embarrassed to be discussing his potential relationship.

"You'll give her a bright point," Fiala said. "You've been upfront with her. It's her choice to take what she can have or not."

"Let's get the day started," Doc said, rising and hoping to spare the dwarf even more embarrassment.

His wives saw the ploy for what it was, but let him get away with it. They exchanged goodbyes and kisses, with Doc thanking Lia again for waking him the way she had. Lia's eyes gleamed as she whispered that she had plans for their date, too.

* * *

Doc had barely settled into his office at the Silver Lily when Harrid knocked on the door. "Doc, you have three already," Harrid told him.

"Send in the first," Doc called back and got back to his feet.

A young woman— barely older than a girl— came slowly into the office, looking nervous. Her stub of a hairless tail twitched behind her.

"It's okay, miss," Doc said softly. "Please come in and have a seat."

Eyes darting around the room, the young woman slowly went to the seating area. She took the padded chair designed for tailed bestials, but she sat gingerly, as if it pained her to do so.

Doc crossed the room slower than he normally would, not wanting to spook the clearly frightened woman. "I'm Doc, miss. You came to see me because there's something wrong, right?"

"Y-yes." The word was barely a whisper.

Doc took a seat a little removed from her so she didn't feel trapped. Rosa knelt beside him, giving the young woman a friendly smile. The bestial shifted a bit when she saw Rosa, but bit her lip instead of running away.

"I'm a faith healer," Doc explained softly, "not a mage. She's my friend and companion. Her name is Rosa; she won't harm you."

"It's okay, child," Rosa murmured. "He can help, if you'll let him."

When the woman didn't say anything, Doc asked, "What brought you in today?"

The rat bestial fidgeted for a moment before she whispered, "T-the w-wounds aren't h-healing."

Doc had seen that her tail was an old injury, so he knew it wasn't the problem, but she obviously had seen hardships. "I can help with new hurts. Lady Luck, this frightened young woman comes to you for comfort and aid. Please, show her your mercy."

Eyes going wide when Doc's hands began to glow green, a small squeak slipped from the bestial, making her seem even more like a girl than a woman. She leaned into the chair when Doc extended his hand to her.

"It's not fire. It won't hurt," Doc said soothingly. "Just take my hand. Lady Luck uses me as the conduit for her healing."

With clear trepidation, the bestial extended her hand, then quickly poked his palm before snatching her hand back. When she didn't feel pain, she glanced at Doc and Rosa and saw only concern. Biting her lip again, she extended her hand a second time, laying hers lightly on his. She trembled as her hand rested on his palm.

Someone whipped her or used a cane, Doc thought once he was informed of all of her problems. *Her teeth are bad, like someone makes her gnaw to grind them down... I can manage this.* With a slow exhale, he touched his other hand to Rosa's hair and let his energy pour into the injured woman.

Tears spilled from the bestial's eyes. The warmth, love, and tenderness that filled her was something she'd forgotten she could feel. Her mother had died almost a decade ago, and she'd lived mostly in the alleys since then. Lost in the warmth, she failed to notice her pain fading away.

Rosa had seen all the times the woman had been hurt. Now, though, she saw the last moments of the mother's life as the then child held her and cried. It was followed by how she'd been forced from the hovel she'd shared with her mother by another bestial family who wanted it.

Doc was sad he couldn't replace appendages; he'd have loved to give her back her tail. Instead, he returned her to as close to perfect health as he could before he stopped. "All done," he said softly, keeping his hand where it was.

Sniffling, the bestial blinked at him, then looked at their hands before snatching hers back. "Th-th-thank you." Swallowing, she managed to ask the question she feared, "Wh-what do I... p-pay?"

"All I ever ask is that you say a prayer to Lady Luck," Doc said gently. "It was her power that healed you."

Blank eyes stared at him— she didn't believe what he'd said. Doctors wanted money or "other" repayments. She'd seen a few back-alley people who'd wanted the basest form of payment before. She thought he'd ask for the same, as she'd seen him go into the Iniquitous Den.

"He speaks truth, child," Rosa said simply. "A prayer is all he asks."

It took a moment before the young woman nodded. She understood. He wouldn't want alley trash like her— he had the dryad, the women of the Den, and who knows who else. Relief washed through her that she wouldn't have to do that.

"Wh-what is the prayer?"

Doc wondered about the stutter; his healing hadn't given him any reason for it. *Maybe it's fear based?* He questioned himself, but knew he'd have to look into things later. "No standard prayer. Just thanking her for the help."

"L-lady L-Luck, th-thank you," the woman said, sniffling and on the verge of tears again.

"Child," Rosa said, knowing what Doc would do if he knew of her plight, "could you do small jobs for a place to stay and food?"

Now, the woman flinched. "M-maybe."

"Rosa?" Doc asked.

"She has no home, Voice."

Eyes going wide, the rat bestial wondered how the dryad knew.

"Oh..." The sympathy in Doc's voice tore at the young woman. "You're afraid we're trying to trap you, and I bet I can guess why."

Standing up abruptly, the rat bestial bowed to them, then fled the room.

Doc sighed as he watched her go. "Damn... I hope she's okay."

"I wanted to help, as you would if you knew," Rosa said, "but I couldn't explain more without her knowing about me reading her mind."

"Yeah... Maybe she'll come back later? I'll hope for her."

Harrid stuck his head in. "Is everything okay, Doc?"

"She was scared," Doc said. "Go ahead and send the next person in."

"Yes, sir."

Doc sat back, stroking Rosa's hair. "You did the best you could, Weed. Thank you for trying. I take it she lived the rough life I think she did?"

"Yes. Not fully as bad in some ways, but yes."

"Luck, please give that child, or woman, a small blessing," Doc murmured.

Another knock preceded the next person into the office.

Doc stood up to greet his newest patient. He knew trying to heal the world one person at a time wouldn't work in the long run, but he would do the best he could as his bigger plans came together.

"Welcome, sir. Please have a seat," Doc greeted the bestial holding his arm to his chest.

CHAPTER FORTY-FIVE

Doc treated four bestials for various problems before noon came. He still worried about the nameless young woman he'd treated first. Pushing that worry down as much as he could, he focused on what he was going to be doing soon: meeting McKenzie. The idea of a half-elf, half-bestial was fascinating to him. He wondered how it had come to be. If it was common, there would be more of them, and they wouldn't strictly be called Hibernians.

"I can ask Mother if you want to know more," Rosa murmured from her spot curled up against Doc.

"Idle thoughts," Doc said. "You're going to have to stay in the carriage when I go see him."

"So he doesn't attack right away. Yes."

"Just sit on the floor and wait. I technically can't leave you alone, but as long as no one notices, it should be fine. After this, we'll be going to the Den."

"I have preferences, if that's okay," Rosa murmured. "I'd like to sample Heliodor, at least, Voice. Snowflake Obsidian would be lovely if she agrees, but we might not get her until others have spoken about us. She was reluctant when you talked to her before. If not her, then Onyx."

Doc chuckled as he pictured each of the women she asked for. "I do try to care for the women I love. We'll see. Heliodor, if no one else. For you, my precious little Weed." Doc kissed the top of her head.

"Thank you, Voice," Rosa moaned lightly. Her eyes blazed as she looked over Doc's thoughts— he was thinking about her keeping the bestial women "occupied" while he checked on them.

The carriage started to slow. "That's for after this meeting. I'll be back as soon as I can."

"I'll be waiting for you," Rosa said. She slipped off the seat to sit on the floor beside his legs.

Doc stroked her hair softly; his love for the broken dryad only grew day by day. He sighed when the carriage fully stopped. "Be good, Weed. I'll reward you soon."

"I will be the best dryad in the world, Voice."

"You already are, Rosa," Doc murmured, giving her hair one last stroke before the door opened.

Rosa watched Doc go, her chest warm.

Harrid shut the door behind Doc, glancing back. "She's just going to sit there?"

"For now," Doc said. "Clyde, if anyone looks like trouble, circle back for us. I left something precious inside."

Clyde, seeing the lack of Rosa, nodded. "I'll keep the contents even safer than a bank wagon."

Doc looked back at where they'd stopped. It was a two-story building, but had clearly seen better days. This entire section of the city was only a step above the bestial area. The buildings were just better than shacks, and while the streets were mostly clear of refuse, the alleys were terrible. No sign denoted that this was a business; only the two-story nature of it being in this part of the city gave any hint.

Harrid walked behind Doc, his eyes roving the surroundings. His neck itched, sure that people— unfriendly people that didn't care to see a dwarf— were watching.

Doc knocked firmly on the door. There was no sign, and he wasn't just going to walk in. After a minute, he caught the grumble of someone heading to the door, so he waited.

A few seconds later, the door was yanked open by a short, broad-chested man. His thick, red hair was cut roughly, as if the owner had done it himself. Bright green eyes stared at Doc with mild anger, but they were vertically slitted pupils. The man's lip pulled back, showing longer teeth than a person should have. His ears were sharply pointed like Lia's, but had red fur on the backs.

"What do *you* want?" he growled out.

"I'm looking for McKenzie," Doc said, not reacting to the anger. "Orville Simpson told me to mention his name. I have work for you, hopefully."

The man was quiet as he stared at Doc. Doc stared back with a polite smile in place. He could see how it would be easy to tell a Hibernian apart from other bestials on sight, and the distinctive accent was clearly what Doc knew as Irish.

Grunting, McKenzie left the door open as he went back into his home. Doc took that as an invitation. He followed him inside, trailed by Harrid, who shut the door behind them. It was dark, as no lights were on and every window was shut, but Doc avoided things he didn't want to knock over. McKenzie plopped himself into a rocking chair, his tail wrapping through the backing rails to keep it away from the rockers, and Doc took the plain chair across from him.

"Dwarves aren't welcome down in these parts," McKenzie said stiffly. "Simpson did say his new employer had one as a guard, though. Holyday, he called you."

"Doc Holyday is my name. I need someone who can plan out a community so that it has all the fiddly bits it should have spaced out in a good setting. Simpson said you're the one I want."

McKenzie rocked a little faster. "I'm Hibernian. You still want me?"

"I don't hold the prejudices most do," Doc said simply.

"Hard to believe from a *human*." The last word was full of hate.

"Considering what's likely going on with your home, yes, I figure it would be. The church blighted your crops, didn't they?"

The chair came to a sudden halt and McKenzie leaned forward, showing his teeth. "How would *you* know that?"

Harrid shifted slightly, ready to save Doc if needed.

"Mother told me," Doc said evenly, not reacting to the threat. "The Darkness spreads, grows, and the world teeters, McKenzie. Mother needs our help to push back. She needs light. Luck sent me here to try doing just that."

McKenzie slowly sat back. He didn't rock the chair, but leaned back, clearly thinking. Doc sat in silence, waiting for the Hibernian to make the next move.

"Mother told you? How?"

"This might get me attacked," Doc said, looking at Harrid briefly, then back at McKenzie. "A dryad told me."

"A *dryad* told you? Willingly?"

"Yes, just as she told me of the blight on your crops. I can't speak with Mother, not yet, at least. Rosa talks to her for me. This way, I know what she would tell me."

"Rosa?"

"Ponderosa Pine."

"Hmm... fitting for a dryad in this area. When did you speak with her last?"

"Just before coming inside," Doc said. "She's in my carriage outside."

"You brought a dryad into the city?!" McKenzie hissed, sitting forward slowly. "That fucker Steward will take her!"

"He can't. She's already mine."

McKenzie stood up slowly, his lips drawn back. "Yours?! You collared a dryad?!"

The door opened, startling all of them. Rosa stood in the doorway, her eyes blazing. "I gave myself to him, as Mother wished. Do not threaten the Voice, fox-touched."

McKenzie tried to leap back, but stumbled over the rocking chair and went crashing to the ground. Rosa entered, shutting the door behind her. She gave Doc an apologetic look before turning her gaze back to the Hibernian.

Scrambling to his feet, McKenzie backed slowly away. "How do I know you aren't just a puppet?"

"Rosa, answer all of his questions honestly," Doc said. "I will leave her with you so that you know I'm not making her say anything specific."

McKenzie blinked at Doc, shocked that the mage would leave his precious dryad with him. It wasn't known that a Hibernian wouldn't hurt a dryad, so this was a blatant show of trust.

Doc paused just outside the door with a deep sigh.

"Sir, she was out of the carriage before I could stop her," Clyde said apologetically. "Is she okay?"

"We'll find out shortly," Doc said. "He was going to attack me. Rosa came to stop him without us having to defend ourselves."

"Hey! What are you doing down here?" someone called out.

Doc, Harrid, and Clyde all turned to look at the speaker. The man advancing on them was shorter than a human, as broad as a dwarf, with a clipped beard and a badge visible on his vest.

"Hays McGee, wasn't it?" Doc asked, thinking he remembered the man's name.

The deputy slowed upon seeing Doc. "Uh, yes, sir. This isn't a good part of the city, sir. You shouldn't be down here."

"I've heard they don't care for dwarves much, either," Doc said when the deputy got closer. "Is it wise for you to be wandering through here?"

Hays grimaced. "This is the beat the sheriff gave me. I've shown them enough that they respect me."

"*Shown* them?" Doc asked with just an edge to his tone.

"Had to defend myself a few times," Hays said stiffly. "Last one standing all three times. Now, they just let me walk through."

"Sorry, Deputy. I know some people would've meant that differently," Doc apologized.

"You're not wrong. Anyway, you should clear out."

"I have business with McKenzie," Doc said. "Does the sheriff give you the assignments no one else wants?"

"I've got to earn my place," Hays said tightly.

"Hmm... I see. Who patrols the bestial area, then?"

Hays shook his head, clearly unhappy with what he knew. "Not my place."

"Would you patrol it, if given the chance?" Doc asked.

"A damned sight better than the ones doing it now, but he won't."

"Not right now, no. In the near future, he might. Just give it some time."

Hays shook his head. "I wouldn't say no. Excuse me; I have to keep moving."

Doc said goodbye to Hays before turning back to face the door when it opened. McKenzie stood there, eyeing the deputy for a long moment before motioning Doc to enter.

"She gave her neck to you," McKenzie said a little stiffly. "It's unheard of, but I can't fault her answers to my questions."

"I'm sorry I went against your will, but you didn't order me and he would have attacked you," Rosa said, turning to Doc and kneeling on the floor.

"It's okay. You did the right thing," Doc said. "Come here." Rosa was swiftly next to him, and Doc took her hand in his. "McKenzie, I came to have you make the new area of the city that I'm building into a proper home for those that others denigrate. Can you do the job?"

"What area?" McKenzie asked. "For who, exactly?"

Doc gave a brief rundown of what he was planning for the land he bought. "Well?"

"You can't be real..." McKenzie said softly.

"He is. He is the Voice of Luck, child, as I said. Lady Luck has given us one last chance to make this world bright again. Doc is doing all he can to make that happen."

McKenzie took a deep breath before he nodded. "Voice, tell me what you need and I'll make it happen. I'll rally those of us in the city."

"Doc, this is Ian McKenzie, part of the fox-touched, the leading tribe of the free Hibernian people," Rosa smiled. "Did I do good?"

Doc chuckled, then pulled Rosa to him, kissing her in front of

Harrid and a truly shocked McKenzie. When he broke the kiss, he met her glowing eyes. "You did good, my beautiful Weed."

McKenzie stared at the pair, then glanced at Harrid, who was looking away from them. His mind was reeling from what he'd been told by the dryad and the blatant display of affection Doc gave her. If Doc was truly a Voice, then it was McKenzie's mission to help him.

CHAPTER FORTY-SIX

Doc gave Onyx a smile, having just come back downstairs from his time with Heliodor and Ruby. Rosa had left both women insensate with pleasure. Doc had to admit that Heliodor was aggressive with Ruby, but quickly submitted to Rosa once the dryad showed her prowess in bed.

"How have you been, Onyx?"

"Good, sir. Would you care for another?"

"Drink, you mean?" Doc asked with a smirk.

"If that's your pleasure, sir," Onyx said, looking down shyly.

"I'd been thinking of waiting for your relief to get here," Doc said as he watched her get him a drink.

Onyx slowed in what she was doing before quickly going back to work. "Oh? I, umm... that would be okay with me."

Rosa kept her eyes downcast, though she beamed. She was upset that Heliodor had also been embedded with soul stones, but was eager to check Onyx. She thought the lovely panda bestial was unlikely to have them.

"Excuse me? Madam would like to speak with you," a soft voice said from behind him.

Doc looked back to find a small rat bestial girl in a clean maid's uniform standing there. "I'm sorry miss, what was that?"

"Madam wishes to speak with you, Sir," the girl said again, the capital on the title clear to Doc's ear.

"Your cognac, sir," Onyx said softly. "If... after you're done...?"

"Unless she asks me to leave, I'd be happy to," Doc said, placing a tip on the counter and picking up his drink. "Please, lead me," he told the maid.

"This way, Sir," the girl said, leading them toward the stairs.

They were taken to what Doc would've thought was just another room for the staff, but when the maid brought them in, he found an office. The woman behind the desk was half-elven, her hair up and showing off the slightly pointed tips of her ears. Her facial features were more Asian than he'd seen anyone have on this world. The dress she had on was figure tight, but went up to her neck. Her arms were left bare, and Doc could see small scars mostly covered by makeup.

"Madam, the member you asked for," the maid squeaked before scurrying out.

Inscrutable eyes scanned Doc before flicking to Rosa, then back. "Doc Holyday, member forty-two, owner of Luck's Holdings. Welcome to my humble business."

"Nothing humble about it, Madam," Doc said, crossing the room to sit across from her. "This place is a treasure filled with lovely gems."

Lips quirking up, the madam nodded back to him. "You may call me Madam Zu. How have you found my business, now that you've been here a few times?"

Doc watched her pick up a long mythrium pipe dotted with precious gems and soul stones, then use a match to light it. "That's a beautiful pipe, Madam Zu. To answer the question, I've found your women to be clean, honest, and wonderfully open to new ideas."

"I've heard that you yourself do not take time with them, just your dryad. An associate tells me she would get nothing from doing so."

"I'm sure that both the sheriff and Steward know some about dryads."

"True. One has knowledge and the other has heard others speak of it. Both are envious of you having her."

"All they have to do is go collar one," Doc smiled.

Madam Zu took a long inhale on her pipe before slowly exhaling the smoke. "You make it sound effortless."

"It's not. A dryad will kill anyone who tries it."

"And yet here you are, with her," Zu said, motioning to Rosa with the end of her pipe.

"I'm special," Doc chuckled. "I've heard that Steward comes by semi-regularly. I was surprised to see the soul stone earring on one of your bartenders, too."

"Ah, Snowflake Obsidian is the one Steward is currently focused on. He favors a single conquest at a time, then uses them exclusively before changing his focus. It's good, because my girls prefer not to see him again after a while. Though that, of course, is not an option for my longest-standing member."

Doc sipped his cognac, trying to find a way to see if she knew what the soulsmith had done to the women without giving it away. "I saw light scarring on a few of them near their shoulders and hips. Just once, I thought it was odd, but more of them have identical scarring. They also seem hesitant if the act of sex touches on blood. Rosa here has sipped from them gently, which is what she gets out of coming here, but I found it extremely odd."

Madam Zu would've been a master poker player— her expression didn't shift at all. "One or more of my members has... unusual tastes. They've paid me and the women involved for the pain inflicted. I'm not surprised they are hesitant to be injured again, but none of them seem to have minded your dryad."

"Dryads are special that way," Doc chuckled. "When the pain is so slight and happens while they are orgasming, well, I doubt they even realize it's happening."

"I'll talk with them. If they are okay with it, I won't have to bring it back up. If they do object, you will have to compensate them for the harm. Steward has paid them all well for what he's done."

"Hmm..." Doc said thoughtfully as he set his empty glass on her desk. "I'd be very leery of letting a soulsmith do anything to me. I don't know what one can do, but it seems like they could do lasting harm."

Madam Zu was silent for a long moment as she smoked her pipe. "Do you think he has permanently harmed my girls?"

"I'm sure you've had a doctor in to check them?" Doc asked.

"Yes, but that wasn't my question, Mr. Holyday. I happen to know you are a spirit healer. Would you check my girls for me?"

Doc stared at Zu for a long moment before glancing at Rosa, who nodded fractionally. "I already have checked the ones I've been with. I have wives to care for and wanted to make sure I was safe, after all."

"And?"

"He's put activated soul stones into each of them. Removing them would rip parts of their souls out. Leaving them in means he can control their limbs."

Zu's eyes narrowed; it was the first real emotion she'd shown. "He has... has he?"

"Ruby, Heliodor, and Citrine so far. Quartz was clear. I was about to take Onyx upstairs before you summoned me, and had hoped to snag Snowflake, as well. If you're going to work with me, I'll check all of them much quicker."

Rosa pouted slightly, and Doc chuckled. "I'm sure we can stop by once a day after noon so you can have some fun, Weed, even if we've finished checking. A few of them would clamor for a repeat."

"What does she do that others cannot do?" Zu asked as she set her pipe down.

"Weed, show her your full tongue."

Zu's eyebrows rose slightly at the sight. "I know men who aren't as endowed as that. No wonder they enjoy her."

"It's also more agile than a man's length," Doc chuckled.

"I have been given a lot to consider, and yes, I will make sure that all my girls are seen by you, if you will see them two a day."

"Snowflake isn't on duty yet. If you would ask her to see me before she does, that would be good. I'll snag Onyx after the changeover."

Zu paused, staring at him with her mask back in place. "Those two are far from similar."

"Every woman is beautiful," Doc said softly. "It's something most people don't understand or acknowledge. My wives include an elf, dwarf, half-elf, and two bestials, one of which is a Sagesse."

"I had heard you had multiple wives, but not the extent," Zu said. "Very well." She pulled a silver rope behind her. "Let me have Snowflake Obsidian informed."

"Why gems?" Doc asked.

"Because they are beautiful and should be cared for properly," Zu replied.

A soft knock came on the door before the same young rat girl opened it. "Madam?"

"Tell Snowflake Obsidian to attend me."

"Yes, Madam." She was gone just as quickly as she came.

Doc sat back. "Does she have the choice to refuse?"

"No. Not the exam, at least. You hold that they should be given a choice? How would I stay open if that was true? The majority of my business is the members. Refusing them would see them leave."

"My wife, Lia, ran a brothel in Deep Gulch. All the women there got to choose their patrons. Now, she didn't cater as you do, even though her women were all bestial, as well. I think your members would be shocked and you'd lose about half. The other half would be happier because they would know the women actually value them enough to agree."

Zu picked her pipe back up, cleaning the small bowl out to refill it. "That's a lot of lost business."

"What's more important: the business or your girls?"

Zu lit the new pipe, clearly not answering him.

"Pity," Doc finally said.

"The girls, but my life is dictated by my business," Zu answered slowly.

"Have you spread out where your income comes from?"

"What do you mean?"

"Diversification means you have a greater chance of surviving a sudden downturn. Or even having a second place to let your gems shine," Doc grinned as he thought of different ways to make Zu see things his way. "What if I let you have a small cut of a few business ventures coming up?"

"A small investment is unlikely to help offset what I would lose," Zu said.

"You think so, do you?"

"Yes, but you seem to think differently."

"My mine in Deep Gulch— not including the other two I picked up recently— brought in over a hundred thousand a month. That's small when compared to what else I have lined up in Furden."

Zu's head canted slightly as she exhaled a long slow stream of smoke. "I would be willing to hear more…"

"Two of my wives will come by to talk to you. Ayla and Sophia handle all the business for me." Doc briefly thought about asking after Citrine, but opted instead to get Sophia to angle it during the negotiations.

"Hmm… I'll be very interested in seeing them."

A knock on the door came a second before it opened, revealing Snowflake Obsidian in a white dress that flowed down her body. It obscured what she looked like, but left her arms from the elbows down exposed. "Madam, you called for me?" Her eyes darted to Doc and Rosa briefly.

"Snowflake Obsidian, Mr. Holyday and his companion here will be taking up at least an hour of your time," Zu informed her.

A frown was there and gone on Snowflake's face before the professional smile came back to her. "Yes, Madam. I thought you were going to save my first time for Mr. Steward?"

"Your first time with a man was being saved for that," Zu said calmly. "I have since changed my mind. Even Mr. Steward will not be having you unless you agree to it. Some things have since come to light, and I will be re-evaluating my business with him."

"Miss," Doc said softly, "I won't be doing anything sexual with you, either."

Snowflake looked at Rosa, then took a deep breath. "Very well, Madam."

"Mr. Holyday, she will see to your needs," Zu said as she exhaled another streamer of smoke.

Doc rose gracefully from his seat, Rosa matching him. "I'll send my wives over in a day or two. Good day, Madam Zu." Doc bowed formally to her from the waist at a slight angle, arms stiffly at his sides.

Zu's eyebrow rose as she watched him leave. No one she'd met in this country had known how to bow formally to her before; her interest went up another notch just from that gesture.

CHAPTER FORTY-SEVEN

Snowflake led them just down the hall to her room. Shutting the door behind them, she repressed a shiver— she was still safe if the man could be trusted. A faint voice told her not to trust Doc; he would lie to her.

Rosa's lips pursed, having been keeping the edge of her eye on the bestial. When she knelt beside Doc, she whispered, "Something is lying to her about you. It's a voice she isn't really aware of."

Doc nodded slightly, taking in that tidbit of information silently. Crossing his leg, Doc waited for the bartender to get comfortable. Snowflake's clear wariness had her sitting on the edge of her seat as far removed from him as she could be, yet still appear to be a good hostess.

"What is it you wanted with me, sir?"

"To talk, mostly," Doc smiled. "I've talked to a few of the women here already."

Snowflake knew that; she'd seen him take Ruby up on his first day to the Den. After he'd left, she'd heard from Ruby herself about how nice, caring, and amazing her time had been with him and Rosa. Ruby swore that Doc hadn't touched her, even when she'd basically begged him to. Rosa had been her only companion, and she'd been quite vocal about how talented the dryad was. A nagging voice told her that Ruby could've lied— Doc might've paid her to lie to the others.

Doc saw the moment Snowflake's thoughts shifted. "You don't believe me, do you?"

Eyes going wide, Snowflake shook her head. "No, sir. I would never say that."

"It's okay to be wary of a man you've only talked to once. Honestly, that's for the best, that wariness."

Off-balance at Doc's easy acceptance of her not being comfortable, she was unsure of what to do or say. "No, sir. I'm fine. Madam only lets the best people become members."

"She lets anyone who can *pay* become members," Doc corrected her gently. "Just because someone has money doesn't make them a good person. Plenty of wealthy people are terrible people."

"Are you saying you're a bad person, sir?"

"I could be," Doc said softly, looking away from her. "It would be easy to become a bad person in my place. I have power, wealth, and influence. I could easily let those change me into a person who would force people to do only as I demanded."

Eyes going wide, Snowflake started to become afraid. The voice whispered that he was telling her the truth, that the man in the room here with her was such a man. It said that she should invoke the clause in her contract to have him removed from her room. It would cause trouble with the madam, but it would be best if she did.

"Instead, I try to do the best I can," Doc went on, not watching her. "I'm in the process of a few projects that'll not only do me good, but will help all those who've been ignored or hated get a step up."

"All because it'll profit you..." Snowflake murmured the words she was hearing, not even aware she did it.

"Profit me?" Doc asked, meeting her eyes. "It's costing me tens of thousands, maybe even hundreds of thousands of dollars. If I'm very lucky, I'll break even, but honestly, it's going to be a loss."

Brow furrowing, Snowflake saw honesty in his eyes. She was a damned good judge of character— always had been— and what she was seeing said he was honest... but she was sure he was lying. She could hear the doubt clearly in her mind, and that dissonance was jarring to her.

"I noticed your earring the first day we talked. Mythrium and soul stone are expensive as hell. Must've been a gift from someone," Doc said casually.

A smile touched her lips as she reached up to play with it. "Yes..." She knew Richard Steward was a good man; she was even warming to the idea of him being her first man. When she'd met him, she'd disliked him, but her thoughts had been changing ever since she'd been given this precious gift. Steward was a good man— a great man — who would treat her the way she deserved. "A friend gave it to me."

"Only man I know of who could give soul stones away so freely would be the soulsmith," Doc chuckled. "I've heard he's a man who visits here often."

The voice warned her again that Doc was trying to trick her somehow. "At times..." Snowflake said slowly.

"Do you always keep it in? I know my wives take theirs out when they bathe. Some metals can cause problems if you bathe with them."

"I have to keep it in," Snowflake said, her tone was a bit mechanical as she said it. "It has to stay in all the time. It'll be fine... just keep it in."

"Doc, may I have my time with her, please?" Rosa whispered. "If she's okay with me?"

The voice that warned her about Doc clamored for her to take the dryad. The more willing she was with the dryad, the better. Face heating slightly, Snowflake shifted. She'd always liked the softness of women, but her thoughts right now were extreme even for her.

"I would be okay with her," Snowflake murmured, eyeing Rosa like a meal.

"By all means, Weed, show her your skills. Miss, you'd prefer to be in your bedroom away from me?"

"Yes," Snowflake said. There was a surge of worry, but having the dryad was all encompassing, enough to drive that worry out.

"I'll sit right here," Doc said. "Have fun."

Rosa rose to her feet, then slowly began to strip. Her dresses were no longer simple sundresses, but they weren't as complicated as most dresses, so she was nude in quick order. Snowflake stalked toward the dryad, who backed away from her submissively, coincidentally toward the bedroom.

Doc met Rosa's eyes briefly, and she gave him a fractional nod before bolting into the bedroom. Snowflake let out a deep growl as she rushed after the fleeing woman. Doc blinked, then shifted in his seat. The sight had been intriguing, but he wasn't about to do anything.

The cries of pleasure that came from the bedroom were hard to ignore. When those cries started coming from Snowflake instead of Rosa, he smiled, knowing who was in charge at that point. Minutes ticked by as the cries grew in intensity, and Doc whistled softly. It was clear Rosa was pushing the white tiger bestial for all she was worth.

A brief scream of pain came from the room before the pleased cries returned. Doc frowned at the closed door— the cry had been Snowflake's. He was considering whether he should check when the sounds died off.

A moment later, Rosa came out of the bedroom. Sweat slicked her body, but she was smiling broadly. "She is free of his influence," Rosa murmured, going to Doc and presenting him with the earring. "Come check her while she is out, Voice."

Doc took the earring and almost dropped it— it felt wrong to him and, for a brief moment, he thought he'd heard a faint voice. "What *is* that?"

"It's enchanted to influence the one touching it to view the soul-smith as the only man for them. Every other man is a liar who will trick and hurt them," Rosa murmured. "It's also enchanted to make the person holding it want to wear it... if they are female."

Doc's blood went cold. "I see."

"Cleanse it, and then we can leave it in the bedroom. When she finds it, she'll put it back on, but it won't do what it did before. She'll never know what happened and she'll be free of its effects."

Doc stood up. "Okay, let's go."

Rosa didn't try to tease him, just taking his hand to lead him into the bedroom. Snowflake was sprawled on the bed. Her legs were wide open and her arms were at her sides; the sheets were ripped where she'd obviously been clawing at them.

"Damn... you worked her over," Doc murmured.

"She was amazing," Rosa said huskily. "After you check her, I would love to help you properly, Voice."

Doc knew he was tenting his pants; he had been for nearly an hour. It'd waned when he'd heard about the earring, but Rosa's offer had him fully ready to let her. Coughing, he summoned his gift and touched Snowflake's foot.

After a minute, he let it go, then quickly left the room. Snowflake was a beauty and, even though he wouldn't touch her without her consent, he'd admit that her body was stirring up thoughts. He'd barely left the bedroom when the door snicked shut. Looking back, he saw Rosa already kneeling for him.

"Was she okay, Voice?" Rosa asked, her eyes glowing brightly.

"No stones, and her minor issues are healed," Doc said as he turned back to her. "Let's not take long. I don't want her first sight waking up to be you and me together."

"As you decree, Voice," Rosa moaned.

* * *

Doc led Rosa down to the private lounge shortly after they'd finished. Snowflake was still asleep, which worked for Doc— he wanted her to have time to figure things out for herself. When he reached the private lounge, he slowed.

Onyx saw him; there was hurt in her eyes before she covered it up with professionalism. "Sir, all done for today?"

Doc crossed to the bar with a smile on his lips. "I hope not. I had someone I wanted to spend time with before I was called away."

Onyx's lips quivered. "I'm sure Snowflake managed to assist you."

Doc wasn't sure how the panda bestial knew that he'd been with Snowflake, but he shook his head. "That was different. The madam arranged that. I had my own choice already picked out. I'm sorry it took me so long to come back."

Confusion dominated Onyx's emotional state, but hope flared brightly in it. "Oh... uh... It's okay, sir. You don't need to act—"

"I'm not acting," Doc cut her off with gentleness. "You're a beauty, Onyx. Maybe others don't see that like I do, but you are. If you don't want me to wait for you to get relieved, I'll go to not embarrass you. But, if you'd like me to wait, I'll be happy to drink and just watch you work until then."

Round furred ears twitching, Onyx shifted in place, her face heating. "Umm. I... cognac!" She hurried off to get his preferred drink.

Rosa giggled softly beside him. "She'll be sweet, Voice. I will treat her tenderly. Thank you."

"I might take a little more of a hands-on approach with her," Doc murmured back. "Not sex, but maybe a bit of light touching. She'll be the only one who can say that."

Rosa's eyes blazed for a moment. "She won't understand how special that is unless you tell her, or she talks to the others."

"She'll talk to the others, or they will with her," Doc grinned. He thought about Onyx finding out that he'd treated her differently, and how she'd smile secretively and keep it to herself, knowing that she was special.

"Yes, she will," Rosa murmured, seeing his thoughts.

"Your drink, sir... please stay... for me?" Onyx asked hesitantly, after rushing back to him.

Doc took a seat at the bar, accepting the glass. "Gladly, Onyx. Gladly."

When Snowflake made it downstairs, she paused upon seeing Doc. Licking her lips, uncertain if he was going to do or say anything, she slipped behind the bar. Onyx murmured to her, thanking her before getting out of Snowflake's way. The white tiger bestial looked away from Doc, unsure if she should approach him. By the time she looked back, Doc was already walking with his arm around Onyx's waist, laughing with the panda bestial.

"Onyx?" Snowflake whispered in shock. Doc hadn't touched her at all, but he was going upstairs with her friend, holding her waist like a lover. The normal voice that told her to be wary of men didn't speak to her, and she wasn't even aware that her earring was missing.

CHAPTER FORTY-EIGHT

Doc kissed Rosa before leaving Onyx's room. "Good girl, Weed."

"Thank you, Voice," Rosa whispered. "She was very happy. I think you're right. She heard that you hadn't touched the others, so when you joined in, she was ecstatic."

"That's as much as I'll do without at least one of the others present," Doc said.

"I will not push you for more. I can see how you view it."

"Thank you, Weed. We should get home. We've stayed here much longer than I intended to."

"As you wish, Voice."

The pair left Onyx's room; the panda bestial was a puddle of bliss on her bed. Rosa had been gentler with the softly padded woman, but she didn't relent, either. Doc let her have her way, as Onyx had clearly been exuberantly enjoying everything.

Making it down to the private lounge, Doc slowed. Steward was at the bar, trying to talk to Snowflake. It was clear that he was upset, and the bartender was doing her best to answer his questions.

"Steward, you were right about this place," Doc said, raising his voice enough to reach the soulsmith at the bar. "Goodness, there are many unique and wonderful women here."

Steward jerked back, turning to yell at who was interrupting his time with Snowflake. He stopped himself, plastering a smile on his face instead when he saw Doc. "Ah, Holyday. Decided to sample the gems after all, did you?"

"You did suggest the place to me. I figured that a man of your keen mind would know what was best."

"Ah, who did you just see?" Steward asked, clearly curious as to Doc's preferences.

Snowflake looked startled— the two men were talking amiably, but she silently snuck away, thankful for the chance to escape. Ruby was sitting off to one side. She'd been staying as unobtrusive as she could with Steward in the room, but had smiled when she saw Doc was still there. Watching the two men, she wasn't sure the conversation was actually as pleasant as it appeared.

"Onyx," Doc smiled. "We spent quite a bit of time with her."

Steward's eyes went to Rosa for a long moment before returning to Doc. "Both of you?"

"Rosa does most of the work," Doc chuckled. "It's rather entertaining to see them try to handle an eager dryad."

Steward's eyes narrowed fractionally. "I would agree. That would be a sight to see. I doubt she gets much out of it, though."

Doc leaned in to act conspiratorial, "Blood. She sips from them while they're distracted. Besides, she can clean up any mess I make. It's not what she'd prefer, but it's about my needs, not hers."

"As it should be," Steward nodded, a hint of jealousy in his tone.

"Just as I tell my wives," Doc shrugged. "A man has needs. If they want to complain about my methods, well, this place has filled the needs they can't or won't touch."

"Sounds like your wives don't understand their places."

"Some of them are willful," Doc said. He hated the way he had to act, but knew Steward would believe it. "Not like I can snip the parts I don't like out of them."

"Hmm, yes... that would be useful," Steward said slowly.

"Might as well ask for the moon with all the good it does. At least I can control this one," Doc said, motioning to Rosa beside him.

"A collar manages to make even the most stubborn dryad obey."

"I didn't mean to interrupt you," Doc said when he noticed another staff member slip behind the bar, Snowflake having vanished. "Just wanted to thank you for the information on this place. Onyx and Citrine have made it very entertaining so far."

"Citrine? Hmm... you've had the elf?"

Doc looked around for a moment, then leaned in. "I love nipping the tips of their ears when I'm behind them."

Steward chuckled. "I haven't tried that. I will soon, now that you mention it. Tonight, though..." He trailed off when he realized that Snowflake was gone. "Apoc be damned!" he hissed.

"Problem?" Doc asked. "She looks good to me."

Steward snorted. "I was almost there with the white tiger. I was sure tonight would be the night she'd be ready for me."

"Oh, I've talked to her before. She seems... reluctant to me."

"For most, she would be," Steward chuckled. "Most women find me irresistible after I've talked to them. Silly cat misplaced the earring I gave her. Ah well, she'll be wearing it soon after she finds it again."

"Hmm? You gave her some jewelry?"

"I felt it would help... ease her acceptance of me," Steward shrugged. "Won't be tonight, I suppose."

"Why don't we sit and have a drink?" Doc offered. "Maybe she'll be back with it shortly." He hoped that Steward would decline, as he hated playing friendly to this creep who should be shot.

"I'll pass. My desire to be here tonight is gone now. I'll come back tomorrow once she's remembered to wear what she's been given."

"I'll see you again. Have a good evening."

"You, as well, Holyday."

Doc waved to the bartender, one of the women he hadn't met yet. "A cognac, please?"

She went to fill the order as the rat-girl maid came hurrying into the room. Pausing, she looked around, then went over to Ruby. Rosa watched the pair before nodding. The maid rushed back upstairs a moment later.

Doc thanked the bartender and tipped her when he took the drink. He walked toward the door slowly, sipping as he went.

"The madam was going to summon Steward," Rosa murmured. "He left before the maid made it down here."

"We have at least a day or two before he finds out things have turned sour for him," Doc murmured back. "Let's go tell our wives what we've found out."

Setting down the half empty glass, he left the lounge.

*　*　*

It was after dinner when Doc finally got to talk about his day. "That's where we are right now," Doc finished.

"So the madam isn't as bad as we thought," Lia murmured. "Still, the fact that she'd even consider selling Citrine's debt is wrong. Us buying it isn't much better."

"Sophia, Ayla, if you can swing that into whatever deal you work out with her, that'd be amazing," Doc said.

"It'll be difficult, but we'll work on it," Ayla replied.

"Did she really consider the offer, or was she stalling Steward at the point Citrine recalled?" Sophia asked.

"Citrine thought she was seriously considering it," Rosa answered.

"We'll see what we can do," Ayla said. "As for our day, David agreed to back the telephone invention. He also agreed that the telegraph running to the other mines is a good idea, and it'll be simple enough since we'll want the railroad to connect them."

"He was very excited about the idea of instantaneous communication between distant people. I think he saw what you did, Doc," Sophia added. "We'll be starting up another subsidiary of Luck's Holdings. He suggested 'Luck's Voice' as the name of the company."

Doc chuckled at the name, but the more he thought about it, the funnier it became to him. He was full belly laughing before he regained his composure.

"I'll let him know you agree."

"It *is* rather funny," Sonya giggled.

"It really is," Fiala nodded, wiping her own eyes free of laughter-tears.

"I'm glad he's an ally," Doc said, wiping away tears. "Things would've been much harder here if not for him."

"Agreed," Ayla nodded.

"You'll be getting busier at the Silver Lily soon," Sonya said.

"The bestials seem to be spreading the word amongst each other," Doc agreed. "The more we help them, the more trusting they'll be when we open up the houses to them, hopefully."

"That would be a hard thing to sell normally, but your goodwill with them is growing rapidly," Fiala smiled. "It's not all bad news in the city, at least."

"The sheriff, Steward, and Strongarm are the major blocks," Sophia said.

"We've put ourselves directly in the path of the soulsmith, at the very least," Lia said. "I think he'll be the one to move against us first."

"Hopefully, we get time to solidify a few more friendships before that happens," Doc said. "The madam might upset him before we can."

"Depending on what she tells him, we'll either get dragged in quickly or he'll blame her," Sophia said.

"True... we don't control that, though. We focus on what we *can* control. I'll be seeing more of the staff there after the Silver Lily tomorrow. That'll give me a better idea of how invasive the problem is."

"Tomorrow, we'll see the madam before visiting David again," Ayla said. "We'll get started on trying to arrange things with her."

"We should head to bed for tonight," Fiala said. "You'll be healing more tomorrow, and we should make sure Rosa is filled for you."

"Yes, please," Rosa said eagerly.

The others laughed at her quick acceptance. They all knew she'd keep Doc in bed all the time if she could. A lot of them would join them for long stretches if that was the case, and none of them would deny it.

"You'll be ready for our date after tomorrow night?" Lia asked Doc as they went to bathe.

"Yes. I've had a helper arrange things."

"Rosa, what's he planning?" Lia asked.

"I can't tell you," Rosa whispered. "He was quite firm on that topic."

"I see. A surprise it is, then. I do trust my husband to know me."

"I'll be doing my best," Doc smiled, taking Lia's hand. "If I do badly, tell me so I can learn?"

"I will," Lia murmured, pulling him closer to kiss his cheek.

CHAPTER FORTY-NINE

The next day was calm: Doc had healed a half-dozen people, five of whom were bestials and a half-dwarf who'd nearly sliced his own thumb off. He also checked two more women at the Iniquitous Den. One of them had also been embedded with soul stones, increasing his reasons to hate Steward.

Ayla and Sophia managed to put together a contract with the madam, but only after they'd cleared up the misconception that Zu was willing in any way to sell Citrine. That'd almost ended the budding relationship before it really began, but it was fixed after some discussion and Citrine being called in to explain.

Fiala and Sonya had tea with the dwarven women, plus Tarbo's wife. When she was told about the housing project, she asked insightful questions. It appeared that she'd never had an outlet to get involved in before, and the idea of others having good, clean homes sparked with her. Fiala and Sonya let Ayla and Sophia know that Tarbo would likely be seeking to talk with them about joining in on that project.

* * *

Doc seated Sonya at the table for breakfast. They were only a little later than normal, as she'd come to wake him early. "Hopefully we didn't delay things too much," Sonya said.

"We told Charles that we'd eat a little later today," Fiala smiled softly. "You didn't delay anything."

"Thank you."

"All of us understand our unique needs," Sophia said softly, "which makes us want to help each other out even more."

"Since we're all here, I can tell you my plans for today," Doc said, taking his own seat. "Lia, after breakfast, we're going out. We'll be back tomorrow."

"An all-day date?" Ayla asked with a smirk.

"Travel time. I'm not taking Lia into the city for her date."

"Meaning you've planned on taking me out into the wilds?" Lia asked with a smile.

"Figured you'd enjoy that more than a fancy dinner and a show. Just the two of us riding out and having a night together."

"Shouldn't you take Rosa with you?" Harrid asked. "If you're going into the wilds, even the ones close to the city, it might be for the best."

"Hmm... Harrid has a point, and while Rosa does get to spend a lot of time with you, she hasn't had a date night, either," Lia said.

"That's very kind of you, Lia," Rosa murmured from between Lia's and Doc's seats. "I wouldn't wish to intrude on your time with him."

"Lia offered," Doc said. "Adding you to one of our horses should be fine."

"It'll make the rest of us feel better, too," Fiala said.

"Agreed," Sonya chimed in.

"It really will," Sophia added. "We know Lia is fully at home off-trail, but Rosa is literally part of nature."

"It reminds me of my first time with Rosa." Ayla smiled as she recalled that night.

"The night you accepted me and I helped you find yourself." Rosa's eyes glowed brightly.

"A lot changed because of that," Doc said softly.

Harrid shifted uncomfortably with the current conversation.

Lia laughed as she watched him. "We'll leave it there, Harrid, but you got your way— Rosa will come with us."

"Thank you," Harrid exhaled.

"What about your date, though?" Lia went on after he thanked her. "What have you settled on?"

Harrid coughed roughly; he'd been taking a drink and hadn't expected the question. Sonya slapped him on the back to help. The others grinned as the dwarf was clearly trying to figure out what to say.

"Nice timing, Lia," Doc chuckled. "We should let him have his dates without us grilling him. It's hard enough for him to ask me for the days off."

"Hmm... there is that," Lia nodded.

"She's good for him," Rosa said. "The two of them will be good together."

A knock came on the door just before Charles led his helper into the room, ready to serve them breakfast. That cut off any conversation; they all felt the edges of hunger and were ready to dig into what the talented man had cooked for them.

* * *

It didn't take long to head out, as the groom, Vic, had arranged the horses for them. The deer bestial was quick to add another saddle blanket onto Doc's horse to make it more comfortable for Rosa.

They went up river, away from the city and the manor. Doc asked Lia to lead, as she had more experience than he did for off-trail riding. It was a quiet ride for all of them— Rosa behaved herself, just holding Doc around the waist and leaning lightly into his back.

If it hadn't been summer, it would've been more pleasant than it was. Doc was still glad he was in his road clothing and not a suit. He knew he'd be dying in a suit. At the moment, he was hot, but not in danger of heat stroke. He smiled at the thought of showing up to the opera in his current outfit. They'd never allow him in, even with all his money, as society had "*standards.*"

"You find the need for specific clothes foolish?" Rosa asked.

"The minutiae of it is what I find foolish," Doc said. "Where the waist of the jacket is tailored, for instance. My bowler got a lot of side-eye at the opera and play. I'll have to get a top hat. Probably should get a cane, too. All the gentlemen had them. I mostly ignored it, but if I'm going to play the part, I should get them."

"Just as we have to pay attention to the cut of our dresses when we go out," Lia said. "Well, more them than me. Wearing my native clothing is fine in most situations, even if it does make people uneasy. If I was going with you to the opera or another major event, though, even I would need to wear an appropriate dress. Ayla and Sophia have done wonders for us in that regard, but I think Fiala is starting to take the lead there."

"Because of the tea club she's involved in?"

"Yes. Fiala seems to be doing better about her role, too. Rosa?"

"She is. Her ability to meet friendly ladies and learn from them has given her a tremendous boost. She knows some of them laugh behind her back, but she has grasped at what she can. You should praise her soon, Voice. When we get back, you will find a gift from her. She took the initiative to get it made for you."

Doc smiled softly at the thought of his lovely wife arranging a surprise gift for him. "I won't even ask. When we get back, I'll make sure to thank her."

"You chose well for my date, Doc," Lia said, looking back briefly. "This is vastly preferable to a night in the city for me. For us," she amended with another glance back at Rosa.

"Agreed," Rosa murmured, her arms tightening briefly on Doc. "Under the stars with our shaman will be much better."

"I want to give you all some special time, especially before shit starts hitting the fan," Doc said. "We've laid the groundwork, but in the near future, some of those against us will move to thwart us."

"We'll deal with them as needed," Lia said. "I was considering just killing Steward, but our wives would balk at the thought. Sophia would have the worst of it, as it throws aside her stance on the laws. I didn't bring it up because of that."

"For the best," Doc nodded. "I'd rather not become a flat killer unless needed. If he'd touched one of our wives, I'd probably do it myself, though."

"We'd do it together," Lia said softly.

"I could help," Rosa murmured. "I can make my nectar take on a killing taint. I think you called it 'anesthetic,' Doc."

"That reminds me, Lia, can you set up to make more Moondew?" Doc asked.

"I have the still and other pieces being put together," Lia chuckled. "It'll be a while before we have it distilled down correctly, but I'm working on it. Rosa can give us the right amounts as needed. Right now, we have a couple of bottles on hand and her undiluted nectar to help us."

"A good wife thinks of everything," Doc laughed. "Just proves that my wives are all very good wives."

* * *

They spent the rest of the ride chatting about the staff, the manor, and other odds and ends. When they finally made camp, it was near a clearing by the river's edge, maybe six hours from the manor.

Doc got the camp set up while Rosa and Lia went into the water to catch fish. He caught glances of Lia in just her underclothes, standing in the water, spearfishing. Rosa had gone further, opting for being completely naked as she stood still in the water.

Life was good. Doc said a silent prayer to Luck, thanking her for this chance to live a better life. By the time he had a fire going, Lia and Rosa were coming back to the camp. They each had a trout in hand, and Rosa's was the larger of the two.

"I see you both had success," Doc said as he got ready to prep the fish for cooking.

"She cheats," Lia chuckled.

"It isn't cheating. I just asked for a fish that wouldn't mind feeding the Voice," Rosa countered.

"You asked nature and nature responded," Doc chuckled. "I can see why Lia says you cheated. If I had a fly pole, I might've caught one, but not as quickly or as easily as you both did."

"You're going to handle them?" Lia asked when Doc held out his hands to her.

"I'll take care of them," Doc said. "I don't get to cook often anymore. Thought you'd enjoy having your husband show that he can care for you in the wilds."

"I do," Lia murmured, handing her trout over and kissing him. "For a tribe, everyone needs to know how to bring in food and prepare it. I'm glad you know how to do this."

Rosa set her fish on the rock Doc was using as his preparation surface. "You washed the rock first?"

"As best as I could with what we had. I'll be cooking it long enough to not worry about it, but I'm still a man of my world."

"Daf told me about your talk with her," Lia chuckled, sitting down where she could watch him. "How you insisted on them scrubbing the kitchen after cutting meat. She was a little miffed, but did as you asked."

"She makes great food and doesn't keep a dirty kitchen, like I told her. It just wasn't as clean as I'd have preferred. Part of that is convenience. My old world had hot and cold water on demand in every kitchen, so cleaning was much easier."

"Tell me more about it, please?" Lia asked. "You say it had a lot in common with ours, but that there were only humans. Were there no elves who lived on the continent before humanity came to it?"

"Native tribes, like yours, but they were human, not elven," Doc said. "Humanity never needed another race to be what you have here. Without others, we isolated specific humans for their differences and attacked them in the same ways."

"A pity," Lia sighed. "I'd hoped your world was better."

"Same or worse, honestly," Doc shrugged. "I'll use what I know of my world to try making this one better. You never had a civil war here, though, which we did."

"Civil war? The country fought itself? Was it the tribes?"

"No, the northern and southern states. Even there, people argued over 'the how's and why's.' The southern states seceded from the Union. It lasted four years and ended with over a million people killed."

"A million people..." Rosa said softly, fearful of a conflict that could see so much death.

"We might see something similar here in time," Doc murmured.

"Because of what you plan to do," Lia said.

"If I get the West to see everyone as people and diminish the church in the process, yeah," Doc said somberly. "They'll have to do something. It won't be a North-South war; it'll be an East-West war."

"What about the dwarves of Tsarrus? If that happens, they would likely also push to remove the church from their lands."

"They might."

"The tribes, if they knew, would fight again, too, Doc."

"I know. I have a hope that we can lessen the Darkness without a war."

"That would be for the best," Rosa said. "If it comes to a war, Voice, Mother would do what she can. She knows how close to the brink she is."

"What could Mother do?" Doc asked, pausing in his work on the fish.

"Let nature run wild in the places that thwart you. Floods, tornados, and the like would happen."

"Lots of innocent people would die that way."

"Yes, but if they move against you, she would make it problematic for them to do so. Would they continue to attack you, or help their followers?"

"Attack me," Doc snorted. "I think McIan proved that. Thank Mother, but I don't want innocent people to die."

Rosa met his eyes, then bowed her head. "I will tell her, Voice."

"That's all far off, I think," Lia said. "For now, we can enjoy our night away."

"Yes," Doc smiled as he finished the first fish. "I'll be cleaning up in the river after I get them done."

"A good idea," Lia smiled crookedly. "I have plans on what I want for dessert, and you being clean is required for that."

"Agreed," Rosa giggled.

Doc just laughed as he got started on the second fish. Tomorrow would come soon enough, and with it, the troubles that were brewing, but his first steps in Furden were complete. Luck's Holdings had taken massive leaps forward with the companies folded under their banner. David Roquefell was a solid ally, as was the Ironbeard clan. Other allies were starting to show themselves with Madam Zu and Tarbo— Doc hoped they would prove to be reliable.

His smile faded a little as he thought of the people who would make life difficult for his plans. Richard Steward, the soulsmith, would likely act once the madam stopped him from controlling her girls. Sheriff Franklin Donadin would hate that the lesser were being treated well; his bigoted tendencies were obvious. The biggest question mark and potential trouble was Michael Strongarm, the rich socialite with ties to many areas in Furden and beyond.

"We'll be with you, Voice."

Doc met Rosa's eyes and he smiled. His family would be with him no matter what, and that gave him hope for the future.

CHARACTER INFORMATION

Doc Holyday- 42
Half-Breed Elf/Dwarf
Voice of Luck
Energy: 19/20 (200/200)
Vitality: 16/20
Health: 15/15
Faith: 1,506 (3,681)

Racial Bonuses:
Natural affinity to nature magic, improved reflexes, keen hearing and sight, resistance to poisons, improved vitality, night vision, natural affinity for metal crafts

Goddess Gifts:
All In, Stand Down, Missed Me, Healing Hands, Cleansing, Energy Reserves, Medic, Unblemished, Lasting Help, Remove Curse (Minor), Immunity Bubble, Cleric (Minor)

All In: When the game is on the line, your luck knows no bounds. The Lady herself will influence things in your favor. Calling on her in this way draws the attention of the Darkness as well. Use this sparingly, or bad luck will swiftly follow.

Stand Down: When you decide the point needs to be made, you can force even a wolverine bestial to step back and calm down. Useable once per day without cost. Using this again on the same day will tax you heavily; within an hour, you will collapse into a short coma.

Missed Me: Who needs to be fast on the draw if they cannot hit you? Able to bend time and space so any single attack misses you. Only able to use this once per hour.

Healing Hands: Use your energy to fuel healing for whoever you touch. If no energy is available, you can use your vitality. If no vitality is available, you will use health. Using health in this way can lead to death.

Cleansing: This gift augments the spell "Healing Hands." Lets the spell cleanse toxins, diseases, the Darkness, and other lingering effects. Energy cost is based on the severity of the condition being cleansed. If no energy is available, you can use your vitality. If no vitality is available, you will use health. Using health in this way can lead to death. You will be asked to verify if you wish to use this ability before it triggers.

Energy Reserves: Doubles your available energy.

Medic: Healing costs ¼ less energy.

Unblemished: Healing no longer leaves scars, and can remove old scars.

Lasting Help: Makes the person healed immune to the toxin purged from their system. This gift uses twenty energy.

Remove Curse (Minor): Remove a single condition from a curse. Energy consumption varies depending on curse and condition.

Immunity Bubble: Grants you ten seconds of immunity from all harm. This gift can only be used once every twenty-four hours.

Cleric (Minor): Grants a chosen person three of your gifts. This person can generate faith on your behalf.

AUTHOR'S NOTE

Please consider leaving a review for the book, feedback is imperative for an indie author. If you don't want to review it then think about leaving a comment or even just a quick message. Remember, positive feedback is always welcome.

If you want to keep up on the latest updates, or the one stop shop for all the links, my website is the best place for that. Remember to subscribe to the mailing list to know when I publish a new book, and you get an exclusive short when you sign up.
http://schinhofenbooks.com/

Other places you can keep up to date on me and my works:
https://www.patreon.com/DJSchinhofen
https://twitter.com/DJSchinhofen
Fan group on Facebook for Daniel Schinhofen
https://schinhofenbooks.blogspot.com/

If you LOVE LitRPG, then check out these pages full of awesome LitRPG goodness. You can interact with authors like me and many more. Find banter, good times, and a lot of like-minded people.

https://www.facebook.com/groups/LitRPGsociety/
https://www.facebook.com/groups/haremlit/
https://www.facebook.com/groups/LitRpg & GameLit Readers

A big thank you to my editors, Samantha Katt and Sarinia Phelps. Also props to Geno Ferrarini and Sean Hickinbotham for being my Alpha Readers. I'd be remiss if I didn't include my beta readers, in no particular order: Ian McAdams, Dame, Jay Taylor, Zee, Scott Brown, Kevin Kollman, Justin Johanson, Kenneth Darlin, Rob Bunting, Aoife Grimm, Peter LaFemina, Tanner Lovelace, Dimitri Shadow, Matt Case, Richard G Stahl, Cheyene Adams, A Madsen, Jeremy Stone, Navdeep Kumar, Megan Grueloh, Aaron Preston, David Hoerner, Todd Kibler, Testsu-nii, Tom Sethre, Brad Schultz, Derek Morgan.

The cover for Luck's Voice 5: Luck's Holdings is brought to you by Anthony Bishop, a very talented artist. You can find him at https://grimmhelm.artstation.com/

A big thanks to my Patreon supporters who have gone above and beyond in their support:

Edward P Warmouth, EvilZetti, Robert Yarber, Green, M. Ahles, Michael Erwin, Robert McCoard, Otis Coley, Thomas Smith, Calidia, Michael Mooney, Jeff Gaebler, Brian Biggers, James Domec, Exempt Pie, Craig Mather, Matt Sensenig, Scott Baxter, Christopher Cales, Patrick Glass, Zachary Johnson, Shakekiller, NooneSpecial, Jeff Kollada, Gian M, Jeff Ford, Khamla Khongloth, James Parker, Tyller James, Tanner Lovelace, Daniel Glasson, Cheyene Adams, IntheRaccon, Kurt Bodenstedt, Stefan Holze, Jeremy Patrick, MadManLoose, General Raith, David Hoerner, Kyle Pettay, Stephan Juba, Scott Hank, Matthew Kelly, James Breaux, Ron Arbitz, James Murphy, Forrest Hansen, Michael Shearer, Jon Bryant, John Cothrin, Charles Demarest, Dedalus Inventor, Stephen Caperton, Tyler Scheibe, Christopher Gross, Kurt Borek, MattMick222, David Taylor-Fuller, B

Liz, Council of Nine, Dances with Kobolds, Christopher B., Charles Henggeler, Top Cat 269, Matthew Parikka, Jose Ibarra, Deme A., Gslice 100, Lgikito, Cody Creager, Zifferix, Brian O., Riley Dunn, David Florish, Logan Cochrane, Allen Deck, Chad Arrington, Kevin Kollman, Michael Moneymaker, Aristo, Michael S Pellman, Orray Mooney, Eric Hontz, Sith, PantherTheory, Brett Hudson, Mark Kewer, JakeTylerPsn, Tetsu-nii, Kevin McKinney, Matthew Caro, Jerrod, Gabe Patton, Richard Papst, Joel Wilkinson, Christopher Edstrom, Adam, Arthur Cuelho, Sean Fitzpatrick, Gregory Johnson, Justin "Johnist" Johanson, Sawyer Williams, Ryan Luttinger, David Fletcher, Kori Prins, Red Phoenix, Dwinald Lint III, Spencer Jefferson, Clinton Wertzbaugher, Joshua McCane, Chace Corso, Chief 37, Tom Richards, Michael Jackson, Masta Matna, Jose Caudillo, William Merrick, Benjamin J Russell, Abraham Madsen, Matthew, Aryan Eimermacher, Rey T Nufable, Eli Page, Barry Dirickson, J. Patrick Walker, Kevin harris, Winston Smith, Matthre Malkin, T3iain, Dn Jinkins, Darkserra, EthanK, Robert Owen, Aaron Blue, Jeremy Cox, Robse, Derek Raines, Malcolm White, Jacob Lawlor, Brad Schultz, Rafnar Caldon, Caleb Bear, Travis Hilliard, Matthias Meilahn, Pamela J Smith, David Morrissey, Lui Adecer, Chioke Nelson, Damien Osborne, Terry Wood-Davies, Oni no chi, Thomas Lindsay, Malcolm Wade, Kenneth Darlin, Morgan C Williams, William Simmons, Ryan A Larkey, Thomas Corbin, Andrew Nevius, David Peers, Brendon Quinn, Michael Browningkoelper, Erin Jordan, Influenza, Tanner Sealock, Josh Holmes, Zachariah Miller, Robert Shofner, Taefox, LarrytheEmu, Eliseo Rios, Gregory Lamberta.

The last big thank you goes to Nick Kuhns who formatted this book for paperback. If it weren't for him you wouldn't be holding this book.

Other Books written by Daniel Schinhofen:

Binding Words:
Morrigan's Bidding
Life Bonds

Hearthglen
Forged Bonds
Flame of War
Lost Bonds
Noble Solutions
Accorded Nobility

Aether's Revival:
Aether's Blessing
Aether's Guard
Magi's Path
Aether's Apprentices
Mages of Buldoun

Luck's Voice:
Suited for Luck
Cashing In
Breaking the Bank
Dangerous Gamble

Dungeon Walkers:
Dungeon Walkers 1
Dungeon Walkers 2
Dungeon Walkers 3

Apocalypse Gates Author's Cut: (Completed)
Rapture
Valley of Death
Gearing Up
Elven Accord
Downtime and Death
Can of Worms
Unexpected Dev-elopments
One Nation, Under...

Alpha World: (Completed.)
    Gamer for Life
    Forming the Company
    Alpha Company
    Playing for Keeps
    Fractured Spirit
    The Path to Peace
    Darkhand
    Gamer For Love

Last Horizon: (Completed.)
    Last Horizon Omnibus

NPC's Lives: (Hiatus)
    Tales from the Dead Man Inn

        Resurrection Quest: (Hiatus)
        Greenways Goblins